BETWEEN EROS

The Love Secret: Book Two

CHRIS NEO

Between Eros
The Love Secret, Book 2

CCNG Ltd
T/A CCNG PUBLISHINGS
Unit 3 Gateway Mews, Ringway, Bounds Green
London, N11 2UT, UK

ISBN: 978-1-7396302-4-9 (paperback)
ISBN: 978-1-7396302-5-6 (ebook)

www.ccngpublishings.com
Author: www.chris-neo.com

All correspondence to: enquiries@ccngpublishings.com

The Love Secret series is fiction based on multiple true-love stories, derived from the clinical experience of the author interweaved with a fictionalised adventure. Names, characters, places, events, locales, businesses, and incidents are either the product of the author's imagination or used in a fictitious manner.

Cover artwork by Art Nedko, www.artnedko.eu
Cover design by www.bookcoverzone.com

DEDICATION

To the two gorgeous girls who encouraged me
to persevere and not only finish but also publish:
my granddaughter Zoe, and Lablin,
and to all those pure hearts around the globe
who know and believe in true love.

NOTE TO READER

This is a work of fiction based on multiple true love stories encountered by the author during clinical hypno-psycho-analysis practise and others from the author's imagination.

As a love adventure, I hope this story entertains readers of all genders and ages, incorporating an abundance of love, action, humour and drama, as well as offering therapeutic benefit.

Though I adore literary writing, I do not write in high literary style, but rather with emotion-filled dialogue. Every sentence is part of the story and moves the plot forward. When I read a book, I am impatient. I do not want to read ten pages if only two sentences are required. So my dear reader, be prepared for a fast-moving tale.

Are those clues of the love secret true, or a combination of reality and fiction? You must decide for yourself. Does this powerful love secret exist? Is it possible?

Only the pure of heart will discover it. It will require hard work, intelligence, and imagination, but most of all faith… to break love's secret code. I cannot guarantee if you will be one of those making a discovery. I will respond with guidance to those who subscribe to my readers list.

I hope you enjoy the Love Secret series. I will be with you all the way!

Subscribe to the email list and discussion groups:
www.chris-neo.com/subscribe
www.facebook.com/ChrisNeo1010
Twitter: @ChrisNeo1010

BONUS!

As a special gift for you,
download your FREE copy of the novella
Assassin's Love.

Two never-fail assassins! Target and client in the same couple. The devil has drawn his double knives. There will be death! But there will also be love. Who can survive when Eros has drawn his bow and pointed his love arrows?

Claim your free copy at this website:
http://bookhip.com/GZKHQLJ

1 RETURN?

Aris folded himself into the passenger seat of Peter's car after it pulled to a stop in front of the airport's arrival terminal. His other grown son, Gerry, was already in the back, leaning over the seat like an excited youngster about to receive a toy from a returning parent.

To avoid an interrogation about his travels, Aris gave them a quick overview of recent adventures—the run-in with the Mexican drug cartel and Katerina's brothers, and the close call with the Central American general and his wife/sister Celia.

With some hesitation, Aris also revealed that he had met some good people, new *friends*, who helped him along the way. Of course he kept the part to himself about how the descendants of the Greek sisters had trusted him with important clues about the love secret.

"So, finally you admit friends are not dead weight!" exclaimed Gerry.

"When people risk their lives for you, they are very good friends indeed." Aris smiled softly as he recalled his escapades with John and Uri. But he added, "That doesn't mean everyone is a good friend."

"What about that crazy idea of crossing the Atlantic at the wrong time of year?" Peter questioned.

Aris confessed that he had been sorely tempted to take on the challenge until their recent call. "After all, nothing is more important than family." Aris then quickly changed the subject to his grandchildren before his sons could push for more information. They happily caught him up to date for the rest of the drive.

When they arrived at the house, Gina was standing in the entryway, skinny jeans barely covering her rear and a crop-top exposing ample midriff. Her purse was slung over one shoulder as if she had been preparing to leave. Clearly she was not expecting him.

Aris pointed to her while turning to Gerry. "This is the woman you said was threatening to commit suicide?"

"I never said that." Gina glanced casually from Gerry to Peter.

"Mum!" Gerry cried.

She waved her arm dismissively. "Maybe as a joke while drinking, but I would never kill myself over this zero man."

Peter's jaw dropped.

Aris merely shook his head. "I told you she was playing you both."

Gina flounced into the kitchen, her high heels clacking. Picking up a stack of papers and a pen, she presented them to Aris. "Since you're here, you can sign these."

Aris looked down at the first page:

Divorce Settlement Agreement

"I'm not greedy," Gina continued. "I just want what I'm entitled to."

Aris turned again to Gerry and waved the papers. "She manipulated you to get me home… just for this."

Gerry's face pinched. "This crosses a line, Mum."

"You lied to us?" Peter asked. "Really? You used us?"

Gina shrugged indifferently. "It got him here, didn't it?"

Gerry shook his head in disbelief. "All this drama for a divorce?"

"Oh, I can get a divorce without him anytime," Gina bragged. "I just needed him for the settlement."

Peter's entire posture collapsed. "Money! That's all you care about?"

"I'm entitled to half of it."

Fury darkened Gerry's face. "So help me, I will cut you off from even whatever allowance Dad already provides for you."

Aris released a bright peal of laughter. He tapped the side of his head. "I told you! You can't touch the family wealth. It's all tied to the children and their offspring."

"I'll take you to court then," Gina scowled. "My lawyer assured me I was entitled to half of everything."

"Ah, but I have nothing in my name," Aris said, now barely containing his laughter. "I'm worthless, remember? I'm the zero man!"

Uri and John sat in their hotel room enjoying the warm sun and the view of the Belize coastline out the window.

John sighed. "Have you seen Aris? I haven't seen him since yesterday afternoon."

"Only one place he could be," Uri leered. "I bet he slept with Kay on the boat."

John smiled so wide his cheeks ached. "Remember how she followed Aris around? Should we surprise them?"

"After breakfast," Uri replied. "I can't deal with him on an empty stomach."

The pair had a quick meal at the hotel and then proceeded down to the marina. The wooden planks of the dock creaked underfoot as they approached the catamaran.

Two women, a blonde and a brunette, were sunning themselves on deck.

"Good morning," John called to them.

The girls waved them aboard.

Pointing a finger at the brunette, Uri smirked. "You naughty girl, Kay. Did you work Aris so hard last night he's still in bed?"

"What are you talking about?" she replied.

John smiled. "We know he didn't sleep at the hotel last night."

Kay's face fell. She extended a finger up to the sky. "Aris wasn't with me... he was up there."

John followed her pointer finger, taking in the sun and the sparse clouds above. "What do you mean?"

"He went home," Kay explained.

Uri glanced at John. "No," he said. "Aris was going to shake the boat this morning. What did you do to him?"

"Us?" the blonde, Lilly, sniped back. "Aris is a coward, abandoning us like that."

Kay slouched against the rail of the boat. "He had to go home. He said his family was his priority."

John bent forward as if he'd been struck. "Why didn't he tell us he was leaving?"

"Because he's a coward," Uri growled. "He abandoned us. *Again.* And he didn't even have the guts to tell us himself."

Kay shrugged. "He asked me to tell you."

Uri's chest puffed up. "Aris never wanted us around from the very beginning."

"But we all heard that phone call yesterday," John argued. "There must've been trouble back home."

Uri spun on Kay. "Did he say how long he'd be gone?"

"Forever. He said you were free to do what you want."

Uri punched the table. "Selfish bastard! Not once has he treated us as friends."

"Well..." Lilly drawled out. "Aris did tell Kay that you weren't his friends... and that friends are only a dead weight." After a short pause she added, "But we can't sail without a captain. I'm going to go talk to the old man. I bet I can sweeten him up."

⋅◊⋅

Varo lounged at a nearby luxury hotel while enjoying the view of the Belize coastline from a quiet corner. After Aris had refused her advances, she had vowed to win or destroy him. How could any man resist a beautiful and powerful CEO like herself?

A female detective joined Varo where she was seated beside her chief security officer and martial arts trainer, Victor. "We've lost Aris," she informed.

Varo threw a spiteful look at Victor, who immediately opened an application on his mobile phone. The muscular man's eyes widened in surprise. "Aris's cell phone just popped up on the grid. He's back home."

Instantly, Varo dialled a number.

Kay picked up her phone in one hand and grabbed Lilly with the other. "It's Mother. Let's ask her."

She stepped away from the group and pressed the button to accept the call.

Varo's voice was sharp over the line. "Why didn't you inform me Aris was gone?"

"I was just about to call you."

"What happened? Why did he change his mind just like that?"

"Trouble at home," Kay replied. "He got a call from his sons yesterday. What should we do?" She dropped her voice. "His friends are here with me on the boat now. Should we go ask the old captain from the other boat?"

"No!" Varo huffed. "It could be something temporary. Especially if his friends are still there. Wait for my instructions."

"Well, Aris said they weren't his friends," Kay refuted. "He said family—"

"Yeah, yeah," Varo interrupted. "Family above all. I've heard that before. Just wait for my instructions!" She ended the call abruptly.

Kay tucked the phone away and turned to the others. "Mother said to wait. She'll give us instructions."

"That's right," John snapped. "We should wait. We know Aris has problems at home. Give him a few days."

Uri groaned. "How many days is a few? Face it, John. He's not coming back. Aris is a selfish deserter."

"Give him a chance," John mumbled. "We can try calling him later today."

"Shouldn't we get the word out for a new captain? Just in case?" Lilly wondered. "I mean, with the amount of money we're paying, we could even charter a plane."

"No." Kay's voice was firm. "Mother told us to wait."

***

Gina stamped her foot on the floor yet again. "I demand that you sign the divorce papers and the settlement," she screeched. "It is only fair. I am entitled to half of everything. I suffered at your hands for so many years. This is my compensation."

Ignoring her, Aris waved his sons over to the couch. "Come on, let's sit. Update me on the business."

Chasing behind, Gina poked Aris in the shoulder. "Stop ignoring me! This is psychological abuse. You're hurting me. I will inform the court."

"Your crocodile tears no longer work on me. Can I just have a few quiet moments with our sons, please?"

"Dad just got home," Peter whined. "Let us catch up and then you can *talk*."

"He's not going to talk to me after you're gone," Gina answered sharply. "He tortures me with his silence. He's cruel and hides when the rest of the family isn't around."

"We took the whole day off, Mum," Gerry interrupted. "We'll stick around for you, so just give us a moment of peace."

"I want him to sign the papers now. I have friends waiting for me and I'm not changing my plans just because he's home."

"I told you I won't sign anything." Aris gazed off at nothing in particular. "Stop wasting our time."

Gina thrust her index finger in his face. "I'm a woman and I have rights, you know! I can send you to prison!"

A sharp ringtone halted the conversation. Aris pulled out his phone but hesitated at the caller ID, putting it on speakerphone. "John, I'm sorry I left so abruptly."

"We understand," came John's voice across the line. "It was a family emergency. Kay explained it."

"Well," Aris muttered, "more like a false alarm."

"Uri and Lilly want to try and get the old skipper to take over," John whispered. "What do you want us to do? Should we wait?"

Aris glanced at his sons, who were sitting tense beside him. "Tell them I'm coming back. A few moments in this house and I already realise that nothing has changed."

"Are you serious? You're coming back?"

"Yes," Aris answered, smiling at the clear joy in John's tone. "I'll get the first available flight." He ended the call and turned back to his family.

"You just got here," Gerry argued. "Why don't you wait a few days? Spend some time with us and Liza."

"We can have a nice lunch, all of us together," Aris said. "But I need to leave tonight. The window to cross the Atlantic is shrinking by the day."

"You're back to that crazy idea? It's suicidal."

Aris stood up and made his way out of the house, his sons rushing to keep up.

Trailing behind, Gina continued to fuss. "That's right," she screamed after him. "Run away, like always. Wouldn't want you to be a man for once and stay!"

Aris ignored Gina and instead tried to pacify his sons. "Walking down the street is dangerous. Besides, I've already been paid, and the boat is stocked. I don't want to let my crew down. Now let's find somewhere more congenial for lunch."

Peter and Gerry exchanged grimaces but followed him to the car.

Aris again commandeered the passenger seat. Gina stood outside shouting, her face ugly and contorted.

As Peter turned the key in the ignition, Aris glanced back at Gerry. "Call your assistant. Have her book me a flight as soon as possible."

The car hummed to life, and Aris switched on the radio to a rock 'n' roll station. Even then, it barely drowned out his wife's howling demands. He recognized the tune from a mid-'80's hair band and smiled. *Yes, indeed.*

Just as the lyrics implied, Gina gave love a bad name.

2 ᴿEUNION

The next morning Aris grabbed a cab from the Belize airport to the marina. He stood staring up at the crew he'd only recently abandoned.

It took a moment, but Kay eventually ran forward with a warm smile. "Welcome back, Captain. Is everything okay?"

Aris gave a shallow nod. "Is the boat ready? I want to test the systems, see how it handles."

John jumped out, engulfing Aris in an embrace. "I'm so happy you're back!"

"Easy," Aris laughed. "I told you on the phone that I was coming back."

"I want a hug, too." Lilly flung her arms around him.

"Enough," Aris chided. "I'm glad to be back. Now let's shake the boat."

The ocean was on their side that day, calm and windless, the sky a cerulean blue. Aris remained hopeful it would be a nice first outing for his crew. He stood at the starboard helm and glided the catamaran out of the marina while the girls enjoyed the ride and later recreated the scene from *Titanic*, their arms spread wide at the bow, heads tilted back.

John hovered over Aris, but Uri took position behind the port helm station. For the next few hours, the water was gentle, and Aris took the time to coach them all in turn through raising and lowering the sails, securing a line, and the different parts of the boat they might need to know.

Before long, the sun began its slow descent. He guided the boat back to port. After a stop for fuel, they docked and made their way toward the marina's main building.

"That was fantastic," John exclaimed. "The boat hardly shook at all."

"It actually was really great," Uri smiled.

"Don't get used to this," Aris chuckled. "The open ocean is rough on the best of days. I still think a flight would be easier for you all." He turned serious when he looked at Kay. "I need you to call the marina's engineers. There are some issues that need to be fixed before we can set sail."

Aris stopped in front of the old skipper to ask when the next shipment of reserve fuel tanks would arrive.

He frowned at the old man's answer.

❖

On the long-awaited morning of the launch, Aris gently guided the catamaran out of the marina, tipping the bow away from shore. His crew stood against the rails, excited to start their journey.

"We will do six hours shifts," Aris raised his voice. "Except for Lilly, who will be in charge of the kitchen."

He kept his eyes on the horizon as he called Uri and John to work. The two glanced at each other, confused, merely staring back at Aris.

"Balloons up and secure," he commanded. "Then collect and store the mooring ropes. Kay, check that all the hatches are sealed. Lilly, confirm everything is secure in the kitchen."

After their initial surprise, everyone scrambled to follow his orders.

When they had finished, the crew gathered under the shade of the bimini near the aft. Aris was still in working mode though, issuing directives and trying to teach them how to use the navigation equipment behind the helm.

"Rule one, never push any button unless you know what it does. If you forget, ask!"

A moderate wind picked up so Aris paused the lesson to turn the boat into the wind, instructing John and Uri to raise the main sail and then the genoa.

Setting the boat to autopilot, he continued his directives with Kay brushing up against him at the starboard helm. As a frisson of heat passed between them, Aris felt his heart thaw just a little. It was good to be back.

❖

The sailing that day was uneventful. New land came into view but they quickly left it behind. Soon they were the only boat out in the water.

"The ocean is endless out here," John whispered. "There's no one else for miles."

Kay, still sitting beside Aris at the helm, echoed his statement. "It's so beautiful."

"I like it," Uri chimed in happily, stretched across the bench under the bimini.

"Don't be fooled." Aris shook his head. "Enjoy the calm while it lasts. Once we're out in the Atlantic, there will be nothing but water for weeks."

Kay shifted, trying to get more comfortable. "Can I rest my head on your shoulder?"

Aris nodded, a smile slipping across his face.

Uri nudged John and the two exchanged knowing glances at Kay and Aris.

Lilly leaned over. "She's just tired, you idiots. But if she wants him, who cares?"

"Don't feel left out," Uri told her. "You can rest your head on my shoulder."

"I'm not that easy, and I don't need your permission," she smirked. Lilly turned to Aris. "I think you were just trying to scare us. There aren't any honking horns or loud car engines out here. This is wonderful. I love it!"

"Of course, you don't scare easily," Aris laughed. "You've already become a sea wolf. Let's see how long until your pants get smelly!"

❖

The first storm crept up on them, blacking out the horizon and swallowing the sky. Aris braced the helm dressed in foul-weather gear, with Kay wobbling at his side. The waves built upon each other until they nearly towered over the hull of the boat, crashing across the bow in a spray of white.

John and Uri huddled beneath the bimini, seasick and unable to stand.

"You should sit by the table," Aris told Kay. "The boat's more stable there."

Kay slipped her arm through Aris's. "I feel better staying with you."

The sound of retching echoed up from the saloon. "Get Lilly," he commanded. "She'll do better up here. It's worse below deck."

Kay crossed the deck like a drunkard at closing time, using the walls and stainless-steel handrails as support.

She soon returned, helping Lilly stagger up the stairs. She prodded the poor girl onto the bench under the bimini, but Lilly leaned directly over and heaved, her back convulsing. Lucky for the boys, there was nothing left in her stomach to expel.

"I want to go back," Lilly wailed.

"It's too late for that," Aris reminded. "Give it a few days. You'll get used to it."

Lilly scowled. "You lied. You never mentioned we would be vomiting for hours!"

The waves grew more erratic, battering the hull from all sides and cresting the bow. The boat surged upward only to plunge straight back down.

Huddled under the bimini, John, Uri, and Lilly clutched each other, taking turns vomiting and shaking inconsolably.

Aris watched while Kay struggled to pull down the sails without assistance. Alone, he raised the storm sail and sent up a prayer to Poseidon, the sea god himself. Was this his penance for abandoning his wife and family?

3 Surprise Them

Eventually the storm broke and the afternoon sun burned away the cloud cover. But the wind held strong, making the day perfect for sailing.

Aris made his way to the bimini where Uri and John were laying down. "You're next on shift," he commanded Uri, shoving a cushion behind his own back. "The sails are in good position, so just maintain course. The weather should hold for a good while, but if there's a big change in wind speed or direction, turn into the wind like I showed you, then wake me."

"I'll stay here close in case Uri needs help," John said, and Aris nodded in agreement.

"Time to rest," Aris called to Kay at the helm. "Uri's on shift now."

At Aris's instruction she rose and followed him to the port hull. At the bottom of the stairs, he turned to head for his aft cabin, but then paused and spun back to watch Kay descend.

They stared at each other for a moment before Kay took one step toward her cabin in the bow. She glanced back at Aris.

He held out his hand to her, waiting.

She grasped it gladly, a smile splitting her face. "Took you long enough," she said, pulling Aris into his cabin and closing the door behind them. The pair collided, their lips seeking each other in a rush of hunger.

Kay inhaled greedily. "Why did you waste so much time? I've been desperate for you." She peppered Aris with kisses.

"I wasn't sure you felt the same as I felt about you," he confided.

Kay merely cradled his face between her hands. "I crave you like crazy."

"I didn't realise." His eyebrows raised in surprise.

"I'm in love with you, Aris! The more I get to know you, the harder you are to resist!"

Aris stood mesmerized as Kay tilted her head and bit his thumb.

"I'm sure this is love," she promised.

Heat pooled in Aris's stomach, a gnawing hunger he usually kept at bay. "That's just the sea opening your appetite. Let's see how we feel after a few days. Lust can be deceiving."

"There is no doubt in my mind," she confirmed. "I know what my heart feels. I'm attracted to all parts of you—your intelligence, your strength of character, your maturity, your leadership. You're definitely an alpha male." She kissed him once with each attribute. "Every day, my love for you grows stronger. As I've gotten to know your personality, your warmth, and your courage, you have my heart, Aris."

She pulled at his clothes, and they undressed each other quickly.

"Don't expect anything grand," Aris warned. "I have a wife and a family. Even grandchildren."

"I expect nothing but for you to want me. All of me. If you don't want me, stop me now," Kay begged. "But if you just want a warm body, Lilly would be more than happy to be of service."

Aris gazed at Kay, taking in her state of undress and the light upon her face. He pulled her close and drew her into a fierce kiss, his tongue slipping between her lips.

Kay tugged off his shirt. "Maybe your marriage is dead, and you don't know it."

"Everyone seems to know that," Aris confessed.

Kay sat on the edge of the bed and lifted her legs for Aris to help with her pants, then knelt before him, tilting her head back to look him in the eyes. "You must know, I would follow you anywhere. No questions asked."

"Don't frighten me off with such a huge declaration," Aris said. "I need to shower first. I'm salty from sailing."

Kay pulled him down and rolled them over, so his back was on the bed. "Salty or not, to me you are sweet. I'm done waiting."

Aris tried to sit up in protest, but Kay pinned him to the bed, wagging her finger. His hands drifted up her thighs, but she slapped them away. "This is my show," she purred.

With a shimmy and a sharp yank, she pulled down his trousers and removed his underwear. Nuzzling into his crotch she began to work him over with her mouth. Soon, Aris was writhing beneath her. She sped up her ministrations, swallowing him to the base as he thrust into her.

Suddenly, she flipped him onto his stomach and slapped his ass hard, biting each cheek until an imprint of her teeth marked his skin, making Aris shout in surprise.

She pushed him back down. "No, no. A bit of pain will stop you from finishing before me." Aris could sense the sly smile on her face as she added, "We're not done until I decide."

◆

Lilly stepped out of the saloon. "Where's Kay?"

"She isn't in your cabin?" Uri asked.

Lilly shook her head.

"Maybe she's showering," John offered.

Lilly yawned, leaning on the saloon door. "No, I was just in there."

"She went down with Aris after her watch ended," Uri said with a smirk.

"I thought we weren't allowed in Aris's cabin."

"Maybe not blondes like you," Uri replied, laughing.

Lilly clenched her jaw. "That bastard! I will have him. No one rejects me!"

"Or," Uri pondered, stretching out in his seat, "you could forget Aris and join me."

Lilly sauntered into Uri's waiting arms. "Why not? I can't sleep anyway."

Uri jumped to his feet, eyes bright, and called to John, "Take the helm for a while!"

"Aris won't be happy!" John shouted after them.

"If Aris is getting some, so should we," Uri snapped back with a grin.

He tugged Lilly behind him and then slipped into the dark entrance of the starboard hull while John sagged into the seat at the helm.

4 THE UNEXPECTED

The days started to bleed together and soon they were nearly two weeks at sea. Aris dozed at the starboard helm until he was jolted by a shrill scream.

"Smoke!" Kay shouted, running out of the saloon. "Smoke in the port hull."

Aris jerked to his feet, the navigation system nearby sparking before shutting down.

He raced behind Kay to the port hull, drawing short when confronted by a coil of thick, black smoke. For a moment, panic locked him in place but he quickly contained it.

"Get a lifejacket and take the helm," he instructed Kay. "We've lost our electrical systems, so maintain course as best you can with the compass."

Aris turned back to see John and Uri, both pale and frightened. "Everyone, get a lifejacket. John, get Lilly out of her cabin."

"I'm here," Lilly called from the settee.

Glancing at the navigation plotter, Aris saw that all the systems were off. His heart tightened in his chest. Aris ducked low and sprinted. At the end of the port hull, dense smoke billowed from the electrical cupboard that housed the entire electrical supply system—from batteries to inverters.

He grabbed the powder extinguisher, shouting, "Fire! Get under the bimini!"

Aris yanked open the cupboard and stumbled back as the fire roared out from the contained space. Flames spat from the master inverter, stretching towards the switches. He aimed the extinguisher, spraying white powder to suffocate the fire, going wide first, then targeting any remaining pockets of heat until the fire died completely.

Aris reeled back to the helm, informing the others that the fire was extinguished. "John, Uri, open all the hatches to get the smoke out."

John and Uri didn't move, standing huddled under the bimini. "Are we stranded?" Uri asked with a concerned wobble in his voice.

Aris took a deep breath and tried to stay calm. "As long as we have our sails, we can always move with the wind. We have the engines and we have generators. I'm concerned about the inverter system, though." He turned from Uri to John. "You know electronics. Are you up to the challenge?"

"What do you need?" John stood ready to help.

"The main concern is the navigation system, but it needs twelve-volt batteries. If the inverters are beyond functional, we'll need a different way to charge the batteries."

John shifted on his feet.

"Kay, go around the boat. Make sure everything electrical is switched off." Aris turned back to John. "Well?"

"I'm more comfortable with household electronics and engines," John confessed. "Inverters are beyond me. I don't think I can fix them."

"Is there a way around them?" Aris asked, trying to sound encouraging. "Some other way to power the batteries?"

John thought for a moment. "Maybe we can charge them directly from the engines or the generators, like jumpstarting a car. I can connect the engine to the battery banks. I know there is a connection because if the engine batteries go down, we can start the engines using the house bank batteries. I'll go down and check."

John marched off and, after a moment, popped back up. "Start the engines, Aris. Let's see."

Aris flipped the switch for the port engine. The crew stood silent behind him but didn't hear anything.

Aris flipped the switch again and again, but the engine never rumbled to life. Taking a deep breath, he tried the starboard engine. The only sound was the ocean rocking the still boat.

"Kay, take the helm," he called. "John, with me. We're checking the engines."

Opening the starboard engine hatch first, Aris stilled. His jaw clenched as he tried to contain a sudden wave of horror at what he saw.

John peered over his shoulder with a gasp. The engine and generator were nearly submerged. The water seemed to be rising still.

Without a word, Aris dropped into the room, instantly soaked to his waist. He leaned down until only his head was above water, reaching out with his right hand.

After a moment of struggle, Aris huffed, "I closed the inlay tap. That should stop the water from rising. No power means no bilge pumps to automatically pump water out. Let's check the port engine."

John helped him up and the two made haste to the other engine. Rushing around, Aris tried to hide his fear under a mask of anger, but the rest of the crew couldn't help but be on high alert.

"What's happening, John?" Uri called after them.

"Not now!" John barked, brushing him off.

When the two reached the port side, they found it in a similar condition—water quickly drowning the engine.

Aris jumped in and flailed around until he was able to seal that inlay tap as well.

He met the crew back under the bimini, drenched in seawater and trying to calm his breath. The others curved around him.

"Both engine rooms are flooded. Until we drain the water, I can't start the generators." He turned first to John. "Under the port helm station is a manual bilge pump. Lower the inlay into the water and use it to pump manually. Just until the water is below the engine's belly. Then we can try starting the generator."

He gazed around the rest of the crew and stopped on Lilly. "Go help John. Make sure the hose stays submerged."

The two hurried off to follow orders while Kay stepped closer. "You're soaked!"

"I'm going to change now," Aris promised.

Later, after getting warm and dry, Aris sat between Uri and Kay as they watched John and Lilly still pumping. The process was slow and agonising.

"Nearly there," John grunted.

"You start doing the same on the starboard side," Aris motioned to Uri. "Drain it till the water is below the engine."

Uri nodded and got up.

Aris made his way over to John. "Is the generator completely out of the water yet?"

"Yes," John gasped, catching his breath. "But the engine appears to be damaged in the right corner above the pump."

"Give Uri the pump, then," Aris commanded. "Kay, go and help Uri."

"I can try to fix the damage," John offered.

"Let's see if the engines start first. But the generators are more important. Lilly, stay at the helm and hold us on course."

Running back to the starboard helm station, Aris jammed the button to start the port side generator, but nothing happened.

He tried again. Not even a flicker of light.

His face sagged. Aris scurried back to the port side engine room and lowered himself down to check over the fuses and switches on the generator.

Next he tried the master power switch on the front. He held it down. Nothing happened.

John watched him from the hatch, frowning.

Aris paced under the bimini, lost in thought. He moved once more to the helm and tried to start the engine. Nothing! Again and again, but there was no response from the engine. He clenched his jaw, making his teeth ache.

"John," he gritted out. "Go down to the engine room and see what's happening. Nothing is turning on."

John went and returned quickly, shaking his head. "The damage is worse than we thought. The engine has a massive hole in the top right corner, straight through to the fuel pump. There's no way I can fix it."

Aris tried to ignore Lilly's cries and Uri's outrage. He sank down into a chair. "The generator?" he asked. "Can it still be used for the navigation system?"

John shrugged, sighing deeply. "I'll have to remove the cover to check the damage."

"This doesn't make sense," Aris muttered, gazing at John. "We hardly used the engines, and everything was inspected before we left. For now, let's keep an eye on the generator. We can deal with the engines later."

John wiped his hands on his thighs. "Even if you start the generators, they're useless without inverters. The rest of the system is fried."

Aris squeezed his eyes shut to concentrate. "One inverter is not burned. We also have a manual charger. We can use that if we can get the generator started. Go!"

John raced off as Aris sank down into a seat beneath the bimini with the rest of the crew to wait.

On John's return, his head was hanging. He wiped his hands on a rag, shifting in place in front of the others.

"It's worse than we thought," he reported. "The generator is totally fried. Battery cable, fuel system, all gone. And there was this box that was melted on top."

"What?" Aris growled, eyes searing. "Show me."

He followed John to the port engine room to inspect the generator himself. A loud bang cracked the silence, followed by a groaning noise. Aris jumped up onto the starboard helm just in time to see the mast start to lean.

"Watch out!" he shouted, pointing upward.

Aris jumped to the left as the mast crashed down, narrowly missing Uri's head and the hard fibreglass roof of the bimini.

Kay had dived away by a good margin, with her hands clutched atop her head.

The mast crunched against the deck, the top hanging down into the water, now attached to the boat only by the shrouds.

The crew gathered around, still stunned. Aris stepped over the boom, only attached to the mast by the main sheet. "Hurry up," he called to the others. "We need to secure the mast before it falls into the ocean."

He steered the boat so the wind was behind them, using it to fill the sail and genoa shroud to help keep the mast from sinking further. Snatching a length of rope from the rail near the starboard helm, he rushed past the others.

"Kay, go back under the bimini!"

Unfurling the rope, Aris quickly threaded it around the mast and cleats, securing the mast to the hull.

"Lilly," he shouted, his voice sharp and sure. "Bring us ropes. Uri, do as I do. Help me tie this mast down."

Aris raced back to the bimini. "John, gather mooring rope and follow me."

The three men worked, backs bent, to secure the mast, the boom and the genoa to the boat. If Aris ever had cause to doubt his friends Uri and John as "dead weight" it certainly was not this day.

5 Pan-pan Danger

Aris hunched over the navigation table, making notes of their estimated position, along with the time and overall path of their course. When he finished, he sat under the bimini with the others, all of them tense and waiting for his report.

Scooting closer to him, Kay leaned in for a kiss. "Thank you. You saved my life earlier."

Uri let out a string of burps, a stress reflex he had more or less conquered before they set sail. "We're in serious danger here, and the two of you are kissing as if nothing's wrong?" He slammed his hands down on the table. "We have no engines, no power, no mast. What are you going to do, *Captain*?"

"I agree," Lilly squeaked. "You need to fix this!"

Aris lunged across the table, slapping Uri.

"What was that for!"

"Don't panic," Aris warned.

John cleared his throat, but his voice still came out high and reedy. "What happened? The mast. The generators and electrics. All these failing at once isn't normal, right?"

"No," Aris replied, sceptically. "Masts don't usually collapse. And this one seems to have broken from the base like it was rotten. Things do break, but all at the same time?"

He stood up, heading into the saloon where the others followed him. "Inverters are known to overheat, though it's very rare. It's happened to me only once before."

The crew listened as he paced back and forth.

"But h-h-how could all this have h-h-happened at once?" John's voice again cracked.

Aris merely stared in silence. His lack of response put everyone on edge.

Uri shivered, another burp forcing itself out of his throat. "Aris is cursed," he said. "Wherever he goes, catastrophe follows. What are we supposed to do now?"

Ignoring Uri, Aris observed his crew, one after another. He could see the fear hanging over them like a shroud.

He took a deep breath to remain calm. "There's nothing we can do. Without an engine or sails, we will just drift. All we can do now is rest." He tried to muster a smile. "But the boat is strong, and we have plenty of supplies and water. There's no need to panic just yet."

"But Aris," John interrupted. "Without electricity, we can't use the VHF radio. We can't call for help."

Aris dipped his head slightly. "We can use the satellite phone. The battery should still be full."

He headed for the navigation centre, pulling open drawers and cabinets to search for the device. The longer he was unable to find it, the darker his mood grew. He stomped back out to the others, anger roiling in his veins. "Where is it? Where's the damn phone?"

Everyone remained silent.

"Who's taken the satellite phone!" he shouted. "It's our only hope to call for a rescue!"

Lilly slipped away using the hand bars to support herself. "I may have borrowed it to call Mother. Let me check my cabin," she called back over her shoulder.

Aris breathed heavily as Lilly disappeared.

She returns silently, handing over the phone. One glance was enough for Aris's rage to nearly boil over. Wary, the others shifted quietly.

He braced himself against the saloon door frame, swinging his right foot back and forth, trying to rein in his rage.

Fearing the worst, Uri cleared his dry throat. "What's wrong?"

Aris turned to face them, the phone dangling from his left hand. With clenched jaw, he whispered, "It's dead."

For a moment, the men appeared too shocked to speak. Then, face flushed, Uri punched the table. "You stupid woman. We were told only to use that phone in an emergency!"

Lilly reclined on a seat, unconcerned. "So? We can just charge it."

John smiled bitterly. "With what power?"

Uri lunged at Lilly, fist raised to strike, but Aris pulled him back. Barely understandable over his burping, Uri choked out, "How long were you on that phone?"

"Not long," Lilly replied. "Just two, three hours. It ended when the battery cut out."

Aris tried to keep his composure. Pulling out his mobile phone, he shook his head at seeing there was no signal. "Everyone, check your phones. Someone might have coverage."

But after everyone did so, their answer was the same. No reception.

Aris stepped back into the saloon and picked up one of the handheld VHF units before moving to the bimini. "These still have a good amount of battery left," he shared. Their faces brightened with hope. "But they have a limited range. Maybe thirty miles. Our only hope now is if another boat is nearby."

He went to retrieve the sea charts, estimating their position, then held the VHF up to his mouth. "PAN-PAN, PAN-PAN, PAN-PAN," Aris called, clear and loud into the radio. "Drifting. No power. No sails. This is sailing catamaran IK, all signs 424242. Five adults on board. PAN-PAN, PAN-PAN, PAN-PAN."

The rest remained silent, their agony increasing as they listened to him relay the message. The severity of their situation settled in.

Aris silently waited for a response.

John cleared his throat, his voice finally back to normal. "Why PAN-PAN? Why not send an SOS?"

"SOS is a mayday signal for when there is immediate danger to life. Since we are not in any immediate danger, this is enough to inform others of our situation."

Uri yanked Aris by the arm. "Is that really all you can do? After getting us into this mess?"

"I told you all to fly over," Aris chuckled. "You insisted on sailing."

Uri paced in circles, clutching his head. "I didn't know something like this could happen. You're the captain, you should know what to do… but you're just sitting around!"

"Me neither," Lilly said, aloof. "With how much we're paying, you should find a solution."

Aris laughed again. "You could always swim back."

Lilly twirled her curls. "I would, but I don't want to damage my hair. One of your men can swim for help."

Kay placed her hands on Lilly's shoulders. "Don't worry. You heard Aris. The boat is strong. We are safe if we stay right here."

⸺ � ◇ ⸝ ⸺

Aris sent another PAN-PAN message the next day. The radio's battery dipped dangerously low.

The others were nearby sitting under the bimini and growing more uncomfortable the longer the silence stretched.

"Is that it?" Kay asked.

"If we get no answer," Aris replied, "we will repeat the call until the radio dies."

Uri chain burped, a shiver running through his body. "Then what?"

"Then you pray to Moses," Aris joked.

"Who's Moses?" Lilly asked, confused.

"Uri's God," John explained.

"What kind of captain are you?" Lilly spewed. "You're the one who's supposed to take care of everything."

John sneered at her. "And you're the one who used the satellite phone. It's your fault we can't call for help."

Lilly held her head high. "It's still Aris's fault. He didn't make it clear that I couldn't even use it for just one call."

Uri glared at her. "I guess we know who we're eating first if we run out of food."

Aris clicked his tongue. "Calm down. I ordered a surplus of supplies. But we will need to start rationing food and water."

Lilly raised her hand, volunteering. "I oversee the kitchen, so I'll make sure to keep track of what we're eating."

Barking out an incredulous laugh, Aris tugged Lilly by her shoulders. "No, Kay will be in charge of the food and water now. Without generators, we have no water purification system, so we need to cut back on everything—showers, washing dishes. All of it."

"But I need to wash my hair," Lilly argued.

Aris snarled. "If I see you washing your hair, I'll shave your head."

"Hey," Kay waved, trying to get his attention. "Who do you want at the helm?"

"No one. We're just drifting. I'll monitor our position, but there's nothing else to do."

"Couldn't we just drift to land?" Uri asked.

Everyone turned to Aris, hope brightening their faces.

"We could," Aris admitted. "We are surrounded by land."

Lilly cheered loudly, jumping up and down.

Aris's smile creased. "We just don't know how long it could take. Could be months or even years."

Aris watched as they collapsed under the reality of their situation, their gazes losing focus.

He paced outside the saloon doors. "We need to establish a watch for a boat or plane. And we need to save any torches. We can use them to signal nearby boats."

He ordered Kay to collect all the lights on board and bring them to him. "John, you take the first watch."

"What are you d-doing?" Uri asked, voice trembling.

"I'm taking a nap!"

"But we're in danger!" Uri jumped to his feet. "How can you sleep at a time like this?"

Aris shrugged. "There's nothing else to do."

"But we might die!"

Aris offered a small smile. "We all die one day."

Lilly sat at the helm gazing blandly at the horizon. Behind her, the rest were lounging around the table under the bimini with Aris bent over the sea chart.

"How long have we been out here?" John wondered. "Must be at least a month and not another boat in sight."

Uri's face sagged. "Even if there was another boat, we'd never see it through all these storms."

Aris kept his focus on the chart, tracing their aimless route across the Atlantic.

"Do you even know where we are?" Uri asked. "Or where we're heading?"

Aris shook his head, sighing deeply. "No, with our drifting and the strong storms, it's hard to pinpoint or even estimate."

Uri tapped his teeth with the jagged tip of one fingernail. "You said you'd be able to captain us across this time of year. Now you've led us to this… a slow death. Might as well just have committed suicide. Probably be less miserable."

"Ah, but Moses wouldn't let you into heaven then," Aris joked. "Though either way, I doubt that's where you're headed."

6 Refusing a Woman

At the top of a glass building that grazed the sky, Varo Theobald sat behind her large desk. Her brow was wrinkled in concern as she glared at the oceanic map on her computer monitor. At the bottom in red font flashed the words NO SIGNAL.

She pushed out of her seat, stalking the length of her office, tugging her ear. Turning back, she hit the speed dial button on the office phone.

"Victor," she snapped. "Where is Aris? Where is the boat?"

"Last I checked, they were about halfway," Victor replied, unconcerned.

"I'm looking at it and there's no signal," she growled. "Check with the engineers, now!"

"On it, ma'am."

◆ ◇ ◆

Victor dropped the phone back into the cradle, leaning back in his desk chair. Beside him, a small, thin man shifted uneasily.

"Is she beginning to suspect something?" the man asked.

Victor waved him off. "Doesn't matter. They will either sink or die from starvation."

"But what if she blames you?"

"Why would she? I've never been near the boat." Victor paused, turning to look at his assistant.

"And the engineer in Belize? The one who did the work on the boat?"

"I've worked with him before. He's never let me down. Relax, cousin. Everything is fine."

After days of pounding the boat with a chilling rain, the storm broke and the waves settled to a more manageable pitch. Aris entered the saloon to find the crew spread out across the settees, their lips wrinkled and faces pale from dehydration.

John lifted his head. "Where are we?"

Aris shrugged.

Kay pushed herself upright. "I've rested a bit. Do you need me to go on watch?"

Aris collapsed onto one of the couches. "I've tied the helm, and with the weather breaking, we should be okay. I need to eat."

"I'll grab you something." Kay moved away then placed an open tin of corned beef and a fork on the nearby table. "There's still a few bites. We're running low on food. Got maybe a couple more days of rations."

Aris whipped around, back taut in alarm. "No, there should be enough for all of us for nearly four months."

"Where?" Kay asked, her shoulders drooping.

"Uri," Aris shouted. "Where did you store the food supplies?"

The man in question looked startled.

"Where is all the food I told you to load on the boat?" Aris repeated.

"I," Uri mumbled, stumbling over the words. "I loaded a few and then took a break at the café. When I got back, the pallets were gone. I thought you guys brought the rest in."

Aris surged to his feet, looming over the crew. "Did any of you load the rest of the supplies?"

"No," John immediately replied, his voice a harsh squeak. "I didn't!"

"Do you mean all those boxes of food that were sitting on the dock in the marina?" Lilly asked.

Everyone turned to where she was laying back, casually twirling a length of hair. "Some guys from another boat said they'd take them since the boxes were blocking the way."

Uri lunged. "You brainless woman!"

"No," she shouted back. "I helped you with the lighter boxes, you useless sloth! You were supposed to do the rest. I assumed you finished!"

Glancing around, Uri finally turned on Aris. "He's the skipper. It should've been his responsibility to check everything!"

Kay shoved him back, stepping between the men. "Uri, it was your job. You were the one who didn't do it."

"Exactly!" Lilly shouted in support.

Aris raised his gaze to the roof in a bid for patience. "Uri is right. I should have checked. Especially since I gave the job to an idiot."

Lilly smirked. "See? It's definitely not my fault."

Uri sank back down, dropping his head in his hands. "Aris didn't check the engines or the electrical system. He didn't check the food supply. He has driven us towards death in every way possible."

Lilly's shoulders pulled back in determination. "Uri said that I should be eaten first, but since he forgot the food, that means we're eating him first, right?"

Aris ignored her, pushing the tin of food back at Kay. "We cut back to two spoonfuls a day," he said. "One in the morning and one at night."

A hush fell over the group. They turned their gaze to one another in silence.

※

Pacing in front of the large windows of her office, Varo tugged on her ear to try and soothe her nerves.

At the sound of a knock on the door, Victor stepped in, standing with his hands behind his back.

"You're right," he conceded. "We've lost the signal. But there's no need to panic right now. It could just be an issue with the satellite. It might be back online soon."

Varo shook her head, doubtful. "Kay had a tracker. You had your men place two more on the boat. We also had the ones in their bags. And all of them aren't working?"

"We had all the signals until recently, except the luggage trackers that are out of range anyway. As I said, I think it's just a satellite problem."

Varo fixed her gaze on him. "I learned that this is not a good time of year to cross the Atlantic."

"My knowledge of oceans ends at the beach," Victor shrugged. "Besides, Aris is a bright man and an experienced sailor. He wouldn't put himself or others in needless danger. Unless…"

"Unless?" Varo prompted.

"He did accuse you of trying to kill him. We know he's delusional. He could be suicidal."

"No," Varo bit back, disgusted by this analysis. "I know him. He's not crazy or suicidal. Check the systems again, and alert me the moment we regain the signal."

◆◇◆

Aris chewed his single scoop of corned beef slowly, watching the crew share wary glances with one another.

John shifted. In a soft, curious voice he asked, "Do you know where we are?"

Aris shook his head. "I can guess, but with the storms and the ocean having no landmarks, it's impossible to be certain."

Uri perked up across from them. "What about star navigation?"

Aris squeezed his eyes shut. "I never learned that skill."

"Another thing you failed to mention," Uri scoffed. "A captain with a handicap!"

Aris practically cackled. "Even if I could read the stars, what am I navigating? We have no sails or power!"

Tears of fright rolled down Lilly's cheeks. "You're irresponsible. You promised you could do this. Everyone said you were the man for the job!"

"I remember telling all of you to fly across," Aris replied, smiling sardonically. "You insisted on coming with me. So shut up and stop panicking." He took a deep breath to clear his mind. Extending both arms, swaying his hands as if to a jaunty tune, he began to sing a Greek folk song. "Phenomenon is not earthquakes and storms, not even the pyramids. The phenomenon is that I put up with you."

Manically slapping his face, Uri burped, his unease escaping in a rush of gas. "The bastard is sick. We're dying and he's dancing to some stupid song! We followed a psychopath!"

Lilly watched in awe. "It's like he's happy we're going to die. And people tell me blondes are stupid."

Aris clapped his hands, trying to pull Kay up to dance with him. Her smile was small and sad. "Come, everybody," Aris called out to them. "It will be a good death. We will have no problems, no worries. We will be completely free!"

Only John, standing off to the side, managed a smile at this behaviour.

Aris slowly finished his song and dance, turning to face his audience. "We are not drowning," he reminded them. "Our boat is still watertight. It is the safest place to wait for any of the many boats crossing the Atlantic."

"What about food," Lilly reminded. "I won't be attractive if I become bony!"

"Don't fret about a few tins of food. The gods provide for birds and other animals. Would they not provide for us?"

"But I'm not religious," Lilly argued. "Which gods? I'll follow them immediately!"

"Right now, we're at the mercy of Poseidon, god of the sea," he laughed. "The ocean is full of his bounty. If you pray and send him kisses, I'm sure he will send plenty of fish. He's fond of pretty girls."

"Does he like blondes?" she asked, playing with her curls. "I can't dye my hair."

"Poseidon is Greek. He loves all women. Especially ones with nice curves."

John and Uri looked on, baffled at the nonsense.

"He's trying to tell us not to lose hope," Kay assured them. "We are surrounded by food."

Lilly struck a confident and seductive pose. "I will go show Poseidon my curves, then. He's sure to love me."

◆ ◇ ◆

Lethargic, the crew lazed around in the saloon, except for John, keeping watch at the starboard helm.

Uri perched in his seat, holding his head with trembling hands. "We are never going to be found."

Kay nodded in agreement. "The weather's getting colder, too. We don't even know where we are."

Lilly glared at the captain. "The famous skipper who can't even cross the ocean."

Aris lifted a hand, flipping her off. "I warned you it would be risky."

"Mother said it was a bargaining tactic so you could get more money," Kay shared. After a beat, she jumped to her feet. "Mother! I forgot… she's watching us! She'll know we're in trouble."

Uri perked up. "What do you mean?"

"She gave me a box to keep under the mast to track us."

Aris jumped to his feet in alarm. "What box?"

Hope illuminated her features. "She told me to keep it under the mast in the front anchor hatch."

Aris pulled on his foul weather gear and flew onto the deck. Wrenching open the anchor hatch, Aris slipped from view.

A moment later, he stormed back into the saloon. "There was an explosion of some sort. That's clearly what caused the mast to collapse." He turned to Kay, anger clouding his face. "You said your mother gave you the box. Was she in Belize with you?"

"It's not Kay's mother, you idiot," Lilly sniped in defence of her friend. "It's the other mother—the owner of the boat."

Furious, Aris grabbed Kay by the shoulders. "Who is she?"

Fear choked her words so she remained silent.

"You placed a device under the mast without telling me? Was this all a set-up?" In a fit of rage he shook her. "What else did you do? Did you sabotage the engine rooms, too?"

Kay burst into tears. "I didn't do anything."

Aris's nostrils flared. "We can't fix what happened but tell me everything."

Kay slumped into a seat, regret coating her figure. "Mother sent her engineers to inspect everything. You saw them on the boat yourself."

Aris collapsed beside her and wiped away her tears with his thumb. "Who is this woman, Kay? Who does this boat really belong to?"

John stumbled into the saloon, drawn by the shouting.

"She was just some woman," Lilly answered. "She told us to call her mother and offered us money to take the boat across."

Aris nodded for Lilly to continue, but Kay stepped in. "She's American. Elegant, rich, young. She instructed us to hire you to sail the boat. She gave me the tracking device to keep up with the journey."

Everyone waited patiently as Kay grabbed a tissue to blow her nose.

"She must know where we are and what happened by now."

Shaking his head in disappointment, Aris asked, "And the father in this little masquerade?"

"There isn't one. It was just part of the cover story to use so you didn't refuse the offer."

"Why would I refuse?" Aris frowned.

"She said she's in love with you but that if you knew it was her boat, you wouldn't help."

Aris's features constricted. "Was she at the marina in Belize?"

"Yes, she stayed at a hotel, driving around in a limousine with a man and some other woman."

Aris attempted to stay calm. "What other woman?"

"A local that was working for Mother."

Tilting her head back by her chin, Aris asked, "You're positive she was American? Late twenties, or early thirties? Tall, beautiful, long black hair?"

Kay seemed surprised, and Lilly confirmed. "Yeah! She was gorgeous."

"The man that was with her," Aris continued, digging for more information. "Was he athletic? Well dressed with a birthmark by his left eye and ear?"

"Yes," Kay admitted. "He's the one that gave us the money and the boat papers. He also sent Mr. Fisher to inspect the boat."

Aris punched the table. "Evil, the both of them!"

John's face twisted with curiosity. "Who?"

"That woman and her henchman that tried to kill me," Aris answered, his voice surprisingly soft.

"Are you serious?" Uri shouted. "Are you saying this was sabotage?"

"Of course," Aris announced as if stating a fact. "How else do explain the engines flooding and the mast falling all within minutes of each other? This was well planned."

Anger bled across Uri's face. "You never told us people were trying to kill you! I mean… beyond that hairdresser related to the drug cartel. And well… that creepy general and his sister-wife. Who's this crazy love-crazed woman?"

"Varo Theobald, a rich and vile woman."

Kay appeared unconvinced. "I don't think she gave me a bomb. When I spoke to her, she seemed genuinely concerned for you."

"Yeah," Lilly agreed. "She was really nice. I wouldn't say no to spending a night with her."

"What about this Mr. Fisher?" John asked.

Aris considered a moment before answering. "Probably a grunt man to do the dirty work. Victor is her head of security. The real question is how she found us in Belize. How did she even know we were looking for a boat?"

"But if she didn't know we were there, then it couldn't have been her," John argued.

Kay stepped up, challenging Aris. "Besides, if she was trying to kill us, why give me her phone number?"

John stood beside her. "Kay's right. If this Varo is so clever, she wouldn't offer any information that could expose her."

The others nodded agreement.

"You don't know how shrewd the woman is," Aris argued. "Think: if we die out here, who will witness it? The risk of her being exposed is negligible."

Kay wiped away the last of her tears. "I just don't agree. I don't think she wants to hurt you, Aris. I think she's in love with you."

"You are too kind to see what a monster Varo is."

"You never said what you did to her," Uri pointed out. "Why would she want to kill you in the first place? Is she also chasing after you for that damn love secret?"

"No!" Aris chuckled. "I just refused her advances. I don't date employees or customers."

Uri scoffed, unconvinced. "Are you sure? Both Katerina and Celia tried to kill us because of the love secret."

Lilly perked up. "What love secret?"

"Something that can supposedly make anyone fall in love with you," Uri volunteered. "It's a myth that Aris fell for."

Lilly leaned forward. "I want to know this secret. I'd gladly kill for it. Does Aris know it?"

"*Pff.* He knows nothing," Uri said. "He risked our lives to get some supposed clues from a couple of old sisters. Now, he's searching for the third sister who migrated to Europe. I think she's dead."

Lilly tilted her head, thinking out loud. "So, that's why Aris wants to go to Europe. But why would Mother want to kill him? Wouldn't she want to know the love secret first?"

Aris waved off the conversation like an annoying gnat. "Varo knows nothing of the love secret. I just refused her sexual advances."

"Are you kidding? We're going to die because you refused to sleep with a stunning woman? What's wrong with you?"

"Serves you right," Lilly snapped. "Who would refuse a rich and beautiful woman? If I was her, I'd kill you, too."

"That's some feminism," John said, "sympathising with the woman trying to kill Aris. You do realise that this means she doesn't care if you die, too, right?"

Lilly sat for a moment, sucking on her index finger. "I need to think about that."

7 Sharks for Dinner

Uri sat at the starboard helm keeping watch on the horizon. On the other side of the boat, Aris stood sentinel while John and the girls rested under the bimini. The silence was thick as the boat drifted.

Jumping to his feet, Uri shouted, "Sharks!"

Aris caught sight of fins circling the boat and quickly lowered a dinghy into the water. The others gathered around, curious as to what he was planning.

He shouted over his shoulder, "John, bring me that thick rope over there."

With that, Aris jumped into the dinghy, catching the rope that John tossed him and deftly tying a noose on the end of one of the dinghy's oars.

"Get the spear!" Uri shouted, excited.

"We have no spear," John reminded him.

"What's he doing?" Lilly wondered aloud.

"He's going to try and catch the shark with the noose he crafted," John explained. "If he can, he'll be able to pull it into the dinghy for us to eat."

A glimmer of hope sprouted on the faces of the crew as the sharks drew closer. Aris dropped to his knees, trying to reach out for one with his noose.

After a moment of silence, Uri announced the obvious. "The sharks are gone."

That fragile glimmer of hope vanished.

Relentless, Aris kept banging the bottom of the dinghy trying to lure the sharks back.

A small fin broke the water's surface nearby. Aris tracked it with a sharp look, an excited gleam in his eyes. He clenched his jaw, gripping the oar, and perching on the side of the dinghy.

In one sharp slice, he snagged the small shark within the noose. The crew shouted in excitement behind him as Aris tensed his arms, trying to lift the struggling shark out of the ocean.

He twisted, yanking the shark up, but the angle and the weight allowed the shark to slip out of the rope.

"No!" Lilly hollered.

The crew lamented the sudden loss of their first real meal in days.

Drained, his arms throbbing, Aris collapsed back in the dinghy. When the last hint of water life disappeared, Aris climbed back into the catamaran.

⸻ ◇ ⸻

Varo leaned back, once again staring at Victor who now shifted slightly in the chair across from her.

"Explain to me how, despite having the best tracking devices on the market and three powerful satellites at our disposal, we have no idea where Aris and the boat are."

Victor cleared his throat. "He might have turned the girls against us, telling them lies to get them on his side. If that happened, and if he found the devices, then he could have destroyed them himself."

Eyes glinting, Varo leaned across her desk. "Sure. But it's been a month since their departure. They should have made landfall by now."

"After you mentioned the timing of their trip," Victor said, "I asked around. It is possible, but the weather is working against them. From the trackers, we know he sailed north-northwest instead of straight across. It might just be taking longer than planned."

Varo's gaze became melancholy. "I did my own research. With current conditions, a small vessel could never make the crossing safely."

"They aren't in some dinghy. They're in a custom-made, top-of-the-line catamaran."

Varo leaned back in her seat, puzzled. "That's what they said about the Titanic, but it sank on its maiden voyage."

Victor shook his head and remained silent.

Absentmindedly, Varo tapped her fingers against her desk, then sat up, a sudden thought coming to mind. "Actually, we haven't checked whether they turned around. Did you try calling the marinas or the Coast Guard? Maybe there's news of the boat on this side of the Atlantic—if it arrived or if it had to be rescued."

"We haven't checked."

"Call around to marinas, ports, the Coast Guard," Varo commanded, eager with the possibility of a new lead.

"Odds are highly unlikely," Victor warned. "If they were on land, the girls would have called."

"Unlikely or not, do it."

Victor nodded and turned to leave the office, a small smile teasing the corners of his mouth.

⁕

Aris once more sat in the dinghy fixing the noose on the end of the oar to be more secure. A heavy metal hammer lay on the floor next to him.

When the rope was the way he wanted it, he began to bang the base of the dinghy to attract any nearby sea life while the crew reclined under the bimini.

"Doesn't the fool know the sharks are gone?" Lilly asked dismissively.

"It's not just sharks," Kay informed. "He's trying to lure any large fish."

The sun set without a single bite.

Disheartened, Kay stood on the aft steps. "Come back. It'll be dark soon. You can try again tomorrow."

Aris climbed out of the dinghy and joined everyone.

Uri clenched his fist, punching the table in a rage. "We survived a Mexican gang and a firing squad only to starve to death stranded in the middle of the ocean! At least a bullet would have been faster."

Lilly curled up. "This is Aris's fault. He's useless. He can't even catch a fish."

"It's no one's fault," Kay soothed. "This just happened."

Aris laid down under the bimini, closing his eyes. "Save your energy. John, it's your turn to keep watch. I'll go after. Wake me if you spot a boat."

"How can you sleep?" Uri asked sharply. "We're all going to die because you wouldn't have sex with a woman. Don't you care? If she was ugly, I'd be on your side. But a stunner? You're messed up. I don't know why my wife Epi admires you."

"Every day is a chance for hope," Aris stated. "Every hour is a chance to be saved. Try to stay calm." He addressed the entire crew. "You all need to save your energy. That's our goal. To be alive when we are saved. To survive!"

"You mean *if* we're even found," Lilly corrected.

8 No Signal

Varo stared out her office window overlooking the skyline. She stretched to loosen the tension in her shoulders before returning to her desk. Hitting the speaker button, she issued orders to her assistant to have Victor meet her at the monitoring department immediately.

She exited her office and walked hard and fast, her unannounced arrival drawing attention from the department. A number of employees scrambled to their feet, waiting silently as if sensing her mood.

When Victor slipped into the room next to her, she approached a large monitor showing a map of the world. Pointing at a place on the screen, she said, "Along with the device I gave Kay, your man installed two more trackers that were connected to the boat's power. Where are they?"

The other employees stiffened.

Victor said, "The last signal we received places them in the middle of the Atlantic. According to satellite imagery, there have been massive storms. If they haven't capsized, then the weather is what is affecting the signal."

Varo tapped the screen to punctuate her argument. "These devices were top of the line. A storm wouldn't be able to block their signal. Someone, give me answers!"

"Power!" a shout rang out.

Varo waved at the employee and waited for an explanation.

In a hushed tone the man began, "Something must have happened to the power supply. Without that, the devices wouldn't be able to beam a signal. It also means they wouldn't be able to charge their cell phones."

Varo nodded, considering the information. "What's your name?"

"Nikos, ma'am."

"Okay, Nick." She pointed at him. "These devices had backup batteries that last six months. Even if the power was lost, they should still be functioning. So, where's the signal?"

He crinkled his brows. "Perhaps the batteries were damaged while connected to the boat's power supply."

"That might explain losing the two devices attached to the boat. But what about the sat phone we gave Kay? It wasn't connected and ran on a lithium battery that should last more than a year. I will ask again, where is the signal?"

Nikos sighed. "Someone might have discovered it and turned it off manually. Or it could have malfunctioned. It could have been damaged from the movement of the boat."

Varo stared at him, unconvinced.

A woman coughed, stepping forward. "Miss Theobald, it is unlikely that all the devices were damaged. Either they were discovered and removed, or the boat sank."

Considering the information presented, Varo's shoulders drooped. "Yes, I have thought of that possibility. Is there any way to confirm this?"

"We can't," Nikos said. "Not until we receive a signal."

Varo returned her gaze to the man. "There's no other way?"

"Well," Nikos hedged. "If we assume the boat sank, we could try and trace the emergency position indicating the radio beacon. Every boat has a unique EPIRB registered to it that releases a signal if a boat goes under. The Coast Guard would have picked it up if this is the case."

"Of course!" Varo exclaimed. "Why did no one think of this sooner?"

"This device, whatever it is, still needs a power source to send a signal," the female employee pointed out.

"Assume it has power. How do we find out?"

Nikos straightened. "The information should be under the boat registration at the marina. We should be able to get the call sign from there. Once we know that, we can use it to confirm if the Coast Guard has heard anything."

"Thank you, Nick. Your expertise has been invaluable." Varo turned to Victor. "At least someone has managed to please me today."

9 Catch of the Day

The sun slowly arced towards the horizon, and Aris sat stiff and alert in the dinghy, once more tapping the floor with the oar and scanning the ocean for a single sign of life. The water was unusually calm and the wind nearly non-existent. Only the odd cloud passed overhead.

"Just our luck," Uri grumbled. "Even the wind has died. We'll be next. Aris is cursed and we're paying for his sins."

"If this is due to bad luck," John chimed in, "then it's ours as well."

Lilly dropped to a squat at the top of the aft steps. "Do something," she cried out to Aris, her voice cracking.

The others didn't move, already submitting to their fate.

Aris glanced up to see Lilly pouting, but otherwise ignored her and kept banging the dinghy with his oar.

A moment later he pushed up on his knees with the noose in hand. "Dolphins," he called out, his voice weak. "Everyone, make some noise! It will draw them closer."

The crew gathered at the aft, hesitant smiles adorning their faces. They began to clap and stomp while a pod of dolphins broke the water's surface.

The creatures circled closer, jumping over the waves and dancing on the ends of their tails.

Aris gripped tight on the noose. "Clap! Yell! Bang the boat! Whistle!"

The dolphins playfully circled closer, and, like a flash, Aris sliced the noose to snare a tiny young dolphin. With all his might and one sharp pull, he yanked the animal clean out of the ocean and into the dinghy.

Behind him, the crew broke out in raucous applause.

Tears streaming down her face, Lilly shouted, "We caught one! We won't die today because Aris is the best captain!"

Aris straddled the young calf, pinning it to the hard floor with his knees and left arm. With his right hand, he raised the hammer over his head, his arm tensed to strike.

Then he glanced at the pod of dolphins flailing in the ocean as they continued to circle the boat. Their screeching pierced his ears.

The calf beneath him continued to flail, crying and gasping in turn.

His grip on the hammer tightened, cocked back and ready to kill. From his peripheral, he caught sight of an adult dolphin close to the dinghy. It rose out of the ocean on its tail, crying to the pinned dolphin.

Aris snarled, actually baring his teeth. His arm tensed further, veins bulging.

He started to swing the hammer down but stopped halfway, again hearing the pleading cries of the dolphin and its calf. Once more he raised his arm high in the air.

An eerie silence descended over their small patch of ocean.

Lilly burst into tears. "Kill it! Kill it! We need food."

Uri's breath came short and fast, his chest heaving. "Do it, Aris. Kill the damn thing."

Aris turned and looked up at the catamaran, the entire crew lined on the aft deck and pumping their fists in their air, urging him to finish the deed.

The pod of dolphins now screeched and thrashed in the water, drawing Aris's attention back to them. Their cries rattled in his ears.

"Goddammit," Uris shouted at the top of his lungs, "it's just an animal. Kill it!"

One dolphin pushed out of the water, calling out in a soft plea. The calf beneath Aris cried out in return, slapping its tail against the floor of the dinghy.

The sound of the baby dolphin reminded Aris of his parents. The hollow clap of his father's hand colliding with his mother's face. How they had argued about money nonstop after his father was released from prison. How Aris once got between them and slapped them both, screaming while he did. How, once, he climbed a tree and stole baby sparrows from their nest, apologising as he snapped their necks so his family could have meat for dinner.

Fighting for its life, the calf struggled, its tail flailing as it tried to wiggle out of the captive grip.

Aris's right arm was still raised when he glanced between his crew on the brink of starvation and the dolphins. Heart pounding in his chest, he clenched his jaw, his attention warring between the two groups.

Gasping in desperation, Aris released a wild scream similar to the one he'd made when slapping his parents.

The crew onboard urged him on. "Do it!" they shouted in unison.

The dolphins, reacting to his howl, called back in an orchestrated cry.

A hesitant smile crept onto the faces of the crew as the hammer swung down in concert with Aris's scream. A loud bang cut through the air and the dolphins fell silent. They simply bobbed along the surface of the ocean.

The four on the boat simmered in their rising hope as they watched Aris, bent over the dolphin in the dinghy. He remained folded, rocking back and forth over the calf.

Lilly and Kay pushed up onto their toes to try and get a better view, while John and Uri climbed out onto the main sail traveller extending over the aft. All were eager to get a glimpse of their dinner, still hidden under the curl of Aris's body.

There wasn't a sound from the dinghy, and the dolphins remained silent.

Aris shifted, beginning to move. Slowly, he unfurled his body while keeping his arms tense around his torso. As he sat up straight, the young calf became visible, clutched tight to Aris's chest. The captain pushed to his feet, his gaze not wavering from the dolphin cradled in his arms.

Leaning down, Aris placed a soft, tender kiss on the head of the calf as the crew watched in disbelief. Their spark of hope flickered out.

The dolphins in the water circled closer to the dinghy, still silent.

Lowering to his knees, Aris gently released the dolphin back into the water.

The calf swam back and forth, keeping its sight on Aris. Bending over, now Aris reached out and stroked it.

The crew dropped to the deck, unable to utter a single word.

"I don't want to die!" Lilly screamed in tears.

Uri was on his knees, crying. "That bastard chose an animal over all of us."

John remained by the rail, sitting on the aft steps in total silence.

"You're a murderer," Lilly screamed at Aris. "You put the lives of animals before the people you swore to protect!"

"Moses sent us salvation," Uri preached. "You had our survival in your hands, and you let it go!" He faced the others. "We should kill Aris. He made his choice, and he should pay for it."

Meanwhile the dolphins danced in celebration of the returned calf. They jumped and somersaulted in joy, clicking and barking. They swarmed the calf, rubbing up against it as if to ensure it was safe and healthy.

Aris remained on his knees petting the calf when it swam by, a childish grin splitting his face.

Two full-grown dolphins approached, lifting their heads out of the water. Aris bent close to them. "I'm sorry," he said, caressing their heads. "I'm so sorry."

The dolphins surged up, rubbing against his head and outstretched hand. Aris smiled with deep satisfaction as they seemed to accept his apology.

Watching him interact with the dolphins, Kay wiped away her tears. She smiled. "Aris really is a special man."

"He's mental," Uri snapped back. "That man is a psychopath!"

Unexpectedly, one of the dolphins surged out of the water and snagged Aris by his shirt, tugging him into the water.

John jerked to his feet. "The dolphins are trying to drown Aris!"

Everyone stared at the dinghy that was now empty, bobbing in the ocean. The dolphins continued to swarm around Aris, jumping and flipping, while he tried to flail his way back into the dinghy. The dolphins circled close together, rubbing up against him and preventing him from getting back in the boat.

Tears slipped down Kay's face. "They aren't killing him. They're playing with him!"

Laughing, Aris surrendered to the dolphins' behaviour. After a long moment in the water, he made his way back to the dinghy. One of the dolphins even came up and pushed him from behind to help him into the craft.

The dolphins danced along the surface of the ocean on their tails while Aris laid back in the dinghy, enjoying the entertainment with a peal of laughter.

When the dolphins finally started drifting away, the young calf that Aris had spared jumped high, somersaulting in front of him and clicking in joy.

Smiling slightly, Aris sent a last kiss its way as it left to join the rest of its pod. He reflected that just maybe the events of the day had shed light on part of the love secret he'd been seeking.

10 Winner of the Draw

Lilly slumped on the settee, her face drained of hope, while the others rested nearby. Kay shifted closer, pulling Lilly into her arms and brushing her hair back. "Have faith, Lilly. We'll figure something out."

At dusk, Aris pulled the dinghy closer to the boat by rope and climbed aboard, joining the others in the saloon.

Uri sat near the entrance, head in his hands. "So, if we aren't eating dolphin, what are we having? Or rather, *who* are we going to eat, since there isn't any other option?"

Aris slid his gaze to Lilly who immediately went stiff. She shifted back in her seat, clinging tighter to Kay. "You can't eat me," she screeched. "Men have more meat. It's smarter to eat one of you first."

Uri and John watched in silence.

Kay tensed, focusing on Aris. "Would you really do that?"

Aris also remained silent.

"How are we supposed to decide?" Uri asked, his face blank and stiff like a mask. "Do we draw straws?"

Aris stood to the side and pulled out his switchblade, flicking it open with his thumb. His drooping eyes filled the crew with an unease.

Finally, he sighed and forced out a laugh. "I have the right to decide who will be eaten first."

Lilly scuttled further behind Kay, while John and Uri exchanged weary glances.

Aris waved around his knife without a care. "Just one of us will be enough."

The air thinned and it was hard to breathe. Lilly clung to Kay, and Uri burped uncontrollably.

Then Aris sat down opposite the girls, placing his knife on the small table between them. He leaned back, folding his hands behind his head and took a deep, calming breath. "What I can't do is cook a person while they are still alive. We'll need to kill them first."

The crew glanced away, unable to look at each other.

"No!" Lilly screamed. "I don't want to be eaten. Kay, don't let him!" Turning to glare at Aris, Lilly continued, "We're the owners of this boat. We should get the final say!"

Kay curled around Lilly. "Calm down. No one is getting eaten."

"It will be fine," Aris soothed. "In the end, we'll all become fish. And you, Lilly, will be a gorgeous mermaid."

Lilly leaned forward, Aris having grabbed her attention. "Can't I be a dolphin? Everybody loves dolphins, even monsters like you. And I've always wanted to be loved by everybody." Then she burst into tears. "I'm not asking for much, just a little love. I want to be loved!"

Aris nodded. "If all you want is to be loved, a mermaid is the best choice. You'd be able to make love with young fishermen and anything in the ocean. Including dolphins."

"How? Dolphins don't love."

Aris chuckled. "Of course, they do. They have emotions like humans. They can laugh, they can cry. They don't forget those who've helped them."

Lilly scrunched her nose. "Dolphins can't make love."

"Dolphins have erections just like men," he told her. "They make love and give birth the same way as well."

"Nonsense," Uri scoffed.

Aris saw Kay also shaking her head.

"It's true," he insisted. "A girl in Scotland used to masturbate a dolphin that befriended her. She even claimed to have stood on its penis. Everyone believed she had sex with it, though she always denied the accusation."

"I like that," Lilly said. "But do you think they do oral sex, too?"

"Shut up!" Uri shouted. "Aris is just trying to distract us, but I'm not playing around. I'm Jewish. We're the chosen people. I can't be eaten!"

Aris glared him into submission. "Nothing—not gender or religion or age—will have anything to do with deciding who will be eaten first."

Losing his mind in a burst, Uri slapped the table. "Jews aren't a good source of meat. We're kosher."

"Stop being selfish," Aris chided. "This is about survival. Kosher or not, we're all a good source of protein. When the time comes, we will sacrifice one of us so the rest can survive."

Uri started pacing the saloon. "This is all your fault. You said so yourself. You didn't check the supplies. You should be eaten first. It's the least you can do."

A beat of silence followed before Aris yawned and rubbed his face. "I've already made my decision."

"Not me, please! I'll sleep with you," Lilly wailed. "I give the best blow jobs."

Uri bared his teeth like a feral animal. "Then allow me to be your last supper."

"You can't eat me!" she screamed. "I'll jump into the ocean and become a mermaid before that happens."

Glancing at the table, Uri lunged for the knife that Aris left there earlier.

Aris jerked out of his seat like a flash of lightning, landing a solid kick against Uri's chest.

Uri stumbled back, slamming into the kitchen wall before crumpling to the floor.

Aris snatched the knife off the table, folded the blade and kept it in his hand.

He turned to Lilly with a stern gaze. "Don't you dare jump in the ocean. I was only joking about you turning into a mermaid."

"You planned this," Uri said, groaning. "You never liked me from the very start and now you're going to eat me. Moses will smite you before you even touch me. Just watch."

Aris stayed calm and kept his voice soft. "Uri, have faith. A boat can still find us at any time."

For a few seconds, everyone stared in silence as they waited for Aris to continue.

"I am the oldest," he said, leaning back in his seat. He folded his legs beneath him and braced his elbows on bent knees. "I've lived a long life. If the time comes, you will eat me first."

"You're serious?" Uri asked, burping.

Aris flipped him off, continuing as if he hadn't been interrupted. "I don't have a gun, so you will need to use a knife."

John's face hollowed. "So, this is for real. We're actually going to eat each other? But I don't want to kill you! I don't want to kill anyone!"

Flicking open the switchblade again, Aris levelled the tip against his chest. "You must stab me here. Grab the knife with both hands, like this, and force it straight in as hard and fast as you can." He closed the knife and set it aside. "That's the easiest way, both for me and whoever does the killing. It's one of the fastest ways to die with minimal blood loss."

Kay became racked with tears. "No," she blubbered. "No!"

Lilly flung herself over the side of the couch. "I can't do that," she insisted. "I hate you, but I can't kill you!"

Uri dropped to his knees in thanks, offering a prayer.

John merely sat frozen.

"I can't do what you're asking," Lilly repeated.

Aris laughed, getting to his feet and walking to the saloon door. "That's okay. Uri is strong enough. He'll do it."

Uri shrugged. "Which knife should I use? Yours or the kitchen knife?"

"The kitchen knife is bigger," Aris replied, amused.

"Okay," Uri said, his burping finally dying out.

John shot forward, whacking Uri upside the head.

Meanwhile, Aris slipped out during the commotion, standing under the bimini and leaning against the bench seat.

"Do you think he's serious, John?" Kay wondered aloud.

"He volunteered," Lilly said, relieved. "And his reasons make sense to me."

Kay got to her feet and went to John and Uri. "He's our captain. How are we going to get anywhere without him?"

From the bimini, Aris called out, "In our current state, there is no use for a captain."

"Who will be eaten after you, then?" Uri shouted back. "Who should be next."

Aris shrugged. "Save your energy. I'll appoint a captain before I die—whoever has the highest chance of survival."

Lilly jumped to support him. "If I have the energy, I'll give you a massage before we eat you… like those cows from Japan."

"Wagyu Aris!" he laughed. "I would like that very much!"

11 Dolphins Dance

It was early morning and the sun was barely strong enough to illuminate the saloon.

"Does anyone know how many days it's been?" John asked slumped over a bench.

"Shut up!" Lilly groaned.

Aris was standing watch at the starboard helm when Kay jumped to her feet. "Did you hear that?"

He turned towards the aft of the boat where she headed.

She stretched an arm out towards the stern. "Dolphins!"

He stood and headed over. A few dolphins jumped and frolicked near the boat. Further behind them, an entire pod moved towards the catamaran in a circular formation.

In the centre of the pod, the water appeared rough and undulating. Peering through binoculars, Aris investigated further. His face split into a smile. "Dolphins!"

Rebellion in his heart, Uri marched out of the saloon, eyes wild, and grabbed the long rod with the metal hook on the end. He set his shoulders in determination. "We have a second chance, and we can't let it pass us by."

The others smiled, catching sight of the dolphins and all they represented.

As the pod drew closer, Aris grabbed Uri by the arm. "Drop the hook," he growled fiercely.

Uri froze.

Lilly took the moment to yank the rod from his hands and turned it on Aris. "Either we catch a dolphin, or we kill you."

Aris approached her calmly, easily wrenching the hook rod from her grasp. He tossed it on the table under the bimini. Pointing to the circle of dolphins where the water was white-capped and frothing, he said, "There are fish in there, you idiots! The dolphins brought us fish."

Everyone rushed to the side of the boat. There, inside the circle, was a school of fish, small and floundering over each other.

Grabbing the fishing net by the long handle, Aris shoved Uri and Lilly out of the way and jumped into the dinghy. The crew watched, curious, as the dolphins herded the fish close to the boat.

Without wasting a moment, Aris leaned out and dipped the net into the middle of the circle of dolphins, scooping out fish with a flick of his wrist and onto the floor of the dinghy. He did this again and again until the boat was nearly full of flopping fish.

On deck, the girls broke into tears, cheering the dolphins for their ingenuity, while Uri and John exchanged a bro-hug over their newly secured future.

"John," Aris commanded. "Pull the dinghy closer and give me that bucket there to fill it up with water. We need to keep these fish alive."

Jumping to attention, John tugged the dinghy close. Uri hurried over with a heavy, black plastic bucket, passing it to Aris who immediately started dumping water over the fish.

"Grab the slipcover from the couch," Aris called out when fish start escaping the dinghy.

Uri returned, slipcover in hand, and Aris tied it down over most of the dinghy's top. Aris then handed over two full buckets worth of fish and climbed back onto the catamaran.

"Eat, hurry!" he urged them. "Don't waste time cooking."

Like wild beasts, the crew huddled eating, hardly bothering to chew.

Coming up for air, Aris returned to the dinghy and, on his knees, faced the dolphins that remained near the boat. Two of the adults kicked up on their tails and Aris leaned out to embrace them, letting out a triumphant yell before breaking into laughter.

He slipped out of the dolphin's hold, cackling like a hyena. Suddenly, the young calf sprang out of the ocean and landed against Aris's chest.

On instinct, he caught the creature and it curled up in his arms like a baby.

Leaning its head on Aris's shoulder, it clicked softly.

Aris dropped a tender kiss on the dolphin's head.

"Man," Kay sighed. "Even the dolphins love him."

"His name does sound like one of those Greek gods," John said. "Maybe he's a descendent?"

Kay shook her head. "I've met many Greek men. None of them can compare."

John watched on with a proud gaze. "He is an extraordinary man. I'm honoured to have Aris as a friend."

Uri scoffed, unimpressed. "I think it might be easier to be his friend if you were a dolphin."

"Maybe dolphins just know how to be better friends," John observed. "They brought us food, after all. Would we have done the same for them?"

Aris gently placed the calf back in the water, nodding to the pod. The dolphins descended on the remaining fish and, after they were eaten, began to swim away.

Aris sent them all kisses, talking to them as if they were humans, calling out, "Thank you, thank you! Be safe, my friends."

When they were out of sight, he climbed back on board and approached the rest of the crew. "We will eat well tonight, but from now on we ration the fish. Don't throw away the bones or skin because we can boil it down on the gas burner and make soup. We also need to start hanging out sheets to try to collect extra water."

⸺ ◇ ⸺

By mid-afternoon, their luck turned as bad as the weather. Everyone huddled under the bimini. "This storm is coming in fast," Aris noted. "We need to secure everything before then."

Pointing at the saloon doors, he ordered, "Keep two buckets of fish there. Even if they spill, the fish won't get into the water. We'll eat the ones that die first, but we need to make sure those buckets stay full of seawater to keep the fish fresh longer."

He stopped short by Lilly who was daintily picking up slivers of raw fish and dropping them in her mouth. "You like our sushi!"

Lilly held her head high like a queen. "I used to hate sushi, but now I love it!"

"Much better than one lousy dolphin, right?"

"It's not like you knew they'd come back," Uri snapped. "It was Moses who answered my prayers."

"Keep praying, then," Aris mocked. "We aren't saved yet. We just bought ourselves a few extra days."

"It was my prayers," Lilly insisted. "The Virgin Mary sent us food."

Aris laughed at their argument. "What does God have to do with this? You should thank the dolphins. They're much more intelligent and kinder than us or even your gods!"

"The dolphins came back for you," corrected Lilly. "They don't care about the rest of us."

Uri stared down at them with the arrogance of a street preacher. "Both of you are wrong. This is the manna of the sea that was provided to me by Moses because I am Jewish."

"Fish is food. Not mana or whatever you are going on about," Lily said.

Aris snorted. "Why don't you two do something more useful and start praying for a ship?"

Lilly put her hands on her hips. "I will!"

"Maybe Lilly should be the next captain."

"I should be," she nodded.

"In that case, you need to promise two things."

The others turned their attention to Aris as he moved to the port helm, a bounce returning to his step.

"First, when you eat me, you must promise to wash your hands and teeth first, so I don't get an infection."

Lilly held his gaze, deadly serious. "I promise."

The others smiled now.

"The second is that you must let Uri eat my dick!"

Without hesitation, Lilly replied, "But I was going to keep that for myself."

Aris nodded his agreement. "I see you've already made some good plans."

Choppy waves battered the catamaran and they soon ran out of potable water. Their desperate edge to get rescued returned.

While most rested in the saloon, John maintained watch at the starboard helm. Jerking to his feet with the binoculars lifted to his face, he yelled, "Ship! Ship on the horizon!"

Aris burst out onto the deck, already shouting orders. "Uri, get me the red bag with the flares. It's under the table."

The others gathered around as Aris took the binoculars, asking John where the ship was.

John pointed off the starboard side and Aris quickly scanned the area. He shifted left and right, adjusting the focus. "I don't see anything."

"Gimme." John yanked the binoculars back. He looked out over the ocean while everyone leaned closer.

Slowly he dropped them to his side. "It was right there. It couldn't have disappeared."

Aris patted his arm in sympathy. "Maybe you were confused. The sea can play tricks on your mind. Like the desert."

John stomped his foot. "I'm sure I saw a ship. Maybe it's just slipped behind some mist. Light a flare. They will see it!"

"We shouldn't waste a flare when we can't see or hear a ship," Aris argued. "We only have so many."

John grabbed Aris by the shoulders, shaking him lightly. "Damn it, I know what I saw! It was large and grey. Just light the damn flare!"

"Do it," Uri prompted. "We can't afford to miss this chance."

Hesitating, Aris licked a finger, holding it up to test the direction of the wind. He took one flare from Uri and raised it.

"You're facing the wrong way!" Uri exclaimed.

"This is correct," Aris insisted. He lifted the flare higher and fired it. It shot straight up before curling slowly back down. "I'm not sure that was worth it, but let's burn a small fender balloon inside the metal bucket just in case. If there is indeed a boat out there, they might see the smoke."

Kay frowned. "We've burned all the balloons. In fact, we've burned everything but the main and genoa sails, which we left like you instructed."

Aris clenched his jaw. "With poor visibility, it's not worth it anyway. When the weather clears, we can gather the bedding— or anything that can burn—in case we have another boat sighting."

He turned to the men. "John, you and Uri unscrew the ceiling panels from the hulls and cut them into small pieces to fit inside the metal bucket. If we run out, then we'll cut the wall panels next."

— ◇ —

The sun settled on the edge of the horizon as Uri kept watch at the port helm. Large waves tossed the boat around like a toy. He scanned the horizon, sweeping over the stern, and coming back to the starboard side, then twisted around to check the aft.

After a quick glance, he started to turn back to port but paused. Lowering the binoculars, Uri sat in shock, mouth gaping open.

"The dinghy's gone," he whispered. Then, running to the saloon in a panic, he shouted, "The dinghy is gone, Aris!"

Aris snapped to his feet. "What do you mean?"

He rushed out on the deck behind Uri. There, tied to the aft, was a length of yellow rope dragging behind them in the water. The dinghy, fish and all, was completely missing.

The crew sank into a depression.

"This means we'll starve to death," John mumbled.

"Why?" Lilly asked, astonished.

"Without the dinghy, we have no fish. We have nothing to eat."

"I don't like this god," Lilly cried. "One minute, he's giving us fish. The next, he's taking them away."

Uri turned on Aris. "It's not God's fault. It's this curse that is plaguing Aris."

Lilly marched up to Uri and shoved him in the chest. "It's your fault. And your God, Moses. Stop praying to him. My Virgin Mary sent us fish. Moses took them away!"

Kay pulled Lilly away, wrapping her in a hug.

Aris dropped onto the port helm seat. "I should have made sure the dinghy was secure. It must have been too heavy when filled with fish and water, or the waves were too strong."

Uri growled. "You stupid, worthless man. It's one mistake after another with you. You are the captain of catastrophe!"

Silence settled over the group. Uri and Lilly walked back inside the saloon, with John and Kay trailing behind.

Aris remained alone at the helm.

Inside, Lilly turned to the rest of the crew. "We need to kill Aris before he gets us killed. He's one disaster after another!"

⸎ ◆ ⸎

A storm had blown in and lingered for a few days, but the calm finally returned. Drinkable water again became scarce and everyone stayed silent to save their energy.

John and Aris scanned the horizon with little hope while Uri sat under the bimini, staring off the back of the boat.

Kay sat across from Uri, with Lilly laying beside her, resting her head on Kay's thigh.

"Aris," Kay called. "Lilly isn't responding to me. She can't even sit up!"

Aris slid around the corner of the bimini. "Move," he told Kay, and she made room for him.

Aris settled into her place and shifted Lilly onto his lap. As the others watched, he pulled the knife out of his pocket and flicked it open.

"No," Kay screamed. "You can't kill her!"

Alerted by the shouting, Uri and John jerked out of their lethargic states.

Kay grabbed Aris's arm, yelling, "Stop it!"

Aris stared at her. "Uri, keep Kay back."

Uri wrapped his arms around Kay from behind and pulled her away a few steps.

Aris passed the knife above Lilly's throat. The girl's eyes fluttered open for a second, alighting on the blade. She groaned, trying to shake her head, but instead just closed her eyes again.

Kay dropped to her knees, covering her mouth. "Oh my god, please. Kill me instead! Not Lilly!"

"Do it!" Uri interrupted. "She's dying anyway."

Aris yanked his sleeve up on his forearm and laid the blade across his own skin just above the wrist. With a gentle flick of the knife, he made a small cut across the vein.

In a catatonic state, the crew watched as he tossed the knife onto the table and cupped the back of Lilly's head with his opposite hand, tilting her carefully and pressing her mouth over his wound.

"Suck, Lilly," he urged. "Blood will help you regain your strength."

With great effort, Lilly pried open her eyes and caught a glimpse of Aris.

"Suck, Lilly," he insisted tenderly. "It's okay." He caressed her head like a sleeping baby and she began to suckle on his open wound.

Aris looked at the others. "The Mongols used to drink the blood of their horses on long campaigns," he explained. "They would drink it straight from the vein."

"But how did you know that your blood types would match?" John asked, puzzled.

Aris squinted his eyes, but then shook it off. "This isn't a transfusion. She's drinking it as a substitute for food."

Like an infant breastfeeding, Lilly continued to lap at his blood, her eyes finally able to stay open for longer periods of time.

The others watched in awe.

"You insane bastard," Kay chastised. "If you give so much of your blood away, you'll drive yourself to an early grave."

"I'm the first to go anyway. This might buy us a little bit more time."

Uri slapped his own head. "She's nearly dead. We should just eat her. Why waste an animal that's going to die anyway? Moses would never allow it."

"I didn't realise you were so religious," Aris said in a sarcastic tone.

"We're in danger! We're dying!" Uri shouted. "Everyone turns to God when they're in danger. Just because I don't practice daily doesn't mean I don't know the basics."

Aris chuckled. "That's all you playboys do. When it helps, you turn to God and your family and friends. But when they aren't needed, you toss them aside."

"Tell him, Kay," Uri pleaded. "Lilly's the one with the lowest chance of survival. We should eat her before we all starve to death!"

Aris glared at Uri. "I've had enough of you and your arrogance. Maybe I'll kill you first."

John lifted his head. "God would never let a man such as Aris die. We can simply take turns offering blood to the weakest of us."

"No one else will injure themselves," Aris commanded. He turned to Kay. "Bring me the first-aid kit."

She nodded, tripping into the saloon and returning with the box tucked under her arm. She pulled out bandages and disinfectant.

Lilly opened her eyes wide, sucking harder on Aris's wound.

He glanced down at her. "That's enough for today, my little Dracula."

He pulled his arm away from her mouth and nodded to Kay who cleaned and bandaged the cut. He put pressure on the wrapping to help staunch the flow of blood.

Lilly reached a trembling hand up and pulled Aris down for a soft kiss on his lips. Then she managed to murmur something.

"What did she say?" asked Kay.

Looking up at Uri, Aris broke into a grin. "She said she'd always promised to suck the life out of me."

12 Mammals vs. Humans

The large military vessel cut through the ocean like a blade as sunlight seeped past the mist.

The admiral entered the bridge. "Are we still following the strange activity of the dolphins?"

"Yes, sir," a navigation ensign replied sharply.

Beside them, the lieutenant on deck slumped at his post. "I think it's a false alarm, Admiral. The dolphins are just messing around."

"Sir." An ensign jumped from his seat. "I've picked up a signal on the radar. It's faint, but there."

The admiral stepped up to the duty officer. "Which heading?"

The ensign pointed across the bow of the ship. "Same direction as the dolphins, sir."

The admiral barked out a surprised laugh. "Do we know the ship?"

"Too small to be one of ours," the officer said, shrugging. "But no reasonable person would be out here in a pleasure boat at this time of year."

The lieutenant waved away the suggestion. "Probably just jetsam or something. We can't seriously think following dolphins is a good use of our time."

"How far is the signal?" the admiral asked, ignoring his lieutenant's complaint.

"Two hours, sir, at our current speed."

Crossing his arms, the admiral's brows creased. "While at sea, we have a duty to investigate. I'm also curious to see what the dolphins are up to. Keep the course."

He stepped to the front of the bridge to take in the view, a milky fog obscuring much of it.

"This mist won't be lifting any time soon. Start blowing the horn regularly on the chance it could be a manned ship. We might get a response."

The lieutenant wilted under the unwanted order, but quickly called out the admiral's commands to the rest of the officers. They leaned into their duty to execute the orders.

* * *

The catamaran swirled across the mist-covered ocean. Onboard, the crew lay scattered like discarded clothing. Uri was slumped over, asleep at the helm where he was meant to be keeping watch. In the saloon, Aris and Lilly slept near the entrance while John and Kay curled up further back.

A low, guttural moan rippled across the silence and startled Aris awake. He hurried out, casting around for the origin of the noise and seeing Uri snoring at the helm.

"Uri, go inside," Aris said, shaking the man. "Get some rest."

Uri slid out of the seat and was plodding towards the saloon when another bellow called across the ocean.

Both men stopped at once.

Uri turned to Aris, a manic glint in his eyes. "Did you hear that?"

Aris snapped up the binoculars, turning out over the edge of the boat. "I heard it before but thought I imagined it. This fog is too thick. I can hardly see!"

Uri twisted Aris around. "Think it came from behind."

"Might be a ship trying to warn others of their position in the fog." Still searching through the binoculars, Aris said, "Grab the air horn from behind the TV."

Shortly, Uri was back, shoving the air horn into Aris's hands. Aris lifted it over his head, releasing the blaring honk in short and long bursts.

He stopped, waiting for a response as the rest of the crew tumbled out of the saloon, drawn by the sudden noise.

Uri bounced on the tips of his toes like an overly eager puppy. "Are you using morse code or something to communicate with whoever is out there?"

"I don't remember the signals, but I think I'm sending SOS. The most important thing is that they hear us." Aris passed off the binoculars to John who was now standing on his other side. "Watch for movement, a shadow, anything."

The low baritone call crashed over them again.

Kay gripped Aris's arm tightly. "It's so loud!"

"That means they're close," Aris interpreted. "Uri, grab the flares!"

Uri tilted his head in confusion. "But they can hear us already."

"Yeah, but… they can't see us through all this mist," Aris replied, a thrum of excitement making his voice shake. "They could pass right by us without noticing."

"Or r-r-run us over," quaked John.

Slipping away, Uri scurried back with the flares in hand. "Can't you just tell how far they are?"

"I'm not Moses!" Aris grabbed and readied a flair.

— ◇ —

A sound cut across the tense silence of the bridge, bringing the lieutenant immediately to attention.

The voice of one of the crewmembers on lookout filled the room. "Horn blasts, dead ahead, sir."

"Verify."

"Some weird pattern, sir. I think they're trying to signal SOS."

"Summon the admiral," the lieutenant commanded before turning to an officer at the navigation station. "How far?"

"Two knots, sir."

The lieutenant called the lookout on the VHF radio. "Can you still hear that horn?"

"Yes, sir. Getting louder."

"Reduce speed," the lieutenant commanded as the admiral took his place on the bridge, a coffee held tight in his grasp. "Course of the radar object?"

"Steady at 300 degrees, Lieutenant."

"Still on course with the horn?" the lieutenant asked the ensign at the door.

"Yes. Straight ahead, sir."

A boyish grin filled the admiral's face. "And the dolphins?"

"Still leading us in the same direction, sir," he replied. "Admiral, the horn means we have proof of life."

The admiral nodded in agreement, sipping his coffee.

❖

Uri now twitched, anxiety sparking in his limbs. He handed the whole bag of flares to Aris. "How are they going to know where we are if we can't tell them?"

Aris handed one flair to Uri. "Shut up. Just stand at the aft over there and pull the string. Keep your aim high above your head."

Buoyed by the hope that steadily inflated his chest, Aris turned to the others as he continued to blare the air horn. "They must be hearing us. Their horn is getting louder. I hope the flare and our horn will prevent them from turning into us."

"There!" John shouted. "It's a ship!"

"Start shouting," Aris encouraged, a shadow of the ship just coming into focus through the mist. "We need to show them we're here!"

The crew yelped, jumping and waving their arms in a manic dance.

"Louder," John encouraged, his arms waving madly like a conductor announcing a crescendo.

A wet slapping sound drew Aris's attention to the port side of the boat. A giggle bubbled up from his chest. "The dolphins are back!"

Around him, the girls embraced and jumped as the vessel pulled closer. Uri stood right beside them, waving his arms like a windmill. "Keep yelling, girls! They might not have seen us yet!"

Lilly started to peel off her top. "I know what can get their attention!"

— ◇ —

The bridge of the naval ship buzzed with energy. The lieutenant jerked forward. "Twenty degrees port."

The admiral peered through a set of binoculars offered to him by a nearby ensign. "It's a catamaran. How many are on board?"

"Seems to be f-f-five, sir," said the young ensign who had originally convinced the admiral to follow the dolphins. "At least one female," he added with a smirk.

"Good work…" the admiral trailed off, waiting for the man to offer his name.

"Joseph, sir."

"Yes. Thank you, Joseph. I just wonder how the dolphins knew. It's phenomenal."

The admiral watched the catamaran bob in the ocean for a moment longer before turning to address his crew.

"Launch the rescue boat. There are estimated to be five survivors, at least one female, but there may be more. Put our ship into a wide turn to stay circling their boat at a safe distance and alert the medics to be on standby."

With smiles all around, the crew enacted their commander's orders without hesitation.

13 Lucky Captain

Aris gazed as the small, inflatable boat surged through the water towards them. He'd followed their progress from the larger ship with relish. "It's Navy." He put down the binoculars. "One of ours from the U.S.!"

Kay's body went limp with relief. "Who cares who it is? We're found. We're not going to die." Then turning to her friend, she added, "Lilly, put your shirt back on."

The blonde pouted but acquiesced. "You're right. I'm so skinny, I've almost lost all my boobs."

The little craft slowed, turning sharply when it neared the catamaran. It circled their boat warily. Onboard, a group of fully armed sailors sat at attention. One held up a VHF to his mouth and then waved it in the air at Aris and his crew.

The girls waved back at their saviours while Uri dropped to his knees in a prayer of thanksgiving, rocking back and forth.

Aris sighed at the sight, knowing they weren't out of the water yet. Stumbling to get around them to the end of their ship, he shouted, "We have no radio!"

The rescue boat rocked closer, welcomed by hoarse cheers. One of the officers focused on Aris, who was standing on the lowest step, bracing himself on the stainless steel rail.

"How many?" the officer shouted.

Aris cleared his throat and raised his hand, his fingers spread wide. "Five. All American citizens!"

"Is urgent medical care required?"

Drawing in a breath to fortify himself, Aris shook his head. "Just dehydrated. And starving."

The officer leaned over his boat, concern etched into the creases around his eyes. "You're bandaged. Are you sure you're all right?"

Aris flapped his hands, shooing off the man's worry. "Just some scratches."

The naval officer relayed information back to his ship, speaking in concise phrases.

Aris smiled wanly, still bracing himself on the rail. "How did you find us?"

The man dropped the VHF, barking out a surprised laugh. He waved over at the pod of dolphins frolicking nearby. "They led us here!"

Dropping to his knees like Uri, Aris's joy felt heavy in his empty stomach. Aris threw his arm up, punching the air. "Thank you, my magical friends! You are phenomenal! I love you!"

"Captain," a young naval officer called. "Admiral McNeil wishes for you and your crew to join him on board, courtesy of the United States."

"Of course. I'd like to request a tow." Aris paused, taking a breath to strengthen his voice. "Perhaps, with your help, we might be able to fix our ship."

The man grimaced, but nodded. "I will pass along the request."

The rescue boat came close to the catamaran and two officers clambered out, reaching for Aris to help him across the small gap.

He shoved them off. "Get the others first."

Acquiescing, they slid past him and took first Lilly and Kay and then John and Uri onto the lifeboat.

Lilly wiggled into a demur position but then started to rise. "Breakfast with an admiral! Could I just grab some makeup first?"

Kay held her firmly in place with a stern hand on her shoulder. "Now's not the time, Lilly."

After the others were safely onboard, two sailors helped a wilted and exhausted Aris off the catamaran.

"Give me a moment."

The men nodded while Aris squatted on the floor of the rescue boat, leaned over and dipped his hands into the water.

He splashed to lure the dolphins closer and they flurried around him.

From the naval ship, an ensign called out to the admiral. "You have to see this, sir. The dolphins are swarming the rescue boat!"

"I've never seen anything like it," the admiral whispered reverently. "Are we recording this?"

"Yes, sir."

Aris leaned further out over the water, caressing the dolphins he could reach. "You saved us. And the calf, where is that little baby of yours?"

He pushed on the inflatable portion of the boat, trying to rise and gain a better vantage of the full pod of dolphins. Halfway to his feet, he tipped forward, losing balance.

Two of the naval crew hooked him by the arms and tipped him back into the boat. The men carefully manoeuvred around the dolphins that followed them while Aris continued to send his thanks out to them for saving their lives.

With the Navy vessel now towering over them, Aris sagged and collapsed.

Kay's alarmed cry cut through the joyous atmosphere. "Help him," she yelled, trying to move Aris into a more comfortable position.

"He went through all that trouble to save us," Lilly whimpered, "only to die when we're rescued."

One of the sailors pressed his fingers lightly against Aris's neck. "He's alive, just exhausted."

"Officer, he needs a blood transfusion," Kay urged, fear blanketing her face. "I think he's O-positive."

"The medics will have a better idea what to do, ma'am," the sailor replied as the lifeboat idled alongside the larger ship.

In a fit of rage, Kay lashed out with her fists. "Listen to me! He put himself between death for us. Look at his arms. He's been draining himself of blood to keep us alive. You need to save him!"

As the rescue boat and its occupants were transferred to the main ship, one of the sailors radioed the bridge with an update. An ensign relayed the information to the admiral without delay.

"Five American citizens: three male, two female. One of the males—the captain—is in need of immediate medical care for exhaustion and possible anaemia. They claim to have been trying to cross the Atlantic to Europe, sir."

"At this time of year?" the admiral scoffed. "Are they crazy?"

"Before collapsing," the ensign continued, "the captain requested a tow and for aid in repairing their boat."

A nearby officer folded in dismay. "Only a fool would try crossing the Atlantic this time of year!"

"He is definitely a character. He kept his crew alive by feeding them his blood. It seems he even ordered them to eat his body if it came to that."

The admiral reared back. "He fed his own blood to his crew?"

"Yes, sir."

"And he ordered them to eat him?"

"Yes, sir."

The admiral shook his head. "Well, I've never come across anyone like that before. Is he sick or wounded?"

"No, sir. All things considered, he seems relatively healthy. Just exhausted and malnourished."

The admiral turned to a nearby officer with white hair. "Have we received any orders from shore?"

"Not yet, sir."

Turning back to the rescue officer, the admiral said, "Have the survivors checked by medical. Let them eat and rest until they've had a chance to recover. And call the high-ranking officers to a meeting so we can discuss our options."

"What about the captain's request for a tow and repairs, sir?"

The admiral fell silent, shifting slightly. He looked around at his officers present.

"Whether or not they are American citizens," the white-haired officer interjected, "we should help as much as we can."

Another officer jerked in surprise. "We can't just tow them around."

"Let's see what the damage is," the admiral said, stepping between them. "Grant their request for now and look into what we can do to fix their boat."

⁘ ✧ ⁘

Around the lunch table, the admiral gathered his ranking officers. "I've never faced this situation of coming across Americans stranded at sea. We aren't a tugboat, though, so once we receive orders, we'll have to depart."

Only silence came from the officers as they glanced at each other.

The lieutenant dropped his fork on his plate with a loud clink. "If we can't repair their ship, we can't bring them with us. We shouldn't have them here in the first place."

The vice-admiral leaned forward, arms braced on the table. "We need to inform Command and await their instructions. We're going to have to report it either way."

"We should repair their ship and get them on their way," the white-haired officer confided. "If we get military orders, we can't carry them with us."

The officer across from him shifted in his seat. "We can't just send them out in their boat at this time of year. That would be homicide. Have you seen the state of that catamaran?"

"They claim it was sabotaged," the vice-admiral pointed out. "Our engineers are still investigating."

The entire table focused on the admiral, awaiting his decision. He bent over the table, slicing a piece of steak with precision.

"If the damage is reparable," he began, pausing to chew, "then we will fix it. Instruct the engineers to work around the clock to do what they can. We won't abandon them on a non-operational boat."

The vice-admiral twitched. "What if we receive orders before we complete the repairs? What if we can't even make the vessel sailable?"

"We'll re-evaluate the situation if it comes to that. Best include this all in the report to Command so we have our instructions ready."

The vice-admiral nodded, turning to address the lieutenant. "Get on it, and pass on the admiral's orders to the rest of the crew. You'll need to get the full details of their trip from the passengers—all about the boat and the events surrounding the possible sabotage."

"If there is sabotage, it's going to bring up a whole other host of problems," the white-haired officer observed.

"Like?" the admiral pushed.

"Where did it take place? By whom? Why? What makes this crew a target?"

"What agency would have jurisdiction over this?"

"I doubt it would be ours."

The admiral shook his head. "There's nothing to be done about these issues until we get instructions from Naval Command. For now, let's not overcomplicate the situation until we have concrete evidence of foul play." A soft smile glimmered on his face. "I'm beyond fascinated to meet this captain. Did you hear what he did to save his crew? He fed them his own blood!"

"But how did the dolphins even know they were in trouble?" one of the officers asked.

"Dolphins are more intelligent and empathetic than most humans," the white-haired officer offered. "They're known to warn other animals about potential danger. Fishing villages are reputed to use dolphins as a sort of early-warning sensor for disaster. Some of the rescued crew mentioned they had previous encounters with the dolphins. Probably realised the humans were stranded and in danger and simply acted accordingly."

The admiral laughed. "What a lucky captain! Saved from being eaten by his own crew by a bunch of dolphins."

He leaned back, contemplating all the information.

Picking up his knife and fork again, the admiral cut into the rest of his steak. "Still… I don't like babysitting civilians. It's one thing to save their lives, but it's another to care for them." Then with a deft elbow to the lieutenant's ribs, he said, "Though I dare say, even a stick in the mud like you wouldn't say no to the company of those two pretty girls for a couple of days."

14 Womanisers

The crew of the catamaran were deemed recovered by the third day. After receiving their cleaned clothes, they were promptly corralled into the officer's quarters, led by a young ensign to a table where the admiral and a few of his high-ranking officers were already seated.

Kay and Lilly sat on either side of the admiral.

Leaning toward Kay, the admiral asked, "Why do you think the dolphins came to help you?"

Kay sat up straight, a smile tugging at her lips. "That was all Aris," she said, then added, "sir," as she'd heard the sailors address him.

The admiral smiled, his voice warm and deep. "I'd like to hear all about it from you, and perhaps the beautiful lady on my other side, as well."

Over the course of lunch, Kay and Lilly recounted their misadventures on the high sea, culminating in the unlikely rescue.

The admiral, floored by the tale, gazed upon Aris with newfound respect. "You are truly remarkable. I'm glad we were able to find you. I've had my engineers looking over your boat. It's almost back to working order." He paused, sipping his drink. "There were some anomalies they came across which are being compiled in a report. The engines and generators were in rough shape."

The doors to the room creaked open and two officers entered, saluting the admiral and passing along a folder. "Everything on the catamaran, sir," the first officer said. "There was evidence of explosive devices used on the mast as well as the generator and engines."

"So, it was sabotage," the admiral replied, dropping his spoon next to an empty bowl.

"We believe so, sir. The device seemed to employ a powerful dissolving agent that eroded much of the mechanics on the boat."

"Sounds like professional-grade work." The admiral flipped through the report.

"We concluded the same, sir." The officer stood at attention. "The devices were positioned for maximum damage. We also discovered the remnants of what appears to be a tracking device near the mast base."

Kay lurched forward in her seat to gain Aris's attention. "You see! That's what Mother gave me, not an explosive!"

The vice admiral frowned at Aris. "Why would her mother want to sabotage your boat?"

Aris hesitated, avoiding the other man's gaze. "It's not my boat. Kay and Lilly hired us to sail it across for the woman they call Mother."

The admiral cleared his throat, turning to the young engineers still present. "Are we capable of completing the necessary repairs to their boat?"

"Yes, sir. It is well underway."

"Excellent. I want it completed as soon as possible." The admiral waved them off with a firm, "Dismissed." Turning back to his guests, he crossed his arms. "The way I see it, either the owner wants to sink the boat for the insurance money, or hopes to send you and your crew to the bottom of the ocean." He turned a sweet smile onto the girls. "But who would want to kill such lovely ladies?"

Lilly tossed her hair. "No one. All men and women love us."

Kay looked towards Aris before saying, "I don't think Mother sabotaged the boat."

"Again I ask, why would she want to kill you?"

Aris sighed. "She tried once before when I refused her."

"Refused her for what?" the admiral asked.

"Her advances."

"Is she that ugly?" He laughed.

"No way," Lilly interjected. "She gorgeous."

The admiral leered at Aris. "You reject a gorgeous woman, but feed your blood to your crew. Are you right in the head, Captain?"

At Aris's prolonged silence, the admiral laughed. "When you get to be my age, the only regret you'll have is all the women you let slip by."

⋄

Aris and his crew remained with the admiral well after lunch was cleared away, providing more information about their journey. The conversation stopped when an officer rushed into the room, saluting the admiral and handing off a communication.

The admiral read it, his lips pursed. "We have orders from Command. It seems we must part ways tomorrow."

Lilly reared back as if slapped. "Where are we supposed to go?"

The admiral tilted a smile towards her. "Back on your boat, off towards your destination."

Leaning over her chair, Lilly slid her hand up the length of his arm. "What if I want to stay with you?"

"I'm afraid that isn't possible. It would be dangerous to take you with us on a military expedition."

"I don't care," Lilly whined. "I'll just sign up for your crew."

The admiral huffed out a laugh, shaking his head. "Captain Aris, we will make sure your boat is topped up with fuel and water. We will also ensure you are ready for departure by the break of day."

Lilly's face went red. "But you know we were sabotaged! You can't just abandon us!"

"I will submit a report based on your statements," the admiral said, turning his focus to Kay. "All relevant agencies will be also informed, though you might be called in for further questioning."

Lilly pressed herself up against the admiral, pulling his attention back to her. "But I want to stay with you. Kay and I are a great team. We know how to make a stressed man like you relax and forget his worries."

The admiral leaned over her. "My dear, I wish we could keep you forever. I hope that after you're home, you contact me so we might get to know each other properly."

"Admiral," Aris cut in, "Perhaps you could keep the girls, just until you reach your next port."

The admiral patted Lilly's arm. "I wish I could, but they can't stay onboard during a military exercise. Your boat should be more than safe by tomorrow."

"What if I just burn the boat tonight?" Lilly asked, jerking out of the admiral's grasp.

"Then I would keep you here…" he replied, "in the brig, detained for sabotaging your own boat."

"I'd rather be in prison than starving to death on that catamaran again."

"The weather is favourable at the moment," one of the officers said. "In all likelihood, you shouldn't have a problem reaching Europe before it turns bad again."

Lilly pinned that officer with a glare. "Aris is insane. He almost led us to death once already. If you send us out there again, he's sure to finish the job."

"My dear," the admiral placated, taking her hand in his. "In all my years I have never come across a captain who was willing to sacrifice so much for his crew. I would trust this man with my life."

Lilly tried to pull away, not wanting to hear him defend Aris. "He's crazy and barely even knows what he's doing."

"You are in good hands. I don't know if I could captain you as fearlessly as he has. Even I might not be a match for Aris."

Lilly threw herself at the admiral, trying desperately to crawl into his lap. "Marry me, then! After everything I've done, everything I want to do with you! Surely, there must be a way."

The admiral pushed her away, depositing her back in her chair, while the others watched in barely concealed amusement. "After everything you've done?"

She jerked to her feet, tears crowding her eyes like a storm. "All you captains are the same—ungrateful, selfish womanisers! I'd rather go to prison than back on that boat!" She stood and ran out of the room.

Kay watched her friend, and in the resulting silence turned to the table. "Don't worry about Lilly. Her fits never last. She'll calm down in a few minutes."

Aris nodded in agreement, turning to the admiral. "We are thankful for your help. You had no obligation to repair our boat."

The admiral waved off the thanks. "We are here to serve. And you are quite lucky, it turns out. Whether by chance or fate, you are just west of Ireland."

"Really?" Aris gasped. "We were just floating at the mercy of the currents."

"The closest ports are Belfast or Galway, though Scotland isn't too far past."

"The wind might be against us," Aris said, pondering the safest path. "I think we'll head for Portugal or Spain, depending on the forecast."

"You'll need to sail port close hull," the white-haired officer recommended.

Aris nodded. "If Mother Nature is with us, that should steer us directly to Gibraltar."

"One Mother or another." The admiral knocked his knuckles against the table in agreement. "Sounds like you have a plan." Then he added, "At least for the sailing. As for Lilly…"

Laughter rose from all the men round the table.

15 One of a Kind

Easing back into the catamaran was an adjustment the first few days after departing the Navy ship. The considerable lack of space caused them to stumble into each other more than they used to, but after a few days, they fell back into familiar habits.

With both the main and genoa sails bursting full of wind, they made excellent time.

Kay slipped into the saloon to find Aris napping in his foul-weather gear.

"Aris," she said, poking his arm to wake him. "It's your watch."

He shuffled out, yawning, and approached the starboard helm. "Where's Lilly?"

Kay shrugged. "Haven't seen her."

Aris twisted, stretching the stiffness out of his joints. "You were on watch together. If she's not in the saloon, go check your cabin."

Kay slipped out and Aris took the moment of silence to admire the gentle rising of the ocean.

"She's not there," Kay said when she returned.

Aris pushed up onto his toes and continued to stretch. "Check with the boys, then."

Kay came back with both John and Uri, but Lilly was noticeably absent. Fear darkened her eyes. "She's not there either!"

"She's not on the front nets," Aris said, his gaze darting around the deck. "Have you checked the bathroom?"

"She's not there, Aris!" Kay stressed.

Aris turned sharply, looking at John and Uri. "What time did you last see her?"

"When we went on watch," Kay offered. "Uri was there when he handed it over to us both."

"I saw her in the kitchen," Uri confirmed. "She was making a drink as I headed to bed."

Kay gripped her hair, turning to John and Uri. "She sometimes slips into your cabin to sleep."

John reached out, trying to calm her. "We were just there. She wasn't inside, remember?"

Aris hooked Kay by the chin. "What other habits does Lilly have?"

After pondering a moment, she said, "She likes to smoke off the aft of the boat."

"Was she wearing her life jacket? Her fouling gear?"

Kay's eyes widened, her lips quivering. "I don't think she had on a life jacket."

Aris turned to Uri. "Was she wearing one when you saw her?"

"I'm not sure," Uri shrugged. "She hardly ever wears it when you're not around."

Aris rounded on Kay, towering over her like a thunderstorm. "You're supposed to make her wear it at all times! She can't be smoking, especially standing at the aft in rough weather. Go check her cabin and see if the life jacket is there."

Kay scurried away, slumping back on deck. The unused life jacket dangled at her side.

Aris twisted, punching the helm, his lips pulled back in a snarl. He pressed the button to signal "man overboard" and switched to manual control. "We're turning back. Sails down, boys. We're going on engines."

John and Uri quickly dropped the sails as Aris threw the wheel and turned the boat in a sudden arc.

"John," Aris called, "take over the helm." He stalked over to the main VHF, hunched over a map and started scribbling down coordinates.

Kay slid up next to him, keeping her head low. "What are you doing?"

"Trying to estimate where she might be floating." Aris sketched out a rough area based on their movements and then flicked back to the helm where John and Uri were waiting. "We'll need to search a large area."

Uri's chest heaved with a burp at the news. "You're taking us back? You said the weather could turn at any moment! We'll be pushed back into the Atlantic again."

Aris ignored him, his gaze out over the horizon. "We'll need to move in a zigzag to cover as much of the space as possible."

Uri smacked his head in frustration. "That's worse!"

Aris clenched his teeth. "We will search for Lilly."

A ringing silence descended.

John looked around before stepping up to Aris. "It's impossible to see anything with these waves."

Uri speared a finger at Aris. "This is lunacy. You're risking our lives again!"

"And what if it was one of you?" Aris shot back. "Would you want me to abandon you?"

John and Uri jerked back as if they had been slapped.

"There's no time for debate. Get your life jackets and secure your harnesses to the boom. One on either side of the mast, and keep your eyes peeled," Aris ordered.

He turned to Kay, huddling behind him like a shadow. "Keep searching the rear of the ship."

— ◇ —

They sailed for hours, the weather deteriorating with the light. Winds blew shrapnel of water over the deck while the engine roared beneath them.

John and Uri sought shelter under the bimini, wet and tired.

When Aris approached, Uri rose and grabbed him by the lapels of his jacket. "You have to give up this search. There's no way she survived in these conditions!"

John wavered to his feet, rocking back and forth. "We need to turn around," he whimpered. "This is suicidal."

Uri punched Aris lightly in the arm. "Come on. We're wasting fuel. We need to get back on course before the storms overpower us again! Better to lose one person than all of us."

Aris turned back to the helm, ignoring them both.

"You're a maniac," Uri said, his voice broken by a series of hiccups. "Hellbent on killing us! There's no chance of finding anyone in this mess."

John sank onto the bench under the bimini. "Uri's right, Aris. You know he is."

Desperation gave Uri's voice a beastly edge. "Lilly is dead by now."

"We're not abandoning the search," Aris insisted.

Kay wailed, "It's my fault!"

Uri slid down next to John. "Lilly was trouble from the start. It's her fault for not being careful, and we shouldn't die for her stupidity."

Ignoring everything, Aris stayed focused on the course, turning to zig and then again to zag.

"You're not Lilly's family!" yelled Uri. "We are not a family. She's just a stupid woman!"

Kay burst into tears, hunching over.

Aris turned at the noise, yanking John and Uri by their arms, and shaking them. "You're wasting time. Stop crying and keep looking!"

He turned back to the helm, expecting the rest to follow his lead.

Before they could move, there was a scuffling at the entrance to the saloon. Lilly leaned out the door, wiping the sleep from her eyes. "What's with all the arguing? You woke me up."

The others remained stiff and shocked. Aris blinked rapidly, taking a deep breath to calm the rage surging through his body. "Where have you been?"

She leaned against the saloon door, twirling her hair. "I was waiting in your cabin. I wanted to surprise you, but you never showed up. I must have dozed off." She stopped, noticing everyone staring at her. "What? Nothing even happened!"

Kay slipped next to Aris and whispered, "I'm sorry. I never even thought to look in your cabin. You told Lilly she wasn't allowed in there."

Unable to stop himself, John broke out in sudden and boisterous laughter. "You are one of a kind, a true masterpiece!"

"I know I am," Lilly replied, raising her head high.

Uri jerked to his feet, jabbing an accusatory finger at her. "We should throw you into the sea right now!"

Aris slapped Uri's hand out of the air. "You touch her, and I'll feed you to the sharks." Then he sighed, turning the boat into the wind. "John, Uri, lift the sails while we still have the wind. Lilly, put on your fouling gear and life jacket, then get me some coffee and sit right here next to me."

Lilly smiled warmly. "I like the sound of that."

❖

Lilly slumped over the side of the bench under the bimini, gazing listlessly at the horizon. "Can we have our phones back now, Aris? Or even let us use the boat phone? I'm bored."

"When we're all off the boat," Aris shot back sharply.

"You're abusing my human rights!"

Aris's mind served up an image of his wife Gina saying something similar.

"The girls will have to communicate with Mother eventually for us to get our bonus," Uri interjected.

Aris waved off the concern. "We don't need her bonuses. We'll get by on the money we have left."

Kay leaned forward. "Are you afraid of Mother?"

Aris laughed. "You heard the engineer. The explosive devices, the sabotage to our boat... We're lucky to be alive. That man who travels with her, Victor, is her henchman. Nothing happens without her command."

John shrugged. "Doesn't mean we can't take her bonus money."

"And keep the rest of it as well," Uri pointed out.

Aris blustered. "We don't need her blood money."

"We earned it! We nearly died!" Uri insisted.

Aris worried his lower lip. "We're talking about Varo Theobald here. The woman is cunning. We can't underestimate her. We have no idea what other surprises she has set up for us."

A hush fell.

John leaned back, looking over at Aris. "Where's our next stop, then?"

"Spain."

"Spain!" Lilly squealed. "I hear great things about Spanish men."

A lazy wind pushed the catamaran at a steady clip. The crew settled in under the bimini, dreaming of land.

"I miss making love to my wife," John mumbled.

Uri snorted. "Me, too."

John whirled around at Uri. "You do?"

"Yeah, I do!"

Aris smiled, watching the two men jostle each other back and forth.

John dived over the couch, wailing on Uri. "You miss making love to my wife?"

"No, I miss my wife! *My* wife!"

Aris laughed at them, his stomach clenching.

16 SPANISH MEN

The sun beat down on the catamaran as it surged over the ocean. John leaned forward at the helm, gazing longingly at the far stretch of the horizon. He sat up suddenly, his heart pounding like a drum in his chest. "Yes!" he shouted, jumping out of his seat and running into the saloon. "We made it! Land, I see land!"

Everyone rushed out onto the deck, leaning over the rail to get as clear a glimpse as possible.

Uri high-fived John and Aris while Lilly and Kay grappled each other, jumping up and down, their mouths pressed together in a kiss.

Uri whistled. "How about one of those for the rest of us?"

Lilly turned in Kay's hold, shooting a glare his way. "You can get a smooch from John."

"We never knew you two were so close," John replied, laughing.

Lilly squeezed Kay tighter. "We're celebrating that we are all still alive!"

"Well, I'm jealous," Uri teased.

Lilly smirked at him. "Go on, then. Don't be shy, boys. No need to hide."

"You never cease to amaze me," John acknowledged. "You've slept with everyone on the ship, male and female!"

Lilly tipped her head in thought. "Not everyone. One of us has a thing against blondes! He doesn't know what he's missing."

Uri's face split open in joy. "You are a star, Lilly."

"I'm a modern girl," she replied, shoulders back and head held high. "I take and give pleasure as I want, for love and to be loved. That's what living is all about!"

Kay slipped away, throwing her arms around Aris and pulling him towards her with a smile. "You brought us here alive. We'll never forget that, Aris." She pressed a firm kiss to his mouth.

John led the crew in a rousing round of applause. "Thank you, Captain," he chanted.

Aris dipped into a theatrical bow, then they gathered to watch the land consume the horizon.

"Which country is that?" Lilly asked.

"Portugal," Aris responded.

"How exciting! What language do they speak?"

John leaned over, a teasing smile gracing his lips. "Chinese!"

"Chinese?" she repeated, raising a curious eyebrow. "I've never dealt with Chinese before."

Aris laughed. "Just for you, we'll stop in Portugal before heading for Gibraltar."

Lilly pouted, cuddling up next to him. "But I've never been to Portugal! I want to get the full experience!"

"Then you'll have to use your charms," Aris joked.

John looked between the two, confused. "So where are we really going? Portugal or Spain?"

"The weather is turning against us, so we should stop and wait for it to pass. We'll moor in Portugal, restock and rest a bit."

"How long?" Uri asked.

"Not long. A few days, depending on the weather."

Lilly wiggled, barely containing her excitement. "Portugal *and* Spain! I haven't been to either of them!"

"Actually," Aris corrected. "We'll make port in Gibraltar, which is part of the UK."

"British?" Lilly sneered. "I'm so over them. All they do is drink beer and complain about football."

Uri nudged her, smiling. "Who cares, as long as we're on land."

The sun had finally peeked out above the catamaran where it rested in the slip of the Portuguese marina two days later.

Aris rose from his seat at the navigation table, yawning like a sun-baked cat. He stretched out under the bimini where the rest were gathered. "The weather is breaking. We should take advantage and head out early tomorrow."

"No!" Lilly wailed. "I still need to experience a Portuguese man!"

Aris shared a smile with the others. "Portuguese men are notoriously shy. Didn't you mention last night that no matter how much you flirted, they never approached you?"

"True," Lilly said, slumping down in her seat with a pout. "No matter what, they just ignored me."

"Don't fret. When we're in Gibraltar, we'll slip into Spain. The men there don't wait for an invitation."

Lilly banged the table as if calling a court to order. "Let's go now!"

The rest cackled like hyenas.

— ◇ —

Detective Joanna Bear strutted through the bullpen, slipping past her colleagues and into the chief's office. The man glanced up and sighed. "It's too early to be raising my blood pressure."

Joanna leaned against the corner of his desk. "You were the one who ordered me to report to no one but you, sir."

The chief leaned back in his chair and waved for her to get on with it.

She dropped a thick folder on his desk, rattling the pens stashed in a coffee mug. "The boyfriend was last seen with Miss Varo Theobald less than a day before he went missing. Early that same day, his mother claims he stopped by. He told her he was going to propose to Miss Theobald," Joanna recited. "Same M.O. with her next boyfriend. His friends claim he was planning to propose on their vacation, but he disappeared during the trip. I know she's a family friend, sir, but the pattern speaks for itself."

"I'm aware of my connection with Varo Theobald, but I trust my detectives, Joanna. That's the only reason I am tolerating your investigation."

"Sooner or later, we'll have to speak to her, sir. We also have that complaint lodged by Aris Theo that she tried to run him off the road. There are plenty of answers only Miss Theobald can provide."

"Are you ready to question her?"

"Yes, sir."

The chief snorted, pulling his cell from his pocket. "Maybe that is exactly what you need." He dialled a number from memory, placing it on speaker and dropping the phone on his desk as it rang.

"Jack, this is a surprise," oozed a woman's voice. "Especially so early in the morning."

"Sorry for the sudden call," the chief began. "Can you spare me a few minutes? I can be in your office in ten."

There was a pause. "Is something wrong? Don't tell me you lost another officer. I couldn't bear it."

He glanced at Joanna who stood firm. "No. All my officers are fine."

"Well, I guess I can give you a few minutes, but not much more."

The line clicked dead, and the chief was already standing, leading the way out. "Varo always donates to the police pension any time we lose an officer. She says it's the least she can do."

"And who does she donate to when she loses a fiancé?" Joanna mumbled.

17 Who You Desire

They moored at the Ocean Village Marina in Gibraltar, slipping between similarly styled sailboats. For three days, they took their time cleaning, restocking, and pretending that their voyage across the ocean was already a distant memory.

The crew lazed under the bimini, Aris perching nearby at the starboard helm.

Lilly flopped back on the settee, kicking her feet in the air. "We've done nothing but chores. When are we going to get me a Spanish man?"

"I thought you had fun last night," Uri argued. "What happened with those two ginger men you were with at the pub?"

Lilly's face scrunched like a used tissue. "The two with beer bellies who couldn't stop belching? Their booze was more important than me."

Aris clapped his hands. "This is the end of the road for us, Lilly. But feel free to head on to Spain if you wish."

"What? You expect me to just leave?" Lilly jerked up. "You wouldn't even have this boat if it wasn't for me!"

"I'm the captain, and it's my contract to deliver the boat to Naples."

Lilly squinted, contemplating him. "And what about Kay?"

"Kay's my partner, and useful on the boat. She goes where I go." Aris nodded at Kay who, like the rest of the crew, was looking at him like he'd grown a second head.

Lilly whipped around to Kay, poking her in the arm. "Can he do that?"

"He is the captain," Kay said, taking a deep breath. "Where are we going after Naples?"

"I'm torn between heading north to Scandinavia—"

Uri perked up like a dog being called to attention. "Yes! The girls in Scandinavia are very free and pretty."

"—or south, to Libya or down into Africa."

"No, no, no." Uri frantically shook his head. "Have you seen the news about those places? Ridden with disease, and the woman are so repressed. Why would we go there?"

"Kay and I will decide when we get to Italy," Aris informed them. He stood up and turned to Lilly. "You need to get your things and disembark as soon as possible."

Kay pulled Lilly to her feet. "Come on. I'll help you pack."

"You're abandoning me for this idiot that nearly got us all killed?"

"Come on, Lilly!" Kay dragged her into the saloon and towards their cabin.

Uri snarled at Aris. "You're a monster! Why would you separate them? Even I wouldn't do that."

Aris responded by shoving his middle finger in front of Uri's face, focusing his gaze straight ahead.

—◇—

Joanna kicked at the plush carpet outside Varo Theobold's office where she and the chief waited to be invited in. The chief stood apart from her, at ease, with his hands clasped behind his back.

The large office door squeaked open as the waif of a secretary slipped out. "She's waiting for you," she said.

The door closed with a hiss behind them.

Arms wide open, Varo hugged the chief, smiling as she pulled away. She turned to the young detective, flashing a similar if somewhat dimmer smile.

The chief introduced them. "This is detective Joanna Bear."

"She's an angel, not a bear!" Varo joked, offering a hand for Joanna to shake. "It's about time you started promoting more female officers. Your precinct was becoming a bit of a frat house."

Joanna gave a perfunctory handshake but otherwise didn't respond.

Sensing apprehension, Varo's smile slipped, but she fixed it back as she faced the chief.

He stepped forward, slipping three photos out and placing them on Varo's desk. She walked over, looking down at them.

"We know you are familiar with this man," the chief said tapping the picture on the left. "But do you recognise the other two?"

Varo's smile fell off her face. "They're my exes."

Clearing her throat, Joanna pushed between Varo and the chief. "What happened to them?"

He began a stuttered apology but Varo waved him off. "It's okay. Us girls love to gossip about failed romances," she reassured. Turning to Joanna, her face was as empty as a dry lake bed. "Same thing as always. They showed such promise, but inevitably fizzled to nothing. I think I might be cursed."

Jonna watched the woman closely, how her eyes kept flickering to her and then away. "I'm surprised that anyone would want to lose you. Gorgeous and rich. Seems like the full package to me."

Shifting her weight to stand taller, Varo narrowed her eyes. "You get used to it. I think they're just intimidated by successful women."

"Have you spoken to any of them since the break-ups?"

Crossing her arms, Varo seemed to consider the question. "No, I prefer a clean break. I'm also a little too busy to be chasing after men." She glanced to the chief. "What's going on? Is there some issue?"

Joanna stepped closer, shoving a finger at Varo. "You—"

The chief placed a restraining hand on Joanna. "The only connection between them is you."

Varo leaned against her desk, picking up one of the photos. "Sounds like a conspiracy. Are they after me for something?"

"It's not them we're looking into," Joanna cut in.

Her patience wearing thin, Varo planted her hands on her hips. "What are you insinuating?"

"These men are all missing," the chief replied.

In her eagerness, Joanna prevented him from going further. "Do you know someone called Aris Theo?"

Varo blinked, nodding. "Yes, but he isn't an ex, nor has he vanished." Joanna saw a trace of something cross the woman's face before she continued speaking. "From what I hear, he's travelling the world. What does he have to do with these men?"

"Mr. Theo filed a complaint against you," Joanna responded. "He claims you tried to murder him."

Varo barked out a laugh. "I should really give up on men. I confessed my love to him, and he turned around and accused me of trying to kill him. How typical. He even attacked me right here in my office, though I fought him off. I'm sure I can get the video pulled for you."

"Miss Theobald has a black belt in karate," the chief explained.

"You've actually met Aris before, Jack," Varo said to the chief. "He was the Greek who accompanied me to the fundraising event. What exactly did he claim in his complaint? Can I read it?"

Joanna shifted under Varo's gaze. "He didn't submit his complaint in writing."

The chief's face grew beet red. "You said he filed a complaint."

"He did," Joanna explained. "He told local traffic cops that someone deliberately pushed him off the road."

"Is that it?"

Joanna held her head high. "Mr. Theo stated he had a fight with Miss Theobald in her office before the attack."

"This is the complaint you have? A traffic accident!" the chief growled.

"Having a fight with Miss Theobald in her office is not enough, sir?" she asked but continued before he could offer a rebuttal. "He also stated Miss Theobald threatened to destroy him. We cannot ignore these facts."

Varo stepped around the detective, placing a hand on the chief. "It's true, he was in my office. When he refused me, I told him I could destroy him. I was embarrassed and lashed out.

Maybe he took it literally. I might have overreacted, because I fell for the idiot the moment I saw him."

"Do you believe Miss Theobald?" the chief asked Joanna.

"I believe she's in love with him, but there's little more dangerous than a woman in love." She paused, smiling at Varo. "Especially one with such a big ego. Miss Theobald just gave us the missing motive."

"Nice," Varo spat. "But you're forgetting something, Detective. Aris might've refused me, but the others didn't. Where's the motive for them?"

"Anyone who refuses you tends to just disappear. Why? Obviously, you can't handle rejection."

The chief huffed, but Varo sank down, bracing herself on her desk. "Aris has this hold over me. He traps himself in a marriage that leaves him miserable with pointless ethics even though I know he loves me. Why can't he just accept that? It burns my soul."

"You aren't usually controlled by your emotions," the chief urged. "You're stronger than that."

Varo offered him a small, fragile smile. "Not with this one. The more I try to forget him, the more he seems to control me. Even work no longer distracts me. He's the only man to ever refuse me. He's different from every other man I've ever loved. He's braver and smarter. And his sense of morality is from another era. Every part of him draws me in."

Joanna's smile flashed like a knife. "She knows you have a soft spot for her. She's playing you, Chief." She stepped away, heading out of the office. "You should know one thing about me, Miss Theobald. I have never left a case unsolved. This one is no different."

⋯ ◇ ⋯

Lilly stomped across the deck, dragging her bag behind her. She swung it up onto the table with a thud before hugging both John and Uri farewell.

Kay slipped out of the saloon a few minutes later, her backpack slung over her shoulder.

The deck fell silent at her appearance.

Aris locked his body in place, only his Adam's apple bobbing as he tried to swallow. His dry tongue stuck to the roof of his mouth.

Uri and John glanced between Kay and Aris. Kay moved forward, dropping her bag next to Lilly's. They watched in silence as Kay clasped Aris's hands between their heaving chests.

"I've never met anyone like you," she confessed, tongue wetting her lips. "You are perfect. Every girl dreams of a man like you."

Aris clenched his jaw, his teeth aching from the pressure. "Just not perfect for you," he bit out.

"You are more than good enough for me. I've never felt this way for anybody but you."

Sliding his hand from her grasp, Aris sighed.

"You are perfect, but I'm not who you desire."

Aris swallowed stiffly, digesting her words.

"You deserve to chase after the love you dream of," Kay insisted, pulling back from his embrace. "Even if you never find her, you deserve the chance for your perfect love. No one— not even me—has the right to deny you that."

Aris brushed her cheek with his thumb. "You are my dream girl, Kay."

Kay shook her head, tears slipping over her lashes. "No, I'm just another girl for you. Liking me, sure. But you aren't in love with me."

Bursting over to them like a raging bull, Lilly beat Aris's back with her fists. "You bastard! You take and take the love we give you, but never give us any in return! You scorn us and toss us aside like we mean nothing." Tiring herself out, she slumped against his back. "There's no such thing as true love. You work with what you're given. What are you going to do when you leave and realise we were the best you could have?"

Kay stood on tiptoe, pecking Aris's cheek. "Then he can look me up," she said, finally stepping away. "Can we have our phones now, Captain Aris?"

"They're in the blue bag on the counter," he replied, face still and placid as a frozen pond. "Both are fully charged. There's also money in the bag for you. Enough to hold you over until Varo sends your payment."

Lilly sniffed back tears. "What are we supposed to do?"

"When you report to her, tell her the boat is safe. I'll find a way to get in touch with her about where she can pick it up."

John grunted. "I thought you didn't trust her. Earlier, you didn't even want her money."

"I'm not trusting her," Aris said, waving away John's concerns. "We're simply completing the job, so we're entitled to our pay."

The girls gathered their belongings and Kay stopped in front of John where he was leaning against the port-side helm. She hugged him, slipping her hand into his and pressing a folded scrap of paper into his palm. "Memorise both of these numbers," she whispered into his ear. "You never know. Having a way to contact Varo might come in handy. The other number is mine. Give it to Aris if he ever wants it."

John nodded, secreting the note in his pocket.

The girls waved wanly as they disembarked. The men fell swiftly into silence. John and Uri refused to even attempt making eye contact with Aris, who slumped at the helm, his body folded in on itself like a snail tucked into its shell.

Eventually, John cleared his throat. "I really thought you and Kay were serious, Aris. It's obvious she loves you, and it seemed as though you felt the same."

Aris shifted, keeping his gaze firmly on the receding forms of the two women. He watched Kay's dark, swishing hair until it was obstructed from view. "I guess she grew on me more than I grew on her."

Uri clapped his hands, standing upright like a professor giving a lecture. "I keep telling you, women don't want love or dreams. Those are intangible things for schoolgirls. They want something more, something physical."

Aris glared at Uri out of the corner of his eye but otherwise refused to engage. He crossed his arms, tightening them across his chest.

"You are both overcomplicating this," John bemoaned.

Uri wagged his finger. "You need to understand. Women are governed by their sense of survival." He marched over to Aris, clasping him on the shoulder. "Their survival instinct is stronger than either their hearts or their brains. Love comes second to this. Once you understand that, you'll never disappoint a woman ever again."

Aris stared at Uri as if he could read the logic of the argument on the other man's face.

"We should follow their example," Uri continued. "Take pleasure while we can, while she's with you. Then, leave her once you're done. Forget love. Seek women for just the simple pleasures!"

Aris nodded, mumbling to himself, "Maybe you're right. Nothing else is simple with them."

18 Porto Torres

Aris didn't give John or Uri any time to rest further. As soon as the catamaran was prepared, they eased out of the marina headed into the Mediterranean.

The three men worked in silence until the boat was cruising. John and Uri settled under the bimini.

A few minutes later John called out to Aris, who was sitting at the starboard helm. "I think you owe us an explanation."

Aris didn't even shift his glance from the ocean. "The girls had to go."

"I'm not talking about them," John said. "I'm talking about where we're going after Naples."

"I didn't want the girls to know our plans in case they would share it with Varo," Aris conceded. "We'll be going to western Greece, then wherever east into the Balkans or the road takes us from there."

Uri lurched to his feet, stomping in childish angst. "But you said Scandinavia! What about the beautiful women up north?"

Aris tilted his head, smirking over his shoulder. "That's so the girls would report it to Varo."

"You're obsessed with that woman!" John criticised.

"Well." Uri shifted forward. "How long to Naples?"

"Depends," Aris shrugged. "We'll follow the coast across Spain and France before heading south. We're in no rush anymore, so we can take our time. Stop along the way and pick up some French and Spanish girls."

Uri grinned now. "That doesn't sound so bad. But why are we heading into the wasteland past Greece? Albania and the Balkans? They're essentially mass graves."

Aris sneered at Uri's characterisation. "That's the best part. They make an excellent place to die. Think of all the company we'll have."

"Bullshit," Uri said with a shake of his head. "You're still searching for your love secret, aren't you?"

"So is Naples the plan or not?" John enquired, looking between the two men.

"Probably. Or anywhere we can find a marina where we can safely moor."

"Let's not be in a hurry," Uri begged. "Italian women are known for their passion."

"You'll have *stiff* competition," Aris laughed. "Italian men are equally charming!"

✧

Varo shuddered when the phone flashed beside her, announcing an incoming call. She spared a glance at the caller's name before lunging for the device. "Kay! Where are you? What happened? We lost all contact with you weeks ago."

Kay's heavy breathing laboured over the line. "We're in Gibraltar, at Ocean City Marina. We nearly died," she whispered. "And Aris knows who you are."

"How?" Varo asked, leaning forward.

"There was trouble. I can get into it later. He forced me and Lilly to leave the ship, and we only just got our phones. He's leaving, Varo. He said they were going to Naples. He asked me to tell you that once he receives his payment, he'll tell you where the boat will be."

Varo's eyes flitted around, trying to keep track of her whirling thoughts. "Has he switched off his phone? I haven't been able to contact him."

"He blocked everyone's mobiles. They probably have switched to local sims and don't even have the same numbers, anyway." There was scratching over the line before Kay continued. "He knows you were tracking the boat. He even thinks you sabotaged it. I told him that was ridiculous, but he was insistent."

"Why would I sabotage the boat?"

"Aris mentioned you've tried to kill him before."

Varo deflated in her seat with a sudden exhale. "He really blames me for everything. You sound tired, but I'm glad you all made it in one piece. Check into a hotel, and I'll call later to see how you are."

"I'm just..." Kay mumbled, her voice breaking slightly. "...disappointed, really. He cast us off like it was nothing. Gave us some cash and sent us on our way."

Varo couldn't help but smile. At least she wasn't the only one Aris refused. "Just take care. I'll have everything organised to get you home. I'll be in touch."

Varo tapped the screen, ending the call. With a deep breath, she sat up and placed a new call. Victor answered before the first ring had the chance to end.

"Victor, I found them. Kay just called. They're in Gibraltar—Ocean City Marina."

Varo waited, but Victor didn't respond.

For a moment, only a deep rush of air was heard on his side, so she continued. "There still isn't a signal from their devices. Try to find a local operative to check. Immediately! Before they have a chance to depart for Naples."

⸻ ◇ ⸻

When they departed Marseille, Aris tipped the catamaran suddenly southward, cutting across the Mediterranean with a definitive arc.

"Are we heading straight to Monaco?" John asked.

"No."

John jerked back. "Genoa, then?"

Aris scanned the horizon. "We have good winds from the east. Cutting this way will be fastest."

Uri saddled up next to him at the helm. "South means Africa."

"I thought we were going to Naples," John gently reminded.

"We are," Aris confirmed without hesitation. "We're cutting across to Sardinia. From there, Naples is just a short jaunt."

"How long?" Uri seethed.

"If the wind keeps? Two days, maybe less."

John glanced at Uri before looking back at Aris. "You said we would stay near the shore."

"I'm just following the weather. This is the ocean, not a motorway! Some things are out of my control."

Uri flopped back under the bimini, murmuring, "Open seas, again."

"We are surrounded by land," Aris reminded him. "The Mediterranean is much friendlier than the Atlantic."

"You don't have another aunt you want to visit in Sardinia, do you?"

"I have aunts everywhere," Aris teased. "Greeks have travelled and settled all over the world. We can be found everywhere. Even the name of Naples is derived from its original Greek—Neapolis!"

Uri bumped John with his shoulder. "Now we know why he wants to leave the boat in Naples. He's still chasing after that damn love secret."

———— ◇ ————

They docked at Porto Torres in northwest Sardinia. Aris eased the boat into the marina, and they made quick work of mooring it securely.

"Wash the boat and fill the tanks," Aris ordered. "I'll run into town and grab supplies. Then we can head to dinner."

Uri jumped to his feet. "We're coming, too! We can do all of that other stuff tomorrow."

Aris shrugged. "Suit yourselves."

The three plodded up to the plaza nearby. On one side was an outdoor café occupied by mostly elderly men.

"Let's have a decent coffee and a quick bite," Uri suggested. "I'm too hungry to wait for tonight."

They settled at an open table and ordered drinks. Aris found himself suddenly drawn into a conversation by the surrounding locals. "I never knew Sardinia was so beautiful. I should have visited years ago," he said, smiling at the other men. "You know, we are practically cousins."

"How so?" one of the men asked.

"I'm Greek. Many Greeks settled in Sardinia. Especially in Iolei in the south. Sicily, as well."

"Don't listen to him," Uri apologised. "Everything good and beautiful is Greek or discovered by the Greeks."

"But it's true!" one of the men retorted.

"You know," John cut in. "I'm part Italian."

A man at another table jabbed his thumb at Aris. "He looks more Italian than you."

"My mother and grandmother are both Italian," John insisted.

One of the younger men smirked, shooting rapid Italian.

John looked at him blinking rapidly, his face twisted in confusion. He nodded quickly, not wanting to be caught out.

All the others burst into laughter.

The younger man repeated but in English, "Like a mule, you make big bubbles with your ass."

Aris did his best to extract John from the mocking. "I have an aunt who moved to Sardinia some years ago. Her name is Garoufalia—it means carnation. Do you know anyone by this name?"

One man thought for a moment before shaking his head. "No. What was her family name?"

"Not sure. She left her husband and child in Guatemala to run away with a Sardinian man. She brought a daughter with her. The girl, Korona, has a long scar up the left side of her face from a knife."

"I would remember someone with such a unique story," the man replied.

"Many women run away with Sardinian men," one of the younger men interjected. "It's impossible to know them all!"

The others burst into laughter again.

Uri slouched in his chair, shaking his head at Aris. "Seriously? You're still looking for this love secret nonsense.

You nearly got us all killed crossing the Atlantic for a stupid myth."

◆ ◇ ◆

"What is this about a love secret?" asked the man who had called John a mule.

"Ignore Uri." Aris waved a dismissive hand.

Uri pointed his finger at Aris. "This hero here dreams of discovering some love secret which will enable him to make anyone fall in love with him."

Bursting into a laughter, an elderly man replied, "Greeks are fond of myths."

The young Italian butted in. "There's something about this love secret. Long ago I overhead the local don's mother talking about it." He gazed at Aris. "So this is why you are here, searching for the love secret? You believe this woman and her scar-faced daughter Korona know the secret?"

Aris sucked in his cheeks. "There's no such thing. The old man is right—it's just a myth. We're on our way to deliver a boat to Napoli. That's why we're here."

The Italian's stare now fixed on John. "So the boat is not yours. You are just the crew delivering the boat?"

John shrugged. "Yes, we crossed the Atlantic to bring it."

Uri rose to say something, but Aris fixed him with a sharp glare. "Nice chatting with you all," Aris said, rising to leave. "It's time to wash the boat and fill the tanks. *Ciao.*"

With a hard nod to John and Uri, Aris walked away.

◆ ◇ ◆

After the Americans departed, the young Italian climbed on his bike and headed out. Within a few minutes he appeared in front of the local don's house, where the man sat enjoying a coffee with his mother, a woman with a faded scar on the left side of her face.

At the sight of him, the mother quickly tied a scarf over her head, covering her cheeks.

105

The older man called out, "What is it that made you race here, cousin Marko?"

"Three men sailed the Atlantic and moored in our marina."

"So?"

"They came to the café."

The man merely raised an eyebrow to show he was not impressed.

"Aunt, do you remember how grandmother kept talking about the ancient love secret… how to make anyone fall in love with you?"

"A Greek myth," came her casual reply.

Marko's voice became excited. "One of these three men is Greek. According to his friend, he is searching the world to find this love secret."

His aunt turned her head sideways, dismissing Marko.

"They risked their lives to find this secret."

She laughed out loud. "And did they find it?"

"No," Marko answered, "but he's searching for a woman who came to Sardinia with her daughter some years ago. He suspects she must know of the secret."

Exchanging a silent glance with his mother, the don asked, "Who is this woman?"

"I forgot the name. He said it meant carnation in Greek. But I remember her daughter's name, which they said is Korona… and she had a scar on her face."

Again the two exchanged a meaningful glance, but the don sternly said, "No such thing. Ignore them."

Disappointed Marko walked away while the don stared deeply at his mother's expression.

— ◇ —

John and Uri spent the next morning scrubbing down the boat until their arms ached. After they had refilled the water tanks, they joined Aris under the bimini where he was tracking the weather and plotting their course.

"Bad sailing weather for the next few days. We should hire a car and explore the island," Aris advised.

"Sounds great." John's voice held a trill of excitement. "It would be nice to take a break from the ocean for a while."

Uri sneered. "Aris just wants to stop in every little village to find his scarred cousin."

Aris tilted a small smile in his direction. "You don't have to come. In fact, you should stay and look after the boat. The mafia is known to still have a presence here in Sardinia."

"No way!" shouted Uri. "I'm not dealing with mafia shit."

The trio spent three days weaving in and out of the villages that dotted the island. By the third evening, even John was losing his patience.

"We've looked at every tiny village on this rock," Uri argued. "Nobody knows of any scar-faced Latina. It's time to move on!"

Aris nodded. "We'll set sail tomorrow, stopping in Cagliari before we cut across to Naples."

"Oy," Uri vented. "So now we have to search the southern half of this island, too?"

⁕◇⁕

The atmosphere on the boat still sparked with tension a few days later when they docked in the marina near Cagliari.

Uri smirked at Aris who was rigid at the helm, refusing to look at anyone. "Told you we'd never find that woman. You were misled every step of the way. I only hope you didn't lose too much money acquiring that fanciful story you were fed."

The longer Aris remained silent, the bigger Uri's smile became. "A married woman running away with a Sardinian man? Any donkey would have noticed that story was bullshit. At least now you understand that this search of yours is pointless."

Before Uri could open his mouth again, Aris launched himself and pinned Uri by his throat. Fist quivering in front of Uri's face he spewed, "You need to learn when to shut up. I paid no one. I wasn't fooled!"

John yanked at Aris's clenched hand. "Guys, enough!"

Aris dropped Uri. "I will search a thousand churches if I feel like it."

"We've already checked every town here," John soothed. "Every village and church. Even the remote monasteries."

Aris now speared John with a glare, but finally he relented with a sigh. "We did, didn't we?"

"The old man was right," John said. "With such a story and noticeable scar, someone would have remembered her."

Aris plopped down under the bimini, his shoulders slumping under the weight of reality. He had no more clues to follow, he had been rejected by Kay, and he was getting nowhere, without any idea of where to head next.

Scrubbing his hands over his face, he said, "Maybe you're right. I'm chasing a myth. There isn't a love secret and there's no village without a name."

John and Uri settled beside him to wait.

"I'm sorry I dragged you both into this."

"Don't worry," Uri gave in, encouraged by Aris's admission. "We just need to find some women and be happy. And when we aren't happy anymore, we find new women!"

Aris stared at Uri for a long moment, his brows furrowed.

"Didn't you feel happy with Kay?" Uri asked. "Or Celia in Guatemala? You said yourself that she had a bubbly character." Uri watching a smile ease its way onto Aris's face. "And what about Katerina, the hairdresser in Mexico? You wanted to marry her. Didn't each of those women make you happy for the short time you were with them?"

Aris nodded, his smile wider.

"Exactly," Uri exclaimed. "That's what it's all about. Make a woman happy and she will make you happy in return. Then, move on."

Aris leaned back, his voice soft and tired. "Maybe you're right. No more searching. It's time to depart."

— ◇ —

Gina was lounging on the couch in a tight tracksuit when the doorbell rang. For a moment, she considered not answering it since she wasn't expecting anyone, but when it rang again she slinked over and opened the door.

"Epi, Leoni. What a surprise! Come in."

Uri and John's wives were wearing flowy summer dresses. They smiled and kissed Gina on the cheek as they entered the house.

"You've both put on a bit of weight," Gina assessed as they settled in the living room. "Are you pregnant? Or competing to see who can get the fattest before your husbands return?"

"I can't seem to stop eating," joked Leoni.

"What about you?" Gina asked, turning to Epi. "It's easy to gain weight, but hard to shed it."

Epi glanced at Leoni before answering, "I eat a lot, too."

"If you were pregnant, I wouldn't blame you," Gina mocked. "We all love the feeling of a man between our legs. If you found a replacement, I'd understand."

Epi glared at Gina, her body rigid and suddenly cold.

Leoni shifted slightly. "You seem to have lost some weight, Gina. You look like a teenager again."

"I like to take care of myself," Gina replied. "Are you sure you both aren't pregnant?"

Leoni laughed. "Perhaps, but we would keep it a secret."

"Who would blame you? Our men are out enjoying themselves. We've only got one life… we should enjoy it!"

Leoni and Epi glanced at each other.

"You're too young to be sitting around waiting for them at home," Gina insisted.

Epi smoothed out her dress. "Some of us are proud to wait for our husbands. It's not a bad thing to miss them, and they'll return soon enough."

Gina flicked her feet to dislodge her slippers. "Epi, you are so naïve sometimes. You're wasting your youth on Uri. Relax and enjoy your freedom while it lasts!"

Epi's face grew harsh. "I'm not interested in that kind of fun."

Tucking her legs under her, Gina smiled wanly. "I used to be like you, always waiting for Aris. Sitting in the house while the world drifted by. But not anymore. There's nothing wrong with going out and having fun with friends."

"We'll have to just disagree on that," Epi said. "Has Aris made contact with you at all?"

"No! And I wouldn't want him to, anyway. I'm at peace, no longer having to listen to him criticise me or threaten me or control me. He used to have me followed, you know."

The two other women listened as Gina ranted. "I think Aris managed to speak to the boys once. That's it. You know how it is—men and their heirs, always more important than the wife. And what about Uri and John?"

Leoni laughed again. "Aris forbade them from making contact."

"That's Aris," Gina scoffed. "Always a dictator."

This made Leoni laugh even harder. "John's cheated a few times, getting in touch with me here and there. I think he might have found a bit of backbone on this trip. Last I heard, they were somewhere in Central America."

"And your little Casanova, Epi?"

"Yes," Epi announced proudly. "A few calls, a postcard here and there."

"You know where they are?" Leoni turned sharply to Epi, poking her in the shoulder. "Tell me!"

"I can't. Uri asked me not to, or Aris might send him home."

Gina barked out, "I never would have expected Uri to be the one to stay in touch."

"You never approved of him," Epi retorted. "But he's a good man. You'll see. Marriage has changed him."

Gina dismissed her with a flap of the hand. "You're only hurting yourself with these delusions."

"You clearly don't understand me, and I will never understand you."

"One day, you will wake up and remember my words," Gina said. "Then you'll understand."

Epi glanced away. "We'll just have to agree to disagree on that."

Bracing her hands on her knees, Gina gazed at them with a sense of detachment. "You're a victim even in your own dreams."

"Let's all relax," Leoni tried to rein in the conversation. "We just dropped by to say hello."

"It was a mistake to come here." Epi stood. "Reminding Gina of Aris seems to have upset her. We should go."

"You come into my house and try to lecture me," Gina railed. "You're fools to wait at home for them."

Leoni stood to follow Epi. "Sorry to have upset you, Gina. We didn't have any intention of doing so."

A grin flashed across Gina's face. "I'm not upset. Where are you running off to? I haven't even offered you a drink yet. I have your favourite sweets as well, Epi. Sit, sit. We won't even talk of men."

The two women nodded to each other. Epi sighed and she and Leoni sat back on the couch.

Gina ducked into the kitchen and returned with a tray of drinks and a little plate of sweets. Standing tall, she held a hand against the flat of her stomach, turning to the side to show off the swell of her butt.

"I started going to the gym again. You two should join! It's great for your health… and look how fantastic I look. Not to mention the trainers there are easy on the eyes."

"I should look into that," Leoni agreed, while Epi just shook her head.

19 Love in Naples

The catamaran drifted into Naples in a spate of beautiful weather. After securing the boat at the marina, Aris headed to the office to provide documents for immigration and customs.

While away from the others, Aris pulled out his cell phone and quickly placed a call. It rang for a bit, causing him to pace.

Then he heard a woman's voice. "Cali?" he asked.

"Aris, is that you?"

"I wanted to let you know I gave your number to Drosita in Mexico and Chrisafina in Guatemala."

"Yes, yes. I've already heard from them both."

"I just left Sardinia to look for your cousin, Korona."

"Did you find her?"

"No, that's why I'm calling. I've reached a dead end. I thought I'd check to see if there's anything we might have missed."

"I'm sorry, there's nothing I can think of."

"Are you sure?"

"I've searched through everything I can find. Even spoke to my mother again. There's nothing we haven't already told you. I'm sorry."

"All right." Aris tilted his head back to watch a cloud drift overhead. "I'll call back in a few weeks in case something comes up."

"I'll call you sooner if we find something."

"No, my American number isn't working and this one is temporary. When I get a new phone card, I'll get in touch myself." Aris ended the call, walking slowly back to the catamaran.

On deck, he joined Uri and John under the bimini. "We should enjoy Naples for a few days. Maybe after this might be a good time for you both to return home."

"Hey now." John punched Aris's shoulder. "You can't get rid of us that easily."

"What about the boat?" Uri asked.

"I've already told the marina that the owner will be picking it up in about a week or so. The boat is no longer our problem."

"Are you going to call Varo?"

"No," Aris sniped back.

"If you don't call," John said, "how will she know the boat is here?"

"I assure you, Varo will have had people watching us. The boat is registered at this marina, so she will find it in no time."

John shrugged. "Where to from here?"

"If you aren't returning home, then wherever the road takes me."

Uri frowned. "You don't trust us enough to say where we're heading?"

"There's no reason to keep it a secret," John agreed. "We aren't Varo's spies."

"When I know, you'll know!"

"Can you at least give us a few days here to relax?" begged Uri. "Maybe have fun with some of these Napolitano girls?"

Aris recognized Uri's single-track mind. "Of course, there's no reason not to enjoy ourselves."

"Hallelujah!" Uri exclaimed.

"What's with you and Italian girls?" John asked. "They're just like any other. Maybe a bit wider in the hips."

Uri slapped John aside the head. "Are you stupid? Girls here are known to be amazing in bed. Hot-blooded bombshells. They take their time and send you to heaven without fail."

John chuckled. "You said you've never been to Europe. These are just fantasies."

"I'm telling you," Uri insisted. "If you get a Mediterranean girl, make sure you last, or she'll drop you fast."

John shoved Uri away. "I don't intend to meet anyone. I'm faithful to my wife."

— ◇ —

They headed to a nearby restaurant after the sun slipped away. There was a bar against one of the longer walls with frescos surrounded by gilded frames on the others, giving the impression they were painted on canvas. Between the tables, waiters flitted by wearing dark trousers and burnt orange t-shirts. Aris, John and Uri grabbed a seat on the far side and ordered immediately.

Nearby, a large group of men sat hunkered over the table slurping down their food. Three women were seated next to the entrance sipping cocktails, and a couple of ladies occupied the table beside them.

Standing at the bar, two women faced each other, gossiping but observant, like they were looking for something.

Uri poked John. "Finish eating first. You can still chat them up when you're done."

John took another bite, his gaze lingering on the girls at the bar.

"If you don't stop staring, you'll choke on your dinner," Uri repeated.

John popped out of his chair. Aris and Uri watched in awe as he sauntered up to the women at the bar. He smiled with a confidence neither of them had seen before.

Approaching the busty girl on the right with black hair and rounded hips, John cupped her hand, bringing it to his mouth for a kiss.

She smiled back, but her companion smirked at John's brazen approach.

"I can't believe what I'm seeing," Aris hooted.

"Neither can I," Uri echoed. "He beat me to the girls! Didn't even say a word."

John stepped closer, flashing a charming smile. "You are the most gorgeous woman I've ever seen, and I can tell your beauty extends well beyond your appearance."

The friend snorted, leaning over and whispering rapidly in Italian, "Shall I kick his balls?"

The other woman just shook her head without looking away from John.

Placing her hand against his chest, John held it there with his own. "I never felt like I do for you right now! Whoever you are, if you become my woman, I'll be your man."

Uri's knife and fork slipped from his grip, clanking against his plate. "Did you hear that? Even I don't come on that strong."

The woman smiled, shifting slightly. "English?"

John tightened his grip on her hand. "American."

She grabbed him by the shoulder, moving him to the side. "Can you stand here, so I can see?"

"I'm here," John said, shifting back in front of her. "There's no need to look anywhere else."

"I wasn't looking at you."

"Yes, you were. You were looking right at me, just as I was looking right at you."

The woman's eyes shifted past him before darting back to John. "Okay, I was also looking at you."

Her eyes darted again towards the table with the men shovelling food into their mouths. The one in the middle whispered something to his neighbour. Instantly, they rose and made their way to John and the women.

The girl's friend nudged her, and the smile dropped from her face. She shoved John to the side once more. "Please," she urged. "Go back to your table."

The men stopped a short distance from the bar. "With the way you keep staring at us, I assume it's because you want to join our table," one said.

The girls shook their heads, but John stepped between them "They're with me," he said. "You can go back to your own table."

Aris dropped his cutlery now too, back going stiff. "I think there might be trouble."

Uri burped, a slight tremor shaking his body. "What an idiot. He hits on the only women who are clearly here with someone else."

Aris dabbed his mouth with a napkin before pushing back from the table.

Uri groaned, a hiccup rattling him. He grabbed Aris by the arm. "Please, not again. Remember our almost-execution? Or the cartel? We're clearly outnumbered, and they might be armed! Besides, John isn't the type to start a fight."

"John isn't," Aris agreed, watching the crowd at the bar. "But I'm not sure about the others."

One of the men shoved a finger at the girl beside John. "Your constant staring is annoying me. Get out of here before we throw you out ourselves."

John hid the girl behind him and shoved the man's hand out of the way. His voice was deep and sure. "That's no way to speak to a lady. Go back to your table. She isn't interested."

The man raised an eyebrow, taking in John's slim build. He started to laugh but was silenced when John's hand sliced the air to slap him across the face.

"What's he doing?" Uri shouted, jerking to his feet. "He's going to get us killed!"

Aris stood, moving behind his chair and taking it in a tight grip. He kept an eye on John as well as the group of men still seated.

Uri's face wilted. "Please, don't."

At the bar, the man pivoted, throwing a hard punch at John. Behind him, the woman seized him by the collar and pulled him away, twisting to deflect the attack with the back of her palm. She slid forward, aiming a kick at his midsection.

The other man stepped forward but was suddenly set upon by John who let loose a series of precise jabs, pushing his larger opponent back. He ducked and weaved around the man like it was a game.

Both women stepped back, watching John warily. Even the barmaid stopped working.

"Amazing," Aris whispered. "Where did he learn to fight like that?"

He and Uri watched in awe as John continued to dance around his two adversaries. In a sudden shift, John tipped sideways and twisted through the air. His feet split apart and he landed a kick against both their thighs before landing deftly in a crouch. The two men wobbled before falling to the ground with a thud.

John stepped back against the bar next to the women, clapping them on their backs.

The men at the table glanced to the one in the centre who was still slowly chewing his meal. He swallowed then waved his hand in John's direction at the bar. "Get them."

Before they had a chance to move, the women at the surrounding tables jumped to their feet and drew guns from behind their backs. One approached the men's table, her face set and determined. "You're under arrest—"

One man rolled out of his chair, grabbing it and swinging wide to knock the gun out of the officer's hand. Two other men surged forward.

The woman skilfully countered their moves. The others remained to guard their boss, who still calmly ate his meal.

Noticing Aris coiled and ready to strike, one of the guards threw a punch that Aris deftly sidestepped, causing Uri to take the hit. He tumbled to the ground.

The man turned, striking out at Aris again.

Aris blocked that attack with his chair, which he then raised overhead and smashed against his attacker.

The boss waved another goon in to help fight Aris.

John kept his position near the bar, retaliating against the advancing forces with kicks and strikes at the knees, the gut, and any weak point he could reach. He refused to leave the woman he'd approached at the bar.

From the corner of his eye, he saw a man headed her way. He jolted forward, slipping between them at the last minute and aiming a swift and sure kick to the ribs.

As if hit by a bolt of lightning, that man stumbled back into the woman behind him. She aimed a kick and then curved around John, striking like a viper.

Uri propped himself off the ground, wincing at the pain in his chest. "You don't seem to need my help," he mumbled before another punch had him bumbling over an empty chair.

"Stay down," Aris shouted as he took out another of the men.

"Will do," Uri agreed from the floor.

John was up, standing next to his woman and punching out another opponent when the door to the restaurant burst open.

A flood of officers, armed with shields and riot helmets, poured in and forced everyone to the ground. The boss remained seated at his table, slicing a piece of steak.

The police kept shouting, shoving guns at Aris, John, and Uri who quickly raised their hands in surrender.

"No," the woman from the bar said, addressing the officers. "They helped us. There's no need to take them in."

The police quickly cleared out the restaurant, leaving only the two women and John, Uri, and Aris behind.

The lady John had approached held out her hand to greet him. "I'm Alexa, I work for the police here in Naples. You put yourself in a dangerous position to help us. Who are you?"

"I'm yours," John replied, his arm clutching his chest.

Aris and Uri watched, smiling, unsure where this sudden confidence was coming from.

"Does my man have a name?" Alexa grinned.

John cleared his throat. "My name is John, and I love you."

Alexa laughed at his sudden confession. When she finally calmed herself, she stepped closer. "You risked your life for me, and you seem to be quite skilled, but getting involved was foolish."

Glancing momentarily at Uri and Aris, John shrugged. "I'm not sure what came over me," he responded, grinning at the confused look on everyone's face. "As my friends will tell you, I don't particularly enjoy fighting. I usually run away. My nickname in school was scared-shit John."

The girls laughed together this time.

"Impossible," Alexa scoffed. "You knocked out most of these men yourself."

"I wasn't fighting, though," John confessed. "I was just protecting you."

Alexa shook her head. "Those skills don't just come from nowhere."

"I was always good at acrobatics as a kid."

"And the fighting skills, which you've never demonstrated before?" Uri asked.

John tilted his head. "I took martial arts classes for years, but I never really got far. I was afraid to hit the other kids."

One of Alexa's fellow officers applauded. "This Mr. Giovanni is definitely your man!"

Aris stepped forward, clapping John on the shoulder. "Did you notice?"

John looked at him, brows frowning.

A smile broke out on Aris's face. "Your voice didn't get high when you confronted those men."

John laughed, turning to Alexa. "When I'm nervous or scared, my voice usually gets really high-pitched," he explained. "But when I saw you tonight, something in me shifted. I fell in love with you instantly."

One of the other officers shoved Alexa. "Is he serious? This sounds like such bullshit."

"Of course, I'm serious." John pulled Alexa into his arms and drew her into a deep kiss.

She froze, caught off guard, before sinking into the moment.

Uri smiled wide. "It's like he's been reborn! He just went for it there, not even messing around." Turning to the other female officers, Uri held out his hand. "I'm Uri, and I also have fallen in love with you."

The women laughed.

"Which one?" the officer closest to him asked.

"All of you," Uri confessed. "I am a generous man."

The moment was cut short when John bent over, coughing violently. He pulled his hand away to reveal a splattering of blood.

"Are you hurt?" Alexa wrapped an arm around him.

"I'm okay, just a bit of pain," he assured, but his knees buckled beneath him when another coughing fit started.

"We need to get you to the hospital," Alexa ordered, throwing his arm over her shoulder as she supported him out of the restaurant.

— ◇ —

Alexa's house was sandwiched between similar stone buildings on a small, leafy residential street. The façade was lined with small balconies from which flower boxes and pots overflowed with greenery. Inside, the high ceilings of the modern furnished apartment provided the illusion of space.

Alexa's well-preserved aunt entered the room, her large bust and rounded stomach leading the way. Alexa, John, Uri, and Aris were relaxing so she served them coffee with a slight glare, untrusting of John's sudden profession of love for her niece.

John nestled against Alexa, laughing at a joke she shared.

Aris looked over the small but happy crowd. "I think it's time for us to move on."

The laughter died suddenly. Nearby, Alexa's aunt pressed her lips together until they drained of colour.

John flicked his gaze from Alexa to Aris, slowly pushing himself to his feet. "I'm still recovering."

Aris shook his head. "You've recovered enough."

John looked back at Alexa, placing a hand on her shoulder. "What's the hurry? We like Naples."

Aris stared at him in silence.

"I should at least see the doctor again before we leave," John added.

Aris laughed. "The doctor cleared you already."

"Not completely."

Alexa smiled, watching the exchange.

Her aunt slithered up next to her. "I told you. Americans always fuck and then leave," she chided.

Everyone turned to the older woman at her sudden pronouncement.

Aris gazed at John. "You don't have to come. Feel free to stay here."

"What if Alexa joins us?" he said.

The woman shook her head. "I can't. I'd lose my job."

Silence descended on the room. Alexa finally shattered it like a thin film of ice. "Go. You can't leave your friends. You need to finish your trip."

John rocked back and forth. "Will you wait for me? If I promise to come back?"

Alexa smiled. "Of course, you're my man, remember? I love you."

The aunt hissed. "How can you love him? He's married. He has kids. He's just spouting bullshit."

"I don't have any kids," John swore. "Only my wife's children from before we were married."

"That's worse," the aunt cackled. "You don't even know if he can have children."

John stepped up to the aunt, staring down at her. "I love Alexa. I will come back and take her home with me to America."

The aunt crossed her arms, head held high. "Empty promises. Thousands of Italian girls fell for similar American lies during the war." She spat on the floor. "They never followed through and the girls were left here with nothing."

"But many did move to America," Aris retorted. "They married and started happy families."

The aunt disregarded his argument. "Fuck off, you clever dick. Most were left here with bastards to raise on their own."

Aris sipped his coffee before addressing John. "I'm leaving in two days. You can stay or you can come along. But I think you should stay. Alexa is a rare find, and you even get the aunt as a bonus."

The older woman pointed her finger at Aris. "*Vaffanculo*, brick head. I'm not for sale."

Uri choked on his coffee, laughing. "It's dickhead, not brick head."

"One stupid language, three dickhead!"

John shifted on his feet. "You're a heartless dictator, Aris."

Aris shrugged. "I'm still leaving in two days."

Alexa caressed John's hand, trying to calm his nerves.

"Only two days?" Uri shouted in despair. "I need more time. The girl I'm after is about to fall."

Aris placed his coffee cup on the small table and rose. "You can stay and keep John company. This might be the perfect time for us to part." He crossed the room and hugged Alexa's aunt. "Pity you don't like married men. I would have fallen in love with you. You must have turned many heads back in the day."

The aunt shoved him off. "I can still turn the head of any man I want."

"Is that an invitation?" Aris asked as the others laughed.

"Unlike some," she said, "I have standards."

◆ ◇ ◆

The crowd outside the train station at Piazza Garibaldi heaved forward while Aris and Uri headed for a bus.

John stood back, clutching Alexa in a tight embrace. "Let me stay," he whispered. "I don't mind."

She pressed a kiss to his lips. "You need to go. It's only a few weeks. You'll be back in no time. Go, my love, and I will wait."

The men piled onto the bus and it rumbled out of the city and away from the ocean.

John rested his head against a window. "Where are we headed?"

"Ancona," Aris answered, watching the scenery through the window. "We'll catch a ferryboat to Greece from there."

They fell silent as the bus rattled closer to their destination.

20 MYTH OR REAL

Flowing streams and soft green pastures dotted the landscape. Uri leaned back under a tree with John and Aris at his side. fanning themselves to try and cool down while they waited for a car to stop and offer them a lift.

Uri groaned and threw a pebble, staring at the rocky mountains surrounding them. "Why did we come to this wasteland?" he asked, swatting a fly away from his face. "There aren't even cars, let alone women."

Aris laughed at him. "Part of the beauty of Epirus in northern Greece is that it is not densely populated."

"It's been hours without a single car," John mumbled.

The men sat in silence.

Eventually Uri yawned. "You're both so boring. If you aren't going to talk, then I will. There aren't restrictions on talking here, are there?"

Aris glared at him. "Only when you're talking out of your ass."

Ignoring them both, Uri began to chatter. "I've been with lots of women. Some were real beauties, some less so. Some smart, some dumb."

Aris snorted. "Like you'd recognize the difference."

"But no one interested me enough to marry," Uri continued. "Why should I? People get married because they can't get women. I don't have that problem."

John seemed to tune in.

"Yet, I don't know how I found myself agreeing to an arranged marriage with Epi." Uri stared off into the distance. "I never even kissed her before our wedding night. We'd met a few times as kids. They told me she was a virgin. What if she didn't like sex?"

John shifted. "Did that bother you? That she was a virgin and waiting?"

Uri shrugged. "A virgin at thirty-three? In this age? I thought it was a joke. When she told me herself, I actually laughed. I made fun of her."

Aris shook his head.

Uri closed his eyes, reflecting on that night.

John nudged him. "Was she?"

"Offended? No," Uri shared. "She has always risen above my antics. It was her choice, she said, to stay a virgin until her wedding."

"How was she in bed, then?" John wondered.

Uri's face twitched before he smoothed it out again. "I found out why she was a virgin," he confessed. "She has a penis. Nearly as long as mine!"

Aris jolted at the revelation but stayed focused on the road.

John shifted closer, eyes wide. "What do you mean? Like her clitoris was large?"

"No, she's intersex. She has both. That night, she did me first."

John jerked back. "What?"

Uri smirked. "I'm saying I got lucky. She has both male and female parts."

"You mean she has balls and a dick?"

Uri shook his head. "No balls. Just pussy and a dick. A thick one!"

"Interesting," John said, leaning back on his hands. "So, does that make you bisexual? How was it the first time?"

Uri slapped John with his hat. "None of your business. I'm not telling what I do with my wife as if she's just some other girl!"

Aris laughed, still scanning the road.

John pushed off the ground, swiping Uri with his own hat. "One minute you tell us you laughed at her, now you're too sensitive to share!"

Uri sat up taller. "If you must know, even that first night she was a miracle. I thought I knew what it was to make love.

Instead, she showed me the truth. We took our time that night. Thinking back, she made me feel something I never had in bed before. The desire to touch and be touched, to hold and be held. It was amazing—craving someone beyond lust. I can't explain it. I still don't really understand."

Amusement brightened John's eyes. "You seem to have found someone you really love through matchmaking."

"Maybe," Uri admitted. "I don't know."

"There's nothing wrong with matchmaking," Aris declared, resting his arms on his folded-up knees. "Some of the happiest and longest marriages I know have been the result of matchmaking. Even celebrities have done something similar through family and friends."

Uri sneered. "Aris the wise finally decides to join the conversation."

"Some people are born lucky," Aris continued. "Epi is your luck. She is truly your dream come true. Everyone loves and respects her at the office. If I hear that you hurt her, I promise I will hunt you down."

"She may be a dream, but it's still embarrassing that our marriage was arranged."

"You need to decide what matters: how you met, or who she is and how she makes you feel."

Uri chewed his lip. "Do you seriously believe that true love exists?"

Aris chuckled. "I'm not the right person to ask. It's rare to love a girl who loves you the same. For me, I think I've given up on love."

John frowned. "Really? Just like that?"

Aris shrugged. "You heard Kay. She dumped me even though I thought we had a connection. Maybe there's no such thing as true love. Maybe I've been wrong this whole time and Uri has been right."

Uri groaned, flopping back on the ground. "The one time I ask for your opinion and advice, suddenly you aren't sure of anything. You need therapy."

They trudged through a small town. John and Aris popped into the café for a moment and when they exited, they found Uri hunched over on the ground by a kiosk that sold newspapers and sundries, scribbling furiously on a postcard.

Aris marched over and slapped him on the back of his head. "You're breaking the rules! A postcard will reveal our location. If your wife knows, then soon even Varo will know."

John watched, his stomach hollow and clenched.

Uri winced, glancing up like a scolded child. "I just miss Epi. I worry about her. I've never worried about someone like this before." He shifted slightly on the ground. "Is it really so bad if she knows that I'm okay? Not where we are, just that we're all safe and healthy? I can't explain it! This urge to reach out to her, even if it's just with this measly postcard. I don't even contact my own mother like this!"

A smile graced Aris's face. "You loved your mom the day you were born. You fall in love with other women whenever it hits you."

Uri cocked his head at Aris. "Is this what falling in love is? This annoying mix of frustration and contentedness? Pain and pleasure? If so, I don't want to be in love; I want to be free!"

"You're a lucky mule," Aris laughed. "You're in love with your wife and you didn't even know it."

Uri scratched his head. "You think so? If that's the case, I need a remedy for this. I don't like to worry and stress so much. I can't sleep."

"There isn't a remedy," Aris mocked. "The only way out is if the other person doesn't love you and kills your love."

Aris held out his hand to pull Uri up. Uri dusted off his trousers and they all sat at the café.

"We'll use the local sim cards when we can," Aris said. "You can call home that way, but don't tell your wives where we are. I don't want unexpected visitors."

John pulled out his phone and Uri packed away his postcard.

"Just remember, you're both free to leave at any point," Aris reminded.

John smiled. "I'm going to call Alexa!"

Aris laughed. "I wonder if you'll be smiling when Leoni gets her hands on you!"

⋄

They had coffee and rested.

Aris wandered over to a table occupied by locals. "We're looking for a peaceful place to relax, with a nice beach and good people. Not too many tourists. Any recommendations?"

The young waitress shook her head. "It's mostly mountains here. Maybe further south on one of the islands."

Aris returned to the table where John and Uri lounged in the sun.

"Well," he said. "You get to choose today. Which direction do you fancy?"

John lolled his head around. "What even is there?"

"West is back the way we came, with Italy and France. We have Eastern Europe above us, Turkey further east, and the islands of Greece to the south."

"West!" John shouted.

"East," Uri decided. "I want to see belly dancers!"

A man with a white beard sitting at the table behind them cackled. His moustache was dyed yellow from cigarettes. "If you're looking for peace, there's a village nestled in a valley in the curve of a picturesque bay. But you won't find any belly dancers or bars or nightclubs. Not even a cinema. Just a single café."

Aris focused on the man. His face was sunburnt despite the straw hat crushed on his head.

Aris stepped closer. "What's so special about this place?"

The old man laughed. "Nothing. It's actually a pretty boring and simple village."

Aris glanced over at John and Uri, who mirrored his confusion.

"It's a multi-ethnic community. They speak all sorts of languages, even English. Only one church that all the religions share. They produce all their own food. Now that I think about it, I'm not sure it's for you."

Aris pulled out the chair next to this man and sat. He leaned forward, asking in Greek, "How are the people in the village?"

The old man gazed out at the horizon. "Simple."

Uri and John rose from their seats and approached, hoping for more information.

"Sounds great," Aris exclaimed.

Uri sneered. "I don't want some deserted village that probably stinks of animal shit."

The old man laughed. "Plenty of manure in that village."

Uri rounded on Aris. "You said it was our choice. We're going east!"

"I gave you the chance, but you couldn't come to an agreement." Aris turned back to the old man, a pen and notebook ready. "Where is this village? What's it called?"

The old man smacked his lips, running his tongue along them. "My mouth is so dry."

Aris summoned the waitress. "Bring this man anything he wants."

"He only drinks beer," she said and retreated inside.

"Two bottles, both large," the old man shouted after her. "And I'm hungry, too!"

The waitress turned to check with Aris, who nodded in agreement.

The old man pointed to his left. "The village is west of here."

"That's east," Aris corrected.

"Is it?" the man smiled. "I must be upside down."

Aris scootched his chair closer. "What's the name of the village?"

"No name. We all just call it the village."

Aris's gaze snapped to the other man's face. "The village?"

The old man jutted out his chin, nodding once.

John and Uri watched as Aris sat ramrod straight, a look of wonder filling his face.

John tapped Aris to get his attention. "I'm not sure this man is right in his head."

The old man flashed his middle finger at John without shifting his gaze from the horizon.

Aris snorted.

"Okay, he might be all there," John admitted. Turning to address the old man, he said, "I apologise. It's just strange that a village has no name."

"Feel free to give it one when you go. I, myself, have only ever called it paradise."

A grin split Aris's face. "How far is it?"

"Head east. When you reach the lake, turn south. Ignore the paved roads. The old roads through the woods will get you there faster. When the road runs out, there will be two hills without any houses. Head straight between them and you'll find the village."

Aris hastily scribbled the directions. John and Uri glanced between the two, unnerved by Aris's sudden focus.

"Are we really going to follow this old fool's directions?" Uri asked . "He's just using you for free drinks.'

The old man glared at Uri. "Where did you find these two mules?"

Aris shook his head.

The old man set his sights on John. "You need to watch out for dragons."

John perked up. "What dragons?"

The old man smirked. "The dragons in your head."

The waitress returned with beers and the old man snatched one up, downing half the glass. "Keep an eye out for wild boars and wolves, too. They are very real!"

John and Uri glanced at Aris, but he was bent over his notebook mumbling the directions to himself.

"Aris," John hissed. "I'm not going through bear-infested woods on some lark for a tiny village."

Aris grinned at them, sending the old man into a fit of laughter. "There isn't adventure without risk," he assured them.

"Bears aren't the big issue," the old man said. "The real dangers are the boars and wolves." He gulped down more beer. "Since you will be shitting a lot, you need to make sure to dig deep to cover it up. They can follow your scent for miles. Just a few months ago, a female archaeologist was killed while hiking alone. All that was left of her were bones. They had to identify her by her passport and phone. Oh, and snakes! Watch out for the snakes."

John and Uri stared in horror at the man.

"Thank you," Aris said. "We'll be heading out."

The old man considered Aris for a moment. "You believe me, then. All this shit I just told you?"

Uri groaned. "He's admitting that he's bullshitting us and you're still falling for it, Aris."

"Are we being sent on a wild goose chase?" John asked.

Aris smiled at them. "It's my kind of bullshit!"

The old man tipped back in riotous laughter. After another long sip of beer, he wiped his moustache on his forearm. "You'll find the village. The footpath over the small hill is shorter."

Aris nodded, scribbling down the extra information. "How will we be sure it's the right village?"

"There's no other village near it." The old man refilled his glass. "It's shaped like a horseshoe that curves around the bay."

Aris hefted up his bag, digging through it to pull out the embroideries from Kali's granddaughter and Droso. He placed them on the table. "Does it look something like this?"

The old man bent over, peering down at the pieces of fabric.

"Forget this half," Aris insisted. "Just here, there is a bit at the end."

The old man furrowed his brow. "The two hills look similar, but there's no open sea. High hills on the far side of the bay though."

Nodding to himself, Aris returned the embroideries and flipped through his notebook to the text Calliope had provided.

"Do you think you could translate this? It's Greek that I'm not familiar with."

The old man pulled it closer. He read through it once then read it again, mumbling to himself. Translating a single word here or there, he shook his head, and worked through it again. "This here, this is land and then after that is the sea." He belched, then drank more beer. "Here, this can be read as brides but also beautiful women. Well, two beautiful women. And this one, it's like the owner or holder of something."

Aris nodded, following along.

"I suppose it's saying two women in paradise, if that's even possible," the old man joked, breaking down into a fit of laughter. "This here—"

"I know that one," Aris insisted, "beside the small hill."

"Exactly," the old man nodded. "Where did you get these?"

"An old Greek book."

The old man grunted but didn't refute Aris's claim. "It says the grandmother was the owner and then something about the sea. The shiny water of the sea, like the surface."

Aris thanked him, pulling the notebook away. "You really know your ancient Greek."

The waitress leaned over, dropping food on their table. "He was a schoolmaster, forced to retire early." She smiled, flitting back to the café as the old man shouted after her.

Aris pressed a wad of cash into the old man's hand. "Thank you, very much."

— ◇ —

The three perched on a short wall by the café waiting for the bus to take them to this very simple village. The silence between them was as sticky and annoying as the heat.

Uri spoke first. "You're something, Aris. Dragging us from one danger to the next. And now you're hauling us into woods that are teeming with wolves. I have to wonder if you're suicidal."

Aris smirked at the characterisation.

"Nothing scares him," John said. "Aris might just have a few screws loose and can't recognise danger. Maybe that's why he isn't scared."

"Then we must have more than a few screws loose if we're willingly following him," Uri murmured. "Make no mistake, I'm enjoying every minute of it. Other than nearly starving to death and the firing squad, I've never had so much fun. The only thing missing is my woman."

John hummed in agreement. "I might have wet my pants a few times, but not for a while. I used to be so scared… but not anymore."

Uri tossed a questionable look at John.

"Okay, at least I'm not scared as much as before. I can even do things on my own!" John sighed. "And I haven't wet my pants!"

Uri grunted. "Not yet."

⁕◇⁕

Aris stood at the base of two large hills, John and Uri flanking him. The land cascaded down into a valley veined with streams of water where the hills were dotted with trees and vines.

John whistled softly. "This must be what the old man was talking about."

Uri nodded, pushing up on his toes to get a better look. "It's even better than he described. But I don't see any village. Are we lost?"

Aris breathed in deeply and let it out with a calm he hadn't sensed in himself for a long time. "We need to keep going down into the valley."

"Hold it, Aris!" Uri glanced at John, hoping for support. "There aren't even signs of civilisation down there."

Aris pushed forward, undeterred. "The idea is to escape civilisation."

Uri grabbed him by the arm, a burp rattling his chest. "You're just as lost as we are. We should go back before we can't find our way. We don't even have cell service if we need to call for help."

Aris pulled out of Uri's grasp and kept moving.

"I'm going back," Uri announced. "I'm not dying out here with a bunch of man-eating beasts."

Aris waved back at him, still moving forward. "You're free to do as you please."

John yanked on Uri's arm. "Neither of us has any sense of direction. We should keep up. Aris will get us there."

The trio trudged on, picking their way down the steep hills and into the valley.

After a few miles of walking, Uri moaned, "I'm exhausted. My legs can't take much more of this."

Aris stumbled to a halt. "Look!"

Below them, two small valleys braided together into a large fertile cradle. The foothills were peppered with fields and woodlands. But at the far end, near a bright shimmer of water, rested the village.

"Exactly as the old man described," Aris gloated.

John cheered. "He was right after all!"

"This must be it," Uri exclaimed, feeding off their excitement.

As the ground levelled out, their pace quickened, as if aware how close they were to their destination. They followed a footpath cresting a small hill and could soon see the entire village as it hooked around the bay, a plaza opening up to the water on one side, houses radiating out from there. At the far side of the bay, the land was an almond green of young pine trees.

"No wonder the old man has such a vivid memory of this place," John confessed.

Aris dropped his pack and took greedy breaths as he admired the view.

John and Uri knelt beside him.

"It's spectacular," Uri admitted.

"Picturesque," John added.

Aris smirked. "Still want to go back?"

21 THE VILLAGE

They entered the village from the rear through the fields. Slipping by short stone houses, they circled closer to the plaza at the centre. The further they progressed, the more they stumbled into residents, young and old, who all greeted them in Greek.

Aris returned their greetings with a nod and a polite, "Hello."

Soon, getting into the spirit, Uri and John greeted the villagers first. They were thrilled to hear a warm welcome and kind words.

Near the plaza, two women were walking towards them on the road—an old lady and a younger woman. Both were tall and sure-footed. The older lady, though clearly entering her twilight years, was slim and held herself upright. The young woman, perhaps in her twenties, was only slightly taller than her companion. A beauty, she had wide sparkling eyes, pink cheeks, and sharp cheekbones that slanted down to full lips. Black hair waved down her back, and a loose summer dress billowed around her, revealing gentle contours. A small basket was looped over the crook of her elbow.

As they approached, John and Uri smiled at the ladies. Aris remained silent, his sight captured by the young woman.

The old lady responded with a welcoming smile of her own.

When the young woman drew up beside him, Aris stopped short and followed her, offering a polite, "Hello," in Greek.

The older woman stopped, causing everyone to come to a halt. "Hello, I didn't take you all for Greeks."

Aris said, "Only I am Greek. We're from America."

"Well, hello and welcome to you all."

The young woman watched Aris for a moment and, when she moved a few paces past, she looked back over her shoulder.

He met her glance and she held it for a moment before shivering, turning forward, and moving a few more steps away. She stopped, turning again to see the old lady now deep in conversation with John and Uri.

"If you're coming this way through the village, you must have entered through the mountain pass," the old woman said.

Aris joined the conversation. "Yes, we fell in love with the view of the village from up there. I'm Aris. These are my companions, John and Uri."

The old lady shook Aris's hand. "I'm Angelica."

"Angeliki?" Aris asked instantly.

"If you prefer," she replied, waving her hand towards the young woman. "That's my granddaughter, also named Angelica. Ever since she was born, the village has called me Granny, so they didn't confuse the two of us."

Aris stole another glance at the young woman, then turned back to Granny with a charming smile. "You must be where she gets her beauty. It almost rivals that of your village."

Granny nodded. "Many call our village paradise. Yet, some think it's a prison, so removed from the rest of the world. During winter, we can be cut off for weeks at a time, and sometimes the only way anywhere is by boat."

"Is paradise the real name of your village?" Aris asked.

Granny grinned, the sun glinting off her white teeth. "It's just a description. Our village has no name. We leave it to the people to name us whatever they want. Are you heading to the café in the plaza? It's just at the end of the road, on the right-hand side. You can't miss it. It's the only one."

Aris bowed slightly. "Thank you, Granny Angeliki."

She turned, heading to meet up with her granddaughter.

Aris tracked the two before he was pulled away by John and Uri. Following them, he couldn't help but peek over his shoulder, catching Angelica glaring at him while she waited for Granny to catch up.

The older woman patted her granddaughter's arm. "What's the matter? You always greet everyone. Why not these three?"

Angelica pinched her lips together. "I said hello."

"You didn't even stop to speak to them."

"I don't know. I didn't feel like talking. Why are they even here? They look like criminals, if you ask me."

Granny shook her head. "The tall man is Aris, very well-mannered. He's Greek but lives in America. There's nothing to be worried about. He even called us both beautiful."

"Sounds like you have an admirer," she replied, her mouth twisting in a frown. "They're strangers, though. What do they want? It's not like we're a tourist destination."

"Who knows? They walked all the way through the hills to get here. Maybe they enjoy hiking."

"I think they bring trouble. That tall one wouldn't stop staring. It made me uncomfortable."

"We have always welcomed visitors to our village," Granny admonished. "You've said many times that we must always offer an open door to anyone who visits."

Angelica shrugged. "I suppose. I'll apologise when I see them next. If they even stay long enough for that to happen."

⁕ ◇ ⁕

The café was located on the right side of the plaza. The inside was wide and open with wooden beams running the length of the ceiling, supporting rows of bamboo covered with a thick layer of grey clay. A terrace with an awning provided shade where most of the patrons were located.

Men sat gathered around tables drinking coffee and playing cards or backgammon. The three travellers were greeted immediately by a few of the elders.

"Hello," John called. "We are Americans. I'm John, and this is Aris and Uri. We just arrived in the village."

A man stepped forward, taking John's hand in a firm grip. "I'm Yiannis, the owner here. What can I get you?"

They all slipped off their backpacks and sat at the closest table. "We're very thirsty," John said. "Three beers, bottles if you have them."

"Our local beer is draught only."

"The local beer is fine!"

Yiannis went into the café and returned with glasses. They toasted, taking a long drink.

"Mr. Yiannis," Uri asked, putting his beer back on the table. "Is there a hotel nearby?"

Yiannis smiled, barely holding in a laugh. "The beach is your best bet. If you haven't noticed, we aren't a resort town. We have no hotels."

Placing his glass on the table, Aris asked, "What about a house? Or rooms to rent for a few days? We might be here for a couple of weeks."

"Not just passing through?" Yiannis asked. "For three, it might be hard."

A man at another table called out to them in Greek. "What about the widow's house? It's empty, and it might be able to fit them."

"We don't mind," Aris cut in. "We'd be willing to pay, as well."

"You speak Greek?" Yiannis seemed surprised.

"I do!"

"No need, as most of the village can speak English," Yiannis informed them. "I'm not sure the widow will rent her old house, even though no one's lived in it for ages. She's a bit of a character."

"I'm sure we can find a way," Aris said, undeterred. "And the condition isn't an issue. The three of us can clean it in no time. Where can we find this widow?"

Yiannis stepped out into the plaza and called over to a bunch of children playing near the water. A young girl ran over, followed by three boys and another girl.

"Who wants to guide these men to Korina's house?" Yiannis asked.

Aris's attention became riveted yet again.

One of the boys shook his head. "Korina's probably resting. I'm not waking her for anything."

One of the girls with a wide forehead, long brown hair, and a heart-shaped face said, "I'll take them."

"Aris," Yiannis motioned. "This is Zoe. She'll show you the way."

Zoe slid up next to Aris, her eyes squinted as she appraised him. "I'm Zoe, and I'm always right because I don't mess around!"

The three men smiled at her antics.

"Come on, it's this way!" Zoe darted off, heading to one of the streets branching off the plaza.

The men quickly downed their drinks, paid Yiannis, and hoisted their bags in an attempt to catch up with the girl.

"If you decide to stay, I can prepare dinner for you," Yiannis shouted after them.

Aris gave the man a thumbs up. "That would be great. Anything you cook, we'll eat! But no onions. I'm allergic!"

The men scrambled after Zoe, who was still scurrying ahead.

"Your English is really good," John called out to her.

She turned, walking backwards to address them. "Of course. I speak four languages. How many do you speak?"

"We speak English," John retorted. "We don't need to speak anything else."

"You think you're speaking English?"

Uri nodded. "Yeah, we're Americans!"

Zoe flipped the hair out of her face. "American English is the worst, but English overall is a weak language. You need a lot of words to explain what a single Greek word can do."

She glanced over her shoulder to check her backward steps before continuing. "Besides, English is made up of mostly Greek words. Maybe as much as half. Some directly, like *mathematics* and *phobia* and *symphony*. Other words are less direct. Therefore, unless you speak Greek, you can't claim to speak English!"

Aris smiled at her. "She's right. Greek is the only language that gives birth to new words. That's why most things that are new are named using Greek terminology."

Zoe raised her hands in victory. "Terminology! That's another word with Greek roots. Do you see? I'm always right because I don't mess around. But I didn't know that Greek gives birth to new words. I'll have to talk to you about this later, Mr. Aris."

⸱ ◇ ⸱

Zoe led them up a short walk to a building set back from the road. She stopped, pointing to the house in question. "This is aunty Korina's house. She is a strong-minded woman. Don't try to mess around or lie with her or she will get upset and refuse you."

Zoe knocked on the door, calling, "Aunt Korina, there are some men who want to see you."

The woman opened her door, wiping her hands on a rag. She had wide hips and shoulders, but a shapely waist. Her rounded face was topped with a boyish haircut.

"They want to rent your old house around back for a few days," Zoe explained.

"A few days doesn't seem worth the effort of cleaning it."

Aris stepped forward. "A few weeks, perhaps. We might extend our stay." He reached out his hand in greeting. "I'm Aris, Greek-American."

She looked at his hand, inspecting it like it might carry an illness. "Greek-American, huh?"

Aris nodded, smiling.

Korina made a choking sound, her neck swelling, then bent over to spit at his feet.

John hurried over. "Only Aris is Greek. Uri is Jewish and I have a bit of everything."

Korina spat at them twice more, widening her stance like she was about to defend her house from an invasion.

Zoe turned to look at him, shaking her head. She placed a finger against her sealed lips and waved for him to back off.

Turning back to Korina, urging her closer, the girl whispered in Greek, "He's not very clever, but I think he's a good person."

Korina looked at Zoe for a moment, then focused on Aris. "Three hundred American dollars for a month, upfront. No refund if you leave earlier."

Zoe waved at Aris, trying to get his attention and convey that it was too much, but Aris ignored her. "Deal," he said.

"Zoe will take you to the old house. I won't clean it for you. If you still want it, send a kid to let me know. I'll bring over bedsheets and towels. The kitchen should still have most of its appliances and utensils, but you'll need to wash them."

Korina slammed the door shut without waiting for a response. The men stared at the door until Zoe called for them to follow her around the back of the building.

A swarm of kids seemed to appear out of nowhere, following in her wake.

They stopped outside a worn, squat house, the exterior chipped and aged but still watertight.

Zoe stood next to Aris. "The widow is very crafty, Mr. Aris."

Uri scoffed. "More like unfriendly. She spat at us!"

"She did that to scare you, so she could overcharge you on rent. You should have bargained her down to a better price," Zoe insisted. She turned to Aris. "Did you not see me waving at you? Three hundred is way too much for this place. It's not as if people are queuing up to rent it. Next time, I'll take care of it."

Aris dug into his pocket, pulling out a few bills and handing them to the girl. "For your help. I promise to consult you next time."

Zoe pushed his money away. "Are you trying to insult me?"

"I'm not insulting you," Aris argued. "I'm giving you a tip as thanks for helping us."

Zoe perched a hand on her hips, pointing at Aris with her other as if scolding him. "First, I have a name. It's Zoe, with the emphasis on the E—it means life. Second, you are a guest in this village. We don't help people for money here!"

Aris stuffed the money back in his pocket. "I apologise. I didn't mean to insult you. Thank you for your help."

"However," Zoe said, holding her hand out to him. "If you were to give me a gift that wasn't money, that would be fine. Like, your hat, for example."

Aris laughed, pointing at his head. "This hat?"

She smiled, nodding her head.

"It's dirty," he told her. "Covered with sweat and dust."

Zoe crept closer, her fingers twitching. "I can scrub it till it's clean."

John nudged Aris with his elbow. "She's got you there."

Smiling, Aris shook his head in disbelief. "It looks like she does."

Plucking the hat off his head, Aris bowed and presented it to her with a flourish.

She took it with a wide smile, turning it inside out. Bringing it to her nose she took a deep whiff, and her face immediately puckered.

"That's disgusting. You should really wash this at the end of every day so it can dry overnight. Remember that for when you get a new one," Zoe lectured, turning the hat around in her hands. "It will take me forever to clean this."

"You can give it back if you don't like it."

"It's insulting to return a gift," Zoe said, holding the hat close. "And I never said I didn't like it, just that it really ought to be cleaned. You need to learn to listen."

John and Uri burst out laughing at Aris's shocked expression.

The widow crept across the yard separating her house from the rental, a stack of linens in her arms. "Better watch out. Zoe is a cunning foe."

Zoe looked from the hat to Aris and shoved it back at him. "I don't want it. I was just testing you to see if you were a good person. Everyone knows it's rude to ask for a gift. As punishment, I will wash your hat and return it to you."

Aris smiled at her fondly. "I see. You really don't mess around."

"But you still owe me," Zoe claimed, pointing at him.

"So," the widow interjected before they had a chance to go another round. "The house is clearly not in the best shape. Been years since anyone lived in it. Needs a lot of cleaning."

"We should be able to handle it with the three of us," John reassured her.

"And with me, it's four, but I don't clean for free," Zoe said, to everyone's surprise, jerking her thumb at the other kids. "And if the price is right, I'm sure the others will be happy to help."

"Zoe!" the widow chastised.

"I'm only joking. I won't take money from our guests." She ran her hands along one of their backpacks. "You know, I haven't had a new bag in a long time."

Korina shook her head, turning to the three travellers. "So, what do you think?"

"We love it," Uri instantly replied. "Anything is better than the beach."

Aris nodded and noticed the widow gazing at him. "Of course, we will take it."

Korina shoved the linens at John, who fumbled with them. She held out her palm, slapping it with her other hand a few times. "Payment in advance."

Aris pulled out the roll of cash and counted off three hundred and passed it over to her.

Korina counted the money twice before folding up the bills and stuffing them in her pocket. She turned to John, holding out her palm again, waiting.

"You said three hundred for a month," Aris declared.

Glaring, she said, "Yes, three hundred per person."

Aris looked over at John and Uri, shrugging. "It's only ten dollars a night per person. Much cheaper than a hotel. Pay the woman."

Once Korina was gone, Zoe wagged her head in disappointment. "What did I tell you? I'll handle bargaining next time!"

"Good thing she didn't ask for three hundred a day," Uri laughed.

"You're definitely Americans," Zoe scoffed. She tapped the side of her head near her ear. "They never listen to advice and always pay the full price."

— ◇ —

Zoe led the horde of kids into the house like a commander leading an army. John, Uri and Aris hesitated a moment before following them over the threshold. They looked around, cataloguing the interior. It was in worse shape than the outside—everything covered in dust and cobwebs. They began to second-guess their decision.

"What're you doing?" Zoe shouted at them, perched on the arm of the large settee. "Drop your bags and get to work!"

"On it, Zoe!" John relieved himself of his bag, stashing it on the dining table. "Come on, guys. Let's move it."

Zoe turned and conducted the swarm of other kids nearby. "Start by removing anything you can carry. Leave the lightweight things for the smaller kids."

Aris opened one of the large windows in the main room to let in fresh air. "What's the plan, Zoe?"

Zoe stood atop the sofa, now as tall as him. "We're going to use the hose to wash down the inside. That would be faster. But the house needs to be empty. You lot should start in the bedrooms, removing the mattresses. They need to be beaten to get the dust out of them."

"That's a lot of work, Zoe. I've never cleaned a room, let alone a whole house," Uri teased.

Zoe levelled him with a look, her nose wrinkled like she smelled something foul. "This isn't America. There isn't time to be lazy. This is Greece, and in my village, everybody works."

Aris smiled at her, his eyebrows raised in surprise. "We'd need a small army for all this. Zoe, we only have one backpack each. We have nothing to trade!"

Zoe grinned at him, her teeth sharp in the afternoon light. She held out her hand. "Okay, pay two hundred dollars. Each, of course!"

Her pronouncement shocked laughter out of the group.

"How about one hundred!" Uri fired back.

Shaking her head, Zoe cut off his offer. "Americans don't pay attention!"

The three men fell silent at her admonishment.

"I've already told you! We don't help people for money or gifts. We do it because it's right! Do you understand?"

Uri bent over, clutching his stomach from laughter.

Zoe jabbed a finger at him. "You, laughing man. After the furniture, take down the curtains to the garden. We'll wash them outside."

Aris smiled as he watched Zoe order everyone around. "Won't we damage the house by hosing it down?"

"We won't let the water sit on the walls long," she reassured him. "And the floor is marble, so no problem there."

Resting a hand against the back of the settee, Aris turned to John. "Remember Zoe is always right. Let's get this couch outside."

Zoe squinted at Aris like she was trying to solve a math problem. "Are you being sarcastic? Wasn't I right about how you should've bargained with Korina? Our teachers and grown-ups always tell us that we must admit our mistakes, or we will never learn. Don't you learn this in America? You, Mr. John, go to Korina's house and ask for her hose." Zoe turned her back on him while he just smiled. "Today, preferably!"

Much to Aris's amusement, John stiffened to attention like a soldier. "On it, just as soon as I take out this couch."

Two hours later, the house was clean and the beds were made with fresh linens. In the garden, the curtains hung to dry in the sun.

With the work done, Aris corralled Zoe and the rest of the kids back to the café. "You all can have any three sweets or chocolates, and one juice or soft drink!" he announced.

Zoe opened her mouth to protest, but Aris silenced her with a wave. "This isn't a payment. It's a treat! You have all earned it."

Nodding her head vigorously, she smiled at him. "I guess, this time, you are right."

22 Lambs Following a Wolf

John, Aris and Uri, having finished settling into the house, stepped out into the cool evening air and headed to the café. They slipped by house after house until they stumbled upon one with three women lounging outside—one by the front door, sorting herbs into baskets, with Granny and Angelica sitting off to the side of the small porch.

The woman with the herbs reclined in her seat. Her belly was plump. She stood up when they got near and waved them closer.

"Good evening," she greeted them warmly. "Welcome to our village! I'm Despo. Sit and join us for a coffee and a sweet."

The three men stopped, returning her greeting but refused the invitation to join.

"We asked Yiannis to cook for us tonight," John explained. "We're starving after cleaning the widow's house!"

Despo smiled at them, a sweet twist of the mouth. "So, you're staying a few days, then? What brings you to our village? We don't get many tourists around here."

Uri answered, "We're just travelling around. A gap year of sorts."

"Ah." Despo eyed the trio. "Just three bachelors, travelling the world."

John gently corrected her. "No, we're all married! Aris has three children, and I adopted two of my wife's children from before we were married. Uri, here, only recently got married."

Aris saw Angelica look up at him, then return her focus to John with an air of indifference. "Your wives must not mean much to you if you can leave your families back home while you jaunt around the world."

Jabbing a thumb at Aris, John replied, "Actually it was his idea. Uri and I are just tagging along."

Angelica smirked. "Two lambs following a wolf on a hunt for pleasure!"

Granny and Despo reacted visibly to her harsh tone, but John merely chuckled. "I guarantee you, it's not all fun and games. We've risked our lives a few times so far. Aris's adventurous spirit gets us into a fair bit of trouble!"

A soft smile graced Aris's face. He hadn't stopped looking at Angelica since they paused.

"Actually," Uri interjected, "it might seem weird to you, being a woman from this small village, but in America, it isn't strange for a couple to take a break from each other and travel."

Angelica cleared her lap of stray herbs. "Just because we are a small, peaceful village does not mean we are backward. Maybe I could understand you leaving your wives, but you also abandon your children. For what? Your pleasure?"

Drawn by the noise, a gentleman joined the ladies on the porch, leaning against the doorframe. A statue of a man with a firm and sunburnt face, he appeared around age sixty, much like the woman who had greeted them. Perhaps these were Angelica's parents.

Uri ducked his head. "I don't have any children, yet. We left very soon after my wedding."

Aris stepped up to the house, smiling widely and extending his hand to the gentleman. "*Kalispera.*"

"Good evening to you, too." The man introduced himself as Manolios and shook each of their hands in turn.

Facing his daughter, Manolios gave her a look of reproach. "Who are we to pass judgement on our guests, Angelica? Don't forget, they come from a very different place," he gently admonished. "While it might seem strange to us, travelling away from their family might be completely acceptable to them. I can certainly see the appeal!"

Angelica stared at her father, her face stiff as ice. "If this is what a modern, progressive society looks like, then it's no wonder their cities are plagued with crime and divorce!"

Switching to Greek, Manolios asked Angelica, "What is wrong with you?"

"He speaks Greek," Angelica replied, nodding to Aris.

Sensing the tense atmosphere, Aris placed a hand on Uri's shoulder. "It was nice meeting you all," he said. "Your village is beautiful, and everyone we've met so far has been lovely both inside and out." He then thanked Despo for her warm offer and tried to usher the others away from the house.

"Perhaps you would stop by for a homemade sweet on your return?" Granny offered. "Angelica makes the best in the village."

"That sounds wonderful," Aris responded. "But maybe another time. We are staying for a few weeks."

Before Aris could retreat too far, Angelica called out, "I'm not trying to be critical. I just think that a man's place is with the woman he belongs to."

Aris lifted his gaze from the road, seeking her out before he even realised what he was doing. "I understand, but not everyone is lucky enough to belong to the right woman."

Aris walked away, John and Uri trailing after him.

Manolios patted his daughter's shoulder. "It's not like you to lose an argument, but it seems Aris is no fool!"

Angelica slumped down in her chair, her heart pounding. "Sometimes I just don't understand people. That's why I came back from the city and chose to live in our village."

23 Life at the Village

The sun was barely visible over the hills as Aris picked his way to the fields. In the past week, he and the others had fallen into a languid and easy pattern. Leaving the confines of the paved paths and stepping onto grass, he stopped at a young man flanked by two horses.

Aris had met Adonis only recently but already befriended him. Adonis was strong, his shoulders wide and heavy after years of manual labour. He lived with his mother in the house next to Angelica.

When he saw Aris, he limped over to a horse. A remnant from an old motorcycle accident, his lame knee didn't stop him from hoisting himself up into the saddle.

Aris nodded at him and mounted the other horse, following Adonis further out of town.

The next day, Uri leaned against the kitchen counter chewing a fresh apple. "I'm glad we came to this village. The people are nice and there's a great beach and hills to explore. The only thing I need now is to bed the widow."

Sitting on the single-seater reading, John closed it and rested the book in his lap. "This place really is amazing, but your widow has eyes for Aris—not you!"

Uris smiled around a mouthful of apple, juice bubbling in the corner of his lips. "Aris already refused her. I think he's afraid of being rejected since Kay left him."

Lying flat on the sofa, hands tucked behind his neck, Aris sighed. "Guys, don't get too comfortable."

"Why not?" Uri asked, head tilted in confusion. "It's like a holiday here. Best of all, nobody wants to kill us."

Aris popped to his feet, his gaze hard and focused. "First of all, don't mess with the widow. There are certain unwritten laws in these types of villages. It's not like other places we've visited. We're guests here. We need to respect their culture."

Uri scoffed. "What nonsense."

Aris chuckled at his friend's brazenness. "It's not unusual for a Greek brother or an uncle to cut your throat for messing around with one of the women in their family."

"She's a widow," Uri replied, waving away Aris's concern. "She has no husband to chase after us. What's wrong with wanting to give her a good time? You're worrying about nothing."

Aris turned his gaze to the ceiling. "Once, in a village like this, I was shot at just for trying to sleep with a widow. And another time, three brothers attacked me for kissing their sister. We need to be careful. If you offend them, they may just shoot all three of us."

"What?" John screeched.

Uri laughed. "Times have changed, Aris. The world has moved on. Relax, Captain. Nothing is going to happen."

Releasing a slow breath, Aris turned his gaze from Uri to John. "This is a small village. It feels like we're intruding. We shouldn't stay long."

"What are you talking about?" John shouted, his voice rumbling.

Uri gestured at Aris with his half-eaten apple. "Is this because Angelica was rude to you? Be honest. Don't hide behind this close-minded village and ethics nonsense."

John began to pace back and forth, his steps harried and quick. "This place is like paradise. If Alexa came, I would stay here forever!"

"This village does have everything," Uri agreed.

"Exactly!" John exclaimed. "It's peaceful, and there's good food and cheap beer. Why on earth do you want to leave, Aris?"

Aris waved a hand dismissively, like he was dispelling a bad odour.

Uri kicked the edge of the couch. "Do you want to drag us into another warzone?"

Hesitating, Aris shifted his weight from foot to foot. "We are intruding. They will get sick of us soon enough. We're not part of their village. To them, we are only drifters."

"Now you're the one who's bullshitting," John shouted. "Everyone, even the children and their animals love us."

"They have their ways," Aris insisted, undeterred. "Soon, they will see us as a threat to that."

John yanked at his hair. "What's wrong with you? You enjoy it here more than we do! We haven't seen you this happy since we left home. You're swimming, fishing, hiking, and napping under the eucalyptus trees in the afternoon. The villagers wait turns to play backgammon with you. They love watching you play cards with the elders. You chat with them for hours, listening to their stories."

Aris nodded, pointing at John. "I agree this village is a small paradise. But this is their paradise, not ours."

"Nonsense," Uri growled. "Did you hit your head? I don't want to leave. I'm tired of your adventures."

"And I'm eager to return to Alexa in Italy," John confessed quietly. "But I'd like to stay here longer, too. Perhaps, you can follow our wishes this time, Aris."

Aris's gaze was firm. "One week, then I'm gone!"

Uri chucked his apple core into the sink. "I've had enough of your ultimatums. Let's stay two weeks more."

Aris glanced at John, who seemed to be in agreement with Uri.

Sighing, Aris relented. "Okay, we'll stay two weeks, until after Easter, and not a minute longer."

"From here, I think I'll return to Italy, to Alexa," John confided. "If that's okay with you, Aris."

Clenching his jaw, Aris nodded. "I can do with some time on my own."

The café was buzzing with patrons when the sun dyed the entire plaza blood red. Aris, John and Uri occupied one of the outdoor tables and made polite conversation with Yiannis as he served them.

Yiannis dropped off a round of drinks. "You've settled into the village quickly. We all appreciate how much you help around here."

John's head bobbed enthusiastically. "We feel the same. It's as if we're already part of your village."

Yiannis glanced at Aris. "What about you?"

Aris smiled wanly. "Everyone here is very welcoming, and the village is amazing."

Yiannis watched Aris biting his lip. "But?"

"We'll be going soon. We don't want to overstay our welcome."

Yiannis's body locked in place. "You can't go now. You've just worked your way into our good graces. If you leave now, everyone will be disappointed."

An old man from nearby leaned closer. "No one in our village sees you lot as intruders. On the contrary. That's why they let you into their lives."

Uri jerked his thumb at Aris. "We already told him, but he's just being a stubborn mule again."

Seeing Adonis limping across the plaza with an older bearded gentleman, Yiannis waved them both over. "Adonis typically avoids strangers. Yet, you have become his best friend in just a few days, Aris. Do you want to tell him you're leaving? He's lost so much since his accident, even shying away from Angelica even though everyone knows he's in love with her."

Aris watched Adonis hobble closer to the café, his body rocking to the side with every step. The older gentleman was more spry.

"I don't blame him," Aris said. "Angelica outshines even diamonds. I'm sure they would be a good match."

When Adonis was closer, he lifted his arm to wave at their table.

Yiannis waved back. "Jacob, the old Jewish man with the white beard, is waiting to challenge you in backgammon," he informed Aris. "You'll have a battle tonight!"

Uri stood, greeting Jacob with a firm handshake. "I hope you destroy Aris today. I want to see him cry!"

Leaning near Aris's ear, Yiannis whispered, "Korina will miss her nightly visits if you leave so soon."

Aris wrenched back, staring at the man hovering over him. "What are you talking about? I don't visit anyone, let alone the widow!"

"It's okay. She needs a man."

"Don't make assumptions that are not true," Aris snarled.

"More than one person told me Korina visits your house at night," Yiannis responded, his voice dripping with confusion. "Who else would she be visiting?"

Aris levelled Yiannis with a bland look. "Maybe Uri. He's the biggest philanderer I know. I warned him not to mess with Korina."

"People think she's visiting you. But if you say she isn't…"

Adonis finally arrived, swaying towards the nearest seat. He eased himself down, settling in to watch the backgammon.

Uri grinned wildly. "I had Aris teach me some tricks, you know. Soon, even I will be able to beat you."

"Challenge me again after you beat my teenage son!" Adonis teased, sending the crowd tittering with laughter. "He hasn't been born yet, but that should give you enough time to practise." He turned to Aris, a smirk firm on his face. "Perhaps the master has time for me tonight, though."

A clatter drew the attention of everyone. Standing by a table at the edge of the café's outdoor seating, a squat man with thick legs and wide shoulders and a pair of binoculars dangling from his neck waited until everyone was looking at him. "No," the man announced. "He's playing me tonight."

"This is not fair, Anastasis," Adonis playful chided the shepherd. "You've had Aris all day helping you with your flock. You need to learn to share."

"What do you say, Aris? Who do you want to play?" Jacob asked, waving his cane in the air for effect.

Aris leaned back and crossed his arms. "You know I love you both, but you're too slow. You take forever to make a move. You'd make a camel lose patience!"

Adonis burst out laughing. "Why don't you play them both simultaneously?"

Yiannis rubbed his hands together like a mischievous child. "That would be a match to watch!"

Aris glanced at Adonis. "Are we still on for tomorrow?"

"Yes, the horses will be ready by first light."

"I better get started, then. Otherwise, I'll be playing these two all night, even if I play them at the same time. Bring me some food, as well. It'll give me something to do while I wait for these old men to make their moves."

Jacob and Anastasis sat at neighbouring tables and set up their boards, the stones clacking against the base of the wooden boxes.

Jacob grinned at Aris's arrogance. "Someone will be getting his backside whipped twice tonight!"

Nearby, Zoe crept across the plaza, drawn by the laughter emanating from the café. She peered over the boards, entranced by the men setting up the game.

"You're playing them both?" she asked Aris. "I won't be betting on you tonight. Jacob is the village champion, and Anastasis is very good as well."

"It was Adonis's idea," John explained.

"They are champions because they're so slow," Aris teased. "Their opponents just let them win, so they can leave."

The crowd erupted into laughter as Aris quickly positioned his pieces on both boards then leaned back to wait for his opponents to throw their dice.

The games proceeded at a sedate pace, the crowd joking the longer it lasted.

Uri was suddenly jostled forward, almost pitching into Jacob's table. He turned to shove the gathering back when he noticed the size of the audience. "Half the village is here, Aris. Your loss will be even better this way."

John craned his head, whistling low as he surveyed the assembled villagers. He caught sight of Granny, Despo, and Angelica joining the group. "What are you doing here, Granny?"

The women slid up near the tables. "Courtesy of Zoe," Granny answered. "She went running all over informing everyone what was happening."

Zoe smiled, her breath heavy and a slight sheen of sweat dotting her face. "Someone had to. This could be a once-in-a-lifetime event!"

"Do you see this?" Yiannis said to John, nudging him with his shoulder. "The village will not allow Aris to leave so soon."

Granny and Angelica turned at this comment. Granny echoed, "Leaving us so soon?"

John shifted his focus to Aris briefly before shrugging. "Aris doesn't want to stay too long. He thinks we're intruding."

The games continued. Aris sat facing the centre of the two tables with his opponents beside one another, bent over their respective boards.

Aris threw the dice with ease, sometimes asking Zoe to blow on them for luck.

Jacob and Anastasis stayed silent except for sharp moans of agony when a roll turned bad. Anastasis took to rattling the dice in his hands longer and longer before chucking them down.

"Anastasis," Aris pleaded. "I've nearly finished a second game with Jacob, but you're still whittling away at the first. Just play!"

Leaning over the board, Anastasis mumbled, "Stop trying to distract me so you can win. I am strategizing my move."

"What's your secret in backgammon, Aris?" Jacob's son, Ali, asked. He was standing behind his father, having already watched Aris defeat him once but hoping his father could eke out a win.

"Like everything in life, backgammon requires—" Aris began.

Zoe interrupted, bouncing up and down on her toes. "Three things. Preparation! No fear! And follow up! Aris already taught me this!"

Aris gave the girl a high-five. "Absolutely right! Well done, Zoe! The point is to practise this advice. Look at these two. Because they weren't prepared, they are now overwhelmed by fear. That's why they are losing."

"Jacob doesn't look too scared," Zoe remarked. "He's beating you four to zero, and first to five wins!"

"It's part of the strategy. Because they are ahead, they will start playing defensively and allow fear to engulf them. That's when I strike."

Jacob laughed at this pronouncement. "You hide your fear very well, Aris."

Aris rolled high on his next turn, earning doubles and locking in Jacob's pieces. With a single move, Aris evened the score.

In the end, Jacob grabbed his cane and lurched to his feet, slamming the backgammon board shut. "You just got lucky."

Zoe rushed Aris, shaking him by the arm. "How did you do that?"

Smiling down at her, Aris said, "Just got lucky."

Jacob wagged a finger at him like he was scolding a dog. "But tonight, I studied your moves. Next time I will beat you!"

Ali hovered behind his father, staring down at the table as if the game was still happening. "He didn't have any special moves. He just confused you. It's like he said—you got scared and changed your game."

Aris clapped Ali on the shoulder. "Your son is right, Jacob!"

"What about Anastasis?" Adonis interjected.

At the other table, Anastasis was bent over his game, head drooped and snoring lightly. Not even the laughter that rippled through the crowd could wake him.

Aris shook his head. "We haven't even finished the first game yet. We'll call it a draw again."

"At least I know how to get a draw next time!" joked Jacob.

Ali stepped up to Aris, crossing his arms. "Aris, I challenge you tomorrow!"

"Are you as fast as the shepherd?" teased Aris.

The rest burst out laughing.

"The only reason I'll be falling asleep is that I will be waiting for you to respond to my moves," Ali taunted.

"You're just a boy," Zoe interrupted. "Aris is unbeatable so far."

"I've seen Ali play against his father, and he's a master when it comes to backgammon," Aris said, Ali preening at the praise.

"You spied on me!" Jacob shouted, laughing. "That explains how you won."

"Did you really spy on his moves, Aris?" Zoe asked.

Aris smiled disarmingly "Studying your opponent is part of preparation."

Zoe nodded. "So, then Ali prepared by watching you tonight!"

Aris nodded back and turned to Ali. "Young man. Your challenge is accepted. Tomorrow, we duel!"

Yiannis retreated inside the café to finish closing while the villagers slowly dispersed into the night.

Angelica slipped up next to Anastasis and gently tapped him on the shoulder, waking him from his slumber.

The shepherd jerked awake, immediately focusing on the folded-up backgammon board. He snorted. "Aris gave up again, huh?"

Angelica laughed softly as she helped him from his chair, threading her arm with his. "Come, I will walk you home."

◆ ◇ ◆

The afternoon sun warmed Granny's face as she sat on the patio preparing medicinal herbs. Next to her, Despo trimmed fresh beans for dinner while Angelica knitted.

Granny picked up a stem of herbs and plucked the leaves with practised ease. "The children seem to love the

Americans—especially Aris. They all run to him for answers, as if he's their favourite teacher."

Dropping a handful of beans into a container at her feet, Despo nodded. "The kids are lucky he puts up with them."

"He's definitely Zoe's favourite," Angelica conceded. "It's always 'Aris said this' and 'Aris said that'. She thinks Aris knows everything."

Granny snorted. "Seems you have competition. Zoe used to come to you."

Despo giggled. "He never says no to them. He goes wherever they ask him to. He seems to enjoy them."

Angelica maintained her focus on the yard. "He abandoned his family, yet entertains these children's demands even when he's tired. He goes out to the fields helping Father and Adonis and Anastasis. Something just isn't right."

Fiddling with a handful of herbs, Granny shook her head. "It's not just the children. Aris is equally popular with adults. Even Adonis, who never befriended outsiders, enjoys his company."

"Same with old Jacob." Despo dropped another handful of beans into the container. "He sometimes spends whole days with Anastasis helping with the flock. Not to mention the widow, who is in and out of that old house."

Angelica pursed her lips.

"She's a free woman!" Despo held up her hands, fending off whatever Angelica was about to say.

Granny cleared her throat. "The other day, John was telling Manolios that Aris is searching for some family secret, but Aris stopped John from explaining. Maybe that's what brought them all to us. To our village. I doubt they'll find a family secret here though."

Angelica lay her knitting in her lap. "Aris seems to have won everyone over. Have you considered that he may just be a very lonely man? Or even a fugitive? No one knows what those men are running from!"

◆

A swarm of villagers fluttered at the end of the plaza near the dock. Anchored in the bay, a small merchant boat rocked as its crew unloaded cargo onto the dock.

The captain approached Manolios, next to whom stood his family. Shaking hands, the captain greeted him in a loud and booming voice. "Georgi wishes to extend another invitation asking for Angelica's hand. She will have servants for her needs, a big house, and her own car. She's not a little girl anymore. She is quickly passing the age of marriage. You are lucky Georgi's still interested."

Stepping back from the captain, Manolios rested a hand on his daughter's shoulder. "She's already thirty."

Aris and Adonis hovered at the edge of the crowd. Adonis leaned over to whisper in Aris's ear, "That spoiled bastard never gives up. He's been after Angelica for years."

The captain turned to Angelica, frowning at the disinterest plastered on her face. "You need to decide. Soon. Having children will be difficult and then who would want to marry you? Georgi is crazy for you. You will want for nothing if you marry him."

"Has Georgi increased the commission promised to you, Captain?" Angelica asked, waiting as the villagers tittered. "Tell him that his wealth is no match to the riches of our village."

Aris tilted toward Adonis, mumbling so others wouldn't hear. "Apparently, men flock here to ask Angelica to marry them? She's clearly waiting for someone to make his move."

Adonis just pinched his lips. "She's the pride and soul of our village," he whispered bitterly. "She deserves someone of equal standing."

"That doesn't mean she isn't waiting for the right man to step up."

"After my accident," Adonis began, his voice raspy and tight, "she left to live in the city. I was told she couldn't bear seeing me crippled and hobbling around. I didn't think I'd see her again. She enrolled in university, graduating with honours. Her life was there."

"But she did return," Aris insisted. "Something brought her back."

"She did, but I don't know why. She's wasted in this village. Soon, she'll get bored and return to the city."

"Were you not listening just now? She loves her village and her people. I'm sure that includes you, Adonis."

Adonis coughed. "Thank you, but you cannot understand. I am an uneducated, crippled farmer. My mother is bedbound. Angelica and I live different lives."

"You're just finding excuses. As I understand it, she already looks after your mother with pleasure."

Aris turned back to the docks, only to find Angelica watching the two of them, her gaze bewitching in the afternoon sun. "I think she may have overheard us," he whispered.

Turning, Adonis caught Angelica's gaze, unable to look away. He tugged on Aris's arm. "Let's help load the goats on the boat. They're less stubborn than you."

24 The Birthday

Aris wandered through the streets, enjoying the weather. Eventually he found himself stumbling into the plaza with a larger crowd than normal. In the corner opposite Yiannis's café, a pedlar's van was parked. The tin roof glinted in the sun while a small horde of people buzzed around picking at the items on display.

The pedlar hunched over, showing off one of his wares to Zoe, who was pouting next to her mother and Angelica.

"I want a special dress. It's my birthday and my mother's birthday, so it's double important. Everything you have is awful!"

Overhearing her wails, Aris shifted his route and squeezed through a small group of women until he was standing beside Zoe and her mother. "I see you are upset," he said. "But you're being rude to the pedlar."

Zoe looked up at him, her eyes glistening with tears. "I'm not. He only has things for old women and tablecloths. Angelica can't make me something nice with any of this."

A small crowd formed around Zoe.

"Remember what you need to succeed?"

Shifting back and forth, Zoe nodded. "Preparation, no fear, and follow-up. But what kind of dress can we make with all that?"

Tugging her through the crowd, Aris brought her to the display at the front of the van.

Angelica followed. "Unfortunately, Zoe is right." She flicked through the fabric. "This is all very basic."

Zoe wilted at the statement. "You see. I'm always right because I do not mess around. But sometimes I hate always being right."

Aris grinned. "Not this time."

Zoe glared at him, opening her mouth to argue.

"First, apologise to your mother. If you do, I'll design something special for your birthday."

Zoe crossed her arms. "You are a man. What do you know about dresses?"

Gently turning her to face him, Aris crouched to look Zoe in the eyes. "I thought you said I know everything."

"Stay out of this," she shouted, jolting out of his grasp. "You don't understand."

"Now you are still being rude. Apologise to your mother or I will walk away."

Around them, the crowd of shoppers stopped, watching the argument unfold.

Angelica stepped forwards. "Can't you see you're upsetting her? And you are promising something we can't provide. You can't just give her false hope."

Aris smiled. "But I'm being serious. I can make something unique only for Zoe. She deserves it."

"Can you? Really?" Zoe asked, her eyes wide with wonder.

"If Angelica is willing to help with the sewing, the rest I can handle on my own."

"Don't promise what you cannot deliver," Angelica reprimanded. "Especially to Zoe!"

Zoe grinned manically up at Aris. "I always expect to get what I am promised, so how can a man know girls' fashion?"

"Some of the most successful designers in the world were men—Armani, Lagerfeld, McQueen. But since you aren't interested, I don't have to help you."

Zoe turned to Angelica. "Men can be designers?"

"W-w-well," Angelica stuttered, caught off guard. "Yes, they can."

Leaping at Aris, Zoe grabbed him by the arm. "Wait! I never said I wasn't interested."

Angelica watched the sudden shift in Zoe's mood, sceptical of what Aris could do but glad he was helping.

"Can you please design something special for me?" Zoe begged.

Aris wavered a moment, pretending to consider the offer, before nodding enthusiastically.

Zoe turned and jumped into her mother's arms, hugging her tight.

Her mother laughed at Zoe's antics. "I know, I know. We are very proud of you!"

After calming down, Zoe turned back to Aris with a serious expression. "I will oversee your design. How will you make something special from these dated fabrics and tablecloths? You better deliver, or else."

"Better not let her down!" Angelica warned.

Aris chuckled. "It's not my first time designing clothes. Back in the '80s in Dusseldorf, Germany, I won an award for best youth designer at a fashion exhibition—beating 2500 fashion houses! I will show you the photos on my phone later. Does that convince you, Angelica?"

"Are you a designer or a businessman?"

"Self-taught, mostly, but I was in the fashion industry. I had to learn to design to survive. I combined taste with intelligence and commerciality. Simple formula, really."

Angelica's mouth went dry.

Aris began to search through the fabric on offer with Zoe glued to his side, watching everything he did and absorbing his advice.

Aris rejected and rejected.

Zoe's hope began to flag. "I told you, there's nothing here."

Finally, Aris selected a few fabrics—a pure white, a light navy with white spots, a navy with white stripes, and a final white one with navy spots.

Zoe stamped her foot and tried to pull them out of his hands. "But these are tablecloths!"

"Do you have any knitted fabric in these colours?" Aris asked the pedlar, ignoring Zoe for the moment.

The man shook his head.

"See?" Zoe whined. "He doesn't have anything."

Aris patted her head. "To the contrary, he has a very good selection."

Zoe looked to Angelica for support, but she just shrugged.

Aris continued to dig through the pedlar's stock. "Remember number three? Follow-up. That sometimes means adapting and finding a new way forward. We'll just have to improvise! Do you have any elastic?" he asked the pedlar.

The man showed him his inventory, and Aris selected a segment of elastic as well as a length of white ribbon.

Glancing around, Aris asked, "Do you have drafting paper?"

"Only plain brown paper."

"It will do. Give me a small roll."

Zoe tugged on Angelica's dress, cupping her hand around her mouth. "What is Aris doing?"

Aris looked over his shoulder to Angelica before she could answer. "Do you have sewing supplies… measuring tape, thread, all of that?"

Angelica was too surprised to do anything but nod.

"I will pay for all this," Zoe's mother said, stepping forward.

Throwing an arm out in front of her, Aris cut her off. "No! This is my present for Zoe." Aris paid the pedlar.

Angelica watched it all in silence, her own mother and grandmother joining her while Aris waited for his change.

Peering over around Aris to get a glimpse at the goods, Zoe cried out, "I'm not wearing a tablecloth!"

Aris pocketed his change and faced Granny. "When you have patients, do they tell you how to treat their ailment?"

Granny narrowed her eyes. "If they knew how to cure themselves, they would not have come to me."

Aris looked down at Zoe. "There you have it."

Zoe tugged at his arm, trying to stop him from leaving. "What does that have to do with anything? I am not going to wear a tablecloth!"

Zoe's mother pulled her off Aris and squatted down to soothe her daughter. "Aris is the doctor of your wish. Are you going to tell him how to do his job?"

Zoe sniffled. "No one can do anything with those scraps."

"Since you seem to have lost all faith in me, how about this," Aris offered. "If you like the dress, you have to run around the plaza ten times screaming 'I have faith!'"

"That's never going to happen. And I am not going to wear old lady clothes," Zoe mumbled.

"Experienced or not, Zoe is right," Angelica conceded. "There is so only much you can do with these materials."

Aris raised an eyebrow at Angelica. "Perhaps, when the time comes, you'd like to run around the plaza apologising, too."

The crowd of shoppers clucked with laughter.

"Very funny!" Angelica sneered.

"Are you going to accept the challenge?"

"I am not a child, Aris!"

He turned to Zoe. "It seems Angelica is not willing to make your dress. We will have to ask old Mr. Jacob."

Angelica jerked as if slapped. "I never said I wouldn't make the dress!"

Aris ignored her, focusing on Zoe. "Jacob will not be needed then. The only thing we need now is a decent-sized table. I will think of something."

"Why don't you use our table?" Despo offered. "It's long and wide. We also have chalk you can use to mark the pattern."

Turning his gaze to Angelica, Aris waited silently. She stared back, lost for a moment, before jumping out of her revelry. "Of course, you are welcome. Our table is ideal."

Aris nodded and turned to Granny. "I will need blue and gold paint at some stage."

"Blue is easy, but gold might be tricky."

"We'll think of something," Aris replied and headed towards the café.

"At this rate, I won't even want a party," Zoe mumbled, sulking after him.

Aris shouted back, "Make it fifteen rounds of apologising!"

25 THE GOSSIP

Aris bent low over a wide wooden dining table that Despo pushed out into the main room where the light was better. He mumbled to himself while sketching out the design for Zoe's dress.

"You were right about this table, Despo," Aris announced suddenly, his hand still arcing over the paper. "It's the perfect size for design work."

Despo smiled. "We use it ourselves when we make dress patterns."

Aris frowned at his progress, waving an arm to the side to grab Angelica's attention. "Can I have the armhole and neck circumference measurements, please?"

"I did not take neck measurements."

"Can you get them for me, please?"

"She can't be far," Granny muttered from her chair in the corner of the room. "Zoe's always trailing after you, Angelica, copying everything you do."

"Okay, I will get the measurements." Angelica headed out of the house.

At her sudden obedience, Granny rolled her eyes. "She just doesn't understand the outside world and other cultures. She spoke out of turn the other day with your friends, Aris."

◆

Angelica yanked Zoe to a halt just outside the open door. At the sound of Granny's voice Angelica motioned for Zoe to stay quiet so she could eavesdrop.

She heard Aris reply, "She was right in everything she said about the three of us. We did leave our families behind." He bent back over the table, returning to his pattern. "She was also right in claiming we could have been criminals running from the law. You trust people too easily in your village."

Zoe groaned, bored from the gossip, and darted out of Angelica's grip and inside to the table, trying to get a hint of the design.

Angelica hurried after her, standing so close to Aris they were nearly touching. Aris shifted slightly, getting a bit more space between them. Only Granny noticed the interaction, never missing anything from her position in the corner of the room.

Angelica stepped closer again, picking up the measuring tape. "How strange… Zoe's head is nearly the same as an adult's."

"The head is the first part of the body to grow to near full size," he said, then saw the girl peeking over at his drawings. "Stop spying, Zoe. It's a surprise, so get out!"

Manolios entered, nearly getting knocked over as Zoe raced out the door. He stopped short seeing the number of sketches on the table. "I thought this would be easy since Zoe is so small."

Granny smiled, leaning back in her chair. "Our designer seems to have complicated ideas."

Aris snorted at the accusation. "Children's clothing has complex dimensions that make patterning for it more time-consuming."

"We have a deadline to meet," Angelica boasted. "We have to work around the clock."

Manolios shot his wife a glance before focusing back on Angelica. "I know. I could hear you past midnight."

Lifting his head from the patterns, Aris said, "I'm sorry for disturbing you. It won't happen again."

Manolios waved off the apology and walked away. "Don't forget it's holy Friday today. Everyone will be at the church. It is Easter Pascha on Sunday!"

Stepping to the back of the house, Manolios caught sight of Adonis looking over the other side of the garden fence. He waved hello, and Adonis returned the greeting.

Gathering the tools and patterns he'd cut, Aris moved it all out of the way. "I think I'm done for the day. The pattern is marked. Angelica, can you finish cutting the sections?"

Aris turned to leave, bidding everyone a good night just as Manolios returned.

"Why don't you stay for dinner, Aris?" asked Despo. "We have plenty."

At the invitation, Manolios looked at Granny who quickly glanced away.

"Thank you," Aris replied politely as he edged towards the door. "But Uri and John will be waiting for me. John offered to cook tonight! Hopefully, I will still be alive tomorrow."

"We can continue working after dinner!" Angelica called out.

Manolios appeared unamused.

Aris gazed at Angelica who seemed caught off guard by her own blatant invitation. "We've made good progress," he said. "There's no need to work late again. Tomorrow is Holy Saturday, but we can work then if that's all right with your father."

⋆◇⋆

Manolios stood at the front door, waiting until Aris was out of sight before turning to his daughter. "What are you doing, Angelica? He's a stranger. You can't have him in the house all day and all night!"

Angelica rolled and continued to cut out the patterns Aris had mocked up earlier.

He stepped closer, lowering his voice. "You need to be a little more distant. Lately, you follow Aris wherever he goes. You take him with you wherever you go. You even chase him at his house."

Angelica glanced up in surprise. "What are you saying?"

"I'm saying that this is a small village. Adonis is watching. Aris is a married man. These things don't go unnoticed here! To his credit, he isn't encouraging you. Like tonight, Aris resisted your invitation. You don't seem to take notice of his message, though."

"He's trying hard to make Zoe happy!" Angelica argued. "We cannot refuse to help him. Mum and Granny are always here. What's the problem?"

"He was here past midnight yesterday!" Manolios fired back. "What are the people in the village going to say? They already talk about his visits from the widow."

To Despo and Granny's surprise, Angelica continued to push back. "The doors are always open! Everyone can see we are working on the outfit. We are not hiding!"

Shaking his head, Manolios took a step closer. "This isn't right. At least stop inviting him around after dark. Adonis has started to watch our house all the time. I just saw him gawking over the fence."

Angelica grimaced. "What does Adonis have to worry about? He came over for a coffee just the other day. He didn't complain then."

Manolios groaned. "Exactly! Why else would he come over for an afternoon coffee—something he's never done before?"

Granny and Despo sat silently as Angelica and Manolios continue to argue.

"Adonis came for coffee because his friend Aris was here. Aris is a kind and principled man. He never offends me nor abuses our hospitality. You heard how politely he refused Mother's invitation for dinner."

"That's worse! Young women are often attracted to these kinds of men."

Angelica's face blazed bright red. "Are you accusing me of something?"

Manolios's body sagged. "I am not accusing you of anything. I am advising you. You need to be careful."

Angelica turned back to the patterns on the table, her mouth set in a firm line. "In case you haven't noticed, I am no longer a teenager. I know how to look after myself."

"You said it yourself the other day. We know nothing about Aris and his friends. Realise, you will be exposing all of us to this gossip."

Sensing the rising tension, Despo stepped between the two of them. "You are both right. It is not long to go, anyway. The patterns are already done. A couple of days more and everything will be finished."

Granny pushed out of her chair. "Enough pointless arguing. She's not a silly girl. Clear the table, Angelica. Let's have dinner." Then with a wry grin towards her son, she added, "Maybe I'm the one Aris is here to woo."

26 The Search

Varo blinked, scrubbing at her sore eyes. The day had only just started, and she was already getting distracted. She looked up from her computer screen and ordered Victor into her office.

He stepped into the room, standing stiffly before her.

"Where are they?" she asked. "They couldn't just disappear… again!"

"The girls reported the men headed for Italy," Victor said. "But they weren't sure of their final destination."

Varo leaned back in her chair, massaging her temples. "Aris knows we've been tracking them. He isn't a fool. He probably fed them false information." She tapped her fingers on the desk, her nails clicking on the hardwood. "He's of Greek origin so try the mainland, the Greek islands, even Turkey. Concentrate your search there."

"We won't be able to track them unless they switch on one of the original sim cards," Victor reminded her.

"Aris wouldn't do something so amateur. He's either banned the use of their electronics, or they're using local numbers."

"We can check with mobile phone providers in Italy, Greece, and Turkey." Victor turned to make his exit.

"Use our network connections," she commanded. "But also find out their wives' numbers. In Aris's case, find his sons' mobile numbers. They're bound to make contact."

"Doesn't that seem a bit extreme?" Victor asked, shifting by the door. "Why don't we wait a while?"

Rising to her feet, Varo approached Victor with a smile. "It cannot be hard to find three American men in a foreign country. We know they left the boat in Italy. Find out where, and from there we can figure out how they would have gone to Greece. They must have bought an air ticket, a train ticket, or a ferryboat ticket. Find the possible routes. Get local teams to search. I will not rest until I find Aris."

"It is a large area… thousands of miles."

"I won't let him outfox me," Varo declared, slamming her hand against her desk. "Find the routes. Narrow the search. Let's be clever."

Victor sighed but nodded and quickly ducked out of the office.

27 The Phobia

Angelica watched Aris as he lined up his patterns, how his hands deftly positioned each fragment of paper. She jerked away from the table when she realised how long she had been staring at his hands.

"Going to feed Snowy," she announced and headed out the back of the house.

"What?" Aris asked the room at large, making Angelica pause at the back door.

"Snowy is the snow-white mare we keep out back," Despo explained. "She belongs to Angelica. Still untamed though four years old."

Aris smiled, eyes glazing over in remembrance. "I grew up with horses. Have even fallen asleep on one a few times."

Pride flushed Angelica's cheeks. "If you like horses, you will love Snowy. Come, I'll introduce you."

He stepped away from the table to follow her outside.

"Don't expect anything," Granny warned. "That horse won't let anyone ride her. Even Angelica can only get as far as mounting Snowy before the animal refuses to budge."

Suddenly, a young boy came flailing into the house. "Aris, quick!" he yelled. "Zoe got stuck in a tree with a snake! She needs help!"

A shiver ran up Aris's spine, freezing his body in place. "Snake," he croaked.

Another boy flew past the first, grabbing Aris by the hand and tugging him towards the door. Aris shook himself out of his shock and started running after the boys.

Angelica hovered at the door, watching them run down the street. "I'm going, too."

"Angelica, wait!" Granny commanded. "If there is a snake, we must prepare. Go for my medicine bag and catch up with me."

Undoing her kitchen apron, Despo and Granny followed the boys while Angelica went off in search of Granny's bag.

⸻ ❖ ⸻

Just past the last house at the edge of the village, Aris found a group of kids clambering around the base of a large tree. He pushed them aside, looking up.

One of the smaller kids jumped beside him, pointing up into the recesses of branches. "There, see?" the boy asked. "One of her feet is stuck. She slipped and is trapped upside-down!"

"Aris!" Zoe yelled. "The snake's getting closer! Hurry up!"

"Where's the snake?"

"Right above me!" Zoe cried.

Catching sight of it, Aris broke out into a sweat. A shiver racked his body.

The two boys jumped in surprise at his sudden flail. "Go get Adonis," Aris commanded one of them.

"Help me!" Zoe screamed.

"Hang on," Aris shouted back. He stepped away from the tree, dropped his trousers and pissed away from the children. Fast zipping his pants, Aris turned back and approached the tree.

A young boy tripped after him. "Are you scared, Aris?" he asked, but Aris didn't respond.

Instead he clenched his jaw, ignoring the sweat dripping down his face, and hoisted himself up onto the lowest branch. "I'm coming," he called out to Zoe.

The sweat came right through his shirt. Glancing between Zoe and the fast-approaching snake, Aris scampered up the tree more quickly.

Zoe was now face to face with a dark-scaled snake with caution-yellow eyes. A tongue flicked at her as if it could already taste her.

"Aris, please!"

"I'm here," he said, steadying himself on the thick branch right below her. He brushed the hair out of her face. "I'm gonna get you out. Hold onto me." He stood up, waiting until she wrapped her arms tight around his body.

"Hurry!"

"On three, I'm going to lift. Don't let go until I get you down on the branch," Aris ordered, his shirt soaked as if he'd fallen into the sea.

"Three!" he yelled, yanking her foot free, keeping hold as he twisted down until he got her steady on the branch.

He looked up, trying to find the snake. "Are you okay?" he asked Zoe without stopping his search. "Can you stand on your own feet?"

Zoe tested resting her weight on both feet before nodding. "Yeah," she responded, not waiting another moment before she quickly began to scramble down.

Halfway to the bottom, Zoe stopped and glanced up at Aris. He was still on the same branch, his eyes focused ahead, his back against the trunk and his legs dangling in the air. He shook the sweat out of his eyes, wiping the excess with the back of his arm.

The snake had slunk down from a higher branch, twisting to face him. Aris was now locked in place, his muscles aching from keeping himself still.

Angelica busted through the crowd, stopping by Granny and her mother.

"Something is wrong," Granny whispered. "Aris is not moving."

Despo cocked her head in thought. "He doesn't seem afraid of the snake. Maybe he is trying to catch it."

"Aris is clearly afraid of something. He's not afraid of heights, is he?"

Angelica's eyes grew wide with a sudden revelation. She rushed forward, clutching the lowest branch. "Hold on, Aris. I'm coming!"

The sound of her voice shook Aris from his stupor. He glanced down, catching sight of a blurred but worried Angelica. "Stay there," he shouted back hoarsely. "I'm climbing down."

Zoe stopped next to Angelica, looking back up where Aris still wasn't moving. She too made ready to start up when a large hand stopped her.

"Girls," Adonis said, his voice strong and sure. "Both of you come down. I'm going up." Like a bolt of lightning, he propelled himself up the tree, pulled by his strong arms even while one leg was almost useless..

Aris felt a rough whisper of a tongue along the side of his face. He jerked, instinctively trying to get away and for a moment forgot where he was. His body flipped sideways over the branch, tumbling down and landing on his crotch on a lower branch.

The impact knocked the breath out of him, causing him to gasp in pain. With effort, he tilted his head back, catching sight of the snake still slithering toward him. Panic chilled his limbs.

"Aris!" Adonis cried out. "Move down or away from the trunk. The snake is getting too close."

Taking a deep breath, Aris slowly began to creep down. He kept his eyes on the branch he was on and tried to ignore the small crowd gathered around the base of the tree.

Glancing down for the next branch, he caught sight of the ground between the gaps. He tensed, breathless at how tiny everyone looked. Clamping his legs onto the trunk of the tree, he saw the snake arch its back.

"Move, Aris!" Adonis shouted.

"Move, Aris, move!" John echoed as he and Uri joined the crowd.

Aris rolled his head back, looking above him. The snake hissed, head up and fangs bright under the shade of the tree. It coiled and launched itself at him.

Aris flinched backwards, flipping away from the tree and crashing through a few more branches.

Adonis flung himself out, snaring Aris in his grip mid-air. The crowd cheered, witnessing the save.

"Give them space," Granny commanded as Adonis cradled Aris back to the ground.

"Is he dead?" Uri asked, causing Zoe to burst out in tears.

Granny knelt beside Aris, casting her eyes for any bite marks.

Aris lifted his head, causing a wave of elation to ripple across the crowd. "He's alive! He's alive!"

Adonis helped Aris to sit up. "Rest here. I'll get the snake," he said.

Wiping sweat from his blurred vision, Aris nodded.

Still in tears, Zoe threw herself at him. "Thank you! Thank you! You saved me! You are my hero!"

Aris sighed, dropping a soft kiss on her head. "You weren't half as scared as I was!"

Watching Aris cradle Zoe, Angelica felt relief wash over her like a soft rain.

"Catch the snake, Adonis!" a boy shouted, causing everyone's gaze to turn back to the tree.

Adonis crouched on a branch, his shirt tied off like a bag in one hand. Patiently, he held it out and waited as the snake moved further into his trap.

Tying off the opening once the snake was inside, Adonis began his descent to the applause of the crowd. Reaching the ground, he offered the snake to Granny. "Here, you can make plenty of antidote from this snake's venom."

"You were amazing," a boy shouted at Adonis. "You weren't scared at all, like Aris."

The crowd turned to Aris, and he huffed out a laugh. "Yes, I'm scared of heights, but snakes are even worse. I'm not sure I've ever been so scared in my life. But I would do it again for Zoe."

Angelica's face filled with sympathy at his confession.

"Were you really that scared?" Zoe asked, shocked.

Aris nodded. "Did you not see the sweat on my face? Look, my shirt is still soaking wet!"

"I am sorry, Aris. I didn't mean to put you in that position. I was really scared, too. I thought I was going to die!"

Aris smiled proudly at her. "It's okay to be scared when there is danger. It's natural. Fear is sometimes necessary."

Suddenly, Zoe's face lit up. "Aris must love me very much! He risked both his fears to save me. Adonis, too, of course. He even caught the snake."

Adonis offered her a gentle smile. "You're lucky it's Easter and we were all around."

The crowd began to disperse, moving towards the village. Aris remained on the ground, stretching his legs out and resting against the tree.

Pausing, Zoe turned to look back at him. "Are you not coming?"

Adonis ushered her along with his usual limp. "Aris needs a few minutes by himself. He will come when he is ready."

28 Multi-Talented

Gina welcomed her sons into the house, but she could feel the tension in the air like electricity. She sat down, fixing her hair as they stood across from her.

"You have to stop this," Peter ordered, his voice hard. "Every day, someone tells us where you've been and who you were with. You're embarrassing us."

Gina snorted. "So what? Do you expect me to just stay home all day?"

Gerry stepped up next to his brother. "Mum, you're putting us in an awkward situation."

Gina rolled her eyes. "I go out for dinner with a few girlfriends and suddenly the whole world is upset!"

"This is not a now and then thing," Peter barked. "It's every day! And it's not always with your *girl* friends."

Getting to her feet, Gina snapped, "You should tell this to your father, not me. He's the one who left! He's out there having fun with his whores, and I'm supposed to feel bad? I deserve to enjoy my life, too!"

"You're both doing the same thing," Gerry replied calmly.

Gina bit her lip.

Gerry stepped closer. "Dad did not leave to have fun. He needed to get away from you. If you were my wife, I would have chucked you out long ago."

Bent over, Gina blubbered through crocodile tears, "You always take his side."

"Mum," Peter said, "this has gone on long enough. If you want to live like this, you need to announce your divorce."

Gina stamped her foot. "It's not my fault! Your father refused to divorce me. You're both like him. All you want to do is cage me like an animal!"

Peter shook his head. "You go out constantly. Who is watching Liza?"

"Look at you!" Gerry added. "Miniskirts and lycra crop tops. Dressing like a teenager does not make you one!"

"Like father, like sons. I free myself from his criticism, only to have you fill his shoes."

The doorbell rang, cutting their conversation short. "My friends are here to pick me up," Gina said. "Come back tomorrow when I don't have any plans. We can talk more."

Peter and Gerry slumped out the door, Gina following behind with a designer handbag dangling from her arm.

⸻ ❖ ⸻

Aris tried to slip out of the house while John and Uri were eating breakfast.

"Aris! Aris!" Uri shouted, smiling wildly. "Where are you going? We're supposed to leave today!"

Glancing between the two of them, Aris finally settled on staring out the window. "You wanted to stay longer. I decided we can stay a bit longer."

The smile dropped from Uri's face. "You were the one who set the deadline in the first place."

"It doesn't matter," Aris replied, shrugging. "We can stay as long as we want."

"But you told us we had to leave." John jumped up. "You can't just change your mind like that."

Aris sighed. "Yes. I changed my mind. I want to stay a while longer. They are nice people and the village is beautiful."

Uri marched up to him. "It was you who said we were intruding and that we must not abuse their hospitality."

"You wanted to stay longer. I'm agreeing with you now. What's the problem?"

"Don't turn it on us," Uri snapped. "You gave us a deadline. You were going to leave by yourself if we didn't leave with you, remember?"

"We agreed to your deadline so we could leave together as a team," John added.

Aris scoffed at them. "If I wanted to have empty arguments, I would have stayed home. You are free to do as you please."

Fuming, Uri kicked the couch. "You're a moron. You're cutting us off again! Do you want to stay? Fine, I have a woman here. I can stay as long as you want!"

"No!" John argued. "I told Alexa I would be coming back in a couple of weeks."

"Then go, John!" Aris shouted, walking out of the house.

"By myself?" John called after him.

Uri slapped the wall by the door. "You're the one who doesn't know what he wants, Aris!"

John moved to stand next to Uri. "I don't think Aris wants to go home."

"Perhaps he's found a reason to stay longer." Uri scrubbed at his face with one hand. "Aris will always do what he wants to do anyway. And I'm pretty sure he wants to get rid of us."

* ◇ *

Zoe rushed into Angelica's house, her mother trailing behind her, to be welcomed by Aris and Angelica shouting, "Happy birthday!"

She smiled at them, hugging Granny and Despo when they wished her a happy birthday as well.

Aris motioned to Angelica, who placed her hand on Zoe's shoulders and guided her into Angelica's room.

"Hurry up, Zoe," Manolios called. "Even I'm curious to see what Aris made."

For a few moments, there was nothing, then a sharp cry filled the house. "I love it!"

Zoe skipped out into the hall wearing the biggest smile. She spun, showing off her new outfit. "Isn't it amazing! I've never seen anything like it."

Off to the side, Zoe's mother wiped away the tears forming in her eyes as she watched her daughter prance around in joy.

Aris waved her over to the full-length mirror in the hall. "Have a look here."

Zoe twirled in front of the mirror, her smile so large it split her face. She turned and ran to her mother. "Look, I'm a princess!"

Zoe's mother laughed, smiling at her daughter.

Zoe giggled, her skirt flouncing with her movements. The golden crown printed across the front glowed in the morning light. She stopped, smoothing out the matching navy jacket and fixing her clothes so that everything was in perfect order, from the jacket to the skirt and all the way down to her striped leggings.

Her gaze surfed across everyone present. "It's really one of a kind. I feel I'm walking on the clouds!"

"Amazing," Manolios exclaimed to everyone's surprise. "You definitely deserve to wear something so special."

Zoe gave Manolios a giant hug.

"Each piece can be worn separately as well," Angelica bragged.

Zoe let go of Manolios and ran to Angelica next, giving her a long and hard hug. "I love you!" Zoe sobbed.

"Bravo, Aris," Manolios cheered. "I guess you really did know what you were talking about."

Aris accepted the compliment with a nod, gesturing to Angelica, Despo and Granny. "This was a joint project. The ladies did most of the work."

Suddenly, Zoe twirled on her foot and stared at Aris. A crafty pout slipped onto her face. "You don't actually think I like this? It makes me look like a little princess in a poor village! I am not five years old, you know."

"What's the matter with you, Zoe? I thought you liked it," Manolios gasped.

Zoe dropped her voice. "I'm thinking about five rounds in the plaza!"

Aris smiled at her, shaking his head. "Ten rounds!"

Manolios glanced between the two of them, confused. "What is happening?"

"They made a bet," Angelica explained. "If Zoe liked what he made, Zoe would have to run ten rounds round the plaza shouting, 'I apologise.'"

Manolios erupted in laughter.

"No. I will be shouting, 'I have faith'," Zoe corrected.

Manolios laughed even harder. "Little fox, you are trapped now. I don't see how you can get out of this one."

Zoe turned to Aris, smiling up at him. "Well, someone told me not to rush when making a decision."

"That's right," Aris fired back. "Take the outfit off and come back tomorrow, or next week. Whenever you decide."

Everyone waited for Zoe's move. With a firm nod, she leaned to the side while keeping her gaze on Aris. "You also told me that if a decision has to be made, I should trust my instincts, while being fair to myself and others."

The group watched, entertained by the back and forth.

"In this case, Aris was not fair, and he could be wrong!" Zoe continued. "He knew he could do this before the bet. If I had known, I never would have agreed to it. But also, there's no proof I agreed to anything!"

Smiling, Aris glanced at the others and nodded, confirming Zoe's argument.

"Zoe is right," Granny adjudicated. "I was there. She never agreed to anything."

Manolios burst out laughing again. "It seems the little fox has found a way to escape. You are in trouble, Aris!"

Aris chuckled. "The little fox princess will make a first-class lawyer. But, as right as she may sound, Zoe never rejected the bet either."

Zoe threw herself at Aris in a hug. "One day soon, I will outthink you!" she promised. "Thank you so, so, so much, Aris. You made me so happy. I love you. I am very proud of you."

"The hard work was done by the ladies. They did all the sewing and decorating. It was impossible to make your outfit without them. Even Anastasis contributed with the stamp to print the crown."

Still hugging Aris, Zoe turned her head to look at the others. "Thank you, thank you. Thank you all! Can I go show my friends now? My party starts soon."

Aris poked her with his finger to get her attention. "You can, but remember the deal? You have to honour my condition."

Zoe gasped, looking around at the others for support, but they all remained silent.

"A deal is a deal!" Manolios commented.

"Fine," Zoe sighed, admitting defeat. "Only because you deserve it, Aris. And to show my appreciation, I will gladly do my rounds!"

Aris gave her a high-five. "Once more, you prove how truly amazing you are. You are fit to be President of the whole world!"

Zoe marched out of the house, her head held high. The others followed her out, watching her journey around the plaza shouting, "I have faith. I have faith. I have faith."

—◇—

After the others cleared out, Angelica and Granny puttered around the room straightening up. They danced around each other, Angelica sometimes stopping and staring at nothing for several moments before returning to what she was doing.

"You seem to be lost in thought," Granny mentioned. "What's wrong?"

Angelica dropped into a nearby chair. "It's Aris."

"What about him?"

Angelica sighed deeply. "He's incredible. I've never imagined a man like him could exist. Now that I got to know him, all my concerns are gone! We can talk for ages, and he listens. Even when we say nothing, just being near him fills me with joy. He's intelligent and thoughtful but as carefree as a child sometimes. And his deep voice makes me shiver. Don't you agree?"

Granny chuckled. "I can definitely see the appeal. But don't fool yourself. Love is full of painful traps. You can't control how others feel. And while it's clear he is attracted to you, keep in mind he already has a wife. Grandchildren even. Don't encourage him."

Angelica pushed off the warning. "I'm just admiring his qualities."

Granny grabbed Angelica's chin, holding her focus. "Never forget that he is just a visitor with a life beyond this village. He will leave soon. Don't confuse admiration for love."

"Do you take me for a fool?"

Granny started pacing the room. "Any woman can fall into this trap! It's not a coincidence that we all enjoy his company."

"Oh, now I see! You really do fancy Aris, don't you?"

"Aris isn't a threat to me." Then Granny dropped her voice and added, "Even though I would not mind a night or two with him!"

29 THE LOVE SECRET

Aris sat across from John and Uri the next morning at breakfast. The open door let in a nice breeze.

A shadow crossed their threshold and John jumped out of his seat. "Good morning, Angelica. Want some breakfast?"

"Thank you, but I already ate." She turned to Aris. "We haven't seen you for a few days."

"Aris has started disappearing early in the morning these last few days," Uri agreed. "He's avoiding everyone."

"I've been helping Adonis in the fields," Aris corrected, levelling Uri with a stern glare. "It's hard work. I didn't have the energy left to go out after that."

"You promised to help design dresses for me and Granny," Angelica said, pouting. "Our name day is soon, and Granny is expecting you to fulfil your promise! Do you want to do mine or Granny's first?"

Aris laughed, pushing aside his finished breakfast. He wiped his mouth, gazing calmly at Angelica. "That was a tricky question you asked there." He left the table and put his dishes in the sink. "I never promised to help you make any dresses. Besides, I'm sure you can do better than I can."

John and Uri glanced between Aris and Angelica, enthralled by their verbal sparring.

Unbothered by his response, Angelica flashed a smile at him. "But you never refused, so you might as well have accepted."

"You're in trouble now," Uri hooted. "Angelica is trapping you the same way you trapped Zoe."

Aris nodded, smiling slightly. "I promised Adonis to help him the next few days. I don't have time. He already left without me today because I overslept. I have to rush to find him now."

"You can always come in the evening," she responded, a smile fixed on her face. "Even just to help us with some ideas."

Aris picked up his hat.

Angelica pressed forward, trying to corner him. "I can ask Adonis if I can borrow you for a couple of days."

John grinned, amused at Aris's predicament. "You've been playing too much backgammon and not enough chess. She's got you in checkmate now!"

Angelica dropped the bundle of fabric in her arms on the settee. "I will leave these here. Stop by tonight if you have any ideas. If not, I'll come back tomorrow to collect then."

Aris smiled, barely holding in his laughter as Angelica waved and walked out of the house.

"I'm a good drawer," Uri crowed after she left. "Give me some ideas. I would love to dress Angelica, though I'd prefer undressing her!"

Aris glared at Uri.

"I can understand turning Angelica down," John mumbled. "But how are you going to refuse Granny? She has the utmost respect for you."

Aris bit his tongue and walked to the door. It wasn't Granny he was worried about refusing. And it wasn't just a dress design that he knew was being requested.

"Where are you going?" John called after him. "By the time you find Adonis, it will be too late."

"I'm meeting Anastasis today!"

"You monster, you lied to Angelica!"

⸺ ⬦ ⸺

Angelica returned the next morning, but the smile she was wearing slipped when she found Uri by himself.

"Aris has gone out," Uri informed her.

"Where is he?" she asked. "I know he's not with Adonis!"

"He promised to help the shepherd today."

"Suddenly, Aris is a farmer and a shepherd and a mender?"

"The more you get to know him," Uri said, "the more you will discover. Aris is a skilled but complex man."

Sceptical, Angelica sighed.

"He didn't forget your request, though," Uri insisted, shuffling some paper over to her. "He drew these for you."

Angelica raised an eyebrow after looking over the sketches. "I know he can't draw, so who did these?"

"Aris made a rough sketch, and I fixed them up. But I promise they are all his ideas."

Angelic gazed at the drawings, a soft smile growing. "Thank you, they are really well done. You even added our faces."

"My pleasure! If you'd like, I can swing by and help out with the designs now that I've got a feel for them."

Angelica pointed to the papers. "I am not that thin, and Granny is not that full."

"If you model for me, I'm sure I can get the proportions perfect."

Angelica tossed her head back, laughing. "Okay… I will send Granny to model for you!"

⸺ ◇ ⸺

The sun was just climbing over the horizon when Adonis walked into the house where Aris was already set up at the kitchen table drinking coffee with Uri.

"Ready to go?" he asked.

"I'll help you today," Uri said before Aris could answer. "Angelica needs him to help her and Granny with their new dresses."

Adonis clenched his jaw, glancing away, but nodded and ushered Uri to the door.

Aris grabbed Uri and yanked him back. "If I wanted to stay home, I would have said so myself."

"It's not good manners to refuse Angelica," Adonis growled. "Even worse to refuse Granny. Don't disappoint them. Let's go, Uri."

Aris felt trapped, watching Adonis stalk out of the house and mount his horse. Aris was left standing in the doorway, watching them ride out of town. Turning, he threw himself onto the sofa, covering his eyes with his hat and taking deep breaths to try and relax.

Soon, Angelica walked in, smiling broadly. "Thank you for the drawings, Aris. Granny and I love the ideas. We just need some help with the lines. Granny asked me to fetch you."

Aris pulled the hat off his face, sitting up. "Who is asking? You or Granny?"

"We are both asking."

Lazily, Aris stood and headed to the door. He waited until Angelica finally followed him out of the house and down the street.

Granny greeted them with a big smile. "We appreciate you helping us with our new dresses."

Aris threw a questioning look at Angelica, who just smiled in return.

Manolios and Despo joined them. "You've become high in demand with the women, Aris!" Manolios joked. "Perhaps you can even design something for me."

Aris smiled politely. "I don't think you need my help. You already have great style with your high-waisted trousers."

"You're just trying to avoid me. Come, we can discuss style while you help me out in the fields."

"I'd be happy to help," Aris said, jumping at the opportunity. "Do I need boots? I can run back for mine."

Angelica stilled, sensing Aris was trying to escape. Manolios glanced between them and then over at Despo, who just shook her head.

He turned back to Aris with a rueful smile. "I wouldn't dare pull you away from helping Granny with her dress. It's all she's been talking about."

"It seems to me that Angelica and Granny have got to you and Adonis both. I'm sure Anastasis won't refuse me tomorrow."

Angelica smirked at him. "The shepherd never refuses me anything. Maybe I should visit him tonight."

"Funny you bring him up," Granny mentioned. "I had a dream of him and my sister, Triantafilo, getting married again."

Aris turned suddenly, his eyes wide at the mention of that name.

"What's so strange about such a dream?" Angelica asked.

"Anastasis is too young to marry my sister—she's even older than me."

—— ◇ ——

They gathered around the large table in the main room, all the tools for patternmaking already assembled on paper that was laid out. Granny looked up from sorting through the designs to find Aris staring directly at her. She held one up, waving it to get his attention. "I like this one the most."

He took the sheet from her, trying to hide his sudden fixation. He bent over, sketching out the pattern to cut. "Granny, I heard that there were six sisters who used to live in this village and four were taken by an uncle to live in America. Do you know of them?"

The smile on Granny's face wilted. "Hard to know without any names."

Aris kept his head down. "I think Garoufalia was the eldest, then Droso and Kali. Aphrodite was the last, but she died soon after arriving in America."

Granny's voice came out tight. "Doesn't sound familiar."

"What about the other two?" Despo asked.

"I'm not sure, but I think they were Antafilo and Liki."

Despo thought for a moment. "We don't have any women with those names."

"They could be nicknames," Aris pressed, trying to stifle his obsession.

"Antafilo sounds like Triantafilo," Angelica offered. "Like the rose."

Aris nodded. "That's logical. Rose, or maybe Rosy." Aris felt Granny's gaze examining him, but kept his focus on Angelica.

Angelica tapped her chin. "Liki can only be from Vasiliki or Angeliki."

Granny glanced away as Despo immediately dismissed the possibility. "There are no such women in this village."

"We have a Vasiliki," Angelica corrected, "but she's only in her mid-twenties." Angelica turned to Granny. "Isn't your name—"

"Let's not keep Aris here longer than we need to," Granny interrupted. "Now, what if we add some pleats here?"

Noticing Granny's panicked look, Angelica bit her tongue, though her hesitancy was noticed by Aris.

Aris cleared his throat. "That's easy, I'd just need your waist and hip measurements."

Granny stood, holding her arms out. "Here I am!"

Chuckling, Aris handed the measuring tape off to Angelica. "Take Granny's measurements, please. If my hands go near those gorgeous buttocks, I'm not sure I can pull them back!"

Granny grinned. "You disappoint me, Aris. I would not mind a man's touch!"

Aris started drawing the new pattern. "I'm sure you've had your share of a man's touch!"

Unable to control herself, Despo collapsed in a fit of laughter.

Aris continued to work, finalising the pattern for Granny. He glanced at her when she approached to check on his progress. "There was a lady who lived in my neighbourhood," he began. "She claimed to have come from a village around this area. Her sister remained here. Strangely, she never said the name of the village. She just called it 'the village' and said it was in Macedonia."

Aris looked up, holding Granny's stare. "Would you know of her?"

Granny pursed her lips. "Many women left our village. What was her name?"

"Rosy. Slim, medium height. She was a beautiful woman, even at her old age."

"Rosy?" Granny repeated, stumbling over the name. "Nothing comes to mind. Are you sure she was from this village?"

"Not sure. She was older than you and lived past one hundred. Petite face, fair completion. They say she was a light blonde before her hair went white."

Granny's body went tense, trying to smother her reaction. "Nothing comes to mind. What about her?"

Aris focused on cutting the pattern precisely and only looked back at Granny when he was done. "Rosy knew the love secret."

Angelica glanced between Aris and Granny. Beside her, Despo giggled. "What's a love secret?"

Aris remained silent for a moment, watching Granny whose gaze dropped to the floor. "It's an ancient secret that can make someone fall in love with you," he said eventually.

Angelica perked up at the claim.

Granny locked eyes with her for a moment before she turned away, chuckling. "There's no such thing. It is a myth."

Offering a smile that didn't reach his eyes, Aris turned back to finishing the patterns. "I don't think so. Rosy knew the love secret. My grandparents told me. Even the priest where I grew up knew about it."

Granny scoffed. "Nonsense. Priests are the first to present false miracles and myths to draw attention."

Aris glanced at Granny, smiling for a moment, and then he once more turned back to his patterns.

Angelica watched their interaction, her brows furrowing. Knowing that Granny was talking in circles, she tried to catch her gaze, but Granny ducked her head.

"Rosy's granddaughter also mentioned something about it," Aris added. "My grandparents and the priests may have been hypothesising, but Rosy's granddaughter knew for sure."

"What do you say to that, Granny?" Angelica urged.

Shrugging, Granny stared at the floor. "There is nothing I can say. I don't know those people."

Finishing the pattern, Aris held it up for them. "There, your pattern is ready. I'm off! If you need help, let me know, Angelica."

Angelica moved toward Aris, but Granny caught her arm and stopped her. "Thank you, Aris," Granny said. "I'm glad we didn't take up your whole day."

Angelica waited until Aris left and her mother headed to the kitchen before rounding on Granny. "What was all of that? You have to know that Aris didn't believe a word you said. Your name is Angeliki!"

Before she could get an answer, Granny slipped away when Despo called for Angelica to help strain the yoghurt.

⬥

Manolios slid up next to Despo in the kitchen as she was plating dinner, peering around to make sure his daughter wasn't nearby. "Angelica is chasing after Aris more every day. It doesn't matter how much he tries to avoid her. I'm getting concerned."

Despo waved him off. "They're just friends. They work well together. That's all."

"Angelica is always one step ahead of him. Our daughter is making it impossible for Aris to escape."

"Nonsense. Angelica seeks advice from him, nothing more. You know she loves to learn. You are beginning to sound like an old woman."

"I am not happy about this, Despo."

"Eat your dinner and stop moaning."

"What are you moaning about now?" Granny asked, shuffling into the kitchen. "You are lucky Despo puts up with you."

They waited a while for Angelica but eventually ate without her. She wandered in after they had finished dinner to find them all sitting in the lounge.

"You missed dinner," Manolios pointed out.

"I'm not really hungry," she remarked. "I will eat later."

Taking a deep breath, Manolios tried to remain calm. "Earlier, I saw you enter the Americans' house by yourself. Seems you have become quite the frequent visitor."

"I am not hiding," Angelica mumbled. "John made me a coffee when I dropped off Granny's cookies. We talked."

"The whole village is gossiping about the widow," Manolios warned. "How she visits their house every night."

"I just delivered some cookies," she argued. "Besides, Aris was not even at home."

"Don't make a fool of yourself," Manolios urged her gently. "It is obvious you are seeking him out despite him trying to make himself scarce. You should ask Granny's advice on these matters. She knows best."

Angelica's throat felt dry and scratchy. "I am neither the widow nor a schoolgirl."

"I am to blame here," Granny interjected. "I should have taken the cookies myself."

"No!" Angelica protested. "Father is right. I understand your concern. Thank you for your advice." She stood, wishing everyone good night. "I'm going to visit Snowy before I turn in."

"She only ever visits that horse when she's upset," Despo groaned after their daughter went outside. "You managed to upset her for no reason, Manolios. Aris was not even at home!"

"She will be fine," Granny placated. "Angelica is a good, strong girl."

Manolios nodded. "I am concerned, though. Aris is not your average man. He attracts everyone. Even men like him. When he came to help me, I could not stop talking for the whole day! Angelica has to be careful. Open your eyes! You women should be advising her, not me."

"Maybe as her father you should tell her to go to Aris, then." Granny laughed. "I mean… when has any young person ever taken the advice of a parent?"

30 The Widow's Visit

In the rented house, John and Uri lounged around. Uri was stretched out on his back across the larger of the two sofas. "Aris is impossible to talk to recently. He has become a mute volcano, ready to erupt."

"Yes," John agreed. "Irritable."

Gazing at the ceiling, Uri smiled. "Apart from mentioning that girl, Melany, he never speaks about his personal life. He is silent as a grave these days."

"I think he's just not happy. He knows he has to go home soon, and he'll have to face everything he left behind."

Uri chuckled. "I think what's eating him is Angelica."

"What do you mean?" John asked, surprised.

"Are you blind? Aris is crazy about her."

"No! They're just friends."

Uri rolled on his side, staring at John. "Haven't you noticed he's avoiding her? She stops by here using every excuse imaginable. She's chasing Aris wherever he is, even when he goes for a walk alone."

"Aris runs into Granny when she's collecting herbs," John argued. "Is she also chasing him?"

"Listen to me. He pretends not to be excited, but he is very attracted to Angelica."

John scoffed. "Who wouldn't be?"

"Correct, but we know what a fool Aris is. While he's trying to avoid Angelica, he's also attracted to her. The question is… how long can he stay away?"

"Why avoid Angelica?"

"Many reasons. Aris is friends with Adonis, who is in love with Angelica. Aris is also nearly twice her age. You know the reason he left Melany was that she was so young. Furthermore, even though everyone in the village respects Aris, they wouldn't be pleased if he messes around with their girl."

John squinted. "He didn't reject Kay or Valia or Katerina. Why would he reject Angelica?"

"Isn't it obvious? Aris is afraid he can't resist her!"

"She's just good company. I think he has more serious issues on his mind right now."

Uri chuckled. "You know his stupid principles. If it was me, I would just give her a good time and wish her farewell when we leave."

"Well, thank goodness Aris is not you! You have no principles at all."

"That's why Aris is a fool. Angelica is the nuclear magnet with an irresistible pull. Aris knows he can't hold out for much longer."

John shook his head. "She may be his dream woman, but don't forget what Aris suffered with his wife. And then Kay dropped him! Maybe he's afraid of rejection."

"Listen, John. Angelica was the reason Aris wanted to leave early. Now she's the reason he wants to stay. When it's time to leave, we'll have to force him."

"If you're right, and if he wanted to, Aris could always take Angelica away from here. That's what I'm going to do with Alexa."

"Take Angelica away to where? That would be like uprooting a young tree, which would die in a new place. Remember, Angelica rejected the city life to return to this village."

"I think you're just jealous. But what if you're right? What do we do?"

"Apart from trying to convince the idiot to leave this village ASAP, there's nothing we can do."

The night simmered with the scurrying of clawed paws and the whoosh of feathered wings. Angelica's face was hidden under a hood. She bent to pass through a small gap in the fence outside Aris's bedroom. On tiptoe, she crept over to his open bedroom window and peered inside. He was sleeping on top of the covers, wearing only boxers, his tan back shining in the silvery light.

At that exact moment, Aris's bedroom door opened. By the light of the full moon, Angelica could make out a dark silhouette, curved and feminine.

Angelica crouched down, peeking over the window ledge as the figure swayed toward Aris where he was laying on the bed fast asleep.

Shocked, the figure in the room became recognisable. "Korina!"

At the noise, Korina twisted to the window, prowling over to it with soft steps.

Angelica ducked down, shuffling behind a bush near the fence before she could be spotted.

Korina stood in front of the window, searching the garden between her house and the rental. Sure that no one was there, she retreated from the window and disappeared into the darkness of the house.

"She really is sleeping with Aris," Angelica whispered to herself.

⊰ ◇ ⊱

Aris woke to a rustling sound at the foot of his bed. A woman stood silhouetted by moonlight through the window. His mind raced, wondering how or why Angelica would be so bold.

Propping himself up on his elbows, he said, "I was wondering when you would finally corner me, but I didn't imagine it would be like this."

The widow turned, her sudden toothy smile piercing like daggers through Aris's heart. She practically floated into his bed and tried to climb atop him.

Aris pushed her away, perhaps too harshly. Korina flew backwards and tumbled off the end of the bed, her nightdress wrapping itself around her limbs.

"You never should have come here," he told her.

The widow pulled herself together, practically hissing in response. "Oh no. I think it is you who never should have come to this village. Mark my words, you will come to regret refusing me!"

31 ANOTHER WOMAN?

Angelica and Granny worked side by side preparing herbs into medicinal remedies. Granny trimmed the leaves from the stems, piling them up and handing them off to Angelica, who crushed them into a paste using a bronze mortar and pestle.

Granny sighed, not looking up from her herbs. "You've been wanting to say something to me for days now. What is it?"

Angelica glanced at her, then looked at the door leading to the kitchen.

"We can speak outside my room, in the garden," Granny invited, standing to lead the way.

Angelica brought two chairs to the rear of the house, placing them next to each other. She sat, still crushing herbs while trying to figure out how to start.

"There's a special bond between us," Granny suddenly began. "Only your late grandfather knew. A week before you were born, I gave birth to a baby girl, too. She died on the third day. It was a sudden death. Then, when you were born, your mother became very ill, so she was unable to breastfeed you. Instead, I took over."

Angelica stopped working, turning to face Granny as she continued.

"Your mother made me swear not to feed you though."

Adonis stayed hidden behind the fence where he had been before they started speaking. He knew he should leave, but found himself pressing closer to hear better.

"Why?" Angelica asked.

"She was afraid there was something wrong with my milk since my baby died." Granny's hands continued to pluck the leaves off the stems. "You didn't take kindly to animal milk.

Not even goat's milk. You became very weak. So I went against my promise, and I breastfed you anyway. I knew my milk was good. That is the bond we share. I am both grandmother and mother to you. So, say what you want."

Angelica's mouth hung open for a moment. "I'm losing my mind. Something woke inside me. I tried to cage it, but it keeps growing wilder. Stronger." Fat tears clouded her vision and spilled down her cheeks. "I feel like I'm possessed and my mind isn't my own."

"Let it out," Granny urged. "Even as a child, you never cried. This must be haunting you."

Adonis pressed his face against the fence, the wood grating against his skin.

"My heart wants him, Granny. I know he wants me, too. I feel it. Yet, he resists every advance I make. I feel he is being tortured, too. The more he resists me, the more I want him. I'm afraid I'd do anything for him. I feel I'd even drop to hell if he asked me to."

Biting his lips, Adonis felt his heart thundering in his chest, rising and falling with his deep breaths. Peeking through a gap in the fence, he stole a glance at the women.

"Carry on, love," Granny whispered sympathetically.

"He is in control, but for the first time in my life, I am losing it. I don't know what to do," she confessed, wiping her tears.

"I'm almost certain, but just to be sure," Granny whispered. "We are talking about Aris, yes?"

At the name, Adonis doubled over like he'd been punched, bracing himself on his knees.

"Who else, Granny? I know he will soon go away. I know he has a wife and grown children. He is twice my age. Yet, I'm desperate to be with him! Help me, Granny. What do I do?"

Angelica dove into Granny's open arms, crying on her shoulder.

"My sweet angel, you are tormented. Have you tried hard enough?"

"I tried very hard. I cannot push these feelings away. I cannot control them. They are torturing my soul. Am I insane?"

Adonis collapsed to the ground, gasping for air.

The two Angelicas exchanged looks. The younger one sighed. "I am dying for his touch. I cannot even understand myself. Help me, Granny. What do I do?"

"You are not insane. You are a woman in love," Granny comforted. "A blessing, and a curse. We all want what's best for you. I've watched you sink deeper and deeper into your torment. I know exactly what you feel. I am not going to try to tell you what's right or what's wrong. Like always, I'll just give you some womanly advice."

Angelica felt a small weight easing off her chest. "My heart is in pain and my body is consumed with the strangest feelings. Sometimes, I find myself touching my body, imagining it is Aris who is touching me."

Adonis's Adam's apple bobbed as he tried to choke down his agony.

"One minute, I feel full of energy," Angelica shared. "Then, within seconds, my knees are crumpling under my weight. When I think of him, strange shivers shoot all over my body. My mouth dries up, but then seconds later I'm drowning in saliva."

"Hush, now. Lower your voice. Someone may overhear you," Granny warned.

"Someone, others, everyone else! What about me?"

Granny offered her a handkerchief, which Angelica used to blow her nose.

"I assure you, I understand. What you describe is only experienced once in a lifetime. Many die without ever having such exploding emotions." Granny tucked the handkerchief away, settling into her chair. "However, sometimes people confuse this with admiration. Are you sure this is the real deal and not due to your admiration of Aris?"

Nodding to himself, Adonis clutched his aching chest, hoping Granny was right.

"I don't understand," Angelica said.

"When two people are in regular contact—whether by physical closeness or exposure—they can develop strong attachments. It can happen between doctor and patient, idol and admirer, and even between priest and parishioner. Eventually though, these feelings wear out. The attraction fades. They may even wonder why they got involved with this person in the first place. In such cases, when rejected by the other person, these feelings can even turn to hatred."

"Go on," Angelica prompted.

"Some don't carry the same emotions, but sensing the vulnerability of the other person, they abuse that temporary weakness. These feelings are indistinguishable from real love. But in the midst of them, the person can't see what's really happening."

Angelica sat quietly for a moment, absorbing all the information. "Granny, I'm sure my feelings are real."

"Yet, Aris is refusing you."

"No, he avoids me because he cannot refuse me. Once I get close to him, he becomes himself. Sometimes, I swear I can feel his heart swelling, and I'm sure he feels the same. I don't think he is engulfed by the feelings you described."

"I am not talking about Aris, I am talking about you. Are you sure this is real and not just a temporary transference of feelings?"

At Granny's question, Angelica turned introspective.

Adonis braced himself against the fence.

"Aris is a very handsome man. He is intelligent," Granny said. "We all have witnessed his warm heart. He is not selfish. He has multiple skills and knowledge that surprises us all. A man's maturity can be magnetic to a young woman like you. You need to ask yourself if you are just experiencing temporary feelings of admiration."

Adonis nodded, his hands clasped before him as if in prayer.

"Granny, I told you," Angelica argued. "I lived a full life when I went to university in the city, but hedonism never suited me. I refused plenty of rich and famous men asking me to marry them."

Granny smiled. "Yes, but your body has its own urges, which can blind the mind sometimes."

"I need to be attracted to the whole person, not just the body, and I need them to feel the same for me. You taught me—beauty will fade but personality and heart remain! That's how I feel about Aris. He loves me. He loves everything about me, and I love him even more. I have already questioned myself every step of the way. Stop trying to tell me this is temporary, or some transference. If I could, I would have done it myself. Please. Help me, Granny!"

"No man can resist an angel like you," Granny reassured her. "You are a beauty that people will speak of for centuries. Even women admires your figure and your warm personality, not to mention your intelligence and charisma. I told you many times, you are blessed!"

Granny paused, gathering herself. "Still, Aris resists you. Have you asked yourself why?"

Adonis furrowed his brow, eagerly awaiting Angelica's reply.

"I don't know," Angelica confessed. "Sometimes, I sense his hand reaching to touch me, only to stop short every time."

"It must be very hard for a man to resist you. I know Aris has plenty of reasons to do so." Granny's voice was filled with concern. "He is much older than you. He is a visitor, who will soon go away. If he truly loves you, he will want to protect you."

Angelica kept her sight focused on Granny, hanging on her every word.

"Aris understands our culture. But we don't know what emotions eat at him, what personal issues he may be facing. Besides, Aris has become close friends with Adonis. By now he knows you are Adonis's unspoken love and future bride. We don't know what Adonis has told him, but an honourable man would not betray his friend so easily."

Hearing Granny's words, Adonis stood up, his legs unsteady.

"Adonis is Adonis," Angelica remarked, shaking her head. "He is my friend and I love him, but my love for Aris is different. I just wish to be liberated from this burning, internal torture."

Adonis froze.

Granny's chest grew heavy. "Only you can help yourself. I cannot help you more than what I'm doing now."

"Yes, you can. You just don't want to."

Granny flinched. "I don't want to? You know I'd give my life for you, my love."

"When I was young, I heard you talking to my mother. You told her there was a secret to love. That's why you dismissed Aris's question the other day! I watched you as he asked about Rosy. You lied to him. I know you did."

Adonis cupped his ear to try and catch more, barely believing what he was hearing.

Angelica gripped Granny's shoulder, but the woman adamantly refused to look her in the eye. "You know it, don't you? You know the secret of how to—"

"What are you two doing out there?" Despo interrupted, her sudden approach sending the other women into silence.

Angelica tried to subtly wipe away any evidence of her tears.

"Are you crying, daughter?" Despo knelt down by Angelica.

"No, just some herbs got in my eyes."

In the distance, Snowy neighed high and clear.

"I think your horse is lonely," Despo mused.

"She's not the only one," Angelica muttered under her breath.

32 You Do Know

The sunset bled light on the streets, glazing the pavement red. Adonis found himself at the café, sinking into a seat next to Aris, who was holding court with some of the other villagers.

Aris turned to greet him with a smile. "When are we going to the fields next?"

"I have to repair the stables and fence around my garden," Adonis replied. Everything sounded far away and staticky, like a radio with bad reception. "A few days, maybe."

"I can help at your house," Aris offered. "An extra set of hands will help you finish faster."

Adonis thought back to his garden and hiding while Angelica confessed everything to Granny. He bit the inside of his cheek until it bled. "No, I don't want to bother my mother with the noise of so many people."

Leaning forward, Anastasis dropped his binoculars on the table. "Why toil in a garden when you can come with me? The view alone is worth the hike, and nothing calms the soul like watching the village breathe from so high up."

Aris smiled at the shepherd. "I'd join you for your bread and cheese alone! Count me in."

Aris didn't notice Adonis's sigh of relief.

⸱◇⸱

Angelica slipped through the liminal space between morning and night, her black dress blending her body into the darkness. She tightened her hold on the black headscarf as she ducked down, sliding through the gap in Aris's fence like a shadow.

She crept across the grass, the soft rustling of the blades sharp in the quiet. Peering over the lip of the window ledge, she quickly hopped onto it and took a moment to rest. Aris was fast asleep, his back to her.

She slunk down like a cat, prowling across the room until she was standing over him. Shifting, she started to remove her dress, the straps falling from her shoulders and slipping off her breasts when Aris lifted his head.

She dropped to a crouch as he slapped his pillow to beat some comfort into it before flopping back down.

Angelica held her breath, her heart pounding, as she waited a moment before backing slowly away and retracing her steps out the window.

Fixing her dress, she steadied her heartbeat, which was rapid as a gallop. Pressing a hand to her chest, she had half a mind to go back to his bed, to remove her dress completely and slip in behind him.

A cat on the widow's roof slipped down and rested on an eave, the glint of its eyes grabbing Angelica's attention. It hopped down, sitting in front of her. They stared at each other, neither moving except the cat's tail swaying in the air.

"I really thought I was going to do it," Angelica confessed.

The cat stared blankly back at her and Angelica felt annoyance rise in her like a tide.

"Either give some advice or leave. Don't just look at me."

The cat flicked its tail once more and turned away. After a moment, Angelica sighed deeply and got off the ground. She slid through the gap in the fence and made her way back home.

⁕ ◇ ⁕

The morning sun was sharp and bright as Adonis tended the garden beside the fence that separated his house from Angelica's. Since the last conversation he'd overheard, he had taken to pruning this section of the yard to the point that most of the plants have been trimmed down to their roots.

His ears perked up at the sound of Angelica's voice, prompting him to press up against the wooden fence.

"Two days," she exclaimed, stomping out of the house and into the back garden where Granny was sorting herbs. "You've been avoiding me for two whole days!"

Granny continued to sort herbs, not bothering to look at her granddaughter. "Why would I do that?"

"Because you don't want to tell me."

"Tell you what?"

"Don't do that. I know when you try to hide something. I'm talking about the secret! The Love Secret that makes anybody fall in love with you," Angelica shouted, shaking Granny. "Look at me!"

Granny lifted her gaze, Angelica's eyes meeting hers like warriors squaring off to duel.

At the fence, Adonis pressed his ear to one of the small gaps in a desperate hope to hear the women clearly.

With their brown eyes wide, the women witnessed each other's pupils dilate.

Swallowing thickly, Granny bent under Angelica's glare.

Angelica's grip loosened and became a soft caress. "I could see how uncomfortable you were when I mention the secret of love."

Furrowing his brow, Adonis anxiously leaned forward.

Dropping her eyes to the herbs again, Granny shrugged her granddaughter away. "I don't know what you mean."

Angelica's hand snapped out, twisting Granny to face her. "Don't lie to me. We promised never to do that. You know what the secret is… you know!"

Granny flinched as if she'd been slapped.

"You do know," Angelica insisted, her voice thready. "I can see it. You can't hide from me."

Her grandmother shuddered and pushed up out of the chair, the remnants of the herbs falling from her lap, then hobbled into her room.

Angelica waited outside the door, fists clenched.

Her mother Despo stuck her head outside, calling, "Come in and help me strain the yoghurt."

Angelica waited a moment more before heeding the summons.

33 People Think It's a Myth

Aris reclined in a chair by a window, relaxing in the sun. The quiet tapping of a mallet against a tack beat a rhythm in the background. He closed his eyes and let the sounds of old Jacob working in his shop lull him into contentment.

There was a moment of silence that drew Aris's attention to the man hunched over his workbench. "You need to be careful," Jacob informed him, keeping his eyes on his work. "I know staying away from such a smart, beguiling woman in her prime is difficult, but you need to try harder. Watch your actions."

Jacob caught Aris's deer-in-the-headlights look.

"This is a small village. It shouldn't be so surprising," Jacob continued, smirking. "You'll be leaving soon, so keep this in mind. Keep up your strength."

Aris stood, nodded at Jacob twice, and walked out the open door of the workshop.

Granny rested in the chair outside her room, idly picking at the herbs in her lap. The sun slipped further down to the horizon but still blanketed the earth in a hazy warmth. She was jolted from her relaxation by Angelica yanking her to full attention.

"Don't think I've forgotten. I know you have what I want. You know how to make someone fall in love with you!"

Across the yard, beyond the wooden fence, Adonis froze. His muscles locked in place as he overheard. Even the possibility of such a thing's existence had his heart ratcheting up.

In silence, Granny watched as the bravado slipped from Angelica's posture. Beneath it, the pain and desperation bloomed across her face like the first sprouts of spring.

"Please," Angelica begged. "I'm losing my mind."

Granny worked her jaw, biding time. "I wish I could help. I know you are in pain."

Tears welled and rolled down Angelica's cheeks. "You can help, you can! Even if it's just to have Aris for a short while! Even just one night. I feel as though I'm burning alive without him."

Hearing Angelica beg, Adonis bent over and punched the ground, barely feeling the impact on his fist. His vision blurred. Then he stopped. Digging his hands into the dirt, he tried to collect himself and focus on the action beyond the fence.

"I just realised it *is* true." Angelica's voice rose. "I had doubts, but now I see it in your eyes. It's written all over your face. You *do* know the secret! Why won't you help me when I need you most? I have no one else to turn to."

Granny's hands stilled. Her granddaughter seemed to be breaking apart in front of her. "I have never refused you."

Angelica continued, unrelenting in her assault. "I have never asked you for anything. Only this one thing! I need you to do this for me. Please, Granny."

Unnoticed, Adonis tensed, ready to fully absorb the secret.

Granny bit back a sob, fighting her own tears.

Angelica knelt, lowering her voice. "I know Aris wants me. I won't be harming anyone."

In a frenzy, Adonis bit down on his arm, blood bursting across his tongue and filling his mouth with the taste of iron.

"I will go to him tonight, regardless," Angelica confessed.

Granny's face flared bright red.

"I've climbed through his window the last few nights, watching him sleep."

Granny snagged the girl by the arm. "Don't you know that the widow goes there every night?"

"I know," Angelica confessed. "I've seen her walking into Aris's room. I don't care. I know Aris does not love her."

"You don't care that he's sleeping with the widow?"

"Actually, since I saw her, my desire for Aris flared up even more!" Angelica actually grinned as Granny gasped in surprise. "I will go tonight, and I won't hesitate. I will give myself to him… whether he rejects me or not is up to him."

At this pronouncement, Adonis put his hand into his pocket and removed a switchblade. He flicked it open, admiring the glint of its sharp edge in the light.

Reaching out, Granny rested a hand on Angelica's arm. "Listen closely," she ordered, her voice sympathetic. "I have seen Aris with you, and it is clear he's torturing himself just as much. Men like him—who are intelligent and kind and put others before themselves—are a rare breed. He resists you because he cares for you."

Adonis leaned back against the fence, nodding at Granny's characterisation.

Leaning forward, Angelica felt a rush of electricity at her grandmother's words. "You agree, then, that Aris wants me?"

"I've watched the two of you since he first entered the village," Granny replied. "Even when he was talking to me, he only ever had eyes for you."

Angelica sighed, her face smoothing over. "Then you do understand, but still you refuse to help me."

"He believes he will hurt you. He's willing to sacrifice his happiness for yours. That is a very precious love—a love beyond eros."

"You just described what I feel about him. I couldn't put it into words before. But that's what I want," Angelica exclaimed, slapping her chest. "A love beyond eros."

"Yet, Aris will continue to resist you because it's what he believes is right."

"Then help me get through to him," Angelica urged. "Tell me the love secret."

Granny gazed at Angelica for a long moment. "This type of love you claim to share is not to be trifled with. If you don't love equally, it will end up hurting you both. Stop, before you do irreparable damage."

"But that *is* how I feel about him, exactly as you've described."

A moment of silence descended between them, like the calm eye of a storm.

"I want to jump him whenever I see him, even in the centre of the village with everyone watching. But I also want him to be happy and protect him from any form of hurt."

At Angelica's confession, a heavy weight clamped down on Adonis's heart, making it hurt to even beat. He tightened his grip on the knife until his knuckles turned a stark white.

Granny squeezed Angelica's arm. "I understand. You feel as though you are even ready to make a pact with the Devil."

"Yes." Angelica dipped her head in embarrassment. "I would do anything to be with him. Even if it meant pain for the rest of my life. That's why you need to tell me the secret."

Adonis dropped his head into his hands, the cool blade of his knife pressed against his face.

Angelica fell to her knees, resting her head on Granny's lap like she had as a child. Granny stroked her hair.

Turning her head, Angelica looked up. "You need to save me before I do something desperately wrong. If you love me, you'll tell me the love secret. I need to break Aris's resistance."

Granny's willpower was crumbling under the weight of Angelica's words. She sighed. "If I tell you the secret," she began, "you must never tell more than one person for the rest of your life."

Angelica perked up, sitting prostrate at Granny's feet like a disciple.

Grinding her teeth, Granny took a deep breath to centre herself. "This secret has been guarded for thousands of years. You must promise to protect it with your life. It can be dangerous. While a just and decent person would not misuse it, a weaker man or woman could bring catastrophe to others with this knowledge."

Adonis banged his hands against his head, hoping Angelica would see reason.

Angelica nodded, eager for Granny to continue.

"Powerful people have killed and tortured to get this secret. It has even ignited a war. The Trojan War was fought after a man stole a woman's heart using the love secret that he learned from Aphrodite."

Angelica's mouth dropped open. "Is that how Paris won the heart of Helen? A married woman who claimed to be in love with her husband, Menelaus?"

Granny tilted her head. "Aphrodite, the goddess of love, traded the secret to Paris for her own gain. It was wrong! Helen was very happy with Menelaus. Aphrodite came to regret it. As a result, thousands died in a ten-year war. You can see how dangerous the love secret can be. Never trade it for your own gain."

Angelica cocked her head, confused at this claim. "In school, we were told that Paris seduced Helen with Aphrodite's scarf."

"A story wrapped in a myth to hide the truth," Granny chuckled before sobering. She looked off to the distance, her eyes glazed and unfocused. "I can't say no to you, even though I've kept the secret from the Devil himself my whole life. I could never say no to you."

Angelica watched a small sparkle of a tear escape Granny's eye, rolling down her cheek and curving over her jaw. It caused Angelica to sit up straight, aware of the shift in the air.

She clasped Granny's hands in her own. "I promise, I will take this secret to my grave."

Heart pounding, Adonis pressed his ear against the gap in the fence in a futile hope to hear the secret.

Granny stood, pulling Angelica to her feet. "You must remember that while the love secret is powerful and can sway any man or woman to fall for you, there is a chance that it might not last forever. If the person is already truly in love with another, then the secret will lose its grip on them until it fades away."

She paused, swallowing to wet her dry throat. "Odysseus's love for his wife, Penelope, was one such case."

Momentarily forgetting herself, Angelica leaned forward like an eager child "How?"

"People think it is a myth, but it is not. Unable to capture Odysseus's heart, Calypso used the love secret. For seven years she kept him on her island. Yet, Odysseus's love for his wife Penelope was so powerful that, eventually, the love secret wore off. This was a rare case but be aware that it can happen. But if there is no other woman, Aris will be yours forever. If his heart beats for you, he will eternally be yours. His love will be beyond ordinary! Beyond imagination!"

"Even if Aris loves another," Angelica insisted. "I'd rather have him for a short time than not at all."

Granny shook her head in disbelief. "You truly love him beyond eros."

"Yes, that is what I feel for him."

"Are you willing to give up everything… for Aris? Your village? Your family? Your life?"

Angelica scrunched her face. "If he does love another, then I would let him go. But I can't let this chance to be with him pass me by. I promise."

"Such love might lead to unimaginable pain for yourself as well," Granny warned.

Angelica nodded, urging Granny to continue.

"I never imagined I would hear you proclaim your love in such a way in my entire life. It is clear there is no talking you out of this."

A contented smile stretched across Angelica's face, while behind the fence Adonis tormented himself.

Manolios startled the two women when he stepped out of the house. "What are you two cooking up?" he teased.

Recovering fast, Granny shot her son an amused smile. "Just some lady talk. Nothing for your ears!"

Manolios nodded. "You better be careful. Someone is listening to your secrets."

Adonis threw himself on the ground, sure he'd been exposed.

"Who?" Angelica asked and Granny twisted around, searching for the culprit.

"Snowy," Manolios laughed, retreating into the house.

Angelica sighed in relief as Granny continued to survey the area to make sure no one was around.

Finally, she turned back to Angelica and waited until she had her full attention.

In the silence, Adonis caught a glimpse of them through the gap in the fence, and he pulled out a notebook and pencil. He watched as Granny leaned forward, wiping Angelica's tears with a handkerchief. She then tore the fabric in two and handed both pieces to Angelica, which the younger woman tucked in the bust of her dress.

"You need to keep that with you," Granny instructed. "Catch him alone, away from distractions, and tell him what's on the handkerchief. Offer him one half. This will help drop his guard."

Their voices fell to a murmur that barely reached Adonis's ear. He watched their mouths move, hoping it would help him understand better. His hand flew over the notebook, recording every snippet of information he could get. It wasn't enough, he feared, but kept scribbling anyway.

When Granny finished, he looked down at the fragments of sound he had captured, fracturing the page of his notebook.

Granny leaned back, feeling lighter than she had in years, no longer having to carry the secret alone. She glanced around once more before focusing on her granddaughter. "When you do that, he is yours. You just lead the way. He won't be able to resist you. He will even follow you to Hell if you order it."

Adonis again looked down at his scribbles, engraving every syllable in his brain. He mouthed the words he had already memorised, carving them deeper into his soul.

Blinking at Granny, Angelica asked, "Is that all?"

Granny nodded.

"Are you sure?"

Granny smiled at her, nodding again.

Angelica chewed her lips, uncertain of the claim. "What if he still resists me?"

"No one will be able to resist you!" Granny exclaimed, staring at Angelica. "His resistance will melt like wax near a fire. All uncertainty will vanish within him. His will be totally at your mercy."

Hearing Granny's final claim, Adonis clenched his fist so hard the pencil snapped in his grip.

Granny searched Angelica's face, looking for some clue as to what she was thinking. "You seem nervous."

"A bit, but I also feel suddenly calm, which I haven't felt for days now. Like hope has replaced my desperation."

Granny grunted in acknowledgement. She looked Angelica over one more time. "Using this doesn't guarantee a happy ending. Whatever you decide, you must protect the secret for the rest of your life."

"I will think about it," Angelica assured. She leaned her head down, resting it on Granny's shoulder. "Was Aris right? About Rosy?"

"Yes. Rosy was my mother, your great-grandmother. She tried to flee the village with her lover. They were both already married. The villages chased her down, but I never saw her again. Her real name was Triantafilo."

"If Rosy was your mother, then who was Angeliki?" asked Angelica.

"Rosy's elder sister. She died just before I was born. That's why they gave me her name."

"But when did Rosy tell you the love secret? Did she come back?"

Granny shook her head. "No, she told me before she left when I was only twelve. She thought she was going to die because during that time they would kill a married woman who broke her marriage vows. I never knew what happened to her. I was shocked to hear Aris speak of her."

Cupping Angelica's face, Granny smoothed the frown from her lips. "If you decide to use the secret, make the most of it.

You don't know if it will last, but the feelings you have at that moment will live with you for the rest of your life."

Angelica shifted. "It sounds like you're speaking from experience. Did you regret using the secret?"

"I don't regret it," Granny confessed. "But like Rosy, I was already married with children at the time. Your grandfather was caught in the middle, and I ended up hurting him."

Granny dropped Angelica's hands, moving away from her. "I need a few moments on my own. Just keep in mind what I've told you."

Angelica watched her grandmother leave, then moving across the yard, she entered the stables and rested against Snowy, trying to find solid ground again.

In the deep dark of midnight, Adonis sat hunched over a table in his house. Papers were spread before him, covered in half-written sentences and fragments of words. Blank spaces littered the lines, gaps in his knowledge.

His pencil scurried across a new page before he hastily erased parts here and there. He corrected his work and started again.

He glanced down once more at the page, no closer to figuring out the riddle of what Granny had shared.

His mother stepped out of her bedroom, her nightgown dwarfing her thin frame. "You've been sitting there all day. What are you doing?"

Adonis scratched his head, turning away from his work. "Nothing, just a puzzle."

"Well, put it away and go to sleep. It's not like it won't be there in the morning."

"You're right," Adonis agreed, stuffing his work into a large envelope. "It might help to come back to this with a fresh mind." If only he could piece together the puzzle and use it on Angelica before she could do the same with Aris.

34 Love Secret Code

The night was warm and windless, the moon a fat egg in the inky sky. The village was asleep, but the chirping of crickets broke the silence.

At the end of the pier, Aris and Adonis sat side by side and let the peaceful scenery wash over them like the tides.

"I'm turning in," Adonis announced. "It's too late for a farmer to be up."

"I will follow soon," Aris responded, keeping his gaze on the water.

Hobbling swiftly, Adonis crossed the plaza and moved through the streets. A blur to his right drew his attention, but he didn't see anything in the shadow of the tree and dismissed it, moving on to his home.

Long after Adonis's departure, Aris was startled by a bat fluttering across his sightline. He decided it was probably time to turn in. He rose to his feet and walked leisurely through the village.

Slipping through the shadows after him, Angelica tracked him through the winding streets where he turned right at a crossroad to continue home. She watched as he drifted down the right side of the junction before she pranced ahead, hurrying down the left path.

As soon as Angelica was swallowed by darkness, Adonis emerged from the shadow of a house. He glanced between the two paths before hurrying down the right after Aris, already regretting his departure. He scurried forward, flitting from shadow to shadow as he closed the distance between them.

Angelica reached the rental house first, sequestering herself near the front door to confront Aris.

He arrived on the scene shortly after, with Adonis pausing further back to remain hidden.

Aris halted, surprised the light above the door was still on. He scoffed to himself, sure that John and Uri must have left it on again.

When he reached the door, he jerked back when Angelica glided out of the dark in front of him, her black dress shifting around her like water. She smiled at him bright as a star.

Aris was enchanted for a moment, unable to do anything but smile back at her. She stepped closer, arranging her body so they were in a relaxed waltz position.

She pushed up against him, her left hand on his shoulder, her open eyes fixed on his. She smiled bewitchingly.

Magnetised, Aris couldn't look away. Enchanted, he subconsciously followed her lead.

She pulled out a torn handkerchief from between her breasts and rubbed it across his face and hair.

"This is drenched in my tears of love," she whispered to him, stuffing it in his pocket. "They are only for you. I want you to have them."

Peering from around the corner of a nearby house, Adonis cursed. "She must be using the love secret."

Still holding Aris's gaze, she caressed his left cheek. Angelica then lowered her right hand, taking hold of Aris's left. "Open your eyes wide, my love. Do not blink. Look into my eyes. Let yourself witness my love for you."

Overcome by her presence, Aris obeyed every word. His eyes found hers without a thought. He felt himself becoming shackled, locking every beat of their hearts together.

Angelica leaned closer, shortening the distance between them.

Adonis clenched his jaw, his hand clutching the knife within his pocket. He refused to look away, desperate to understand what was happening. He watched as Aris opened his mouth to speak, but Angelica silenced him with a finger pressed against his lips.

Two sets of hearts pulsed in synchronicity. Lifting herself onto her toes, Angelica moved still closer, a breath away from his lips.

"Just listen," she urged. "Just listen, my love."

She whispered a phrase to him, then repeated it again and again until Aris felt his mind becoming foggy, like he was on the edge of sleep and the only thing anchoring him to wakefulness was the sound of Angelica's voice.

Her hand grasped his as she continued to murmur to him.

Adonis pressed his own hand against the wall, mimicking the way Angelica tapped the back of Aris's hand. His heart beat fast and loud in his chest, sweat beading on his forehead.

Overtaken mind and soul, Aris's physical and psychological resistance crumbled. Like a child waiting for his treat, Aris willingly obeyed Angelica's every word.

Her right hand slid down his left side. She curled her fingers into his palm and again whispered in his ear.

Subconsciously, Adonis pulled out his knife, clenching the switchblade in his fist.

Angelica snaked her left hand up Aris's arm, wrapping it behind his neck. She pulled his head down, pressing her lips against his for the first time.

She trailed her lips from one corner of his mouth to the other, urging him to kiss her.

Ensnared, Aris felt his restraint snap. He surrendered himself to her command and returned her kisses, now pressing firmly against her.

Chest pumping, Adonis mechanically flicked open the blade.

"Kiss me. I am yours and you are mine. We are one, forever in love!"

The urge to hold Angelica built inside Aris like a pianist who just discovered a harmony for his own melody. Aris returned her feather-light kiss and repeated her exact words back. "Kiss me. I am yours and you are mine. We are one, forever in love!"

Filled with murderous despair, Adonis tightened his grip on the knife and banged his head on the wall. Then he paused, pointing the blade at Aris. *I will get you,* he thought.

Aris embraced Angelica, pulling her closer until they were flush from chest to hips. Their kiss deepened, urging the other on.

Watching them had long since become torture. Adonis raised his knife and prepared to throw it.

He wavered, his breath hitching in his throat.

Lowering his hand, he braced himself against the wall of the house. *Damn it. You did this, Angelica! Not Aris. You!*

His mouth opened in a mute, painful howl.

Angelica pulled back, barely shifting away, but Aris leaned forward, chasing after her lips, unwilling to end the kiss.

Sinking from her tiptoes, Angelica smiled at him. He remained dumbfounded, his lips slightly parted. She pressed one last fast kiss to his mouth and then tugged him by the arm. "Follow me," she commanded, leading him away from his house.

Ducking down into the dark, Adonis hid. They passed without noticing him and he silently crept after them through the deserted streets.

◇

Hand in hand, Angelica and Aris followed their shadows as they headed out of the village and up a small hill, Adonis shifting through the night after them.

They crested the rise. Beneath them, the village slumbered. In the distance, the small pier cut through the moonlit reflection of the bay.

They made their way to an oak tree, huge and ageless. Angelica led them to a branch that scooped low to the ground like a cradle with tufts of leaves on either end of the curve. This is where she urged him to sit on the branch. She followed, bunching her summer dress up over her thighs. A light breeze swept her hair across her face.

Beguiled at Angelica's glowing charm, Aris was enslaved by every twitch of her hips and bounce of her bosom. He tugged her to him and they melted into a long, tender kiss.

Above them, two snow-white owls gazed down upon the lovers. The male had a ring of golden feathers around his neck.

Adonis crawled across the ground on his belly. He witnessed their embrace, the sound of their kissing erupting like bombs in his ears.

Aris pushed against the ground, thrusting the two of them into a gentle rhythm. They clasped each other tighter, locked in their kiss.

Angelica shimmied out of her dress, the fabric falling around her sides and pooling in her lap. Moonlight shined on her pert nipples.

The same moon highlighted Adonis, his eyes fierce as he watched the two undulating on that tree branch. Again, he pulled his knife out of his pocket, flicking it open, the silver blade bright. Eyes burning, he crept closer, lifting his arm and positioning it to throw. He focused on his target.

Aris dragged his hand down Angelica's back, slipping it under her dress and cupping her bottom. Her fingers twitched over his chest, prying open his shirt and dropping her hand down to his crotch.

Face tight, Adonis snapped his arm forward like a whip, releasing the knife at the unsuspecting couple. It sliced through the air. Adonis watched its trajectory with rapt attention.

Above the couple, the owls sensed the danger. Their necks swelled in anticipation, fluttering their wings.

The knife twirled through the air.

Angelica finished unbuttoning Aris's shirt, running her hands down his bare chest.

The knife glinted through the night, and without breaking his focus, Aris shouted in pain as it sliced sideways across his back and buried in the tree trunk.

Adonis sighed, relaxing his stance. He watched as Aris slipped off the branch and landed hard on the ground, letting out a yelp of pain.

Angelica scrunched her knees at the change in position, but otherwise didn't stop in her ministrations.

Aris laid down, pulling Angelica with him. She lifted her arms as he pulled the dress over her head to reveal her fully naked body. The moon reflected off Angelica's back, exposing her full breasts and her hourglass figure.

Overcome with helplessness, Adonis punched the ground as he watched Angelica remove Aris's trousers.

Aris pulled her down, rolling them over and kissing her as he removed his open shirt. He entered her, rocking forward as he swallowed her gasp.

Unable to stomach another moment, Adonis retreated into the dark, limping towards the village. The way was long, and his pace was slow, suddenly exhausted from the day.

Up on the hill, with the danger gone, the two white owls settled back onto their perch to watch over the lovers.

35 THE FOOL AND THE LITTLE FOX

Spotlighted by the moon, Angelica's face broke open in pleasure.

"I've never seen a smile as beautiful as yours," Aris said. "It sends your beauty to new horizons, new dimensions, beyond human understanding. Which god fathered you? Aphrodite must be jealous of your sweet beauty!"

"If there is a god here right now, it is you. You are beyond what I could imagine possible."

Surrounded by her scent, Aris tugged her down for another round and they lost themselves in their lovemaking.

Angelica's body clenched as she reached her climax, tightening around Aris and milking him to completion.

"I'm overwhelmed," she whispered. "I've never felt anything like this before!"

The afterglow of their orgasms rippled out, crackling through the earth and perking the greenery around them to life. The two peppered kisses on each other, slowly catching their breath.

Unwilling and unable to part, they continued to press their lips together. Aris rolled over onto his back, tugging Angelica on top of him. She rested her cheek on his chest, enjoying the feeling of his heart beating under her.

"I've never experienced anything like this. Never even imagined I could!"

Moved, the pair of white owls turned their heads and shared a secretive glance.

Aris caught sight of them. His hands continuing to caress Angelica's back, he leaned closer to whisper, "We are not alone, gorgeous!"

She startled, then followed his gaze and tilted her head, looking up into the branches. "Ah. We call them *night lovers*. They are known to mate for life and never part after meeting."

"It's said they bring good luck," Aris murmured.

Angelica cupped his face and ran her fingers through his hair. "Here, we say that if they witness you make love, it heralds a new life, but also painful joy or turbulent times."

Like thieves sighted, the owls lifted from the tree and flew away. They turned towards the bay before swooping down to the village and out of sight.

⁕ ◇ ⁕

After twenty minutes or so, Angelica rolled off Aris's body, landing on her back next to him. She dragged her fingers up his side, tripping over his ribs, gazing up at the moon above them. Leaning her head over, resting against the left side of his chest, she asked, "Are you happy, Aris?"

"I am happy just having you in my arms. I feel fulfilled. But you are a fool."

"Sometimes it's good to be a fool, Aris," she replied giddily. "Being too serious traps the soul."

Aris ran his hands across her body. "I was afraid I would hurt you. I still am."

She pressed a kiss to his chest. "You cannot hurt me. This is the happiest I've been in my whole life."

"We don't know how long this will last."

Gently massaging Aris's neck, Angelica met Aris's gaze. "Stop worrying about me. Our love will last, no matter what everyone else might say."

She bit Aris on the nipple, causing him to jolt. "You see, this is real! It will last as long as I live and even beyond."

Aris let out a deep sigh.

"I am a grown woman. I can take care of myself. What's meant to be is meant to be. This is our destiny. Just think. You travelled across the world, and out of all the towns and islands, you just happened to arrive at this nameless village. What else could it be but fate?"

He pulled her hand to his mouth, kissing the inside of her palm. "What else do you see in our future?"

She placed another kiss on his chest. "Even if I knew, I can't tell you. If I did, you might try to change it. Besides, I don't think anyone can foresee the future. But I know what will happen in a few moments."

She rolled, presenting her back to him. He quickly crawled over her, his knees pushing her legs apart. Kissing her on the back of the neck, he nipped her lightly with his teeth.

The guttural roar of a boat engine shook them from their revelry. The first of the fishing boats streaked out from the harbour.

"The boats," he warned. "We must return before daybreak."

But they remained wrapped in each other's arms until the owls returned, landing nearby and interrupting their comfort.

"We really should go," Angelica said, kissing his cheek.

They dressed quickly and ambled down to the village holding hands.

When they reached the first line of houses, they kissed again briefly. "Tonight," Angelica implored. "I'll be waiting with the owls. Don't leave me waiting."

"Your smile is breath-taking."

"You exaggerate," she giggled. "But I'm not complaining."

Aris smiled broader. "You make me say things I've never said before."

"This deserves a reward."

Angelica kissed him and he groaned, caressing her hair.

At long last, she pushed him away. "You'll have to wait till midnight for more."

⋯ ◇ ⋯

Adonis sat atop his black steed, the horse's velvet mane and tail shining and proud. They crested the hill, and he pulled the horse to a halt by the oak tree. The stallion neighed, stomping uneasily as Adonis dismounted.

At the tree, he reached for his knife which was sticking out of the trunk. Extending down from it hung the limp carcass of a dead snake. He yanked the blade out and held the snake at arm's length.

The horse stomped the ground again.

Adonis settled it with a firm, "Hold."

He bagged the snake and lifted the knife up to the midday sun, admiring the light along its thin blade.

Angelica jerked awake when Granny shouted for her. She dragged herself from bed and headed to the bathroom. Still half asleep, she startled when Granny cried, "You're hurt!"

"What?" Angelica asked, rubbing sleep from her eye.

Granny ran her hands up and down Angelica, over her arms and face. "You're covered in blood!"

Angelica pulled away, looking down at herself, stunned to see crusty dried blood flaking over her arms.

Granny squinted. "You don't look injured. Where did all this come from?"

Angelica's mind replayed the previous night. "Aris!"

Eyes narrowing to slits, Granny grabbed her by the arm. "What do you mean? Were you with him last night?"

Granny leaned forward, sniffing her, then plucking a leaf from her hair. "Wash up, quick… before your mother sees you like this."

There was a clattering at the entrance of the house before Zoe burst through the door. "Granny, hurry! Aris is hurt!"

Granny quickly gathered her supplies and reappeared at the front of the house with Angelica by her side.

"He was sleeping face down and I saw this huge wound down his back," Zoe explained. "His shirt is entirely red with blood."

Exchanging a quick glance with Angelica, Granny ushered them all out the door and down the street to Aris's house. Upon entering, they found Aris, hair wet and freshly dressed in a clean shirt.

"Zoe said you are injured." Granny set her bag down.

He glanced over at Zoe for a moment before focusing on Granny. "It's just a scratch."

Mind spinning, Angelica watched in silence.

Undeterred, Zoe stepped forward. "I know what I say. Your back is a mess!"

Aris glared at her, but Zoe ignored him and raced into his bedroom. She scurried back, the bloody shirt clenched in her fist. "What's this, then?"

"It's just a scratch!" Aris insisted.

"How do you know?" Zoe pushed. "You can't see it! Show it to Granny."

Aris refused, shaking his head.

Zoe stepped up to him, not backing down. "Open wounds can lead to infection. You need to let Granny take care of it."

Granny approached him, whispering, "I might as well look at it while I'm here."

He looked over at Angelica who, after a moment, nodded. He yanked off his shirt, turning around.

"Oh my," Angelica gasped.

"I'm afraid Zoe is right." Granny shook her head. "The cut is deep. How did you manage this?"

Zoe pointed her finger at Aris in a haughty manner. "You see! I am always right because I don't fool around!"

Aris shrugged. "I tell you it's just a scratch. From a tree that I was leaning against."

Directing him into a chair, Granny eased him down so he was straddling it backwards. "We need to disinfect the wound."

Granny secreted a glance at Angelica, whispering, "Matching blood!"

"Matching with what, Granny?" Aris asked.

Amused, Granny started pulling medications out of her bag. "It matches the blood on your shirt. How did this happen?"

"I slipped on a tree branch last night."

Peering down at him, Granny looked back at Angelica then cleaned his wound.

"Now that Granny fixed you, get ready," Zoe ordered. "A scratch on your back can't stop you from walking."

Aris shook his head. "You little fox! That's why you brought Granny… so you could force me to go."

Zoe scolded, "Stop pushing your luck!"

———— ◈ ————

Granny and Angelica walked back to the house without looking at each other once. "I suppose this explains why you were covered in blood this morning."

Angelica froze, turning to look at her grandmother. They stared at each other for a moment before turning and continuing on their way.

"So the love secret worked then?"

Angelica remained silent all the way to the house. At the door, Granny pulled Angelica to a stop. Without a word, Angelica nodded and smiled brightly.

Joy and concern waged a brief war on Granny's face. She grinned, but it didn't quite reach her eyes. "Well, it is done now. You jumped into the fever. I beseech you to listen to me. I want you to be very careful, my angel. You need to gather all your strength and take control of the situation, both physically and emotionally, before it controls you!"

"Don't worry, I've never felt so in control," Angelica replied, brightening. "I've never felt as wonderful as I did last night. I feel complete for the first time."

"As long as you are sure," Granny said, shaking her head.

Angelica shifted her weight from foot to foot.

Nodding, Granny pressed a hand to Angelica's face. "Seems like you both are swept up in the blaze of love. I worry that it isn't going to end well, though. Perhaps I shouldn't have given you the love secret."

"To tell you the truth, I don't know if the love secret was even needed."

"If that's true, then Aris must already be in love with you. The love secret will make your connection that much stronger! Aris will be willing to kill for you."

"And I for him!" Angelica replied, but then grew contemplative. "Earlier, you seemed to be speaking from experience. What happened to you, Granny?"

The front door pushed open and Despo stuck her head out. "Where did you two disappear to?"

"Long story, my angels," replied Granny to both their questions.

36 My Love Will Never Fade

For over two weeks, Angelica and Aris met in secret under the oak tree to make love through the night. During the day, the lovers completely hid their emotions and even avoided contact as much as possible.

Well after midnight, Aris stretched out beneath the tree, the moon soft overhead. Angelica curved around him, resting on his chest. He slipped his fingers through her hair and trailed his other hand up and down the length of her back.

Above them, Aris noticed the two white owls perched, watching over them. He whispered in her ear, "This is truly paradise—the village, this nature, but most of all you. I hope to die like this, with you in my arms."

Pressing a kiss to his chest, Angelica pulled him closer. "You being here makes it paradise. As long as I am with you, even hell will feel like paradise!"

"The moon is dim tonight. I can't even see the sweet golden-brown colour of your eyes."

"I don't need any light to see you," Angelica replied, lifting her head to look at him. "I know what you look like even with my eyes closed."

"Being here with you is like a dream come true."

"It is, isn't it?" She rested her head back on his chest. "I dreamed of something like this as a child, but now I know it can be real."

Aris sighed. "We don't know how long this dream will last, though."

Rolling herself over, she straddled Aris and dipped down to kiss his lips. "This dream is forever! I will follow you anywhere. Nothing scares me when you're by my side."

Aris chuckled. "At some point, we both will need to wake up. Or maybe I should say that we'll both need to *sleep*."

"It's no dream. This is reality," Angelica reassured.

"There are so many things working against us—our age difference, the other villagers…"

"I'm not pushing you, but if you decide what you want, then we won't have to hide anything."

"I love you like I've never loved before," Aris confessed. "Beyond eros, beyond the physical attraction… but I'm worried about you."

"There's no need to worry. All I want is to be with you, wherever you choose."

"How do you know you will feel the same about me after the initial spark fades?"

"I assure you," Angelica urged. "My love for you will never fade."

"That is the promise of a child. You couldn't even stay away from your village for long."

"Stop worrying. I understand your concern, but I'm ready to face anything and anyone. Time will prove you wrong. I will prove you wrong."

Aris tipped his chin to look at the top of her head. "I like your child-like certainty."

Her eyes opened and she grinned up at him. "It is not childish to love completely. Now, how about I take your mind off these worries?"

37 THE LIE

A ris walked into the living room in the afternoon, sun streaming through the window. John and Uri were already there, lounging across the furniture.

"There he is," Uri exclaimed. "Lover boy is finally awake."

Aris ignored him, yawning as he dropped down onto the couch.

John grinned. "You were out late last night."

Aris looked up but didn't respond.

"And the night before that, and the one before that," Uri droned.

Aris sighed. "What's the problem?"

"The problem isn't what you're doing," John reprimanded. "It's who you're doing it with."

"Fine, I was with the widow."

Uri waved around a pair of white knickers, smirking. "How weird, because the widow left in a hurry just a few minutes after you came home."

Rubbing his face, Aris tried to hide after being caught in the lie.

"The only one other woman you could have been with is…" John prompted.

Aris walked to the window and gazed across the yard, remaining silent in the face of their accusations.

John stood next to him, dropping a hand on his shoulder. "You need to be careful, Aris. If we know, then the widow knows, too. And if the widow knows, then others will soon find out."

Aris remained still, looking out the window.

"You told us we were disturbing the balance of the village," Uri reminded him, his face serious and stiff. "We know you have trouble at home, but Angelica has everything to lose here."

Aris turned to face Uri. "Stop fantasising. I've just been having a hard time sleeping recently, so I've been going on long walks."

"Everyone knows how close you and Angelica have become," Uri stated. "The widow is not blind. You refused her and she's been jealous ever since."

"How does the widow know I'm out?"

"She's seen your bed empty most nights."

"You idiot. Why would you let her in the house?"

"Korina's a strong woman! How am I supposed to refuse her?"

John stepped forward hesitantly. "You should cut it off until we leave, or make it official. Otherwise, you're inviting disaster."

Aris turned back to the window. "I have nothing to lose, but she does."

"But do you love her?" John wondered.

"I don't just love Angelica… I adore her," Aris confessed, turning to face them and leaning back on the window ledge. "I've never felt like this about anyone before. Maybe I found her too late. And I know this isn't affecting just us."

"Yeah," John pointed out. "We are getting caught up in this as well."

"I'll deal with it!" Aris promised, walking to the door. "But Uri, you have to do something about the widow. I don't want her spreading rumours. Just tell her I can't sleep, and leave it at that."

"I've just been trying to give her something else to think about," Uri bragged.

Aris clenched his jaw and walked out the door without reply.

⸺ ◇ ⸺

The moon tipped past its apex. Beneath its glow, Angelica sat on the low branch of the oak tree with a frown worrying her face. She watched the path leading up to the tree with intensity, but nothing changed.

Above her, an owl hooted.

"I know. I don't think he's coming either. This is the third night in a row."

She stood up and headed home, waving farewell to the birds. "I'll be back tomorrow. I'll make sure he's here."

Well past midnight, Aris trudged back into the village and reached his house. He slipped out of his shoes and held them in his hand, creeping through the entryway and into his room.

He dropped down into his bed, leaning forward to rest his elbows on his knees. He scrubbed at his face with his hands.

Suddenly, he sat bolt upright in the dark, a hand covering his mouth from behind. He felt the soft squish of a woman's bosom against his back and a whisper in his ear urging him to keep quiet.

A pair of soft lips ran down the length of his neck. He relaxed, recognising them and reached around to pull a hand up to press a kiss to it.

"You shouldn't be here," he said.

"If the mountain doesn't come to Mohammed, then Mohammed must go to the mountain," Angelica replied. She continued to press light kisses to his neck.

Standing abruptly, Aris pulled Angelica upright. "The bed is too squeaky. We'll put the mattress on the floor."

"I ought to punish you for this."

After he'd shifted the furniture, he asked, "How are you going to do that?"

Angelica straddled him high on his chest, pinning down his arms. She gripped his hair, twisting it in her fingers. Leaning down slowly to make Aris think she would be gentle, she bared her teeth and bit down on his lip.

"Say you're sorry," Angelica mumbled, maintaining her toothy grip. "Say it."

"I'm sorry," Aris whimpered. "I'm sorry!"

Angelica released his lip.

Aris smirked. "You're a sadist." He pulled her down, not wasting a moment as the two of them began to make love.

At the first crow of the rooster, they were roused from sleep.

"It's time to go," Aris whispered, gently pushing Angelica to get her moving.

She threw her arms around him, hugging him before dropping a kiss on his cheek. Without complaint, she climbed out the window and slipped away through the hedge.

Aris dropped back down onto his mattress, falling fast asleep.

◆ ◇ ◆

Well after the sun cleared the horizon, John poked his head into the bedroom to find Aris sleeping on the floor. "Did you miss camping?" he joked.

"What?" Aris mumbled, half asleep.

"Why are you sleeping on the floor?"

Aris pushed up on his arms, looking around. "I'm sleeping on a mattress, not the floor."

"But the mattress is on the floor."

"The floor is better for my back."

John grinned leeringly. "I get it."

"I'm not in the mood for this. Just go away."

There was a moment of silence before John burst out laughing. "I've never understood how a woman could just forget her knickers."

Aris twisted in bed to get a better view of the white panties hanging on the end of his bedframe. He glared at John. "Not sure how anybody is just okay with barging into another person's room."

38 GAVE YOU MY SOUL

Aris curled around Angelica on the mattress on the floor, his arm thrown over her and their hands intertwined.

Outside, just beyond the window, two white owls perched in a tree.

"They must have been looking for us," Aris said, kissing the back of her neck. "They must still be watching over us."

As the first light poured through the window, Aris sat up and watched as Angelica got dressed. When she was ready, she dipped down to kiss him goodbye, fast and firm on the mouth.

"Wait," he called suddenly when she was already half out the window. He balled up the pair of panties and tossed them to her. "You forgot these the other day. John found them."

Angelica glared down at the undergarment then swung back into the room. She chucked them back at him in a rage, tears burning her eyes. "These aren't mine. I don't even wear any when I come to see you. Besides, they aren't even my size!"

Looking down at the panties with fresh sight, Aris reeled.

Angelica kicked him repeatedly. "I thought you stopped sleeping with her!"

Jumping to his feet in alarm, Aris grabbed Angelica to get her to stop. "What are you talking about?"

Angelica yanked away from Aris, glaring at him. "We promised not to lie to each other."

"False accusations are worse than lying."

"Don't deny it. I know what I saw!"

"Saw what?" he hissed. "What did you see?"

"The widow! Before we got together, I watched her come into your room. Everyone knows you were sleeping with her!"

Aris jolted back as if he had been burned.

Tears dripped down Angelica's face as she stepped closer, cupping his cheek in her palm. "I could understand before, but now? You've betrayed me!"

She raced back to the window, but Aris seized her before she could leave. He shook her in frustration. "I didn't betray you! I never slept with her. Maybe you dreamed it up in jealousy."

"I'm not a jealous woman," Angelica sobbed. "Besides, I'm sure if you check, those knickers will be a perfect fit for Korina."

Aris clenched his jaw. "The widow has never been in my bed."

"I've seen her standing here! You were obviously expecting her! I didn't stick around to see what happened."

Aris tried to coax her back in. "I'm not lying to you."

"I'm not lying, either! I know what I saw," Angelica insisted. She pushed him away, spitting on the floor. "I can't share you with anyone. I'm never coming back."

"Please, I swear. I've slept with no one else."

Wiping off her tears, Angelica smiled wanly. "You told me you never forgive or forget. Well, you aren't the only one."

"I love you no matter what! Even if you slept with a hundred men, I'd still love you!"

Angelica jumped out the window, keeping her back to Aris. "I can't stop loving you, but I will never touch you again! I surrendered everything to you! I gave you my soul and you sold it to the devil! To the devil!"

Angelica quickly ran away.

◦◇◦

Aris stormed out of his room, the panties balled up in his fist. He burst into Uri's room to find him alone in bed. Throwing the garment at Uri, it smacked him in the face.

Jerking up in bed, Uri stared at the panties. "What?"

Pinning him to the bed by the throat, Aris loomed above him. "The widow is no longer welcome in this house. If I catch her in here, I'll break both of your legs!"

"Okay," Uri gasped, face turning red. "Okay!"

Attracted by the shouting, John hurried into the room and watched as Aris smashed a chair to splinters, holding the hard wooden back in his hands. He moved back to the bed, standing over Uri who was now shaking, his arms folded over his head in a flimsy attempt at protection.

John threw himself between the men. "Calm down, we're all friends here."

Throwing the remains of the chair in a fit of rage, Aris bent down and flipped the mattress, sending Uri flying to the floor.

Uri scurried away, crawling across to the door, his body hiccupping uncontrollably.

John tugged at Aris. "Please, let's just get out of here."

Aris lets John pull him from the room.

⸻ ◇ ⸻

Uri sat hunched over in the doorway, waiting for the widow. His leg bounced with nerves.

When she arrived, a smile graced her face.

"You need to go," he urged.

Her face fell, confused at his sudden refusal.

"Aris found your underwear. He went crazy and nearly killed me! I'll come to you instead."

She dismissed him with a wave of her hand. "No, I do not want my daughters to see you… or any man in my house. I want to come to you. What's the big deal?"

"I just said! Aris found your panties in his room. He'll kill you if he sees you here!"

The widow grinned maniacally. "Of course, he found them! I hope his lover did as well. You know, I saw her once, lurking outside his window."

"You don't understand," Uri hissed. "He's gone crazy! He flipped my bed while I was still in it. He's out of control."

Her smile widened. "This is my house. So if he has a problem with me being here, then he can just leave."

"Aris will break our legs!"

"If he lays one finger on me, my brothers over in the next village will kill him," she retorted, pulling a knife out of her pocket. "If I don't kill him first. If he comes at me, I'll slice him open till his intestines spill out on the floor."

She pulled Uri along inside the rental property. "You've got me all excited now. Let's celebrate. I want you to be a bull tonight!"

Uri let her lead the way. "I guess you can come in as long as you promise to be quiet and leave early."

"Well," she replied, pushing him down onto his bed. She stabbed her knife into the top of the small bedside cabinet. "I promise to leave… but I don't promise to be quiet!"

39 THE CATCH

Angelica stood off from the oak tree and watched Aris as he sat, unmoving, on the branch where they had once made love. Hidden, she waited until he rose and then followed him back through the village to his house. There, she stood watch outside as he settled into a restless sleep.

Tears gathered in the corner of her eyes as he tossed and turned. She counted off the number of days that she had been watching him, five fingers for five days, and the widow still hadn't made another appearance in Aris's bedroom.

⸺ ⸭ ⸺

Aris sat astride his horse alongside Adonis. The morning light was sharp and bright.

Adonis refused to look at him. "How do I win over Angelica?" Adonis asked suddenly.

Aris glanced over at the man, his face tight and stiff.

"You have plenty of experience," Adonis pushed. "Surely you have some advice."

Aris shook his head. "I'm no expert when it comes to women."

"But you are married! Don't you love your wife?"

"I used to, but not anymore. Now there's only emptiness. Nothing. Absolutely nothing. She burnt even my heart to ash."

"Even that is an experience. Surely you have some advice on how to win Angelica's love."

Aris tugged on the reins, turning his horse to follow the path. "Maybe she loves you already."

"She loves me," Adonis scoffed. "Just not the way I love her. I've protected her my whole life, even got stabbed fighting off a man who tried to force himself on her."

"What are you talking about?"

"It was a long time ago," Adonis said dismissively.

Aris chewed over his friend's words carefully. "How can you be sure you truly love Angelica?"

"Real love takes time to cultivate."

Aris's chest tightened at the claim. "You could just ask her to marry you."

Adonis turned on him, eyes wild. "No, if I ask her right now, she will definitely refuse me."

◆ ◇ ◆

The house was calm and still when Angelica crept out of her room past midnight. She moved through the house to the front door, flinching as it creaked when she pushed it open.

She made it down the first step before she was halted by a hand on her arm.

Taken by surprise, she saw Granny standing in the doorway. "What are you doing here?"

"I was waiting for you," Granny whispered. She led Angelica back through the house like a thief. Closing Angelica's bedroom door behind them, she said, "You haven't been yourself recently."

Angelica hesitated, shifting her feet. "I've had things on my mind."

Granny cupped her cheeks. "Don't lie to me."

"I'm not," Angelica insisted, her shoulders stiffening under the questioning. "I've just been a bit distracted."

Granny nodded, looking into her eyes. "You are having problems with Aris."

Angelica shifted her gaze, looking over Granny's shoulder.

"Sit," Granny said, leading them to the bed. "Tell me what's wrong."

Chest heaving, Angelica kept her head down. "I don't want to see Aris anymore."

"What?" Granny gasped. "Why?"

Angelica shut her eyes for a few seconds then hopped to her feet. "I don't want to talk about it. Just leave it alone."

Granny gently pushed Angelica to sit back on the bed. "It's okay. You can tell me. At least try."

Chest heaving, Angelica finally relented. "Aris is refusing me."

Granny froze in astonishment. "That's impossible! The love secret should prevent him from refusing you. What really happened?"

Angelica choked on her words, causing them to escape in a jumbled mess. "It's me, Granny. I'm the one refusing Aris. I can't stand watching him but I can't go near him. It's painful."

"Go on… I'm listening."

Angelica stood up, speaking urgently. "Not now, Granny. I'll tell you everything tomorrow. I need to go now. Please!"

Hesitantly, Granny finally gave in. "As you wish, my angel."

Hurrying out of the house, Angelica looked up at the moon. It was as if someone had taken a large bite out of it. She moved quickly down the road and found herself, as usual, outside Aris's window.

Squatting down, she peered over the window ledge and watched as he tossed in his bed. She ducked when he jolted upright, head tilted as if listening to something.

Slipping out of bed, Aris crept out of the room, trying to place what he was hearing when a loud moan broke through the night. He tensed, his blood rumbling to a boil, and marched out of his room.

Kicking Uri's door open, he flipped on the light, immediately seeing the widow rolling on top of his "friend."

Uri screamed as the widow dove for her knife still sticking out of the bedside table.

Aris halted her mid-lunge, dragging her from the room by her hair as she kicked and screamed.

Drawn by the shouting, Angelica jumped through Aris's window and stopped at the threshold leading from the bedroom into the rest of the house.

She saw Aris marching towards the front door, the widow flailing behind him. Angelica covered her mouth, shocked, having never seen Aris in such a rage before.

Uri stumbled out after them, having thrown on a pair of shorts. He grabbed Aris's shoulder. "Stop. Enough!"

Aris twisted, landing a solid kick to the chest that had Uri flying back and landing on the ground with a grunt. "I told you I didn't want her in this house anymore."

He slammed the widow against a wall, her head bouncing on impact. He pinned Korina there by her neck, arm cocked back, hand balled into a fist.

Uri grappled with Aris, trying to keep him from punching the widow.

Aris elbowed him off, whipping his fist back and breaking Uri's nose.

Uri crumpled to the ground, blood pouring down his face.

Aris focuses back on Korina, pressing her against the wall firmly. His nostrils flared, but after three breaths he relaxed his grip. He slapped her hard across the face. "Are you done messing around, leaving your panties in my room?"

She cackled. "If I can't have you, then she can't either."

John stepped groggily out of his room.

Aris grimaced at the widow, disgusted, and dragged her across the floor.

"I'll tell the whole village about you and that girl!" Korina bellowed.

He shoved her back, clamping a hand tight on her throat. "You have seen nothing. You know nothing. You say one word and I'll cut your tongue out."

Angelica stumbled back, squeezing her eyes shut to try and forget what she'd just seen.

Aris dragged the widow out of the house.

She was feral, kicking and growling, as he tossed her onto the street completely naked.

"If I see you here again, if you say even one word about anything, I'll kill you."

All around them, the neighbours peeked through their windows, watching as Aris tossed the widow into the street. They gasped, hearing his threats loud and clear.

Uri tried to slip out with her clothes but Aris shoved him against the doorframe. "You want to fuck her, then you go to her house."

Uri nodded, blood from his broken nose seeping out.

Aris pushed his way back into the house, his skin hot and tight. He crashed into the shower, still partially dressed, and blasted it on cold.

After a long moment, he caught his breath and twisted the water off, towelling himself dry.

John hovered just outside the bathroom, frowning. "Are you okay?"

"This isn't a good time." Aris stomped past and returned to his room, kicking the door shut.

He stood before the open window, breathing the cool night air in deep. He tried to hold it in to soothe his burning lungs.

At the touch of a hand on his shoulder, he spun and grabbed the person by the neck, his arm raised and ready to strike.

Angelica thrust up her hands, trembling. "It's me. It's just me!"

Aris's grip tightened briefly before he relaxed and let her go.

"I heard everything she said," Angelica whimpered. "I never should have doubted you. Please, can you forgive my weakness? That woman just—"

Aris wrapped her in a tight hug, shushing her. "We will speak no more about her." He leaned down, kissing Angelica softly. "Not here," he said. "This place is tainted. Our tree, please."

He changed quickly while she waited. When he had dressed, she headed to his door but he stopped her. "Not that way. I caught a glimpse of movement by the neighbour's window. I'm sure they saw everything, and I don't want them to see you here, too."

"If the widow's family learns you hit her, they will come. Father, brothers, uncles—all of them are all killers. You will have to leave!"

"Let them come. Nothing can make me go away from you."

"But they're killers!"

He pressed his finger against Angelica's mouth. "No more talk of that evil woman. It is done."

With that, Angelica led him out the window by the hand, returning to their tree atop the hill together.

40 THE GOSSIP AND A MAN IN LOVE

A short, stout woman waddled down the street on oddly thin legs. Her grey hair glinted like steel in the sun. She bounded up the steps to the house and hurried in to find Angelica, Despo, and Granny sitting around the table having a coffee.

She stopped, leaning against the table to catch her breath.

Granny offered her a seat, but she waved it off. "I can't stay. I left a casserole in the oven."

Noticing her barely contained energy, Granny settled in for a bit of gossip. "What's the news, Josephina?"

"There was a fight. Last night at the widow's old house."

Granny glanced at Angelica out of the corner of her eye, but just calmly drank her coffee.

"The tall American dragged her out by her hair," Josephina continued. "She was completely naked and her face was covered in blood! He even attacked one of the other Americans."

"What time was this?" Despo asked.

"Well past midnight."

"Are you sure it was Korina?"

Josephina nodded, eager to share her findings. "It's not the first time she snuck over there. Most nights she's in that house until the next morning."

Despo shared a look with Granny, leaning back in her chair.

"Do you know why they were fighting?" Granny wondered.

Josephina flicked the air between them. "No idea. Maybe she slept with one of the other ones and Aris got jealous. He was so vicious, though. He didn't seem the type. He even threatened Korina!"

Despo's jaw dropped. "Aris? Violent? I don't believe it."

"He beat up the widow like it was nothing! I think she must have said something about his wife because he said if she spoke another word, he'd kill her!"

A thick silence fell over the room

Josephina looked around at the other women, waiting to see if they asked anything else. "Well, I need to get back home. But just imagine if this gets back to Korina's brothers. Well, anyway, I just thought I'd let you know because I never thought Aris could be so violent!"

The front door clicked behind her as she left.

Granny shook her head.

Despo looked at her daughter. "That man just can't seem to help himself. First, he uses the widow and now he's beating her up."

"I don't think he was involved with the widow," Angelica argued.

"Then how do you explain that fight? The last thing we want is her brothers coming back here."

"They are an evil family," Granny agreed. "Always in and out of prison. It might be best for Aris to leave quickly."

"I'm sure Josephina is exaggerating," said Angelica. "You know how she gets."

Despo slapped the table. "This is serious. Soon, the whole village will know."

"Maybe she was involved with Uri," Angelica supplied. "He hits on everyone, even me!"

Despo narrowed her eyes, studying her daughter. "Then why would Aris throw her out? Was he jealous of them?"

"I don't know. Maybe they had an argument. We all know how vicious the widow can get. It's best if we just stay out of it."

"Regardless," Granny interjected. "Aris needs to be careful with her. Anastasis insists to this day that she killed his brother."

This time it was Despo who shook her head. "The widow did not take kindly to Aris spending time in our house when he was making Zoe's dress. You better be careful, Angelica. Keep your distance from him and the widow."

Angelica waved her mother off, indifferent to her concern. "I don't have anything to share with the widow. I'm friendly enough when I talk to her. Let her fight with the Americans. It's not our problem."

⸰◇⸰

Despo walked down the street carrying a large bowl covered with a dishcloth. Entering the rental house, she found Aris relaxing on the couch reading a book. "Good morning," she greeted. "I brought over some cookies."

Aris hopped up, marking his place in the book with his finger. "Thank you, they smell just like the ones Angelica makes."

"Well, I made them today. Angelica is not feeling well." Despo's smile was small and tight. She placed the cookies on the kitchen table. "Do you have a moment? I was hoping to talk."

Aris set his book aside and joined her at the table, snapping up a cookie to munch on.

Despo sat across from him looking down at her lap, wringing her hands. Finally, she gave a small, mournful smile. "We've noticed Angelica sneaking out of the house recently," she began, causing Aris to pause in his chewing. "Manolios was worried, so he followed her a few times. He saw her climb into your window. And, once, when you met under the oak tree. If Manolios had caught you sneaking into our house, he would have killed you."

Aris swallowed, his mouth dry. He stared awkwardly at Despo. "Angelica is not a schoolgirl. You have no reason to be following her like a criminal."

"Don't misunderstand us. Manolios admires you. We all know how hard you tried to resist her. That is the only thing holding him back from coming here himself."

Aris frowned, returning his half-eaten cookie to the bowl. "If you had so much respect for us both, you wouldn't have followed your daughter. Does she know?"

Uri yawned, walking lazily down the hall, but a yank on his arm halted him. He glanced over to see John shaking his head and holding a finger up to his lips.

John pulled Uri closer, whispering, "Despo is having a serious conversation with Aris."

"Of course not!" Despo categorically denied. "You need to think about our position. Manolios is like a cornered animal right now. The whole village is talking about what you did to the widow. We're just worried about our daughter."

"The two issues aren't even remotely the same. The widow was here for Uri, and I only hit her because she hurt Angelica."

"And with his weird behaviour lately, we think Adonis knows as well," she continued, ignoring him completely. "You've hurt two men already. I don't even want to mention the widow's brothers who aren't that far away."

Uri and John exchanged worried glances.

"Were you sent here to threaten me?"

Despo reached out, patting Aris to try and defuse the situation. "Of course not! I thought it was best to just warn you."

Aris chuckled. "Definitely sounds like a threat."

Uri waved his hand. "Big trouble! We better pack!"

"Honestly, we thought you'd be gone by now," Despo continued. "And Manolios has such respect for how you fended off her advances. It's unfortunate that it has come to this."

Aris pushed away from the table. "The respect, I appreciate. The threats, not so much."

Despo jumped up, standing close to him. "Please, you'll be leaving soon, and this is such a small community. Just stop seeing Angelica."

Aris scoffed. "Just stop seeing her? Do you even wonder how I feel about her? Or how she feels about me? You and Manolios are out of line. She is an adult."

"You don't understand," she retorted. "The last time she was in trouble like this, we couldn't do anything. And it took a long time before the villagers were able to move past it!"

"What are you talking about?"

Despo looked at Aris, noticing his entire focus was on her. "When Angelica was attacked by a group of men. Manolios was in the fields. If Adonis hadn't been there to fight them off, I hate to think what could have happened." She looked into his eyes before adding, "I thought you knew."

"I knew of the fight," Aris whispered, his mouth dry. "But not the reason."

"Angelica left soon afterward for university. She couldn't bear to be in the village while everyone treated her so suspiciously. So please, stop seeing her. Leave before the widow's brothers come or Manolios explodes. It's best for everyone."

Aris sighed, leaning against the kitchen table. "You keep assuming that I will leave, but what if I want to stay?"

Despo offered him a sad smile. "Just don't tell Angelica. There's no need for her to know we talked."

"Are you asking me to lie to her?"

"No, just to not hurt her." Despo nodded one last time and then left, closing the door behind her.

⸻ ◆ ⸻

The house was quiet until John and Uri crept out to stand near Aris.

John had to bump into him to get his attention. "Sorry, we heard everything."

A burp escaped Uri's mouth. "We should start packing. Korina's family is no joke. They're all killers! We've messed with death too much already on this trip."

Aris sneered at him. "Then just pack and go."

"We r-r-really can't stay," Uri replied, voice shaking. "The widow's brothers might be coming for us!"

"I told you to stay away from her," Aris bit back.

"Forget that. We need to go!"

The two glared at each other, refusing to submit.

John stepped between them. "Uri's right. We've overstayed our welcome because you didn't want to go."

Aris turned on him in a flash. "I'm not leaving!"

"This isn't the ocean. These are hurt and embarrassed men," Uri pleaded. "We have to go before they snap."

John paced back and forth. "And you already know Adonis is in love with Angelica. You've taken the one thing he's always wanted. He might call you his best friend, but hate and love are closely related."

Aris's face burned the more he listened.

"We can't postpone our departure forever," Uri asserted. "We've already been here longer than planned."

Aris clenched his jaw, struggling under their joint assault. "You're right. You two better pack up."

Uri groaned at the despondent look on Aris's face. "Don't be like this. We had a good time. We've already used up all their hospitality. Let's go before we ruin it."

"I'm not in the mood for a lecture," Aris spat, heading for the door. "It's best if I don't see either of you here when I get back." Then he slammed the door behind him.

⬥ ◇ ⬥

Aris wandered out to the fields and waited for Adonis to canter over.

Dismounting, Adonis guided his horse by the reins as he and Aris picked their way across the land.

Adonis eyed Aris as they walked in silence, noticing his friend's stiff posture. "What's bothering you? You've been avoiding everyone lately."

Aris gazed out over the horizon. "Nothing. I just felt like being on my own for a bit."

"It's great how we have all opened up to you, but you keep us at a distance. Very strong foundation for a friendship."

"I'm not in the mood."

"Your mood seems to have preferences."

Aris scoffed. "My mood is not up for anyone these days."

"That's not true. You always have time for certain people."

"Don't push me, Adonis."

"I'm just trying to talk, and you accuse me of pushing you."

"I'll see you at the café later," Aris promised. "Maybe my mood will improve after a few drinks."

"When? Every other time you leave before anyone else even gets there. Your nights are clearly booked."

Aris paused, turning to look at Adonis. "If you have something to say, then say it."

"I've said my peace." Adonis held up his hands. "You are the one with secrets, sleeping all day and being out all hours of the night."

Aris twisted around and marched back across the field.

Adonis watched him leave, like a man possessed, a man consumed. A man in love.

41 The Call

Aris reclined in the living room, spinning his cell phone like a top on the small table next to him.

Uri stretched out on the sofa while John read a book at the table.

"You've been playing with your phone all day," John said, lifting his eyes to look at Aris. "If you want to call home, just do it."

As if by fate, Aris's phone illuminated, notifying him of an incoming call. He hesitated as it continued to trill loudly.

"Just answer the damn phone," Uri shouted. When Aris still refused to budge, Uri jerked up and accepted the call on speaker phone.

Aris sighed. "Yes?"

"I need money." Gina's voice was high and whiney.

Aris shook his head in disbelief. "How did you get this number?"

"I'm not as stupid as you think I am, and don't change the subject. I need money."

"You have four credit cards."

"Don't play dumb," she yelled. "You've blocked all the credit cards."

The mobile phone rattled on the table from her volume.

"I didn't do any such thing. Just call them and unblock the cards. You have my information."

"Information?" Gina screamed. "You disappeared, travelling to God knows where to enjoy your whores, leaving your family behind. I don't even know when you're coming back."

Uri and John looked on, sad and withdrawn.

"Come back to what?"

"To nothing, that's what. I don't want you stepping foot in this house again. You are nothing!" Gina's voice was grating and sharp. "I'll file for divorce and take you for everything you have."

Unmoved, Aris smiled bitterly.

"Even your sons realise what a hypocrite you are. They're here, and so is your daughter, and none of them want you to come back! Just stay away from us!"

John and Uri flinched as if they had been slapped, but Aris merely folded his hands behind his head and made himself comfortable.

"I'll sign the divorce papers with pleasure."

"Liar," she snarled. "First you refused to sign, and now you have no problem? What, did you find a whore? I hate you! You were the worst. I want a man who makes mistakes and likes to drink and have fun, but instead I got stuck with you. Always working or watching those boring documentaries. I don't ever want to see you again!"

Aris's voice rang loud and clear. "Don't worry. You won't see me again. You are a cancer, Gina, and the only way to treat a cancer is to remove it. Do whatever you want." Leaning forward, he tapped the red button to immediately end the call.

He leaned back, glancing at John and Uri before turning his attention to the ceiling.

⋯ ◇ ⋯

Gina screeched in frustration. She turned to her sons, teeth bared. "The coward hung up on me! He's afraid to hear the truth!"

Peter and Gerry could hardly believe the way she had spoken to their father.

"Well," she finished ranting, finally puttering out. "At least the coward isn't coming back."

"You told him not to!" Gerry wailed. "That's not the same as him not wanting to come home."

Peter frowned, standing up to his mother. "You crossed a line. Who do you think you are, telling him we don't want him around? He's our father!"

Gina huffed, waving off his concerns. "You're still brainwashed by his notion of family. What family is he talking about? Where is it?"

"She's impossible! Let's go," Gerry said, motioning for Peter to come along with him. "This place has become a madhouse."

"Run away," Gina yelled after them. "Just like your coward father."

Gerry raced outside with Peter following and slamming the door shut behind them.

◆ ◇ ◆

The silence was thick. Finally, Aris sighed, unable to bear the weight of it. He looked over at John and Uri. "Now you know. There's nothing for me to go back to."

Uri's face was slack. "If that's what being married is like, I want a divorce."

"Epi isn't like Gina," Aris soothed. "You have nothing to worry about."

"Maybe," Uri hedged. "But what if she changes? Especially if we have kids… they change everything."

"Absurd. You said yes for a reason. You know that you love her. That is enough."

John leaned forward, bracing himself on his knees. "What about you and Angelica?"

A smile lit up Aris's face. "She is my angel, but I can't be with her. And I can't ask her to leave with me. No matter what I do, she will be hurt. I think I might have found her too late. And you're telling me I must leave now? After finally finding true love?"

John grinned at him. "This is the first time you've ever told us how you really feel."

"Well, now you know everything." Standing up, Aris made his way over to the front door. "I think I'm going to go for a swim alone. It'd be wise for the two of you to leave, so I don't have to worry about you."

42 The Signs Are Visible

Manolios sat across from Adonis at his kitchen table while Angelica and Granny rushed around completing their chores.

"We haven't seen Aris recently," Manolios probed. "Is he still working in the fields with you?"

Adonis put his coffee cup on the table. "Something is bothering him. He's been avoiding everyone, it seems."

Angelica paused her ironing, steam billowing around her as she looked over at Granny.

"Perhaps he's just missing home," Granny suggested.

"He must really be missing it." Despo entered with a basket of laundry. "He even refused Zoe today. She was crying earlier about how he had promised to take her fishing."

Granny shrugged. "It's not like him to let Zoe down. Maybe he forgot."

Adonis waved to get Angelica's attention. "You two are close. Any idea what's happening?"

Angelica glared at him, pinning him like a spear to the ground.

"I thought you'd know," he said. "He's my friend, too."

"That's right," Angelica sniped back. "He spends more time with you than anybody else. You should know better than the rest of us."

The other three stepped back, unwilling to get caught up in the middle of an argument.

Adonis shrugged. "I asked, but he didn't tell me anything."

Angelica crossed her arms. "And you think he'd share it with me?"

"Recently, he's been spending less time with me, so I figured he might have been spending more time around here."

Angelica slammed the iron down in a hiss of steam and ran out the back of the house without saying another word.

No one moved. Finally, Despo picked up the iron and took over where Angelica left off. "She's not been well these last few days. She's been spending a lot of time out with Snowy."

"If the master is depressed, the horse is as well." Adonis decided to leave. "Thank you for the coffee."

As soon as the door closed, Manolios said, "What did I tell you? Suddenly, our entire lives revolve around Aris. This must stop!"

⋄

The next morning, Adonis was hunched over in his garden, spying on Angelica and Granny. In a basket balanced against her hip, Granny carried the washing and Angelica took out one article at a time to hang on the line.

They worked in silence until Angelica collapsed to her knees.

Dropping the basket and falling to the ground beside her, Granny asked, "What's wrong?"

Angelica bent over, vomiting onto the grass, one hand pressed against her abdomen.

"Are you in pain? Are you dizzy? Are you…?"

Curling up like a turtle in its shell, Angelica hid from Granny's probing gaze.

At the prolonged silence, Granny finally asked, "How long?" Patting her arm, Granny tried to unfurl Angelica into a more comfortable position. "You need to decide what to do. An unmarried pregnant girl in our village will be a disaster."

Adonis sank to his knees, realizing what must have happened.

Angelica caught her breath and wiped her mouth clean. "This can't be happening. I used your herbs!"

"Nothing is fool proof. Not even the herbs. You know that."

Angelica averted her eyes.

Granny watched her, unmoved by her display.

Unnoticed, slumped against the fence, Adonis slipped sideways, no longer able to support himself under the weight of the revelation.

◇

The moon was a sliver in the sky, the light almost drowned out by the surrounding stars. Angelica leaned on a branch of the oak tree, head tilted back to observe the pair of white owls perched a few branches above her.

"I don't think he's coming today," she confessed to them.

She stood, slowly working her way down the hill back to the village. Behind her, an inky mass slipped after her. Once she was in the village, Adonis continued his pursuit, tracking her through the streets.

Reaching Aris's window, Angelica found it locked. Gently, she knocked but got no response. Undaunted, she walked around to the front door and entered the house.

Adonis watched from across the street, barely able to believe she would go to such extremes to see Aris.

Creeping through the hall, she arrived at Aris's door. She turned the knob and went in.

Barely visible in the faint light, he was curled up and facing the wall. She shimmied out of her dress, pausing as Aris mumbled in his sleep and repositioned himself.

Angelica crawled into bed with him, wrapping around him and pressing a tender kiss behind his ear.

"I know you're awake," she whispered. "You seem worried even in your sleep. There's no reason to be so stressed. I'm here now."

Aris rolled over to face her and wrapped his arms around her. He tugged her closer, kissing her gently.

She smiled at his ministrations. "Take your time but stop trying to get away from me. Just spend the time we have left together."

He rubbed away her tears.

◇

Granny stepped out the back door and searched over the fence to find Adonis pruning his trees. She crossed the yard, watching him cut off the dead branches and toss them aside. Leaning over the fence, she called, "You seem to be spending more time in your garden lately."

Adonis approached her, eyes flitting around. "Not much more than usual."

She smiled softly. "I noticed you here the other day while I was talking with Angelica."

"Have you been spying on me?"

"Who's doing the spying here?" She chuckled at his panicked expression. "Don't worry. Angelica has no idea. Did you hear anything interesting?"

Adonis scratched his face, considering his options. "It wasn't intentional."

Granny remained silent, waiting.

Adonis dug his toe into the dirt like a boy being chastised at school. "I heard that Angelica could be pregnant. Don't worry. I won't say anything to anyone."

Granny patted his cheek. "You are an admirable man. It is you who has the heart of a child and the courage of not one but of a hundred dragons."

She stepped back, pressing her hand to her breast. "I'm sorry your heart is so broken right now."

He turned away, unable to stomach her sympathy.

"I hope one day Angelica will make you happy. I know she loves you. But sometimes love doesn't move in a logical way. I know that doesn't do much to ease your pain."

"I don't really feel anything, to be honest," Adonis replied, chewing his lip. "I know Aris isn't to blame, that no one is, but now I'm just floating in this drab world."

Granny nodded, leaning closer. "Aris really did try to avoid her. The road he travels is even more painful than yours. He has nothing to offer her in this life."

Adonis choked out a bitter laugh. "I know, and yet things happened!"

"A lesser man would want to hurt them, but you don't want that, do you?"

"No," he mumbled. "I love them both. He's my friend, and she's the woman I've loved since I was a child. I couldn't hurt them even if I wanted to."

"I believe this will bring you and Angelica closer than ever," Granny confided.

Adonis offered her a small smile. "I don't have the flight of fancy I had as a child. I know I've missed my chance. I should have confessed to her years ago."

Granny grasped him by his forearm. "I think this is merely an infatuation. It is bright but fleeting. It will pass. And then you will be there for her."

Heeding her words, Adonis felt his pulse quicken.

"You must understand," she continued. "Angelica is drifting. Have faith that she will find her way to you. This is a test. Hold fast to your love."

"You talk as sly as the Devil," Adonis said, leaning against the fence. "I don't think there could be any truth in your words."

Granny turned and walked away without a second glance back.

43 The Call of the Sons

Beneath the branches of the oak tree, drenched in moonlight, Angelica rested next to Aris, her head on his bare chest, their legs entwined.

"It's past midnight," she murmured, "but the owls are still watching over us. They must be starving by now."

Aris turned them over, spooning Angelica and pulling her back against his chest. He pressed a kiss to the soft back of her neck. "I'm starving, too." He punctuated his point by nipping gently at her neck.

She pulled his hand over her chest, cupping her breast with it. "I love how you wrap your entire body around me. The way you pull me back against you."

Aris groaned, biting at her neck. "I can't get enough of you."

Angelica stayed silent for a few minutes, enjoying the weight of Aris behind her. "You must know how much I've wanted you. I would have been yours the moment we met. Why did you resist me so hard?"

Aris nuzzled her shoulder. "It was the most difficult thing I've ever had to do in my life."

"But why? Men are supposed to be the hunters."

Aris stretched his neck, resting his chin on her shoulder. "I've never felt for someone like I have for you. It frightened me. You frighten me."

Angelica stared off into the distance.

"Yet," Aris continued, "I felt the most powerful urge to care for you. Something quite odd to feel for a stranger. It shook me. I didn't understand it."

She kissed his hand that was pressed against her chest. "I thought I'd make a fool of myself chasing after you."

"I only had enough willpower to stop myself from coming after you—but refusing you was beyond my control."

"I thought you were waiting for something, Aris."

"In a way. At first, I wanted to run away. Uri and John stopped me. Then, I wanted to see if your attraction was strong enough."

"What do you mean?"

"To rise above our circumstances," Aris explained. "I didn't know if you just wanted me because I was new. Of course, I was worried about the same thing but in reverse."

Angelica laughed, thinking of Granny's similar worry. "My attraction for you grew, day by day. By the end of the first week, I was totally overwhelmed! The more I fought it, the faster I lost control. And making love with you is something I can't explain in words. Does that make my feeling for you clear?"

Aris opened his mouth, pressing his teeth into the soft skin of her shoulder. "No! I want more!"

She tilted her head to look back at him. "Do you feel anything half as much as what I feel for you? And don't lie to me—not with the owls watching overhead."

"More," he reassured her, pausing his kissing. "Much, much more! I'm not just attracted to you. I also care for you. I barely understand it myself. I love you beyond physical desire and sex! *Peran apo ton agapi erotan*—I love you beyond the flesh."

Above them, the two owls gazed at each other, as if they understood everything.

Angelica felt Aris lavish her shoulder with a kiss. "When I explained to Granny how I felt about you, she said the same thing… *agapi peran apo ton erotan… love beyond eros*. That's how I feel about you, as well."

They fell silent, Aris grinding harder against the small of her back. Tenderly, she rested her cheek on his upper arm.

"Why did you leave your family? What are you looking for? Just a beautiful woman?"

"All women are beautiful," Aris answered. "Everyone has their charm. But I didn't know what I was looking for until I met you. I had given up on finding true love. But I knew what

I didn't want! I did not want another empty heart, another selfish person in love with herself."

"And?" Angelica prompted.

"Then I found you. Everything I've ever wanted. Even your mind draws me to you like a magnet. My grandfather once said that winning a woman's heart meant nothing. Winning both the mind and the heart, you have a perfect love!" Aris laughed. "At the time, I brushed it off as nonsense. Now, I understand what he meant."

Aris wiled away the next day on the couch, basking in the remaining glow of Angelica's confession. A book rested unread in his lap as he watched Uri and John bicker over the backgammon board.

"You're never going to learn to play this game," Uri shouted. "You're so damn slow that I lose my concentration!"

"He beat you the last three days in a row," Aris teased while staring at the blank screen of his cell phone. "Makes you wonder who's teaching who."

"What I wonder is why you haven't switched on your phone," John snapped back. "It's not like you're expecting a call. Stop messing around and distracting me."

Aris waited until Uri's turn to switch on his phone. "You shouldn't blame others when you're losing. Besides, I am expecting a call… from my son, Gerry. I called him earlier, but he was too busy to talk."

When his phone rang, Aris put it on speaker and walked to the windows.

"Peter and I are both here," Gerry answered in lieu of a greeting.

"Are you both okay? How are the girls?"

"Everything is fine except the situation with you and Mum. That's very upsetting."

Uri and John froze, the dice clattering to a halt.

Turning his back on the window, Aris rested his rear on the ledge. "Forget about me and Mum. Ignore us."

"How can we? Every time you two talk, you rip each other apart. We were there. We heard your last phone exchange."

"I'm not there anymore," Aris replied, trying to downplay the situation. "We hardly talk, so we can't argue."

"Mum said you told her you weren't coming back," Peter said. "Are you coming home or not? We miss you. You're both our parents, and we love you both."

Aris clenched his jaw, hardening his voice at Peter's declaration. "Don't put me in the same league as your mother. She manipulates everybody. She's just playing you. If you heard our last conversation, you'd know she doesn't want me to come back."

"We did hear that," Gerry confirmed.

"She's filing for a divorce, which is fine. She wants all the properties, like her friend. But everything is in a trust, safeguarded for you and your kids," Aris explained, sighing from a sudden wave of exhaustion. "She says she doesn't want a worthless man like me. If she fights for more, she'll get nothing at all. So, there's nothing to worry about. She can't touch anything."

"You're agreeing to a divorce?" Gerry asked.

"Of course I am. I'm done with her."

"How is she going to live if you give her nothing?" Peter asked, concerned. "You're starting a battle that could rip the family apart. Is that what you want?"

"The men she flirts with will have to finance her. I'm not going to pay for other men to bed your mother."

"Come on, Dad," Gerry pleaded. "You can't just throw her out with nothing!"

Aris huffed. "I'm not leaving her with nothing. She has a trust I set up, enough to keep her very comfortable if she stays within her means."

"Who are you?" Peter roared over the phone. "She's our mum. You can't just throw her out. When she runs out of money, who do you think she'll turn to?"

Aris shrugged, unconcerned. "I told you, I already made provisions for her. She shouldn't be begging you for anything."

"Who's destroying the family now?" Gerry snarled.

"I see," Aris said, his voice frosty. "I thought she was lying when she said that you two didn't want me back."

Peter groaned. "You're so stubborn. You're not even listening to us. Maybe Mum's right. Maybe we are better off without you. Maybe it's best you never come back!"

Still huddled over the backgammon board, Uri and John exchanged worried glances.

"You don't want me back," Aris spat bitterly. "Fine, I won't come home. She's clearly poisoned you against me. What's there to even come back to?"

Gerry sighed. "We didn't mean it like that, Dad."

"It might be the best solution," Peter said.

Aris tensed, tightening his grip on the window ledge. "Don't worry. I've moved past your mum. I'll move past you, too. You're both grown up now. I can't worry about you forever. You can take care of yourselves."

Peter lashed out. "You've lost it, old man. You—"

"Goodbye, boys," Aris interrupted, his tone sharp. "Call me when you have something positive to say. Otherwise, don't bother!"

Aris ended the call. Within seconds, his phone was ringing again. Seeing Peter's name flashing on the screen, Aris hesitated. He glanced over at John and Uri, who both nodded in encouragement.

"They are your sons," John whispered.

Reluctantly Aris answered and put it on speaker again.

Peter's voice was deep and harsh across the line. "Don't you dare hang up on us. You said you'd be back in a few months. It's been nearly a year. You've been galivanting around the world while the family has been falling apart."

"You always said we were your priority," Gerry added. "Your children, your family. Where are you to save your family now? We're not taking sides. We're in this together, equally."

Aris took a moment to try and breathe through his mounting fury. "I gave you everything, and your mother wants to take it all away. I am nothing like her."

"What do you expect from us, Dad?" Gerry mumbled. "She is our mother!"

"I always told you to love her no matter what, but telling me that you see us as being equal is a spit in the face of everything I've done for you. You've questioned my devotion and betrayed my sacrifices. I'm done!"

"We are grown up and can take care of ourselves," Peter shouted back. "You should worry about yourself and your wife… that is, if you still want to have a wife."

Aris bit the inside of his cheek, giving himself a moment to control his voice. "You know I don't respond to threats. In case you failed to notice, your mother was hardly a wife. She wasn't subtle with her extramarital affairs."

"We aren't threatening you," Peter retorted. "We're just telling you how it is."

Gerry laughed, soft and anxious. "You're losing it, Dad."

"This is embarrassing," Peter continued. "I don't care if you divorce. Maybe Mum's right. Maybe you never coming back is for the best."

"Great! I can do that for you, no problem. Don't bother calling again," Aris exclaimed, heart pounding in his chest as he ended the call.

Uri hesitated a moment before breaking the silence. "I don't think I want children after that."

"Children are a treasure," John said, "but they have their moments. As we all do. They were just venting. They clearly love and miss you."

Aris slumped down, the conversation playing over in his head. "I've never raised my voice with the boys before. We've argued, but always with good intentions. This was not the same."

"We all lose it from time to time," John soothed.

"Maybe the boys are right. Maybe they are better off without me." Aris took a calming breath. "Everything I have is in their name. I taught them all I could. They can take care of themselves. They don't need me anymore."

John and Uri allowed Aris to continue to work through this on his own.

"Maybe I needed the children more than they needed me. I'm sure they will do well without me," Aris began, chewing his words thoughtfully. He meandered over to the door. "I'm going for a walk. I need to get out for a bit."

Uri waited until he couldn't hear Aris's footsteps anymore. "That's what I'm afraid of," he finally said. "Family is not always rosy. I'm getting a divorce the moment I get home. I don't want to be chained in marriage. I don't want children sucking the tits I want to suck and then growing up to tell me what to do!"

John chuckled. "When we decided to travel, I thought the time away would strengthen our marriages. It seems the opposite is true."

<hr>

Uri sat across from Aris, the morning light soft as they ate breakfast. John was nearby on the couch.

Uri kept glancing at Aris, his jaw flexing as he tried to find the right words. "Aris," he finally began. "You have to free yourself from your motto of 'family and love above all'."

Aris grunted, barely glancing over before focusing back on his food.

"Your sons will still love you, and you will still love your sons," Uri plodded forward. "Epi told me of your habit of putting your family before your own desires. But you can't keep drinking from a broken glass. Even careful drinkers will get cut. You gave your family everything. It's time to free yourself from family obligations."

Aris stood, moving away to clean his dishes in the kitchen sink.

"You keep company with this village's children," Uri called after Aris as he headed to the door. "You can't force your motto onto everyone. Time to face the truth. Families break all the time. People learn to move on."

Aris left without saying a word.

Uri looked over at John, crestfallen.

John frowned like he tasted something sour. "You may be right, Uri, but you can't change deep-rooted values so quickly. It will take time."

"Well, someone had to tell him the truth and wake him up."

John shook his head. "You forget Aris is fighting on two fronts now—his crumbling family and his love for Angelica. They're warring in his mind and soul. Aris will come out of this, in time. He'll find his way."

⸺ ❖ ⸺

Gerry slipped into Peter's office and closed the door behind him. He sat at the large round table near the windows. Reclining, he propped his legs on the table and waited for his brother to finish what he was working on.

Finally, Peter got up and walked around to where Gerry sat, hitching a leg up and perching on the corner.

"What was so urgent that we needed to talk during work?"

Gerry frowned, picking at the seam of his trousers. "We should call Dad and apologise for yesterday."

Peter shifted uneasily. "We should leave him be."

"We were too harsh on him. Why would he come back after the way we treated him?"

"Dad can decide for himself."

"Would you want to come back to Mum's nagging and arrogance?" Gerry asked. "Not to mention her dalliances with other men."

"He can come back without being with her. You heard him. He's ready to divorce her now."

"And we gave him a perfect reason to not come back at all," Gerry retorted, glaring at Peter. "Dad was right. Mum twisted us around until we took it out on him. We were fools."

"No, we were not!" Peter replied sharply. "Besides, what good would it be to call him? You know he hates being told what to do. His pride always gets in the way."

"What would you do at his age if your family suddenly turned against you? What does he have to come back to?"

Gerry took a breath before continuing. "Our sister doesn't speak to Dad. Mum just wants to bleed him dry to pay for her lifestyle. The more I think about it, the more I realise we crossed a line yesterday."

Peter considered his brother's words carefully. "Maybe, but Dad should have divorced Mum a long time ago. They're both to blame. You're being too easy on him!"

Gerry lurched to his feet. "Just think about it from his perspective. He gave us everything and kept nothing for himself. Then we battered him, levelling him with mum. If it was me, I'd be raging, too."

"No," Peter snapped, jerking to his feet and stepping up to Gerry. "This matter must end. We were right yesterday. Dad needs to divorce Mum and give her whatever she needs to make this madness stop."

"We were wrong," Gerry muttered. "Wouldn't you expect more from your sons? Hell, I would. Dad deserves better."

Peter shrugged. "Maybe we went too far, but now this is affecting us as well. Dad shouldn't have left without straightening out this mess. He can't just disappear on us."

Gerry sighed. "I'm telling you. We need to be the ones to reach out and apologise. You know how his pride can make him stubborn. I think we've hurt him more than he's willing to admit."

"No, we should give him some time. We're all upset right now, but maybe what we said will spur Dad into action. He probably won't even answer our calls at the moment, knowing him."

"Then we should go and speak to him in person."

Peter chuckled. "Go where? We have no idea where he is."

"The country code he called from is for Greece."

"Where, though? Greece is massive. Not to mention there are hundreds of islands. No, let's not push him. We should wait."

Gerry sighed, moving to the door. He paused, looking back over his shoulder. "Fine, just a day or two and then let's try again."

44 The Sacred Marriage

In the oak tree, two white owls shifted uneasily on a branch, their feathers ruffling with their movements. Below them, in the faint moonlight, Aris and Angelica lay together, Aris dragging his hand up and down her arm.

"We are both very quiet tonight."

"Yes, but even the silence with you is wonderous," Angelica reassured him. "This is our sacred time and we can spend it together however we want."

Aris turned on his side, facing Angelica. He lifted her hand, daintily kissing her fingers. "I'm sorry, my mind is like poison these last few days."

"You don't have to talk, my love. I don't care what we do, as long as we do it together." Angelica leaned forward to meet him with a kiss. "I only hate when we must part."

Looping an arm around her waist, Aris rolled over and pulled Angelica on top of him. He began to caress her breasts, cupping them gently. He tucked his head close to them, whispering, "My gorgeous twins, you seem to be fuller tonight. Earlier, too, I noticed you were more sensitive."

Listening to Aris, a playful smile bloomed across Angelica's face.

He continued to tease her breasts, captivated by them. "They are so similar. I can't remember which one I named Carnation, and which one is Rose."

"That one's Rose," Angelica said, jutting her chin to the one in Aris's right hand.

Aris dipped forward and pressed a kiss to her neck, sliding his hand down her back. He dug his fingers into the flesh of her bottom. "And these?"

"Rhodopy and Olympus, the mountains."

"Hmm, they seem to have grown as well."

Angelica giggled at his antics. She stood up and picked her clothes up off the ground. "We should go. It will be sunrise soon." She pulled on her dress and started down the hill.

"I feel like staying here on my own for a bit longer," Aris called behind her.

"All right, but I should go. I need to be home before daybreak." She returned and kissed him once more before heading back to the village on her own.

— ◇ —

Angelica sat on her front porch, Granny and Despo nearby. The sun was strong and warm. The low murmur of conversation pulled her attention to the road where Aris was walking with John and Uri.

They called out a greeting, telling the women they were on their way to the café. As they moved on, Aris glanced at Angelica, then the sky. She waited until he was looking at her before she nodded.

Beside her, Granny huffed but didn't say anything until Despo went inside to get lunch started.

"You're meeting again tonight, aren't you?" Granny asked.

Angelica shifted in her seat, glancing inside to make sure her mother wasn't nearby.

"Have you made a decision yet?" Granny pressed. "You can't keep pushing this off. Soon, it will be too late to have an abortion and you won't have a choice but to carry it to term."

Angelica frowned, Granny's warning chaffing at her. She abruptly stood and stalked into the house.

— ◇ —

Aris shifted to the side, pulling out of Angelica but held her close as they rode out the lingering twitches of their orgasms. The leaves of the oak rustled above them while they caught their breath.

273

Aris rubbed her back, light and circular. "What are you thinking about? And don't lie."

"I'm just listening."

"To what? My heart?"

"No!" Angelica replied, playfully shoving at him. "Tonight is very special."

"What do you mean?" Aris asked, shifting closer.

"Tonight's crescent moon is making way for July—the night of the nine Greek muses."

Aris squinted through the tree branches to see the moon. "You're right. So, what is special about tonight for the muses?"

"This is the night that they transform to come to Earth. They become frogs or owls, flowers or the wind. Sometimes even a human. Then, they get married in secret."

Aris shifted closer, resting his head on her shoulder. "What are you listening to, then?"

"The wind. It's asking questions about you."

Chuckling in amusement, Aris prodded her. "Do you still hear the wind? The muses? Tell me what they're saying."

"Don't ask me," Angelica retorted. "I must not tell."

"Wait," Aris stopped her. "I hear them, too. It's so clear now."

"What are they saying?" Angelica asked.

Aris smiled, the skin around his eyes creasing in mirth. "The muses are telling me that we should leave our world and join them. We should marry each other tonight as they do, or they will steal you away!"

"But we need a church, a priest, and witnesses!"

Aris waved his arm out, gesturing at the bright moon and the glinting stars above them. "This is our church, the moon is our priest, and the muses are our witnesses."

Angelica smiled up at the sky, the moon like a diamond in the night.

"Can't you see? This sacred wedding will bind our hearts and souls."

She kissed him on the mouth. "You are especially romantic tonight!"

Aris shifted to his knees, pulling Angelica to kneel opposite him. "The muses say we must do it now before they have to depart."

"Okay, let me pull my dress on."

"No, the muses are nude as well."

They clasped their hands as if in prayer. Aris leaned down until his forehead was against Angelica's. "We only need to touch our foreheads together."

They were silent for a few minutes until, finally, Aris moved back and kissed her face. "It is done! The muses are happy!" Aris sweetly dropped a kiss on her lips and she tugged him closer, deepening it.

Angelica pulled away first. "I feel like I'm floating away. It's like we're bound to each other by the most sacred of vows."

"Come, get dressed. Let's walk with the muses tonight," Aris prompted.

Once fully dressed, they circled around their tree to the edge of a cliff on the far side of the hill. Below them, water washed against the sheer cliffside. They stood, silently enjoying the warmth of their embrace until Aris shifted his weight and said, "I'll walk you back to the village."

— ◇ —

Angelica brushed the brilliant white coat of her horse, pressing her cheek against Snowy's, lost in the churn of her thoughts.

Granny approached, recognisable from the shuffle of her step. "You spend so much time with this horse, and yet she still refuses to let you ride her."

Angelica shrugged. "We have a connection. She understands me! When the time comes, she'll let me ride her."

Granny shifted. "The day is already mostly gone. Are you really going to spend the rest of it here with Snowy?"

On the other side of the fence, Adonis emerged from his house and noticed the two women in conversation. He crouched, moving swiftly across the yard to get closer without being noticed.

"I feel like you're losing yourself," Granny confessed, running her fingers through Angelica's hair. "I'm afraid it's my fault since I revealed the love secret to you. All this pain is like blood on my hands."

Angelica ignored her, focusing on the comfort she felt while taking care of her horse.

"How late are you, Angelica?" Granny's question cut through Angelica's thoughts.

Adonis tensed.

Tilting her head in thought, Angelica continued to groom Snowy. "About six weeks, maybe. Not that it matters."

Adonis bit his lip at her flippant tone.

Granny counted her fingers, calculating. "So, you're probably around nine weeks along."

Angelica seemed unbothered.

Out of sight, Adonis's face flared red hot.

"Are you going to tell him?"

"No," Angelica snapped, rounding on Granny. "He has problems of his own right now. I don't want him to make any decisions just because I'm pregnant."

Granny raised an eyebrow. "You can't hide it forever. Eventually you'll start to show. What are you going to do?"

Angelica turned back to the horse. "I'll figure it out."

"You can't be thinking of keeping the baby, are you?"

"What do you mean?" Angelica replied without hesitation. "I'm a grown woman. I can take care of a child."

Adonis shifted closer to the fence, holding his breath.

"You are not married," Granny insisted. "You cannot believe that keeping this baby is a good idea."

Angelica glared at her. "I would kill to keep this baby."

Adonis dropped his head.

"You're still just a child yourself!"

"And you're just an old, provincial woman. You don't understand."

"I don't understand?" Granny scoffed, her voice sharp. "I'm still paying for the same mistake you're about to make."

45 Granny's Sin

"It was during the war," Granny began. "I was younger than you but just as spirited. One day, during an air raid, one of the Russian pilots was shot out of the sky and crashed just outside the village where the small church is now.

"My mother was called in to treat the pilot's injuries, and I went to help. That's how I met Dimitri. My mother and I took turns nursing him back to health until he regained consciousness. Then I was left in charge of his day-to-day care."

Granny paused, blowing her dripping nose in a handkerchief. "He was so much livelier than me and so handsome. Even while injured, he was positive, playful, and teasing. He was always laughing! And we fell in love. God knows, we both tried to resist. But we couldn't, so we fell. And we made love, whenever and wherever we could. I've never told anyone the full story until you. Please, take this to your grave."

Angelica nodded, breathless.

"We somehow managed to keep it a secret," Granny continued. "No one witnessed us together. Or at least, that's what we thought. And then he came to me, begging, 'Run away with me.' But I told him I couldn't. He didn't care, so I finally had to tell him the truth—what I had been avoiding telling him for weeks. You see, a man had to pull Dimitri out of the wreckage of his plane—a man that was caught in the explosion after the fuel line caught fire and ignited the engine. A man who was now bedridden. A man who was my husband."

Angelica gasped. "Grandfather?"

Granny nodded.

Adonis slumped down against the fence, feeling both guilty for again eavesdropping, and overwhelmed at Granny's confession.

"When I told Dimitri, he broke down, beating his chest and pulling his hair. He was like a feral beast. It took everything I had to stop him from hurting himself. For the first time, he scared me."

Horrified by the description, Angelica shivered just imagining the scene.

From his position beyond the fence, Adonis understood Dimitri's anguish perfectly.

Granny dabbed at her eyes. "Overnight, the Dimitri I knew disappeared. His shining red hair burnt out to white ash. He stopped laughing. He couldn't even sleep. That was when I realised," Granny confessed. She grabbed Angelica's arms and made sure she was paying attention. "I was pregnant with Dimitri's child, and with my husband still bedridden, there was no way it could be confused as his."

Nodding, Angelica finally saw the depth of Granny's despair. She pulled Granny into a long hug, nearly breaking into tears herself.

Granny stepped out of the hug, offering Angelica a small smile. "It wasn't long before Dimitri realised I was pregnant and he demanded to know if it was his. I found I couldn't lie to him, so I told him the truth.

"He begged me again, 'Now you have to come with me,' but I still refused. It was then that I recognised I had backed myself into an impossible situation. No matter what I decided to do, I would end up hurting everyone I loved, including Dimitri."

Angelica bit her nails, trying to stave off her anxiety. "What did you do?"

Unnoticed by the two women, Adonis pressed closer to the fence, eager to know himself.

"I told him very plainly, 'I love my husband, and he loves me too.' It was true. I loved them both. I simply could not choose between them. I was drawn to both of them!"

"You were?" Angelica prompted.

Adonis nodded, eager to hear what happened next.

"With my mind clouded and no idea how to proceed, I confided in my mother. She was furious, of course, and despite her beliefs, she pleaded with me to get an abortion."

"You killed your baby!" Angelica blustered.

Granny threw her a heated glare. "No."

Adonis frowned.

"Soon, your grandfather recovered and discovered I was pregnant. One night, during dinner at which the whole family and Dimitri were present, your grandfather bravely announced, 'By my calculation, our baby is very late'.

"I was so shocked I couldn't speak. Except for my mother and Dimitri, the family was relieved. They thought my husband Vasilis was fooled, but my torment was consuming me. Of course, naturally, Dimitri and Vasilis became close friends. They both admired and respected each other greatly."

Angelica leaned in closer. "Did Grandfather know it was Dimitri's baby?"

"Your grandfather had a sharp mind, but an even greater heart. The pregnancy was difficult, and my mother fell so ill she couldn't stand. Your grandfather looked after me. He nursed me day and night, taking better care than when I was pregnant with his own children.

"Dimitri insisted on staying until after the baby was born, and while Vasilis took care of me, Dimitri worked our fields and looked after the animals. He wanted to make sure your grandfather was free to help me without worry. Their devotion to me brought them even closer."

"What happened to the baby?" Angelica asked.

Tears pooled and spilled over Granny's cheeks. "The baby was born a healthy boy. He had ginger hair and blue eyes—the spitting image of Dimitri."

Angelica felt her heart break open at the truth. Hidden beyond the fence, Adonis's jaw dropped.

Granny sighed, pulling herself together. "Your grandfather cradled the boy in front of everyone, including Dimitris, and proudly said, 'He looks just like my great-grandfather'."

Angelica smiled, overcome by admiration for her grandfather. "That is a truly honourable act."

"Your grandfather turned to me, showing off the strength of the babe's grip. 'Look how strong he is!' he proclaimed to me. 'He must be a descendent of Alexander the Great. He is destined to be a military force.'

"I remember being overwhelmed by this generosity and I pulled him into a fierce kiss and poured all my love for him into it. He filled me with so much love. It burst my soul, how much I loved him."

"And Dimitri?" Angelica prompted.

"I loved him, too. But it was different. I still can't explain it. Your grandfather knew how important he was to me, Vasilis even asked Dimitri to be the godfather."

"He did? Then what happened to the boy?"

"Dimitri suggested we name the boy Angelov, after me, which your grandfather happily agreed to. Dimitri spent most of his time with the baby. The afternoon before Dimitri was due to leave, Vasilis invited him around for a final coffee. Your grandfather and his generous heart had one final surprise for us."

"What was it?" Angelica asked.

Granny smiled at her granddaughter. "He turned to me and said, 'We are already struggling to raise two children, and I'm not sure we can afford a third. I think we should offer Angelov up for adoption... give him a chance in a place where he can have an education. A future'... of course, I was shocked, and I immediately protested. Who could ever care for a baby as well as their mother? Dimitri was right next to me, face red and jaw clenched, ready to defend me to the bitter end."

"Did they fight?" Angelica asked.

Granny nodded, bursting into tears. A small, wan smile glimmered on her face.

"I don't understand. You nod, but you seem happy your baby was given away. I could never do that."

"Your grandfather knew Dimitri was the father. That's why Vasilis offered him the boy. This way, the child would at least be with his real father. He told us that if we agreed to the adoption, then the boy would have his blessing."

Granny choked on tears, barely able to continue. "I m-m-made the choice, in the end, and told Dimitri to love the boy as his own."

Angelica wrapped Granny in a hug, giving a safe haven to shed her tears, not daring to interrupt.

"Of course, Dimitri accepted. He was always loud and happy, freely joking with everyone and everything. Especially after a few glasses of alcohol. So when we celebrated the adoption, it was no different. He told us that if his son ever returned to the village that we should know him as Vasilis, after your grandfather, and Angelov after me, and Dimitrov after his godfather. He lifted the boy up in front of all of us, shouting, 'General Vasilis Angelov Dimitrov, reporting for duty!'"

"Where is Uncle Angelov now?" Angelica whispered.

A shadow passed over Granny's face. "I've never seen or heard from my baby, or Dimitri, again. Our love was pure and erotic. It consumed my very being until nothing else mattered. I have still never experienced anything like it."

She blew her nose and coughed to clear her throat. "But I also loved your grandfather. He was a great man. His love for me was as constant as the tides. He understood me better than anyone. He was both a husband and a friend. Until the day he died, he never complained about the baby or Dimitri. Even though I hurt him, he still loved me. I was lucky to have your grandfather. He knew I loved him with all my heart. And I still love him, even though he's gone."

Angelica leaned against the fence, letting the story sink in. "You've carried this cross for a long time, but it seems as though everything worked out."

"Giving up my baby after such a risky pregnancy, I assure you, was a thousand times more painful than an abortion. I can only hope that I will see my boy one day. But I'm running out of time."

"At least he's alive!" Angelica said, trying to be supportive.

"I'm still not sure if I made the right choice."

Angelica caressed Granny's face. "I don't have a husband. I don't even know if I will ever get married, and I know I have upset my parents. My own happiness feels like it's drifting away on sour water. But I promise you, I will never abort my child, and I will never give my child away."

Hearing Angelica's declaration, Adonis's face pinched in concentration.

"I understand. This is your decision, and I will support whatever you do," Granny promised. "I'm going for a walk. I need some time alone."

"I think I'll stay with Snowy for a bit."

Beyond the fence, Adonis sank to the ground, clutching his head, buzzing both with Angelica's determination to keep the child and Granny's secret.

46 Silent Talk and Father

Edging into the early hours of the morning, Aris lounged with Angelica under what had become their sacred tree. He rolled to his side, her leg slung over his hip as she caressed his back. Her touch was light and slow as it travelled down to his ass, causing him to groan.

"We speak less and less every time we meet," she said, kissing his shoulder.

"No! We are speaking more."

Angelica pushed him down onto his back, resting her head on his chest. "How is that?"

Aris danced his fingers along her soft skin. "We absorb each other through our senses."

"But we don't actually talk."

"We speak with our bodies. We smell and touch and feel and look. This is the way lovers communicate," Aris explained, his fingers climbing the slope of her buttocks. "We can't sense each other as much when we use words. They interfere."

She circled his nipple with the tip of her finger. "You're right. Words of the mouth block the words of the soul."

"The unsaid is sometimes more powerful."

"What do you mean?"

Aris dragged his eyes over the growing curves of her body. "Your breasts seem to be swelling by the day. And you keep growing around the middle like you're eating for two. Has your appetite grown?"

"My only craving is for you." She laughed, deftly changing the subject. "How first impressions can be deceiving. When I first saw you, I thought you were a handsome drifter—attractive but dangerous."

Aris nuzzled Angelica's head. "When I learned you were married, I thought you were a male chauvinist for leaving your family to travel."

"Logical conclusion," Aris whispered.

"And yet, everything about you from your smile to your words made me feel such a strange and strong attraction. You grew on me!"

Aris tangled his fingers in her thick hair. "Like any man, I was attracted to your beauty."

The flapping of the pair of owls landing on a nearby branch drew their attention. Aris waited for them to settle before continuing.

"I confess, I came to this village looking to find the love secret. But instead, I found you."

A smile burst across Angelica's face. "So, it wasn't love at first sight?"

"Most times, love at first sight is only physical attraction. Both men and women are driven by their hormones to mate. Sometimes, even a woman's cycle can affect this." He dropped a soft kiss on her forehead head. "Unfortunately, the majority of such cases don't last. Soon, they discover their personalities are totally incompatible."

"Now I understand my girlfriends at university," Angelica said. "Every few weeks they were in love with a new boy. They swore it was the real thing. Then, a few weeks later, they didn't even want to speak to the guy."

Aris pulled Angelica in for a kiss. "This is why our love is the strongest—the kind that lasts forever. When two people are attracted to the personality first and appearance second, mutual attraction grows as they get to know each other's character, personalities, and faults. This kind of love will always outlast physical attraction.

"You see marriages of forty, fifty, sixty years, and they still love their partner as much as when they first fell in love. Even when they can't have sex, they still kiss and cuddle for hours. Their love outlasts their physical appearance. I'm generally not a jealous person, but I truly envy such couples. I am even proud of them."

Angelica gazed up at the sky. "I agree. While I do think you are handsome, I like you as a whole person."

"People are sometimes surprised when a beautiful woman is with an ugly man or vice versa. But it's because they were attracted to each other's personalities. They grew on each other."

The owls hooted, calling the couple's attention up to the gently brightening sky.

Angelica sat up. "Our guardian angels are warning us that it's time to go!"

⸺ ◇ ⸺

Aris perched on the bench of a small boat, his fishing pole held loosely. A rhythmic splashing drew his attention. He frowned as another boat approached, recognising the occupant as Manolios. Aris noticed the man's oars slapping the water hard. He clenched his jaw, preparing himself for an irate father.

Manolios propelled his boat next to Aris, reaching across the water to grip the other boat and bring them closer together.

Aris greeted Manolios with a small nod.

Turning to face him, Manolios leaned closer. "Despo said she talked to you already. It seems you've ignored her pleas."

Aris glanced at Manolios and reeled in a bit of his line.

"Now, I learn that Angelica is already pregnant," Manolios continued, eyes wide and alert. "She's running out of time to still have options. I know it's hard to lose a pregnancy, but sometimes we have to make painful decisions."

Aris tensed, squeezing his jaw as he continued to stare at Manolios.

Manolios yanked the boats tight together, water sloshing between them. "I know how hard you tried to resist Angelica, and I respect you for that. However, I will not stand by and allow my daughter's life to be ruined by an unwelcome pregnancy."

Manolios watched Aris's lips pinch. "She can't keep this child. You must convince her to abort it before it's too late. Soon, you will be going, and Angelica will have to live with the stain of an unplanned pregnancy for the rest of her life."

Aris's face burned.

"We know you love Angelica," Manolios continued, nodding to himself. "That's why we're appealing to you. Don't let her ruin her life over some fling. You are mature and experienced. It's your responsibility to not take advantage of her innocence. Tell Angelica what to do. She'll listen to you."

Aris squared his shoulders, his gaze firmly on Manolios. "I understand your concern and appreciate your tolerance, but you are wrong. Angelica isn't some fling for me. My love for her is once in a lifetime."

Manolios squeezed the side of the boat hard, veins bulging in his hands.

"This is Angelica's choice," Aris said, his voice deep and calm. "She is smart and independent, and I won't betray her by taking this choice away. I will support whatever decision she makes, no matter who tries to come in my way."

Snarling, Manolios shoved the boats apart. His chest heaving, he hissed at Aris. "If I have to deal with this myself, I will. Don't test me, Aris. I've turned against my own brother in the name of honour. Do what must be done before you regret it."

Digging his oars deep into the water, Manolios swiftly rowed back to shore.

Aris watched until Manolios reached land before he set his fishing pole aside and made his own way back to the dock.

Tying the boat off at the pier, he grabbed his catch, but was almost immediately approached by a group of children.

"You caught so many today," one of the young boys admired.

"You can have whatever you want, except those red ones," Aris replied.

Nearby, Zoe sat by herself watching all of this in silence.

Aris approached, the red fish dangling from a length of fishing line. He squatted down next to her. "I'm sorry, I know I let you down. I have a lot on my mind and I needed to be alone."

"You promised to take me horse riding, and then you went fishing," Zoe whined. "You even refused to take me fishing with you. You didn't even look back at me when I was calling you."

"I didn't hear you! I told you. I've been distracted."

Zoe looked at him, her face sorrowful. "You made me look like a fool."

"I am so sorry," he replied, hanging his head. "You know you are my best friend. Bear with me, please."

"I understand. Sometimes, my mind gets busy and I want to be alone, too." Rising to her feet, Zoe jabbed a finger at him. "But I won't forgive you if you do it again! And you still have to take me horse riding!"

Aris smiled, patting Zoe on the head. "Thank you for understanding."

Aris began to walk away.

Zoe shouted after him, "You owe me double now though! What about a horse ride later today?"

"Double, it is. But not today. I'm not good company," he called back to her over his shoulder. "Go help the kids share the fish."

Her footsteps thumped on the wooden dock as he continued into the village, the red fish slapping against his thigh.

Shortly, he reached Angelica's house. The front door was open as usual. He poked his head inside. "Anyone home?"

Despo stepped out of the kitchen, drying her hands on a towel. "Of course, Aris. Come in."

He held out the fish, still wet from the ocean. "I promised Granny some red fish for soup."

Handing over his catch, Aris followed Despo into the kitchen. "Angelica will love to try making your fish soup. We all enjoyed it when you made some a while back. Even Manolios liked it, and he hates fish."

"Where are they? Manolios and Angelica?"

"My husband is working the fields. Angelica must be with Granny. She spends a lot of time with her and Snowy these days. Want me to tell them you're here?"

"No! Actually, I wanted to talk with you. Do you know what happened between Manolios and his brother?"

"I see you heard of that, too." Despo smiled. "There's not much to it. He shot his brother in the leg with a shotgun. It wasn't serious, as far as a bullet wound is concerned. Not even a limp. You've met him, actually. He was just here a few weeks ago. The pedlar with the fabric you bought for Zoe's new outfit, remember?"

"They don't even look alike!" Aris shifted, glancing down at Despo. "What did his brother do?"

"He refused to marry a girl he knocked up. As the older brother, Manolios felt punishing him was the only way to keep the family's honour." Despo shrugged. "That's just how it was in those days. Sit, would you like some coffee?"

"No, thank you," Aris quickly answered before backing out of the house and down the street.

47 Rosy's Story

Aris burrowed his nose in the soft hairs on the back of Angelica's neck. He sniffed her, enjoying her scent and how it mingled with the smell of the grass and the oak tree above them.

"You are unusually quiet tonight," he whispered. "You keep sighing."

"Hmm, I guess I feel a bit guilty. It's been weighing on me, recently. So much that I feel like I'm drowning."

"Did you lie to me about something?" Aris asked.

"No! I didn't, but we all have our secrets. I'm sure you do, too."

"That's true. We all have secrets. So why would you feel guilty?"

She sighed again. "I don't know if you truly love me."

"That's more of a concern than a reason to feel guilty."

"You don't understand."

Aris pressed a kiss into her shoulder. "Then, explain."

Angelica rubbed his arm that was tight across her belly. "I was losing my mind before, thinking that no matter what I did you would just reject me. So, that night outside your house, I used the love secret to make you fall in love with me."

Aris hid his smile in the curve of her neck. "So, you manipulated me into falling in love with you?"

"Yes… no. Maybe?"

"So, I'm a victim of the love secret? Because of this, you think I might not truly love you?"

"You have an idea what it can do. You spoke to Granny about it days before. Aren't you upset that I manipulated you?"

Aris erupted into a fit of laughter.

"Seriously," she persisted. "I really used the love secret on you."

Aris peppered her neck with kisses and pulled her tighter. "I might have suspected something."

"You don't understand!" Angelica insisted.

"I do, though."

"What could you possibly know?"

Aris hooked his chin over her shoulder. "It was May 8th the first time we kissed, and the moon was nearly full and very bright."

Angelica tried to turn, but Aris held her too tightly so she stopped struggling. "How do you know that?"

"Because I do! Anyway, it was too late for the love secret. I was already in love with you." He bit her neck gently. "But it did help break my resistance. I completely surrendered to you."

"What? Did you speak with Granny?" Angelica asked, surprised.

"I didn't know who told you the secret, or if you even knew what you were doing. But I knew Granny lied to me when I asked her about Rosy."

"You're messing with me."

"No, I am not!"

"Don't lie to me!"

"I'm not."

"What do you know? And how do you know it?"

"Long story."

"But if you knew what I was doing, why didn't you stop me?"

"I didn't want you to stop. Not that I could, anyway! You were a force. Not even a god could stop you. It was breathtaking seeing you like that."

"While I don't like being played a fool, at least now I know you really love me and not just because I used the love secret."

He teased her neck with his teeth. "I don't know about that! I might have loved you, but the love secret allowed me to welcome it."

"This removes the biggest question in my mind," Angelica said, relieved.

"I'm sure that the love secret will never work on me again."

Angelica shifted in his arms, getting more comfortable. "I've been wondering, how do you know about Rosy?"

"She was a lovely old lady from my hometown. What do you know about her?"

"She was my great-grandmother. No one else knows this, so keep it to yourself."

"Tell me more about Rosy's story."

Angelica shook her head. "First, tell me how you knew about the secret. Do you know how to use it? And did you use it on me?"

Wiggling her hips provocatively, Angelica turned around to face him, then pulled him closer until her breasts were pressed tight against his chest.

"I first heard about it when I was around nine," he said. "When I asked my grandparents, they laughed and sent me to ask Rosy, who knew the love secret."

"Did you find her?"

"Yeah, she was six feet under in her tomb."

Angelica giggled. "What did she do? Speak to you from the grave?"

"I thought Grandfather was messing with me. The priest heard me cursing. When he asked what was wrong and I explained, his comment made me realise that the love secret really existed."

"So, you don't know it?"

"Patience," Aris chided. "Years later, one of Rosy's granddaughters arrived. She wanted to pay her respects at Rosy's grave. When no one else was brave enough to take her there, I offered to show her the way. When we arrived, she dug a small hole and buried a letter right next to the tombstone. Then, she prayed and left. I never read the letter. I assumed it was a wish. But now I wonder if it had been the love secret."

Aris rested his head on her bosom as she carved her fingers through his hair.

"On the walk back to town, she asked me how I knew where Rosy's grave was, and I told her I went there looking for clues about the love secret. I told her I used to help carry Rosy's groceries."

"Did the granddaughter believe you?"

"Hush! The girl told me Rosy often spoke fondly of a boy in the village—the only one she liked—and that his name was Aris. She asked if that was me."

Aris pressed a small kiss in the valley between Angelica's breasts. "The girl told me that Rosy was impressed by me and that, because of that, she wanted to pass the secret on to me. You see, she couldn't have children of her own, so she wanted to pass it on to someone her grandmother had trusted. She started explaining how it worked to me, what to do with my hands, what to do with my eyes, and what to look for."

"Carry on, Aris!"

Angelica's face was bright and open, a smile stretching across it. Aris couldn't resist sucking a kiss on her breast again. "We were interrupted by her husband before she could finish. She promised to stop by the next day to finish, but I never saw her again."

"So, you don't know the rest of the love secret?"

Aris shook his head. "That's all I know."

"That's why you were convinced the love secret was real. You just didn't know how to use it."

"I knew some of the early steps or signs."

"Did you come to our village looking for the love secret?"

"Yes!"

"Why would you need it?" Angelica asked.

"I'm not sure. Maybe I thought it would help me find true love. What I really needed was to find the right person, which I found in you. What I wanted and what I needed were two different things."

"Would you have used it on me?"

"It depends on how it works, but yes, probably." He raised his gaze to the horizon. "But then again, maybe not. I was looking for true love beyond eros, what I believe you and I have now. If I used the love secret, I would never know for sure."

Angelica sank her teeth into his shoulder, making him jerk. "The love secret couldn't make me love you more than I already do."

"Will you tell it to me?" Aris prompted.

Angelica laughed. "No way. I promised to only tell one person."

"Well, I'm one person so it's fine!"

"Yes, but I can only tell a person I absolutely trust."

"You don't trust me?"

"Never."

"You know, I have all your long-lost family's contact details from my travels. I might not give them to you unless you reveal the love secret to me."

"Blackmail?" she cackled. "That would automatically rule you out!"

48 The Fight

Adonis waited outside his stables, two horses saddled and grazing nearby.

Zoe came flying across the field, Aris trailing behind her, and headed directly to the large black horse closest to Adonis.

"I'll ride Blacky!" she demanded.

Aris reached past her and took hold of both sets of reins. "I promised to take you horse-riding, but not for you to ride Blacky. Can you even handle him?"

Zoe petted the horse's thick neck. "Of course, I can. He's my best friend. He loves me!"

"I thought I was your best friend."

Zoe smirked. "After you, of course. You are number one!"

Aris lifted her onto the other horse, and they cantered through the fields. He laughed at all of her stories.

When they stumbled across Manolios, mending the small wooden bridge over the stream, Zoe pulled her horse to a stop. "Hello, Manolios."

Aris dismounted, handing Blacky's reins to Zoe. "Wait for me further down. I need to talk to Manolios."

Suspicious but obedient, Zoe nodded. "If you wanted to come out here to speak to him, you could have just told me."

She spurred the horses on, crossing the bridge and continuing for a distance before stopping again.

She looked back, narrowing her eyes at how Aris was hunched near Manolios as he worked on the bridge. "What could they possibly be talking about that they didn't want me to hear?"

— ◇ —

Manolios grabbed another nail, choosing to focus on his work instead of Aris, lining up the hammer and pounding the nail into place.

"I know about your brother," Aris announced. "Stop ignoring me and listen."

Manolios stopped mid-swing, turning to look at Aris.

Aris refused to look away. "I respect and love your family, and this village, but I don't respond kindly to threats. Especially if they're directed against those I love very much."

Manolios closed his eyes. "Your actions show you respect nothing but your own pleasure."

Aris glared at him. "Stubbornness, pride, and archaic values are a potent mix that can turn anyone into a vicious animal. Open your eyes. Wake up!"

Standing abruptly, Manolios returned Aris's glare. "You're the one who needs to wake up. How dare you come into our home, abuse our hospitality, and tell me what to do!"

"I have my values, too. In this case, it is Angelica's choice. You should respect and support whatever decision she makes."

Manolios's face darkened. "You're one to lecture us on how to behave. You're rude and arrogant, disrespecting our values and beliefs. The best thing you can do for everyone's benefit is to leave our village immediately."

"I respect you, Manolios. But know that I would do anything for Angelica. I'd even kill for her. I will not warn you again."

Manolios tightened his grip on the hammer. "I will not hesitate to kill for my daughter and my family's honour. You better understand my warning."

Aris's eyes burned with conviction. "At the first hint of retaliation, I will strike first without hesitation. You have my word."

From her perch on Blacky, Zoe's attention turned back to the bridge at the raised voices. She watched, dread pooling in her stomach, as the two men faced each other like snakes coiled to strike.

Manolios's sunburned face was stiff. He took a step towards Aris.

Without hesitation, Aris stepped forward to meet him. "You asked me not to provoke you, but you've already pushed me too far. I won't warn you again. Leave Angelica alone."

Eyes widening in shock, Zoe leaned forward in the saddle. "They look like they're about to fight."

The two men remained poised to pounce, both their chests heaving.

Manolios could feel his blood burning. "We don't want a bastard in our family."

Aris shoved Manolios. "If Angelica decides to keep the baby, I will recognise the child under my name."

Rage erupted in Manolios's belly. He raised his hammer high over his head.

Seeing the attack about to happen, Zoe kicked her horse into a gallop. "Stop!" she yelled at them. "Stop!"

Aris grabbed Manolios's arm, stopping the hammer from caving in his head.

Manolios struck fast with his other hand, still aiming for Aris's head, but Aris slapped it to the side.

Aris twisted Manolios's arm, bending him to the breaking point until he was forced to drop his hammer.

"Stop it!" Zoe continued to scream, urging the horses to go faster.

The two men struggled across the footbridge, kicking Manolios's tools into the river.

Aris shoved him up against the rail. It snapped with a loud crack, unable to support both men's weight. They tumbled into the water, landing in a heap of limbs in the stream. Grappling, they stumbled across the streambed, continuing to lash out.

Zoe pulled the horses to a halt with a sharp tug of the reins. "What are you doing?" she demanded. "Stop this right now!"

With a grunt, Manolios lost his footing and dropped under the water.

"Aris, stop!" Zoe screamed. "Help Manolios!"

Aris plunged his arm under the water, grabbing Manolios by the arm and yanking him out. He dragged him from the stream and up onto the bank.

"Why are you fighting?" Zoe shouted, making Blacky and the other horse neigh and stomp their hooves.

Ignoring Zoe, Aris helped Manolios to sit up. "Just catch your breath."

"I said, why were you two fighting?" Zoe pushed.

Aris shrugged, refusing to look at her. "We weren't. The rail gave in. I tried to grab Manolios so he didn't fall over, but we both ended up falling in the water."

Zoe levelled a flat look at them. "I love you both, so I'll pretend I believe you."

Aris mounted Blacky, pulling up alongside Zoe. They turned the horses back to the village and kicked them into an easy trot.

Aris glared back at Manolios one last time before they rounded a bend and went out of sight.

Excited, Zoe asked, "Can we race now?"

"No!" Aris snapped. "We're going back. I need to change out of these wet clothes."

"Oh, come on. It's just a bit of water!"

Aris shook his head, feeling cornered by her accusation. "If we go too fast, we'll miss the view. Let's take our time getting back. We can continue to ride after I change."

"You'll be dry before we get back," Zoe argued.

49 Taste of Death

Aris leaned back against a small, windswept tree to find relief from the afternoon sun. Next to him, Anastasis peered through his binoculars every so often to keep track of his flock while his stallion grazed nearby on the short grass.

Having finished lunch, the two men sat in silence. Aris stretched out his legs, groaning at the burn of his muscles.

"Most look down on a shepherd's life, but we should probably be jealous of how peaceful it is. Even in villages such as this one, there is always some stress. Out here, none of that exists."

Anastasis smiled at his friend, nodding.

Aris turned his gaze to the wide horizon. "The sheep never fight or argue. There's no competition or jealousy or greed. Just peace, fresh air, and a breath-taking view. This is nature at its best."

Anastasis laughed. "You could join me and raise your own sheep. I can give you thirty percent of my flock for free."

Aris chuckled. "Very tempting!"

⸻ ◇ ⸻

Angelica stopped at the outskirts of the village, the widow a few feet away. She pulled the scarf tighter around her shoulders and stepped closer to the older woman.

"Why did you want to meet out here?" Angelica asked.

Korina tilted her head to the side. "Thought we could go on a walk. It's beautiful today and it's been ages since our last walk together."

"Your girls are more beautiful every day, just like their mother," Angelica flattered.

Korina scoffed. "I was never as beautiful as they are."

Angelica tried to keep up the pleasantries as they walked, but Korina hardly participated.

Angelica looked around, noticing for the first time how far they had strolled. "We're nearing the snake well. Do you still come here often?"

"Yes," Korina confessed, the smile slipping from her face. "I come and talk to my husband."

⟡

Anastasis bolted up, his binoculars held firmly to his face. "I don't believe it."

Aris leaned forward, a hand shading his eyes from the sun. "I don't see anything."

Anastasis adjusted the focus of his binoculars, his jaw clenched. "Angelica and the widow are together. Korina hates Angelica because she is loved and respected by the whole village."

Squinting, Aris could just make out the shape of two women off in the distance. "Are you sure it's Angelica with the widow?"

"Yes! They're walking towards the snake's well." He handed over his binoculars to Aris. "See for yourself."

"Where is the well?" Aris asked, grasping the lenses to his eyes.

Taking Aris by the chin, Anastasis angled his head slightly. "To your left, straight ahead of the women. You see the stone mouth of the well?"

"Why would Angelica go there with Korina?"

Anastasis groaned. He yanked the binoculars away from Aris, keeping an eye on the women. "Angelica doesn't hate anybody. If someone asks her for something, anything—even the widow—she happily agrees. The real question is, why would the widow want to spend time with Angelica? Lately, Korina won't even greet her when they pass in the street."

Aris kept his eyes shaded as Anastasis detailed the women's movement across the field to the well.

Anastasis tensed next to him, his hand flailing at Aris. "Go!" he yelled. "Hurry, take my horse."

Aris jerked away, startled. "What are you saying?"

Shoving at Aris's shoulder, Anastasis urged to him move faster. "They're fighting at the well. Hurry!"

Flinging himself into the saddle, Aris leaned forward and whipped the horse into a full gallop.

"Be careful," Anastasis shouted after him. "The widow is a killer. She killed my brother in that same well!"

Despair rattled in Aris's hollow chest as the women came into view, struggling with each other.

⊷◇⊷

The widow snarled, spit dripping from her lips. "I'll send you to the bottom of this well, just like my husband!"

Angelica twisted, pulling herself from Korina's grasp. Baring her teeth, she stood her ground. "Anastasis was right. You pushed your own husband down the snake well!"

Korina lunged at her with a roar, but Angelica twirled out of the way.

"Stay away from me," Angelica pleaded. "Why are you even attacking me? I haven't done anything to you."

Korina sneered, pulling a knife out of a fold in her skirt. The blade was wicked and sharp and the widow swung it wide.

Angelica stumbled back, dust spraying where her feet dragged across the ground.

The blade's tip aimed straight at Angelica, the widow launched herself forward.

Both women screamed as they fell to the ground. Flat on her back, Angelica had one hand cradling her belly and the other holding the knife at bay.

The widow bore down, throwing her weight behind the knife and trying to skewer Angelica.

The hand around Angelica's belly twitched as the knife licked closer to her chest until finally she reached up and used that arm to halt the knife's progress with a cry.

The widow laughed, lashing out with her other hand, battering Angelica's chest and stomach.

Angelica tried to turn away, shifting her hips as much as possible to escape the beating. "Please," she begged. "My baby!"

Aris drove the horse with all his might. "Hold on, Angelica!"

The widow leaned closer, a hand pressed against Angelica's throat. Her smile was maniacal. "You will not have his baby. The snakes will eat you both!"

With a cry, Angelica bit down on the widow's arm, blood erupting in her mouth.

Howling in pain, Korina flailed back, throwing her full body weight behind the knife. She pushed down, her smile widening as the tip came ever closer to skin.

Angelica closed her eyes, her arms shaking. Thinking of Aris, and of their child, she did the only thing she could think of. She spat in the widow's face.

It sprayed across Korina's lips, and the widow lapped it up with her tongue. "I will drink your spit and your blood, you secret whore," Korina screeched. "That bastard in your belly won't see the daylight!"

Horrified, Angelica began to thrash under the other woman, but the widow pressed her advantage. The knife snagged Angelica's dress. She could feel its point digging into her chest.

With a sudden roar, Angelica threw her body left and knocked the knife back enough for her to breathe again. But the widow's larger frame meant Angelica remained firmly pinned beneath her.

Whimpering, Angelica's arms were growing numb from the effort to keep death at bay.

The widow smiled when she noticed Angelica's arms begin to bow. "I should have killed you a long time ago. I've always hated you."

The pounding of hooves drew Angelica's attention. From her angle, the horse looked impossibly tall, and its gallop shook the ground beneath her. "Help!" she cried out.

Blood bloomed across Angelica's chest where the knife pierced her skin. The widow grinned seeing the red spread and pushed harder.

The blade slipped deeper. Angelica wailed, gathering all her strength to push back against Korina.

There was a buzz of silence and a rush of air as the widow was yanked off her feet. Above her, grasping the widow by her hair, Aris stood like a hero of antiquity.

Seeing the bloodstained knife in her hand, he snarled, kicking at her arm and sending the blade flying from her grasp. "You don't touch Angelica ever again."

Aris lashed out at the widow once more then released his hold, causing Korina to crumple to the ground.

Immediately, he turned to help Angelica up.

She pressed a hand against the wound on her chest. With a gasp, she felt a sharp pain when she moved too quickly. "She tried to kill me," Angelica whispered. She looked up at Aris, her eyes widening. "Aris!"

The widow, knife in hand, stood behind Aris, her arm raised. She brought the blade down in a lightning quick glint of silver.

With a flash, she buried it hilt deep in his back near his shoulder.

Aris bellowed in pain, mournful and deep like a whale song.

Spinning, he punched Korina in the face and forced her backward, the knife still lodged in his back.

She bent, yanking a small penknife from her boot. Grinning at him, manic and wild, she charged like a beast.

Aris dipped forward, pivoting into a kick that landed solidly against her chest.

The widow stumbled backwards, gasping for breath. Then her feet clipped the stone lip of the well. She wheeled her arms, back arched, as she tried to remain standing. Her mouth dropped open.

Eyes widening, Aris stumbled forward, tripping on loose stones, scrambling to try and catch Korina's arm.

A scream ruptured from the widow's throat so loud that Aris couldn't hear anything but the blood pounding in his ears when Korina fell into the open mouth of the well.

He dove forward, ignoring Angelica's sharp cry, and crashed into the stone lip of the well. He swore he could feel the fabric of Korina's shirt, his fingers tingling with the ghost of her breath.

He bent over, arm stretched down into the darkness of the well where the widow's scream built and echoed, then finally faded to silence.

In the distance, Anastasis jumped up and down, having witnessed the entire event through his binoculars. "Finally! The snakes will make a meal of her."

Angelica moved closer to where Aris was still bent over the well, tugging on his arm. "We need to step away from this poisonous well. Come on!"

He moved back with her, his gaze far away and vacant. Then something caught his eye, and he pushed Angelica away. "Stay back," he ordered.

Aris scrambled over and picked up the bucket attached to the well's rope. He tossed it into the well. "Korina, grab the bucket! I'll pull you up!"

There was no answer. Aris tugged on the rope, testing the weight to see if she was holding on. The blade still embedded in his back made his muscles throb. His arms felt heavy and slow.

He pulled the rope some more, but it was too light. He again dropped the bucket, calling, "Grab the bucket! The rope! I'll bring up you!"

"Step back," Angelica begged. "She'll pull you in with her. Please, step back!" Angelica tugged him by his belt. "It's too late. She met her fate!"

Aris turned to her, stumbling a few steps from the well in shock when the rope in his hand grew taut. Aris twisted around and started to pull.

Angelica watched in fright.

He yanked on the rope until the bucket finally crested the top of the well, only water sloshing out. His face fell, pulling the bucket over and resting it on the perimeter wall.

Aris turned back to Angelica. Taking the rope from his hand, she pulled him away from the well.

"Enough now. You're tired," she murmured to him softly.

His gaze lingering on the well, he allowed Angelica to draw him further away. He finally looked at her.

She smiled at him, sad and fond. "She's not coming back. That well is full of snakes. Just like others in the village, they're all connected to an underground river. There's no escape. She's gone."

Aris nodded, remaining quiet. He opened his left arm to pull her into a hug, his right arm hanging limp at his side.

"She stabbed you. You must be in pain."

"I killed her," Aris confessed.

"She tried to kill you first. It was self-defence. Now, come on. We need to see to your wound."

"I don't feel even the slightest bit of remorse."

Angelica moved away from Aris, tilting his head to look her in the eye. "You did not kill her. The widow fell into the well. You even tried to save her."

Aris chuckled. "I did reach out for her. But in my heart, I wanted her to fall."

Angelica shook her head, praying for him to see reason. "She tried to kill me. She wanted to kill our baby. She was a threat to all three of us."

Aris sighed, wilting in the face of her conviction.

She grabbed his face, holding him firm, repeating, "She tried to kill you. It was self-defence."

"For you, I would do it again," he replied, his voice firm. He brushed his fingers over the bruise on her face. "Okay, my love? Are you hurt?"

Angelica lifted his hands, kissing his palms. "I'm fine. Just a bit scratched up. You saved me. And our baby."

Angelica gasped, stepping back with realisation. "You weren't surprised to hear that I'm pregnant!"

Smiling, Aris pressed a kiss to her hand. "I already knew."

"How?" Angelica asked.

"Later, please. Seeing the blood on your breasts, I realise how close she came to killing you. I'm horrified."

"You saved our lives," she reminded him. "You cared enough to kill for me and our unborn child!"

Aris laughed, barely paying attention. "When it comes to what I feel for you, I don't know what's more important— loving you or taking care of you."

He pulled her to his chest.

"Anastasis was right," she said. "The widow told me she pushed her husband down this well, killing him."

Not thinking, Aris reached to caress Angelica's cheek with his right hand but hissed, clutching his arm as pain rippled across his back.

Angelica circled around him, gasping. "The knife is still in your back! Let me take it out."

"No!" Aris shouted, jerking away.

Stunned, Angelica stared at him.

"Don't touch it with your hands," Aris warned. "You'll get your fingerprints all over the weapon. Besides, it's stemming my blood loss. We need to keep it in until someone can clean and close the wound."

Angelica chewed her lip in concern. "We can't go to the village with a knife in your back. It would draw too much attention."

"First, we need to get out of here," Aris said, pulling her with him to Anastasis's horse. He helped her up and then mounted behind her painfully. He kicked the horse into a trot, heading back to the shepherd.

Angelica ran her fingers along the arm around her waist. "This is the first time you've held me during the day. It's nice, being able to do this with no one watching."

"I assure you, someone is watching."

Angelica smiled. "Who? The owls?"

"No. Anastasis."

Waiting to make the most of this, regardless of someone watching, Angelica leaned back in his embrace. "Anastasis is very special to me. He has always helped me. He's never refused me, no matter what I asked of him. He can watch us any time."

"He's the one who noticed you were in danger. He's the one who really saved your life."

"Take me to him!"

"That's where we're heading. I'm sure he witnessed everything that happened with his binoculars."

Angelica's face tightened as she remembered the widow. "He warned me many times to watch out for Korina. I knew he was right. I shouldn't have ignored his warnings."

❖

Aris pulled the horse to a stop when they reached Anastasis, waiting for him to help Angelica down before holding out his good arm for assistance.

Once Aris was safely on the ground, Angelica rushed to throw her arms around Anastasis. "Thank you. You saved my life. I should have listened to you and stayed away from the widow."

"I'm so happy you aren't hurt. Sit on my stool under the shade," he responded. He pulled back to take a look at her and frowned. "Are you hurt? You have blood all over you!"

"No," she replied, turning Aris around. "Korina stabbed him in the back. The knife is still there."

"She's gone now. Let's focus on Aris," Anastasis replied, taking a closer look at the knife wound. "You're lucky the stab is high, but you're losing a lot of blood. Does it hurt much?"

"Nothing was as painful as when Angelica was in danger."

Anastasis sighed. "The knife must be removed, even though I don't want to risk infection or further blood loss. We should probably get Granny's help."

"No, Anastasis!" Aris ordered.

"I can pull the knife out to clean the wound, but I only carry a little anti-poison paste with me."

Aris pulled away but winced at the sudden movement. "Don't touch the knife. It has the widow's fingerprints. It's the only proof that backs up our story!"

"No one else needs to know," Anastasis retorted. "Besides, no one would believe you. For years, they didn't believe me when I witnessed her push my brother to his death."

"At least let me take a look," Angelica pleaded, slowly approaching Aris. She turned him around again, prodding at the wound. "We can't just leave it like this, but I don't have anything to stop this bleeding or to disinfect the wound. Maybe we can use a shirt to bandage it until we get to the village."

"Fine," Aris bit out, feeling cornered. He waved his hands at a small plant with large leaves. "Cut a few big leaves from that. It will do the trick for now."

Returning with the leaves, Anastasis handed them to Angelica.

"You need to remove the skin on top of the leaf," Aris instructed.

"I know how to use these," Angelica responded, already peeling the thin outer layer of the plant leaf. "It's a temporary fix, but it will work."

"Why didn't I think of this? I even use them to treat my animals." Anastasis stepped forward as if to just take a closer look, but grabbed the handle of the knife and yanked it out in one quick motion, eliciting an awful shout from Aris.

"Lay on the ground face down," Anastasis commanded.

"You just got your fingerprints all over the knife," Aris grumbled, lowering himself to the ground.

Anastasis ignored him, slicing open Aris's shirt around him, then unscrewing the cap to his water and pouring it over the knife, wiping it clean with the fabric. "There, no fingerprints. Now keep your mouth shut."

Bending down, Angelica laid the skinned leaves over the wound like a bandage, their sticky interior adhering to his skin.

Beside her, Anastasis tore a thin picnic blanket into long strips, handing them to Angelica for her to wrap around Aris as a second layer to bind the wound.

"We need to agree on a story," Anastasis announced. "It's so sad, isn't it? First, the widow pushed her husband down the snake well. Now, overcome by guilt, she jumped into the same pit to atone for her sins!

"Or perhaps my brother's spirit reached out and pulled her in, finally taking his revenge. He loved her, you know. Even though she tortured him day and night, always threatening to sic her murderous brothers on him. A poisonous, one-sided love."

Aris shifted so he could see Anastasis. "I pushed the widow down the well."

"I saw it, clear as day through my binoculars. The widow jumped on her own. There was no one else there! I was standing in this exact spot when I saw her push my brother. Nobody believed me then and the villagers will wonder if I'm having hallucinations again. They'll probably laugh at me. Again. The most important part, though, is that neither of you was here. I was alone. Only I was a witness."

Aris grunted, trying to get up, but stopped when Angelica pressed him back to the ground.

"What if someone saw Angelica meet with the widow earlier today? Someone could have seen them together. I won't risk her being blamed. I will explain what happened."

"No, there's a chance no one will believe you because you are a foreigner. This is our best chance for everyone to get out of this without issue," Anastasis argued. "You remind me of my brother, actually. Handsome, strong, intelligent—yet too pure of heart. The evil woman nearly killed you, too." He looked at Angelica. "Aris risked his life for you. He really loves you. Does such love belong here in this village?"

Leaning forward, Angelica landed a kiss on the shepherd's cheek. "Thank you for watching over me, but I'm grown now. You don't have to worry so much anymore."

"You say that, but even after I warned you about the widow, you still didn't listen."

"You were right, you know," Angelica shared. "Korina admitted to killing your brother."

Anastasis smiled, broad and bright. "Finally, someone believes me."

"I'm sorry we all doubted you. We did you a disservice, Anastasis."

He just shook his head, his chest feeling light for the first time in years. "You are such a rare jewel of a girl. You deserve all the happiness. At least now I won't have to worry about the widow hurting you or anyone ever again."

Scurrying around, Anastasis began to pack everything up.

After his wound was dressed and wrapped, Aris struggled to his feet, throwing his torn shirt over his shoulder.

Angelica cried out, causing them both to stop.

"The bleeding hasn't stopped," she exclaimed, pressing the bandages hard against the wound. "You've lost too much blood already. We need Granny urgently."

"Go get her," Anastasis commanded. "Tell her I cut myself. Bring her to my stable outside the village. We'll meet you there."

"Can you make it back with him on your own?"

"I will walk back with him on my horse," Anastasis explained, tossing her his canteen. "Wash yourself before you go. All that blood will draw attention."

Angelica scrubbed herself clean and then raced to the village, while Anastasis helped Aris mount the horse, tying him into the saddle so he wouldn't slide off. "Lean forward as much as possible. It should help keep the pressure off your back."

Marching forward, Anastasis led his horse quickly through the fields and back to the village.

50 Happy Berry Taste

Granny burst through the doors of the stable, stopping short at the sight in front of her. Aris was laid out facedown over a bench, with Anastasis holding a wad of fabric against the wound on his back. The bandages were already stained through and weeping.

She turned to Angelica, just behind her. "You told me Anastasis was injured. What's going on?"

Stepping back, Anastasis made space for Granny to get a better look. "Maybe we should focus on patching him up first."

Examining the wound, Granny pressed for information. "I need to know what happened to be able to treat him."

"He was stabbed with a knife," Anastasis answered.

"Did you two get in a fight? I thought you were friends."

Pulling the knife out of his pocket, Anastasis showed her the weapon. She looked at it, her face wrinkling in confusion. "This looks like the widow's knife! Why do you have it?"

"Granny, enough," Angelica pleaded. "Can we deal with this first? We can explain later."

"We don't know if it's poisoned, so let's assume the worst," Granny ordered. "Be honest, is this the widow's knife? Is this Korina's revenge for Aris beating her up and throwing her out of the house?"

"Yes!" Angelica shouted back. "The widow stabbed Aris. Stop the bleeding."

Granny jerked back in alarm. "We will need to fully disinfect the wound before we close it. It's going to be painful."

Aris's face pinched. "Just do what you have to do. I will self-hypnotise myself to think of pleasant thoughts and memories under the moon."

"You don't know what pain I mean," Granny responded unhappily. She administered a poultice first, rubbing it into the wound.

Aris's body tensed as she ran her hands over his back.

"I thought you hypnotised yourself to not feel pain. Pleasant memories and all that."

"That really hurt," Aris replied.

"That was nothing compared to what's to come! I have to scrub the wound to remove any debris. I suggest you double your hedonistic hypnotism!" She turned to Angelica. "Give him the berry paste, now. He's a big man, so give him plenty."

Jumping to follow her instructions, Angelica opened a small jar. She scooped out a portion of the paste with her fingers and pushed it between his lips. "Chew before you swallow. It works faster that way."

"That's too much," Granny shouted as Angelica fed him more.

"You said to give him plenty."

"Some pain is good. Let's see how sweet his moon memories are against this pain."

Angelica frowned at her, but Granny ignored it, focused on mixing together an antiseptic with the ingredients on hand.

Moments later she nodded for her granddaughter to come closer. "I need you to pull the wound open slightly so I can clean inside."

Sensing Angelica's hesitation, Granny snapped at her, "Either you open the wound, or you clean it. I can't do both."

Angelica sucked in a breath and spread the skin apart.

Granny bent low, working with a practised hand.

When she leaned away, she said, "We just need to stitch him up now. Grab me the curved needle and thread."

As soon as the needle pierced his skin, Aris burst into peals of laughter.

Granny kept her hand as steady as possible. "Someone got too much berry paste," she teased. "Are you enjoying yourself?"

"You're gorgeous," Aris announced, giggling as he caressed Granny's thigh.

Angelica promptly slapped his hand away, though it didn't stop his flirting. "You are a stunner! Definitely the sexiest doctor I know."

Angelica and Anastasis smiled at his antics.

"Is there some way I can thank you?" Aris's hand went back to caressing Granny's thigh.

Smiling, she continued to stitch him up.

Angelica slapped his hand again, harder. "Stop that!"

"You stop that. She likes my touch!"

"Angelica, get me the antiseptic oil," Granny requested.

As Angelica went to Granny's bag, Aris's hand drifted back to Granny's thigh, circling around to grope her ass. "When was the last time you had a man touch you?"

Granny shoved him off with a grin, but Aris's hand returned almost immediately.

Anastasis sniggered, watching the back and forth.

Drawn by the commotion, Angelica marched over with her hand poised to swat Aris.

At the last moment, as her fingertips sliced through the air, Aris removed his hand and Angelica slapped Granny's ass cheek with a loud smack.

"What are you doing?" Granny turned to glare at her granddaughter. "I was enjoying that! I haven't been touched for years."

Anastasis laughed even harder. "Can I have some of that berry paste, too?"

Angelica leaned closer to the wound. "He's still bleeding!"

"It will stop soon," Granny assured her, covering the stitched-up wound with a cotton bandage. Then she spun to look at Anastasis and Angelica. "Now, tell me what really happened."

Granny tensed as Angelica walked her through the events of the day in excruciating detail.

"Aris wants to confess," Angelica concluded. "But Anastasis and I disagree. He can get into trouble, especially if the widow's wild family gets involved."

Nodding, Granny sighed. "Aris's fight with the widow at the rented house will also come out when the police show up. People witnessed Aris hitting Korina and throwing her out of the house. No part of this is good."

Granny turned back to Aris, testing his muscles to make sure there wasn't any lasting damage. She started at his feet, tapping against his legs as she slowly moved up. Reaching his inner thighs, they were all surprised when he released a loud, erotic moan.

"Granny!" Shock erupted across Angelica's face. "What are you doing? You're making a fool of yourself!"

"Don't all the older ladies have younger lovers in the city? Why not me?" she teased.

"Are you sure you didn't have any of the berry paste?"

"It seems as though he's regaining control of his senses. He'll come to in a few minutes, but he'll still be out of it for a bit." Granny stepped back and started to clean her hands. "At least the bleeding has finally stopped. Sit him up and finish dressing his wound. Make sure to tie it tight. He'll need a clean shirt. He can't go through the village in that bloody torn-up one."

"I have a loose overshirt that I wear in winter. I'm sure it will fit," Anastasis offered.

Angelica took Aris by the arms, rolling him over and pulling him until he was sitting up.

"Be careful," Granny warned. "He lost a lot of blood, so he'll be dizzy for a while. No sudden movement, plenty of rest, and no moon memories! Take it easy the next few days so the wound doesn't reopen."

"How long will he be like this?" Angelica asked, trying to keep Aris sitting up.

"It will take a few hours for the berry paste to wear off. He shouldn't be left alone, or he may tell what really happened."

Aris's head lulled to the side. "I'm not in pain. I feel a bit numb, but how lucky am I that I have two sexy Angelicas looking after me?"

Struggling to tie off the bandage around his chest, Angelica snapped at him. "Stop fooling around!"

Aris frowned at her. "Does Granny know I killed the widow?"

"You did nothing to Korina. You were nowhere near the widow. She fell while dancing on the well, just like Anastasis said."

Aris leaned away, shaking his head. "I cannot lie to Granny."

Angelica glanced at Granny before focusing on Aris again. "I did not lie. I told her the truth."

Aris peered around to look Granny in the eye. "I kicked the widow into the well and she fell to her death. I tried to save her, I really did, but I wanted her to fall. I'm glad she did. She nearly stabbed Angelica. Now she can't hurt Angelica. Or our…"

Angelica slapped him across the face. "You're hallucinating! You don't know what you're saying. Just keep your mouth shut until you recover."

"Why would you even go to the well with her?" Granny asked Angelica. "You know she's the devil. This will get out eventually. The police will have to be informed. Her murderous family will find out. There will be big trouble."

"Keeping it a secret is too risky," Aris argued. "I have to report what happened. I don't care if people find out. I'm happy I killed the bitch! I'll gladly kill anyone who threatens Angelica. Tell that to Manolios so he knows I'm not lying."

Angelica looked at him, confused. "Why would you tell that to my father?"

"You aren't in a sound state of mind to make such a decision," Granny warned him. "This is not a joking matter. No, we stick with Anastasis's story. She fell in the well on her own." Granny picked up the knife and handed it to Anastasis. "Go throw this in the well, too. Get rid of it completely."

"No," Aris argued. "We just leave Angelica out of it. Focus everything on me. The widow lured me out to the well. She attacked me with this knife and the other one she had. I kicked her into the well to save my own life. My wound is proof enough it was self-defence."

Anastasis turned to Aris in shock. "A second knife? Where is it?"

Aris shrugged. "I don't know. Probably fell down the well with her."

"No! I saw very clearly," Angelica said. "Both her hands were empty when she fell."

"I'll go back to check," Anastasis offered. "And make sure the area is clean. I'll even bring my sheep with me to cover any footprints."

"People would have seen Angelica walking with the widow," Aris persisted. "They are an unusual pairing. Someone would have taken notice."

"No!" Anastasis bit back. "Only I witnessed the widow dancing on the wall of the well, which she does very often. She tripped and fell. That's it. You keep your mouth shut!"

Angelica pulled at her hair in a near panic. "You can't confess to this. You could be arrested! I won't lose you to this."

Aris looked her firmly in the eyes. "And if someone saw you with the widow, they will arrest you!"

Grabbing him by the chin, Granny turned his focus to her. "Being honest is different from knowing when not to speak."

Tears welling in her eyes, Angelica slapped Aris across the face. "Get over your pointless morals."

Anastasis nodded. "Our story is solid. I always see the widow dancing on the well. I mention it often at the café. I'll tell everyone I saw her fall in. They all know I watch the well. It will not be anything unusual."

"They never believed you before," moaned Aris. "Why will they believe you now?"

With conviction, the shepherd said, "They will have no choice but to believe me. The important thing is that I was the only witness!"

"Enough," Granny cut in before anyone else could speak. "Let me talk to Aris alone for a moment. Anastasis, if you could grab him some clothes to wear, that would be perfect."

Angelica scowled. "I wish we had some forgetting paste so we could just wipe his memory clean."

Granny waved them both off. Anastasis headed back to his house, while Angelica retreated to the horse a few feet away. She ran her hands up and down its coat, her eyes glued to Granny and Aris.

⬥ ◇ ⬥

Granny settled down next to Aris on the bench. "The paste may make you feel loopy, but you understand exactly what's happening. You know of Angelica's state. Your decision will affect two lives."

Aris glanced at her but remained silent.

She sighed. "Even if the police believe you, Angelica will be marked by this forever. Getting pregnant out of wedlock is already bad enough. Don't weigh her down with more than she can bear. Everyone has their breaking point."

Aris tried to stand up only for Granny to push him back down.

"Did you save her just so you could ruin her later?"

Aris hunched in on himself like a berated child.

Taking his hand, Granny patted it gently. "The horizon is full of storms for Angelica. Soon, you will leave. Don't make more mistakes that will haunt her and your child for the rest of their lives. Promise me now… let Anastasis handle this."

Aris looked at her, nodding reluctantly. "I promise to think about it."

Like a clap of thunder, Granny shook Aris until his head wobbled. "You promise now, for Angelica's sake! For your child's sake! You must say nothing."

"I promise to do whatever is best for Angelica," Aris grunted between clenched teeth.

"At least promise you won't do anything until we speak again."

"That, I promise."

"After resting, you will see things more clearly," Granny insisted. "You lost a lot of blood. Get some sleep."

Packing away her medicine, she left the stable. Just outside the barn door she stopped next to Anastasis and Angelica. "He promised not to say anything until he speaks with me again. That's the best I could do. He will come to his senses after a good rest. Let's go, Angelica."

Angelica shifted restlessly. "Someone needs to be with him."

"I left him some of the sleeping paste and told him to use it for the pain. He will sleep like a baby until tomorrow." Granny turned to Anastasis. "He's free to go home, and it's best if he goes alone so you aren't seen together. Make sure you clean all the blood out of the barn. And go throw that knife in the well."

Anastasis nodded, moving past the women and into the barn.

He approached Aris, holding out a spare shirt. "Go home and get some good rest. Everything will be fine."

Slipping his arms into the sleeves of the shirt, Aris started to walk away. At the door, he paused and glanced over his shoulder at Anastasis. "Thank you… for everything. You are a true friend."

51 The Announcement

Anastasis herded his sheep down a winding path. When he arrived, he made a circuit of the area, walking in concentric circles around the well. He kept his eyes trained on the ground, looking for anything that could tie them to the widow's death.

Trampled in the dirt, he found Angelica's blue scarf, which he picked up and tucked into his pocket to return later.

He searched the area twice more but found no trace of a second knife.

When one of his sheep let out a helpless bleat after getting separated, Anastasis saw a glint of metal from the grass next to the animal. After picking it up, he stepped to the well, running his fingers along the rough stones.

"I hope your soul can rest easy, brother," he whispered. "I'm glad that karma finally came for its payment."

He dropped the second knife so it fell into the well with a distant splash, then lowered the bucket for water.

Anastasis reeled it in when full, carrying it over to a nearby trough. The sheep gathered around. He dumped in the water and watched as they drank their fill.

When there was nothing left to do, he mounted his horse and herded the flock to circle the well a few more times, roughing up the ground.

Afterward, he was sure there could be no trace of Aris or Angelica having been there.

⸺ ❖ ⸺

The café was busy in the warm evening. Locals gathered for the opportunity to savour the last dregs of sunlight, lounging at tables, playing cards and backgammon. At one table, Manolios held court with Jacob and Yiannis. Adonis limped up, joining them.

This was what Anastasis observed when he finally arrived, standing in the middle of the crowd and calling for their attention.

"Earlier this afternoon," he announced. "I was watching my flock through binoculars and witnessed Korina jump into the snake well."

A hush fell over the café.

"Which well?" one local asked.

"The same one she pushed my brother into. I told you, the snake well!"

The locals glanced at each other. "Did she jump in," one finally spoke up, "or did you push her?"

"I was sitting under my tree. I was nowhere near her."

"Did you see her with your miraculous binoculars?"

"Yes, I did. They have never failed me before."

Yiannis leaned over to Adonis. "Why don't you go check if she's home?"

Nodding, Adonis stood and limped out of the square.

"Did she jump or did she fall?" another villager enquired.

"I'm not sure. She was dancing like she usually does and then she was just gone."

"Why should we believe you this time?" another local asked.

Anastasis shrugged, settling into a chair. "Believe it or don't. I know what I saw. Just like I know I saw her push my brother into that same well. If you don't believe me, that's on you."

Leaning forward, Jacob cleared his throat. "It's true that she often visits the well. I've told her to be careful, since it doesn't have a cover, but she just laughed at me."

Adonis returned huffing. "Korina's house is empty. Not even her daughters are home."

"I brought the girls to my house," Anastasis explained. "I told them their mother went away and that I would be looking after them."

Yiannis's face turned hard. "Why have you done that?"

"I am their uncle, their only living relative in this village. I am their guardian now that their mother is dead. I only came to inform you what I have seen."

John and Uri wandered up, intrigued by the crowd.

Jacob looked over at them, shaking his head in wonder. "The old fool was telling the truth about his brother's death."

Yiannis waved Adonis over again. "Why don't you lead a search party, just in case he's right?"

Anastasis laughed. "Check what? Nothing that ever fell into those wells has ever come out again. Besides, I ran down there as soon as I saw it happen, but I couldn't even hear her down there."

"It doesn't hurt to look. Uri and I can help with the search," John volunteered.

"Where's Aris?" Adonis asked.

"He's in bed, already asleep," John informed.

Adonis nodded. "I'll grab a light and have a look inside the well, but if Anastasis already searched I doubt I'll find anything."

⸺ ❖ ⸺

Adonis was the first to arrive back at the café and report what he found. "She was last seen leaving the house she rented out earlier today."

"What time was that?" Manolios asked.

"I think she left about two," Uri responded.

One of the older locals leaned forward. "We all know about the fight between Aris and the widow. He warned her not to step foot in the house again. Have they reconciled? Perhaps she's with him and not at home."

"I'm sure they haven't," John answered, glancing at Uri. "She never visits when Aris is home."

The local cocked his head. "How does Korina know when Aris isn't home?"

John shifted in his seat.. "Well, Uri closes all the doors and windows. Aris likes to keep them open even when he's sleeping."

The entire café shifted to look at Uri, finally realising who the widow had been visiting all those weeks. A number of interested murmurs could be heard.

"Besides," Anastasis interjected. "Aris was helping me in the fields today. We had lunch together. I told him what happened, but he laughed at me just like the rest of you."

"We better inform the police," Yiannis said. "They may want to get involved."

Manolios shook his head. "Let's wait until the morning. The widow may show up. It wouldn't be the first time she's disappeared for hours only to return out of nowhere."

⁂

High up in her luxury office, Varo worked as early morning light streamed through the windows. She kept shifting through documents, distracted until she finally stood and started to pace, squeezing a stress ball in one hand.

It had been weeks, but she was no closer to tracking down Aris. She tapped the intercom button, ordering her secretary to summon Victor to her office.

He entered silently, standing at rest and waiting for her to speak.

"Whoever you hired locally is not delivering results," she snapped. "These are three grown men. They can't just disappear."

Victor remained still, seemingly unfazed. "We are narrowing in on them. It was a lot of ground to cover, but there isn't much left to search now. They will find Aris soon."

"How hard can it be? It's three foreigners. They should stand out."

"Be patient. We will find them," Victor assured her.

"Something's wrong," Varo insisted. "Hire another team and double the reward. If that doesn't get results, I'll just go find him myself."

Victor sighed but nodded, walking out of her office as quietly as he'd entered.

52 The Pregnancy

Aris led John and Uri on a hike outside the village. The path was clean but steep, and by the time they reached the summit, it was already well past noon.

Dropping to the ground for a rest, John ignored the vista, focused entirely on his phone. "There's a pretty strong signal up here."

"Either call the girl or put it away," Uri urged him.

John looked over at Aris, but he just shrugged. Smiling, John tapped his phone a few times and held it to his ear. "Hi, Alexa!"

"John? What a surprise! How are you?"

"I'm sorry I haven't called earlier. Aris doesn't like us using our phones. All is fine with me. How about you?"

There was a rustling over the line before her voice came through again. "I'm late. The tests have all come back positive."

"Positive for what? Are you sick?"

"No," she repeated. "My period is late, and the test is positive."

"You mean you're pregnant?" John asked, eyes wide in excitement.

"Who's pregnant?" Uri gulped, drawing Aris's attention.

"Alexa! She's pregnant!"

"Yes," Alexa replied, her voice shaky and hesitant. "With our baby."

"Our baby? Like, my baby?" John's voice became squeaky.

"That is what 'our' means," Alexa replied.

The smile on John's face slowly died. He turned to Aris and Uri, placing the phone between them and putting it on speaker. "Are you sure it's mine? I was told I can't have children."

"Of course I'm sure," she snapped back.

"Alexa," John replied, his voice dropping low. "Every doctor I've ever been to has told me that I can't have children."

Her voice became brittle and sharp. "There's no one else that I've slept with."

Uri and Aris flinched.

Confused, John scratched his head. "I was your first? But you definitely weren't a virgin."

"My body wasn't," she said, her voice stretched thin like a rubber band. "But my soul was! I've never had a love before you!"

John squeezed his eyes shut, his face scrunched up. "That doesn't make any sense."

Aris and Uri leaned closer to hear better.

John started pacing back and forth in front of the phone. "You don't have to lie to me. It doesn't matter either way. We can overcome this."

Alexa's sobs pattered like rain. "I'm not lying!"

John sank down into a crouch, cradling his head. "The baby can't be mine."

"You don't believe me? Sorry I brought it up." A loud buzzing cutting through the call.

"Alexa, Alexa?" John called out, hunched over the phone. He looked at Aris and Uri in shock. "She hung up!"

Uri chuckled, sliding closer to him. "This is a common trick. Foreign girls who want to go to America claim to be pregnant. That's their ticket. They do the same thing to get married. If I had to marry every girl that claimed I got them pregnant, I'd have a harem by now."

Dismayed, John's entire body seized up.

Aris's lips puckered. "Not all women are like that. Alexa has a good, secure job. She doesn't need to go to America."

"Here we go again," Uri leaned back. "The woman-whisperer, come at us with his hot take! He instantly believes any woman at the first sight of tears."

"Shut your stupid mouth, you fool," Aris snapped. "Can't you see this is serious? They're both distressed."

"Do you believe her, then?" John asked, eager to hear Aris's opinion.

Aris smiled softly. "Alexa is not a cheap, easy girl. She could be telling the truth."

John slumped down. "But the doctors told me I couldn't have children. I never used protection with Leoni, and she didn't get pregnant."

"It's not unheard of. Science isn't infallible. Frankly, I'd be shocked if Alexa is lying."

John gripped his head. "What about the story of her soul being virginal?"

Uri sat up. "Oh, she's definitely trying to use you. Next, she'll be asking you to send her money for the baby, even though there isn't one!"

"I disagree," Aris retorted. "Call her back. Just keep an open mind."

Uri smirked. "That's a big mistake. I would never call her back."

John hesitated, looking between the two before lurching for his phone.

She answered after the fifth ring and John immediately started to babble. "Alexa, I told you, I love you. I will take you to America. You don't have to lie to me if that's what you want."

"What? I don't want to go to America," Alexa insisted.

"Is this about money? I am no fool."

Aris shook his head and waved a hand in the air.

"You are a fool," she snarled. "I don't need you or your money."

Not sure what else to do, John ended the call himself.

He stewed in silence for a moment before rounding on Aris and Uri. "She doesn't need money. She doesn't want to go to America. She's pregnant with someone's baby. And here I was ready to drop everything to be with her. Forget her. Forget Italy. I'm staying here."

Aris sneered at him. "Afraid to confront again, John?"

John spun around. "I am not afraid. There's just nothing left to say. Listen to my voice—it is full and normal!"

"Yet you seem scared to death! Uri has poisoned your mind. Follow your own heart, your own feelings, your own instincts for once."

Face burning bright, John spat at Aris's feet. "Like you did? You're the biggest mess here. A wife that doesn't want you. A lover you can't have. Maybe you should sort your own life before you offer other people advice."

John stalked back down the path toward the village, Uri trailing behind.

Picking at the dry grass until it crumbled in his hand, Aris finally stood and followed at a sedate pace.

❖ ◇ ❖

Aris lounged on the couch reading a book while Uri sat across from him, cutting his nails.

John had been pacing the length of the room for the past hour. He stopped, kneeling before Aris. "It's been two days now, and Alexa hasn't called back. Should I call her? What do you think?"

"Classic chick move," said Uri. "She's just messing with your mind, waiting for you to break first. Don't call her."

John remained focused on Aris.

Still intent on his book, Aris said simply, "Only you know what to do. Trust your instincts."

"But I don't know what to do. I've never felt like this before. I can't even sleep. It's torture. I need your advice."

"I thought my life was too messy to offer advice."

"God, I'm sorry, all right? I was angry and confused. I didn't mean it. You know I value your opinion. Please, tell me what to do."

Aris peered at John from over the top of his book. "If I loved the girl, I would run to her and clear this up before she does something you'll both regret."

"I can't just jump on a plane right now," John shouted.

"You must make your own decision. Forget about me and Uri. Have a cold shower and make up your mind."

⸺ ◇ ⸺

Angelica trailed behind her grandmother as they collected medicinal herbs to restock Granny's supply.

"At some point," Granny called over her shoulder, "you will have to ask Aris what he wants."

"I won't tell him what to do. It's his choice whether to stay or go."

Granny raised her brows. "Unless you tell him to leave, he will remain right beside you."

Angelica looked down, focused on the best leaves to pick. "I'll never ask him to leave."

Shaking her head, Granny turned her gaze back to the herbs.

Angelica smiled, thinking about Aris. "He's given so much meaning to my life. He is everything I've ever wanted."

Granny scoffed. "Have you ever asked him about your pregnancy?"

Angelica tensed. "Like what?"

"Well, he may not want you to keep it."

"He would never ask me to abort our baby."

"What if he did, though?"

"Even if Aris asked me, I would never give up my baby!"

"Well, you've clearly made up your mind."

Lifting her head high, Angelica refused to look away from her grandmother. "Yes, I have."

Sighing, Granny bent down and pulled a handful of leaves away from a bush. "Even so, you should at least prepare yourself. You may have to let Aris go. He could decide to leave tomorrow."

"No," Angelica screamed, her voice harsh. "He loves me as I love him. It's beyond physical attraction. We care for each other. He told me I command his will, but it's the same for me. I would do anything he asked of me." Her voice dropped and she added, "I'd even kill."

Granny stood stock still and ceased her line of questioning.

After a few moments of standoff, the two women continued to pick the plants.

"I feel responsible for you," Granny suddenly confessed. "Do you remember my warning before I revealed to you the love secret?"

"I do. When Aris was absorbed in his thoughts a few days ago, I asked his friend John what happened."

Granny stopped with her hand mid-air, turning to look at Angelica.

"John said that Aris's wife told him never to return. She doesn't want him back."

"Couples argue and fight regularly," Granny warned. "This can be something temporary between Aris and his wife. Don't be surprised if one day you discover him gone."

"If Aris decides to go without asking me to go with him, I won't try to stop him, no matter how much it hurts. But I will never give him up!"

Granny eyed her wearily. "Yet, you have not discussed the baby with him. You're running out of time."

"Aris already knows. There is nothing to discuss. If he disappears, then it's one more reason to have something to remind me of him."

"Let's turn back. We have enough," Granny announced.

53 THE POLICE

At noon, most of the village was gathered in the square as the police lieutenant paced before them.

"In other villages, I deal with the mayor or a committee. But since you don't have either, who should I start with?"

Yiannis stepped forward. "We searched everywhere. There isn't a single trace of Korina. The widow just disappeared, the same way her husband did ten years ago."

"It's a reservoir well," Anastasis interrupted. "The kind connected to an underground river. Once something falls in, there's no chance of it being found again."

Aris pushed his way through the crowd, his palms sticky.

"Who is this?" the lieutenant asked when Aris stumbled out in front of him.

Jacob, the old Jewish man, stepped forward next. "This is Aris," he explained. "One of our three guests."

"Three guests?"

Across the crowd, Angelica went pale.

Granny leaned in and whispered in her ear, "What's he doing? Why is he up there?"

Angelica tried to swallow. Her throat was desert dry. "He thinks telling the truth will protect me."

Grabbing her by the hand, Granny started dragging her through the crowd. "Well, let's stop the fool before he ruins everything."

Aris cleared his throat. "I want to——"

A way back, Anastasis threw his arm high in the air and waved. "Lieutenant, I saw everything. I am the only witness to the event. I saw her die."

The crowd turned and focused on the shepherd who shoved his way to the front, pushing Aris behind him.

"So, Korina isn't missing," the lieutenant pressed. "She's dead."

"That's right."

The lieutenant raised an eyebrow, taking in the man's clothes, the heavy binoculars hanging from a cord around his neck, and the eager demeanour. "Unless you killed her, how do you know for sure that she's dead?"

"I saw it happen through my binoculars. The widow liked to dance around the well. I've seen her do it a bunch of times before... ever since my brother—her husband—died in the same well."

Turning to the crowd, the lieutenant scanned faces before resting on Jacob.

Jacob jolted upright, raising his cane like a pointer. "Yes, that's true. She was known to visit the well where she claimed her husband fell in years ago."

"No," Anastasis shot back. "He didn't fall. Korina pushed him."

Stepping closer to the shepherd, the lieutenant loomed over Anastasis. "If she pushed her husband, who pushed her?"

"No one pushed her," Anastasis stated firmly. "I saw her fall in. I don't know if it was an accident or on purpose."

Angelica and Granny sighed in relief, but Aris appeared ready to spring across the square. Granny caught his eye and shook her head, praying he would hold his tongue.

"So, we have two murders," the lieutenant decided. "But neither Korina nor her husband's body has been found."

"You're not listening," Anastasis said. "Only my brother was murdered. Korina fell into the well herself."

"But no one found your brother's body, and no one has found the widow's body."

"Right, like I said earlier, the well is connected to an underground river. Whatever falls in gets washed away with the tide."

"And you witnessed both of these events?"

Anastasis nodded.

"Wouldn't the widow's role in your brother's death be enough reason for you to want to kill her?"

The villagers went still, tension heavy like heat in the air.

Anastasis shrugged. "As I said, I only saw it happen through my binoculars."

"Did you, or anyone, try to see if she was still alive after she fell?" the lieutenant asked.

"Yes—" Aris blurted out.

Angelica latched on to Granny for support.

The lieutenant pivoted on his heel, giving Aris a quick once-over. "You did?"

Anastasis stepped forward again. "Yes, I did."

The lieutenant tilted his head to look back at the shepherd. "And?"

"I lowered the bucket and shouted for her to grab it so I could pull her up, but there was no response. I did it a few times, pulling up buckets until I filled the stone trough for my sheep to drink from."

Yiannis frowned, turning to Anastasis. "You didn't tell us this."

Anastasis barked out a laugh. "Would you have believed me if I told you I tried to pull Korina out? You didn't even believe me when I told you she fell in."

"So, you rushed to the well."

Anastasis nodded.

"Did you see anyone else around? Any signs of a struggle or another set of footprints?"

Angelica stared at Aris, her body tense. She pinched her lips together.

"I told you," Anastasis insisted. "I saw her through my binoculars. There was no one else around."

"You said so. But you also just said your herd followed you to drink water from the trough. So, any evidence is most likely gone," the lieutenant snapped. "Did you not think I would need to examine the scene? Or did you drive your sheep there on purpose to destroy any evidence that might have been incriminating?"

"I told you exactly what happened. I can't help the fact that sheep get thirsty."

"How long did it take you to reach the well?"

Anastasis shrugged. "Maybe five minutes. I wasn't counting."

"Five minutes walk? You must have been very close. Why would you need your binoculars?"

"I was on my horse. That's how I got there so fast."

Granny slipped through the crowd to Aris, taking his arm and gently pulling him back from the front of those assembled.

The lieutenant turned fast, noticing Aris's departure. "Sir, wait. What is it you wanted to say earlier?"

Granny stepped forward, partially concealing Aris. "He suggested that we build a cover over the well so there wouldn't be a chance for an accident like this to happen again."

"That's really more of a decision for you all to make on your own," the lieutenant replied crisply. "For now, we need to examine the well and see if there are any signs of a struggle. Maybe bring divers in to dredge the well."

Anastasis glared at the lieutenant. "If you send men into that well, they will never come up."

The lieutenant's lips curled in a cunning smile. "You seem to not want me to search with divers."

"I can't stop you, but at least remember that I warned you," Anastasis replied, turning to walk away.

"One last thing," the lieutenant called after the shepherd. "When you were at the well, did you find anything on the ground? Anything the widow could have left behind, like a hat or a scarf. Anything?"

Anastasis shook his head, sucking on his lower lip. "No, but I didn't think to search the ground."

The lieutenant looked over the crowd of villagers. "Perhaps one of you can show me the way to the well. I'd like to see the scene while it's still light out."

"I'll take you," Adonis volunteered.

"And Anastasis," the lieutenant called. "Make sure you don't leave the village. I might need to speak to you again."

Anastasis shrugged. "I've never left here before. There's no reason to leave now."

⸺ ◇ ⸺

The lieutenant prodded Adonis to leave immediately, and with that the rest of the crowd began to disburse.

Anastasis trailed behind Angelica. Tapping her arm, he pulled her scarf from his pocket. "You left this the other day at my house," he told her. Leaning in, he dropped his voice and added, "The scratches on your neck are still noticeable."

Quickly, Angelica wrapped the scarf around her neck.

Walking quickly, they caught up with Aris and Granny. The four gave simple nods to each other, but Aris offered a small smile to Angelica.

Anastasis patted Aris's shoulder, his hand warm and comforting. "It's done," he tried to reassure his friend. "Just keep your mouth shut and no one will be in any danger."

Shaking his head, Aris glared at Anastasis. "You should have let me speak. Now you can get into trouble for providing a false statement. We can both go to prison." Aris let out a sigh. "I've lived my life. You're still in the height of your youth. You need to look after yourself. Besides, I killed the widow!"

Anastasis yanked Aris closer. "The only evidence they're going to find is sheep shit from when I herded them out there the other day. I even disposed of the weapons. Don't do anything foolish. The case will go cold before long."

Seeing her father just ahead, Angelica turned and gave Anastasis a fierce hug.

Manolios laughed at the display of affection. "I'm jealous. I no longer get such kisses from my daughter."

"I am sorry for your loss, Anastasis, and that we didn't believe you before."

Patting the shepherd on the shoulder, Manolios smiled at the shorter man. "Accident or not, the widow's gone. Nothing any of us can do now."

Manolios maneuvered between Angelica and Granny, wrapping a possessive arm around each of them.

Angelica peered over her shoulder at Aris as they parted company.

54 Take Her

Aris trotted into the kitchen, his eyes blurry in the morning light. After pouring a cup of coffee, he joined John and Uri at the table.

Uri sat picking at the remains of his meal while John was hunched over, spinning his cell phone, tapping on the screen only to let it fade to black with a sigh.

John spun the phone again.

Uri slapped his hand down over the device. "Relax. If she isn't lying, she'll call first."

Aris took a sip of his coffee, setting the cup down with confidence. "Stop messing with John. An honest woman wouldn't call back after the way he spoke to her. Even if a woman doesn't want an abortion, she might do so, just because she wants the man to stay with her out of love, not as an obligation."

"That's what happened to Le…" John cut himself off. "…a girl I know. She had an abortion despite being vehemently opposed to them. The decision has haunted her ever since." John jerked to his feet, his whole body vibrating. "That's it. I'm calling Alexa. Keep quiet. I'm going to put it on speaker."

He jammed the numbers with his thumbs. His shoulders tensed with each ring.

When she finally picked up, John eagerly started babbling. "Alexa, I'm sorry that I upset you. Let me explain."

"No, I will speak," she cut in. "When my parents died in the accident, I joined a monastery to be a nun."

"You already told me that," John said.

"At the monastery, when I was sixteen, a priest came to me," Alexa continued, ignoring him, her voice brittle.

Aris laid a hand on John's arm.

"So, you made love with a priest?" John squawked.

"No," she cried. Her tears echoed over the loudspeaker.

Uri leaned closer, whispering, "She's playing you."

Aris slapped Uri on the mouth like a clap of thunder, silencing him.

Shocked, Uri stumbled back, burping.

There was a rustling before another woman's voice came on the line. "Listen, you American bastard. When my niece Alexa was sixteen, a priest forced himself on her. That's why she broke her vows and left the monastery. That's why she's never had a boyfriend. We don't need you or your money. We'll take care of this child ourselves. Fuck off and never call back."

The bitter silence of the call ending sliced through the room.

Aris rubbed his neck, not sure how to help.

John dropped into the nearest chair, rigid like a robot. He slapped his head, muttering, "I'm such an idiot."

Uri leaned back, crossing his arms. "That still doesn't explain how you're the father of the baby. Their story doesn't make sense."

John glared at Uri, his fists clenching. "I never should've listened to you. You made me into an even bigger idiot than you are. I'm going back, right now," John announced, pushing to his feet.

Aris patted John on the shoulder. "Finally standing on your own two feet. Do it! Pack and go right now."

John offered Aris a wan smile. "Now it all makes sense. The first time Alexa and I made love, she froze before bursting into tears and locking herself in the bathroom."

"What happened after that?" Uri asked.

"An emotionally stunted buffoon like yourself would never understand," John spat at him. He breathed deep, a faint smile gracing his face. "I coaxed her back and I just loved her. I made her feel good as a person! Then we made love again and again and again. Priest or no priest, I love Alexa! Even if the baby isn't mine! I love her even more now that I know the truth."

Aris grinned. "Then go to her!"

"Are you coming?" John asked.

Aris shook his head. "No, I'm not ready to leave. I don't know if I will ever be. Call Alexa back. Tell her you're returning."

"The village festival is the day after tomorrow," Uri said with a burp. "We owe it to these people to be there. If you wait, I'll leave with you, the day after the festival."

John glanced at Aris, looking for an opinion.

Aris shrugged. "It's your decision. Whatever your choice, make sure to call Alexa. Don't leave her in her current state of mind."

Pacing the length of the house, John muttered under his breath, trying to work out what to do.

Uri rose and gripped him by the forearm. "After the festival, we can hitch a ride with one of the visitors. It will be faster than walking for days."

John set his jaw. "Okay. But not one minute more. The morning after the village festival, I'm gone… with or without either of you!"

⸙

That afternoon, John and Uri grabbed empty seats at the café. Adonis was seated a few tables over, chatting with Yiannis.

"This will be our last meal here, since you're closed tomorrow for the festival," John informed Yiannis with a smile. "We're leaving the morning after."

"Just like that? What's with the sudden departure?"

"We were supposed to leave a while ago," John explained, "but we lengthened our stay because of all of you and the village."

"This is it, then," Yiannis mumbled, hurrying off to the kitchen.

A frown settled on Adonis's face like a heavy blanket of snow. Waving over Yannis's son, he paid for his lunch and made his way out of the café.

⸙

On the road leading out of the village, Granny was resting on a large rock. She turned her head at the sound of a horse clomping up the road.

Blacky jerked to a halt in front of her and Granny smiled up at Adonis in the saddle.

She waved up at him. "Climb down and I'll walk with you back to the village."

Adonis swung a leg over and jumped to the ground. "Have you been waiting to ambush me?"

Granny smiled back at him. "I confess nothing!"

"Is there something I can do for you?"

Granny patted his arm, nodding toward the village. "Come, let's talk about you and Angelica."

Adonis froze. "There's nothing to talk about there."

Frowning, Granny moved closer and peered into his face. "What are you going to do about you and Angelica?"

"Do what?" Adonis asked, scoffing in disbelief. "There's nothing I can do. She's gone."

Granny shook her head and started to walk away. "When are you going to take her?"

Adonis reached out for Granny. "Take her? Who do you think I am? I'm not a rapist."

"You take her," Granny corrected, gazing calmly into his eyes. "Not rape her."

"You know how I feel about Angelica. Don't play with me."

"Who's playing?"

"What are you saying?"

"When are you going to wake up?" Granny asked. "When are you going to stop pining for her and tell Angelica how you feel?"

Adonis clenched his jaw. "Don't mess with me."

A smirk deepened the wrinkles on her cheeks. "If you stand and watch while Angelica slips through your fingers, then you are a fool."

Adonis's skin itched. "My love for Angelica is not a joke."

"Is it not? That's exactly what it seems like."

Adonis twisted away from her.

Granny snatched him back by the arm. "If anyone thinks love is a joke, it's you. You just watch and do nothing!"

Adonis's face burned. "I'm a crippled farmer with nothing to offer her. Plus she's pregnant with another man's child. What is there left to do?"

Granny beamed at him, her voice firm and strong. "Confess! Ask her to marry you! Offer her every part of yourself before you lose the small part you have left."

Adonis scoffed. "Just like that?"

"Yes, or you'll forever be sucking your thumb in regret."

"You've lost your mind. I don't want to talk about this again."

Blacky's hooves clacked against the paved roads as they continued winding their way towards the village.

At a split in the road, Adonis went one way while Granny turned the other.

After just two steps, she stopped and backtracked to the bend, shouting after him, "I thought I could shake some sense into you, but clearly I was wrong. You've all but lost Angelica!"

Adonis whipped around to face her. "I didn't lose her. You drove her away. You revealed the damn love secret to her. That's what broke Aris's defences. This is your responsibility, and no one else's."

With that, he grabbed Blacky's reins, tugging the horse down the road without bothering to look back.

55 Mind Made Up

Aris relaxed on the couch, gazing out the window while his companions scurried around packing their belongings.

"Are you almost finished?" John asked. "I don't want to miss the festival."

Casually lifting to his feet, Aris walked across the room and leaned against the window ledge. "I've made up my mind."

John tilted his head in confusion. "About what?"

"Alexa is not the only pregnant girl."

Uri slowly turned to look at Aris, his eyes wide. "Angelica?"

Aris nodded. "I'm not going back. I'm staying here."

"No way!" John responded, his jaw dropping. "This is so sudden."

Smiling broadly, Aris squared his shoulders. "I'm going to stay here and build a life in this village. This is where my future is."

"A new life with Angelica?" John asked.

"Yes!"

"Are you sure?" Uri chewed on his lip anxiously. "Have you told Angelica?"

"I'm going to tell her today," Aris replied, eyes shining.

"What if," John began, clearing his throat, "what if she doesn't want you to stay?"

"Angelica loves me completely, and I love her the same."

"What if the other locals don't want you to stay?" Uri pointed out.

Aris waved off the concern. "They're all friendly and decent."

John stepped towards Aris hesitantly, like he was approaching a wild animal. "Maybe now. But you're stealing the jewel of the village. They might not take that so well. And what about Adonis?"

"Adonis and the rest will respect Angelica's decision."

Uri bounced forward, engulfing Aris in a hug. "You lucky bastard. You finally found true love! I'm glad. You deserve Angelica."

"I hope you find the happiness you deserve," John added. "Angelica is a blessing in every way."

Aris smiled at them, feeling sure about where his life was heading. "Let's go to the festival!"

⊰ ◇ ⊱

They arrived at the plaza where the entire village had gathered, greeted by cheers and laughter. The space was strung with lights, and various pedlars lined the path on the far side leading down to the pier. Their goods—clothes, toys, traditional sweets, nuts, cheeses, sausages, and smoked meats—were on display and for sale. On the opposite side, long tables extended from the front of the café, loaded with food and drinks.

Locals brought their dining chairs and tables, arranging them around a raised platform where musicians played for the crowd. Villagers called out to each other and to visitors from the surrounding area as if they were long-lost lovers.

John's gasp of surprise was barely heard over the applause. "I didn't expect so many people to come so far. The crowd is huge!"

"I haven't been to a *panigiris* like this in years!" Aris looked around the festival atmosphere.

John laughed, watching as more people arrived. "Incredible. They're coming here even on tractors, four-wheelers, and mules!"

Catching sight of them, Yiannis wandered over to greet them. "Aris, John, Uri, help yourselves to food and drink. We have your favourite… barbecued lamb and pig."

Uri spun around, taking in the scenery.

John wiggled to the music. "With kids playing games and all the people dancing, it feels more like a party."

"At village festivals like this," Aris commented, "there are always games, singing and dancing, and little competitions like for the best food."

"Stop being Americans," Yiannis chastised. "Go on and mingle with the people."

John bounced on his toes. "Don't have to ask me twice."

Aris smiled. "I'm going closer to the stage to watch."

"Good luck," John replied. Moving closer to clasp his friend's shoulder firmly, he said, "This would be the perfect time to surprise Angelica."

John and Uri meandered off to check out the merchants and pedlars.

High-pitched children's screams filled the plaza. Angelica had just arrived, shining in a sky-blue dress..

Aris watched her from a distance.

John nudged Uri. "Let's move closer. I want to hear what Aris tells her."

Uri tugged on John's sleeve as he followed behind. "I bet Aris's is shitting bricks right now."

Angelica worked her way through the crowd, smiling and accepting kisses from friends and relatives along her path, but her gaze remained firmly on Aris.

Yanking him by the arm, Uri pulled John to a stop. "We're close enough. We don't want to intrude."

"But I want to hear Angelica's response! What if she refuses him?"

Aris, distracted by flailing in the corner of his vision, looked away from Angelica to see John and Uri jostling for position. He smiled when John offered him a thumbs up.

Turning back to Angelica, he reached out his hands, fingers brushing hers.

At the last second Angelica was pulled away and swallowed by the crowd, vying for her attention. She shot Aris a sad smile, holding up her hand and begging him to wait.

His shoulders sagged, but he nodded back at her.

She cycled through the crowd, hugging and laughing in equal measure until she was finally able to extract herself. Momentarily lost, she craned her neck to find Aris again.

Back at his side, she reached out to him, their fingers sliding together into a firm grip.

Angelica giggled. "We never had so many people at our festival!"

"I think it's happening," John exclaimed. "Go, Aris!"

Aris pulled her closer, grinning wide. "I have something to tell you!"

Angelica focused on him, taken by his smile and the strength of his voice. She smiled encouragingly.

Uri tugged on John's sleeve. "Has he told her yet?"

John brushed him off like a fly. "I don't know. I can barely even see them. We need to get closer."

Angelica was yanked away again by two young women who jumped around her with a youthful energy Aris could only admire. He let her go, watching patiently.

Uri whistled in admiration. "Angelica sure is popular. Everyone wants her attention today."

Angelica danced and laughed, finally shoving the other women off to celebrate as she slipped back to Aris. "Sorry, it's crazy this year. What did you want to say?"

Aris cleared his throat, overcome for a moment. "I decided to…"

"He's going to tell her!" John whispered hoarsely to Uri. They both stood on their tiptoes to watch.

Angelica tipped her head, cupping a hand around one ear, waving at Aris to repeat what he said.

"I said," Aris raised his voice over the din of the festival. "I decided to—"

Angelica whipped around as a body collided with hers. She laughed, greeting a cousin fervently before focusing back on Aris. "One moment," she said. "I'll be right back. Will you stay?"

Offering a brief smile, Aris nodded. "I'll be right here."

Uri shoved John to get his attention. "Did he tell her?"

"No, I don't think so," John confessed. "At least, it doesn't seem like it."

"Maybe she didn't care," Uri offered.

"Shut up. Why do you always have to be negative?"

"It is possible," Uri insisted.

Aris watched Angelica again get pulled through the crowd. She twisted and turned, dipping out of sight before surfacing even farther away.

"I doubt he'll be able to tell her today." Uri pointed over to where Angelica had reached. "She keeps getting pulled away."

"Maybe we should grab her," John suggested. "Bring her back to Aris."

"Sometimes, you just don't think things through," Uri chastised. "How are we supposed to get to her? With the way this crowd is acting, we'd be lucky not to get trampled."

John watched the revelry unfolding around them. "I'm glad we stayed for the festival. It's nice to be able to end our visit on a high note."

Electric feedback came over the speaker system surrounding the stage. The merriment stopped instantly.

"What's happening?" John wondered, craning his neck to see the stage clearly.

Uri squeezed his arm. "It's Adonis. Seems like he's got some sort of announcement."

56 The Claim

Adonis smiled out at the crowd from the stage. He tapped the microphone a few times, making sure he had everyone's attention.

"On behalf of all of us in this village, I thank you for joining our celebrations."

He paused, waiting for the wave of applause to recede.

Raising his arm like a conductor, arm outstretched over the crowd, he said, "We are not only celebrating our village, but also honouring some special guests. Our friends, whom we invited into not only our village but also into our hearts."

The crowd turned, following his command to look at Aris, John, and Uri.

John raised his arm slowly in acknowledgement of the recognition. Aris and Uri followed suit, grinning at the attention.

"From the first day," Adonis continued, drawing the attention of the crowd back to him, "Aris, John, and Uri became a part of our village. Part of our lives. They have forever left their mark here. They will always be in our minds and in our hearts. For those who don't know yet, our three friends are leaving us tomorrow. So, let's raise our cups in farewell to our three brothers."

Upon hearing this, Angelica gasped, clutching her chest.

John and Uri continued to wave their hands at the crowd, not realising what had been said.

Behind them, Aris felt a breaking apart beneath him, like the earth threatening to collapse. "Not me," he choked out. "I'm not leaving."

Angelica tried to force her way through the crowd, calling out to him.

He saw her lips ask, "You're leaving?"

Pushing against the crush, Aris tried to reach out to her.

Off to the side, at a table on the far edge of the crowd, Granny, Despo, and Manolios sat grinning, relieved at Adonis's announcement of the Americans' impending departure.

John punched Uri's shoulder. "Look at Angelica. She doesn't seem too good."

Uri peered through the crowd at her. "What happened?"

"I think she believes Aris is leaving with us tomorrow," John replied, glancing between her and Aris.

Uri turned to John. "But he said he's staying here."

Aris lurched forward against the wall of people, reaching his arm out, trying to shout for Angelica's attention.

She had wilted, her hands tucked against her chest. She stepped back, legs wobbling like a frightened deer.

"You decided to leave?" she called out, her words disappearing before they could reach Aris.

He shoved against the bodies in his way to get to her.

"This is bad." Uri prodded John in the side. "What should we do?"

John shouldered his way into the crowd. "We need to help Aris get to her."

"It's not like she's doing any better than him. She's barely standing," Uri muttered, following John.

Angelica wiped her tears but was barely able to make out more than a distorted image of Aris reaching through the crowd for her. Her friends jostled her, shifting her towards the stage and away from Aris.

From his perch, Adonis watched as Aris fought the throng. He turned to the drummer near him. "Can you give me a couple of beats to get everyone's attention?"

The drummer immediately obliged, and Adonis raised his hand once more. "Today is a great day for our village, but especially for me. A new life will soon be born here, with more to hopefully follow. Our village is growing."

Adonis paused as everyone waited for clarification. Murmurs filled the air around the plaza.

Granny glanced at Despo and Manolios, seeing her concern reflected in their faces.

Hearing Adonis's words, Angelica looked back for Aris but he was buried in the crowd. Her vision blurred, brimming with tears. She brushed them away so they wouldn't obscure her view of him.

John shifted nervously in place. "This is really bad."

"She can't honestly think Aris is leaving, can she?" Uri asked.

"Who's pregnant?" a voice cried out, echoed quickly by many more.

"Before I tell you," Adonis answered, scanning the faces beneath him until he found Angelica, "I want to announce my engagement."

The crowd erupted into a cheerful uproar.

All around, people were shouting out questions, asking who the mother was and when the baby was due.

Finally, one voice cut through the rest, shouting, "Who's the bride?"

Angelica tensed, her face puckering like she tasted something sour.

Adonis looked directly at her.

She unconsciously covered her belly with her hands.

Twitching, Adonis wiped the sweat from his brow. His throat clicked as he swallowed, dry and scratchy. "I'm honoured to be marrying the smartest, most beautiful woman I've ever known. She is the love of my life."

Torn from his desperation to reach Angelica, Aris stared up at Adonis, flinty and unwavering.

"Oh no," John whispered.

"Shit," Uri mumbled back.

The crowd's response went wild. On stage, Adonis smiled at the increasing fervour, pleased with the support of the masses.

57 All Is Lost

Adonis watched the crowd undulate around him, smiling at their reaction before raising his arms to bid them quiet. "My friends, I'm thrilled to announce my impending marriage to Angelica. My Angelica!"

Angelica froze as he held his hand out to her, beckoning her to the stage. He smiled, wiggling his fingers as if to entice her.

The crowd turned, all focusing their sight along the line of his arm to her. She could feel their eyes burning holes through her.

"My Angelica," Adonis repeated, turning the attention back to him, "will soon give birth to our child and the newest member of our village."

A roar of cheering went up for Adonis and Angelica. The musicians launched into a jaunty tune. The plaza fell into pandemonium until Adonis raised his arms again asking for silence.

Turning back towards Angelica, he saw her stumble and fall to the ground.

At the edge of the stage, his breath caught while he watched the people around her try to help her stand.

Aris's feet went numb beneath him, the energy slipping out of his body.

"We have you," John reassured, coming up behind Aris, he and Uri lending support before he could collapse. "Just take deep breaths."

"Look!" Uri exclaimed, pointing towards the stage. "I think Angelica is searching for you!"

At the chance of seeing her, Aris pulled himself together and looked up. Rising over the crowd, raised from behind and pushed along by happy hands, Angelica ascended to the stage.

The entire time her gaze stayed fixed firmly on Aris. She shook her head, crying out for everything to stop.

John leveraged Aris more securely under his arm. "This is mad. Angelica really believes you're leaving tomorrow, Aris."

Finally, when Angelica was dropped on the stage, she looked out at her family.

Her father's face was bright and her mother smiled with relief. Only Granny seemed to notice Angelica's pain, reflected in her bitter frown and tense shoulders.

Uri shook Aris, trying to get him to focus. "What are you going to do, man?"

Aris widened his stance to gain a sense of stability. He clenched his jaw, glancing between John and Uri before looking down at the ground.

"You don't have to be embarrassed," John reassured him. "It's us. We've got your back."

Aris gazed out at Angelica, still beautiful in her blue dress but tearful on the edge of the stage. He took deep breaths, trying to regain the colour in his face. "I am fine. Really, I'm okay."

"What are you going to do?" John asked, wringing his hands.

Uri punched Aris lightly on the arm. "If you don't do something now, it'll be too late!"

Aris shifted his gaze between Adonis and Angelica. "Maybe this is what she wants, and that's why they were all congratulating her."

"Are you blind? She's crying up there!" John argued.

Uri shrugged. "Could be tears of joy."

Aris stared at Adonis, refusing to look away as their gazes locked. They remained like that, unmoving, trying to gauge the other's next move.

"Look at him. He's already won," Aris said. "The village believes him."

"Are you going to do something?" John wondered. "Or are the three of you just going to keep staring at each other?"

"Did John and I miss something?" Uri asked.

Aris ground his jaw, his face tensing from the pressure. "What you're missing is that it's too late. She already thinks I'm leaving."

"Bullshit. It's not too late. She clearly doesn't want this. She's bawling her eyes out. They had to force her onto the stage. Are you blind?"

Deep creases shadowed Aris's face, ageing him noticeably. "I don't know what to do. I can't think. It's too much. Everything is blurry."

Angelica pushed up off the floor of the stage, standing on her own. With her gaze on Aris, still so far from her, she refused to look at Adonis until he held out his hand.

Her eyes tipped down to stare at his fingertips. The sight of it made her cry more for the simple fact that the hand wasn't Aris's.

A woman next to Aris sighed, soft and long. "Look, she's so happy she's crying."

John snorted, leaning closer to Aris. "She's clearly in pain. You need to do something! Look, even Angelica's family realises something's wrong. Just look at Granny's face!"

Angelica, suddenly noticing the focus of the crowd on her, gazed back to Aris. Everything faded to a dull hum. The band sat still, silent and waiting for her to make some move and join Adonis.

She remembered Aris's comment to her earlier, that he had decided something. In her head, she filled in the remainder of the sentence on her own… he was leaving.

Convinced it could be nothing else, she made a choice, opening her mouth and, without a sound, forming words with her lips for Aris to read: "You can go, my love." She repeated it again and again without sound, just barely biting back her howl of despair.

Uri stepped closer to John, bending to whisper in his ear. "What's she saying?"

John squinted. "I don't think she's doing anything."

Aris slouched, his back curved as if from a heavy burden. "She's telling me I can go."

Finally turning towards the centre of the stage, Angelica accepted Adonis's hand.

He smiled unrestrainedly when her fingertips brushed his. Adonis guided her across the stage and offered her a cup of wine that was waiting nearby. He pressed it into her hand, which she accepted without thought. He raised his own cup, tapping her hand with a finger till she did the same.

"To us," he cheered. He brought the wine to his lips and took a large sip, watching Angelica as she remained still. "Have some wine."

She complied without thought, bringing the glass to her lips, but refused to open her mouth. It spilled down her chin and stained the front of her dress. She angled herself to look over the rim of her glass, seeing Aris in the crowd as tears joined the wine spilling down her face.

Aris held her gaze, shaking his head. "I don't want to leave. I decided to stay," he whispered.

"But you never told her," John retorted angrily. "You never finished explaining. How could she possibly know what you want?"

Uri poked Aris, causing him to stumble forward. "You need to act now before it's too late."

Frowning, Aris rubbed his heavy chest. "It's already too late. Adonis announced I was leaving."

"For once, Uri is right," John said. "You need to act now."

"No, there's nothing to be done," Aris replied, clenching his jaw. "She has made her choice. She must have accepted a proposal sometime this morning before we arrived."

"But why would she do that?" Uri countered.

Aris shrugged. "Perhaps she thought it was for the best."

"This isn't like you," John argued. "You are a fighter. You don't just give up. How can you just stand here and do nothing?"

"Because there's nothing I can do. It is their village. They have their way of doing things."

"I've never seen you like this," Uri grumbled. "Even stranded on the ocean, you refused to give up. How could you just walk away from Angelica like this?"

Aris pursed his lips. "For whatever reason, she has accepted Adonis's proposal. I left it too late. I should have acted a long time ago."

John grabbed Aris by the wrist, spinning him around. "Wait, Adonis said she's pregnant. But there's no way he's the father, so why announce it?"

"Just shut up. It's probably to stop any rumours spreading now that she's showing, but it doesn't matter. None of it matters anymore." Aris pushed John and Uri away. "I'm feeling suffocated. I need space. Let me go."

On stage, Adonis raised his glass in another toast. "To your tears of happiness, may they never run dry!"

Instantly, the crowd joined in the celebration, their voices lifting together in congratulations.

At their table, Angelica's family sagged into their chairs in relief. Granny smiled dimly as villagers stopped by to offer their congratulations on the engagement.

Even John sniffled, his eyes filling with tears. "I can't believe that Angelica slipped away from just a single missing word."

Aris clutched his head. "Maybe Uri's right… I am cursed."

On stage, Angelica watched as Aris curled over in pain. He sank down to the ground between John and Uri, disappearing.

She saw John and Uri, faces creased in worry, drop down to help him. Taking a step away from Adonis, she felt compelled to rush to Aris's side, but was stopped suddenly by Adonis grabbing her by the arm.

She struggled against his grasp until she noticed that Aris was back off the ground, supported by John and Uri. For three brief seconds she smiled, before doubling over as a stabbing pain ripped through her stomach. She pressed her hands against her lower abdomen, screaming out like a wounded animal.

Her howl could be heard above the crowd, and her family jumped up from their table in concern.

Confused, Adonis held her upright in a tight embrace.

Angelica turned her head, finding Granny standing over by her parents, crying, a wrinkled hand pressed to her mouth to muffle her sobs.

"What's wrong," Manolios asked. "What's happening?"

Granny wiped away her tears, offering her son a wobbly smile. "It's fine. I'm just happy for her. See? I'm crying because I'm happy… same as Angelica."

"Well, she should at least sit down," Manolios argued, and waved for his daughter to join the family.

On the other side of the plaza, Aris shoved away from John and Uri and moved towards the pier. "Let me go. I just need to be alone for a moment."

John watched as Aris dragged his feet. "Just earlier today he seemed like the happiest man in the world. Now look at him."

Uri sighed, crossing his arms. "He's lost everything. No home to return to, and no home to build here. Love is stupid. It gets you nothing but pain."

"Adonis pulled off a real coup," John observed. "What is Aris going to do? How's he going to survive this?"

"We should persuade him to come with us tomorrow. He can't stay here now."

"You're right," John agreed. "Let's follow him. We don't know what he might do in this state."

"Be careful to keep your distance," Uri pointed out as the pair tailed Aris around the edges of the festival. "He needs his space right now."

They followed him like shadows as he circled the plaza then suddenly turned right back to the festival.

"Where's he going now?" Uri asked.

"Seems like he's heading straight for Angelica's table."

The pair watched from a distance. Aris slowly approached the family table where they were happily accepting everyone's good wishes. Even Zoe was present, jumping around Angelica and peppering her with questions.

Uri bit his lip. "I hope Aris doesn't make a scene!"

John tilted his head in consideration. "You know how his temper is… rare but ferocious. I don't want to think about what he's capable of right now."

"Hurry, let's catch up with him. We d-d-don't want another f-f-fight," Uri stuttered, his burps bursting between his words.

On stage, now alone with the band, Adonis watched as Aris approached Angelica with a steady gait. He snapped at the drummer to kick up a beat so he could regain everyone's attention.

Tightening his grip on the microphone, he cleared his throat. "I don't think we should end these festivities without hearing from our three friends who are leaving us. Please, come and join me."

John and Uri exchanged a quick glance at Aris who hesitantly walked to the stage while they followed.

Aris reached the stage first and Adonis shoved the microphone into his hands with a grin.

Turning to the crowd, Aris scanned the faces—both familiar and new—until he found Angelica. "I just want to say thank you, on behalf of all three of us. You have helped us see ourselves in a new way. Your love and wisdom have illuminated our dark souls. Though we come from an advanced civilization, it was here that we found true culture and belonging. We will never forget this place."

Everybody applauded as Aris gathered Adonis in an embrace. Afterward, they both climbed down from the stage platform.

John continued to applaud, not even bothering to dry his tears.

"Why are you crying?" Uri asked.

"I have feelings," John retorted. "Unlike you, you stone-faced mule. Aris is clearly in unimaginable pain, but he still offered such a heart-warming farewell to the village. I am very proud of Aris!"

"Maybe you've forgotten that every word was addressed to Angelica. Don't envy him. We need to get him out of here before it's too late."

58 ALREADY MARRIED

Angelica let Granny pull her down into a seat next to her and Manolios at the table in the plaza. Her mother sat across from them. Angelica looked down, running her fingers along the wine stains that mingled with tear marks covering the front of her blue dress.

Manolios leaned back in his chair and scratched his chin. "I'm not sure I could be so level-headed in Aris's situation. He's just lost the woman he loves. But he did the right thing for us."

"As always," Granny responded. "Aris has risen above every one of us."

Fresh tears worked their way down Angelica's face. "This is ridiculous. You're all hypocrites. You interfered without care for how much I love Aris, but here you are singing his praises!"

"Be brave," Manolios said, patting her shoulder. "Things will work out for the best."

Angelica glared at him. "For whom, Father? If it wasn't for my unborn child, I would jump into the snake well."

Despo leaned across the table, cupping Angelica's hand with hers. "Time will heal your heart, my love."

Angelica choked back a sob. "I know this is your doing. You've all been talking to Aris. Whatever you did has led him to leave without even telling me first. I will never forgive your evil!"

Her family twitched back, unaccustomed to her speaking like this. She even pushed Granny away. "Whatever you've done," she continued, "you didn't just kill Aris. You've killed me as well! You had no right."

Granny clasped Angelica's other hand with hers. "Adonis is your man. He's loved you his whole life. He just needed to win you, as much as you needed to be won by him."

Angelica shook her head wildly. "I only love Aris, and you've pushed him away!"

Manolios clenched his jaw.

Granny squeezes Angelica's hand. "I beg you. Let go of your pain. Whatever you feel, making your child happy is your priority now. You might not believe it at the moment, but soon, Adonis will love you just as Aris claims, and his hands will spark your body alive in the same way."

"I belongs only to Aris," Angelica growled with such ferocity her chest heaved. "I swear, no other man will ever touch my body. No one!"

Manolios frowned. "This is a day of celebration. Don't ruin it."

"You took away my chance at happiness. I'm going to leave this village and never come back. You'll never see this child! You've turned my paradise into a living hell."

Her mother reeled back in shock. "Angelica, what are you saying?"

"You only pretended to care for my happiness."

Silence fell over the table as Angelica noticed Adonis approaching with his mother, both smiling broadly.

Manolios jumped to his feet, shaking hands with the man. "With my blessing, my son!"

Adonis then fell into Despo's open arms. She kissed him, saying, "I was wrong. You don't just have the courage of a dragon, but of a thousand dragons. I always knew you had it in you."

Adonis came around the table and kissed Granny's cheek. She pulled him into a hug. "Well done, my son. I know you will make each other very happy."

With a cold detachment, Angelica watched her family welcome Adonis further into their lives. But when his mother approached her, arms wide and welcoming. Angelica sighed and turned away, pretending not to notice.

Seemingly unperturbed, Adonis's mother leaned down to kiss the top of her head, but she cast a concerned look at Adonis.

Adonis finally caught Angelica's sight. They stared at each other in silence until Adonis dropped to one knee and kissed Angelica's hand.

Granny fixed her gaze on Adonis's free hand hanging loosely by his side. One by one, his fingers curled inwards, forming a soft fist. Granny smiled as she mimicked his action. She nodded, whispering to herself, "Now!"

Gently, Adonis pulled Angelica's face close until their foreheads were pressed together. His breath ghosted over her mouth, and she instinctively matched his breathing pattern. Her eyes glazed over, and she tilted her head slightly as he leaned in closer for a kiss.

From the corner of her eye, a shadow caught her attention. She followed its pull until the details of a face solidified in her mind's eye. The vision she'd conjured was Aris. She yanked her hand out of Adonis's grasp and jumped to her feet.

As Adonis was pulled away once again by well-wishers, Angelica whirled around on Granny and yanked her close. "You had a hand in this, but it doesn't matter that he knows the love secret. It will never work on me. My heart belongs to Aris!"

Granny gripped Angelica by the arm. "The only person I've ever told the secret to is you."

"Your hand is all over this," Angelica hissed. "You've betrayed me like Judas betrayed Jesus. I could never have imagined you capable of this." She spat at Granny, spraying her across her breast.

Angelica stepped back, turning to face her entire family. "You all conspired against Aris and me, but nothing you can do will stop me from loving him!"

"Aris is the type of man most women dream of," Granny conceded. "But he is just that—a dream. You need to wake up to reality."

"I am not you!" Angelica sneered, shifting her eyes between Granny and Manolios. "You all conspired against me and Aris. Aris is my miracle! None of you can make me stop loving him!"

Granny stood and brought her hands up like she was trying to calm a wild beast. "Right now, you're simply adrift in emotions. Tighten your heart. After Aris is gone tomorrow, you will see that everything will be okay."

"I'm lost in a dark storm I can't control." Angelica's gaze was frosty and unyielding. "And I don't know if I'll ever find my way out. But when I do, I assure you I will not be the Angelica you knew."

"I never should have shared my secret with you," Granny said. "It causes nothing but heartbreak."

"The love secret has nothing to do with Aris," Angelica insisted. "With or without it, our love was meant to be."

Manolios and Despo exchanged confused looks.

Angelica's chest heaved and her blood began to boil. "If you want to find something to blame, then maybe ask yourself why Adonis decided to do this today of all days. Why now? What convinced him to act? And what evil tongue forced Aris to suddenly decide to leave?"

Granny tensed.

"Not that Adonis's announcement matters. It's too late," Angelica continued. She kept her voice low. "I already married Aris in a sacred wedding. And I will never break my vows!"

A shock rippled through the family as Granny and her parents exchanged looks of horror.

59 Competition

It was only the sudden arrival of Georgi the pedlar—Manolios's younger brother—coming over to congratulate them that caused the family to shake off their conversation.

Georgi extended his arm to Manolios, and the two of them faced each other for the first time since Manolios had shot him.

"The least you can do is shake his hand, Father," Angelica scoffed. "You're acting like a child."

Sighing, Manolios took his brother's hand. "Join us," he asked.

Before Georgi could even search for an empty chair, Angelica pointed, "Use mine. I need to change out of this stained dress anyway," and she quickly left the table.

Adonis made a move to follow her, but Granny stopped him with a firm hand on his arm. "She needs a few moments alone."

Adonis craned his next to follow her departure.

Instead of walking towards her house, Angelica ducked down a side street. Once out of view, she leaned back against the wall, her breath fast and thready. She softly banged her head against the solid surface as tears streamed down her face.

Losing all control, she folded her knees, her buttocks nearly touching the ground, and wrapped herself in a tight hug. Mouth stretched wide, Angelica released a long, mournful howl.

That was the same moment when the music in the plaza fell silent.

— ◇ —

Aris tensed, knowing instinctively that the woman's cry was Angelica. Coiled to rush to her side, Uri placed a hand on Aris's shoulder just as the band kicked back in and drowned out the moans.

"We're leaving tomorrow," Uri encouraged. "Hold strong."

Zoe suddenly darted out of a nearby throng of children. She planted herself right in front of Aris, hands on her hips, her face pinched in anger. "You liar! You promised I'd be the first to know if you were leaving."

Seeing the hurt behind her flimsy façade, Aris pulled Zoe into a hug. Tucking her in close, he whispered, "I didn't lie. Only Uri and John were leaving. But after everything that happened today, I think I should go too. But if I do decide to leave, I will keep my promise and come speak to you first."

Zoe leaned back, inspecting his face. "Okay. But you've promised twice now, so don't forget."

With the resilience of a child, she took him by the hand, chatting about what she'd been up to during the festival. She dragged him along behind her across the plaza.

When they reached the table where Adonis was still sitting with Angelica's family, John and Uri rushed up beside Aris. Fortunately, Zoe kept up her banter and entertained them all.

Shortly afterward, Angelica re-joined them. She had changed into a flowing black dress, her hair damp from washing it.

"You shouldn't wear black," Manolios let slip. "You're not in mourning."

Angelica shrugged, looking directly at Aris. "It's the sexiest colour on a woman. Don't you agree, Aris?"

The table tensed until Adonis finally spoke up. "You are beautiful in any colour."

Raucous cheering drew their attention, and John made use of the distraction. "Look! Arm wrestling!" He grabbed Uri and tugged him in the direction of the small audience.

Aris moved to follow them. "If you'll excuse me, I think I'll join them."

"Nonsense," Adonis commanded. "Stay with us."

Aris shifted, skin itching with the need to escape. "I will come back later."

Adonis sat up, a smile stretching across his face. "Why don't we have our own arm wrestling match here if you're so interested? If you win, you can leave. If I win, you stay to drink with us."

Without waiting for a response, Adonis whistled for John and Uri's attention, waving at them to come back to the table.

Unhappily, Aris rocked back and forth.

Angelica crossed her arms, her face frozen like the Arctic. She stared down her nose at Aris. "Mr. Aris wants to leave. Don't you see? He made up his mind. He is going. Nothing can stop him."

Adonis's enthusiasm waned at Angelica's insinuation.

Unwilling to let the mood last longer, Manolios finally broke the ice. "Nonsense, let's have some fun."

Aris sighed. "Adonis is stronger than me. This won't be much of a contest."

Uri frowned. "Yeah. At this stage, even Granny could beat Aris."

"Are you really scared of Adonis?" Zoe asked, grinning slyly. "I thought you were only scared of snakes and heights."

Angelica's face remained as firm as cold granite.

Aris stared down at Zoe. "It's not a matter of being scared. I'm simply being realistic. Adonis is stronger. He is also younger and in better shape."

"You're being ridiculous. Of course, you're strong," she said. "Manolios is stronger than Adonis, but the other day you threw him off the bridge!"

Aris tensed further as the small group focused on him.

He stepped closer to Zoe, who tried to duck away. "You know that isn't what happened. The fence collapsed and Manolios lost his balance. I tried to stop him from falling, but we both ended up falling in."

Zoe nodded slowly, her eyes darting from Aris to Manolios and back. "I'm just teasing. But you were stronger. You were able to pull him out of the water all by yourself. I know you're not afraid. Please do this as a last favour before you go."

Alarmed, Angelica fixed her father with a penetrating gaze.

"Zoe, the truth!" Angelica commanded, keeping her gaze anchored firmly on her father.

The rest watched, wondering what happened at the bridge between Aris and Manolios.

Adonis plopped down at the table where the women cleared everything else away. He popped his elbow up, hand open and in the air waiting.

Manolios tore his gaze away from his daughter. "It will be a good match!"

Aris glanced at Angelica, but she shrugged indifferently.

John slapped Aris's back. "Come on, I've yet to see anyone beat you at this."

"That's only because you've never seen me arm wrestle before," Aris corrected, causing the group to break into laughter.

"Aris doesn't want to fight," Angelica cut in. "He doesn't even want to be here. It's obvious that he's given up. He doesn't fight to win."

Her words pierced deep. Aris hesitated only a moment longer before taking the seat across from Adonis.

Zoe slipped in next to him, kissing his cheek.

Adonis smirked, confident, as the two men locked hands between them with their elbows firmly on the table.

"Adonis has a dangerous side," John whispered to Uri. "What kind of friend purposely tries to humiliate the other person?"

"When it comes to women, there is no friendship," Uri responded. "We're no different than animals killing to be the stud of the herd."

Jumping up, Zoe sprawled across the table and cupped their hands with her own. "When I remove my hands, the match begins."

She looked between the men a few times and then threw her hands in the air. Someone snagged her by the waistband to pull her back so the others could see.

The two men flexed their forearms, veins pulsing as they tested each other's strength. Their clasped hands shook but did not move to either side of the vertical.

John and Uri began to cheer.

Aris started to push Adonis's hand down towards the table.

"Push!" Zoe shouted at Aris. "I told you that you're strong. Push!"

Adonis gritted his teeth, hissing out a breath. Their hands came back to the centre. Adonis stared over at Aris with a grin. He forced another breath out between clenched teeth and started to push Aris's hand down, making slow but steady progress.

"Go, Adonis!" Zoe shouted.

Georgi bent down and chastised Zoe gently. "You can't root for both of them."

Zoe smiled, keeping focused on the ongoing match. "But I do support them both. That way I will always be cheering for the winner."

The smile adorning Adonis's face slipped out of place. His face turned red.

Lifting his unoccupied hand, Adonis slapped Aris hard across the face.

The crowd gasped as Adonis released Aris's hand and pushed out of his chair.

"What are you doing?" Manolios gaped. "You were just about to win."

The crowd nodded, equally surprised.

Uri and John stared in wonderous silence.

"He's letting me win," Adonis growled. "He's not fighting."

Aris smiled calmly. "No, you are just better than me. You won."

Adonis dove across the table, slapping Aris again.

Aris took the hit like a child accepting deserved punishment.

John lurched forward, recognising the look on Aris's face. "Stay cool. Don't give him the pleasure of provoking you."

Aris glanced over at Angelica, her face stiff and unyielding. He nodded at her, waiting for her verdict.

Angelica's mouth twisted in distaste. "You're leaving us, without warning or reason. Don't depart on such a cheap note. It's disrespectful to the people who have grown close to you. Compete properly or not at all."

The crowd shifted uneasily.

"What difference does it make if Aris wants Adonis to win?" John asked. "It's his choice and you should all respect it."

Zoe's hands fisted in her lap. "If Aris doesn't want to fight, we shouldn't force him. The last thing I want to do is make him unhappy. This could be his last day in our village."

Hearing Zoe's deeper meaning, Angelica's brows furrowed.

Aris's nostrils flared as he continued staring at Angelica.

"He's clearly not in the mood for this," John continued. "I've seen what he's capable of. Maybe he just doesn't want to crush your hand and embarrass you on such an important day, Adonis."

Aris raised his hand, silencing John and anyone else who might chime in. His eyes narrowed, his jaw clenched.

Lowering back down in his chair, Adonis and Aris positioned their elbows on the table and gripped hands once more.

Adonis met his gaze without falter. "I can take you," Adonis insisted. "Give me a chance to prove it."

Aris remained unresponsive.

Zoe leaned back over the table, holding their hands as she had before.

Aris peeked sideways at Angelica. She pursed her lips and nodded at him. When he still ignored Adonis, she finally smacked the table, then reached in and pushed their hands apart, holding each by the wrist. "You will both compete honestly with all the strength you command, or you don't compete at all," she ordered.

Adonis quickly agreed, but Aris remained silent.

Angelica shook him. "Promise me! Swear on my unborn child you will fight honestly!"

"What's the matter with you people today?" Uri blustered. "You're no friends of Aris."

Aris waved him off, focusing on Angelica.

"She wants Aris to win," John whispered to Uri.

Uri nodded. "Now he has no choice. This is too important to walk away from."

Angelica stared directly at Aris now, peering into his soul, and seeing something that convinced her, she offered him a soft smile. "May the best man win."

Aris relented with a nod. She immediately brought his and Adonis's hands together, her own hand on top to hold them in place.

60 Judas Kiss

Angelica glanced between the two men, her hand poised on their tense fists. She lifted her hand away and both men threw their entire strength into the contest.

The crowd watched in silence.

Adonis and Aris's faces turned red from exertion, but neither made a sound.

"It's been five minutes, and no one's gained an advantage," John observed. "It's nice to see them battling for real."

Uri shook his head. "I think they're both still holding back. Aris should make his move before he runs out of energy."

John elbowed Uri in the ribs. "Look, Aris is pushing ahead now. He might win this!"

Uri leaned forward. "Not so fast. Adonis is already pushing back!"

Angelica's face remained impassive as the two men battled it out before her.

The crowd had grown larger and there were roars from both sides of the table as the arms returned to centre, both men now shaking from the strain. With every tiny movement, the audience crowded closer, barely managing to remain a respectable distance from the competitors.

Manolios tilted his head towards his brother. "Equal strength. They're stuck."

Georgi the pedlar rubbed his chin with his hand. "Ah, but they're getting tired. Look how their nostrils are puffing wide."

"This will be won by stamina, not strength," Manolios observed.

In his effort to motivate his friend, John shouted, "I bet one dollar on Aris."

"I'll take your bet," Manolios replied immediately.

"I bet two dollars on Aris," Uri shouted.

Georgi laughed. "And I will take your bet… and double it if you like."

"I bet a kiss for whoever wins," Zoe exclaimed, "and two kisses for whoever loses," sending laughter rippling through the crowd.

Both Aris and Adonis were drenched in sweat, completely focused on their battle. Their right arms trembled, wavering back and forth as their left arms gripped the table for leverage.

Adonis grunted, arm flexing, as he finally gained the upper hand and pushed Aris's hand down, millimetre by millimetre.

With a feral growl, Aris forced his way back to centre.

As Adonis lost his lead, Manolios and Georgi fell into hysterics while John and Uri jumped at the comeback.

Angelica alone remained unmoved, her face blank as she stared intently at the hands locked before her.

Aris snarled once more, pushing Adonis's hand past the vertical.

The veins in Adonis's neck flared as he tried to fight back.

"Now they're all in," Uri acknowledged.

"Come on, Aris!" John urged.

"One more push, Aris!" Uri echoed.

"Hold on, Adonis. Hold on!" Manolios called from the opposite side.

Georgi leaned to his brother. "Someone must give in eventually."

Manolios nodded. "If Adonis can hold a bit more, he'll find an opening."

Angelica shifted her weight, anxiously gnawing on her lip. Beside her, Zoe had stopped cheering for either man, but her laser gaze was practically drilling a hole in those two wavering fists.

Aris slapped the table with his left hand, the hollow sound echoing in the plaza. "Prove you aren't just waiting for a favour."

Adonis returned the table slap with equal force and pushed back against Aris's arm. "I don't expect anything from you. Fight me fairly and I'll beat you just the same."

"Stop," Zoe screamed. "Stop fighting! This isn't fun."

Immune to her pleas, the men persisted.

Adonis let out a snort, his eyes wide and manic as he gained back his advantage over Aris.

"Aris must be getting tired," Uri remarked.

Granny smiled. "Fought with honour and strength."

"Damn good friends!" Manolios added.

"I don't know about that," John said.

"Fight," Aris snarled, grabbing Adonis by the ear using his left hand. "Prove you're fit to be a father."

Adonis's face flared in rage. In a mirror image, he snatched Aris by the ear, pulling him close. "You prove you're a man worthy of naming our child after."

Zoe's eyes went wide. She turned to Angelica and tugged on her dress. "You have to do something! They're hurting each other!"

John leaned close to Aris. "Just beat him. Don't show mercy. You have nothing left to lose."

The men released each other's ears and returned their focus to the arm wrestling. Both of their chests heaved with the effort.

"A thousand dragons!" Despo cheered. "A thousand dragons in your heart, Adonis!"

Adonis glared at Aris, his head held high. "Win or lose, I will still be a fit father and husband!" He pushed against Aris, forcing the other's hand down ever so slightly.

Aris pushed back, refusing to give in without a fight.

Adonis dropped his gaze to the table, then looked over at Angelica. With his free hand, he made to reach out and touch her.

"Keep your hand on the table," she advised him.

Aris smiled at the rejection. Turning his own gaze to Angelica, he seemed not to notice as he steadily lost ground in the match, Adonis forcing his hand closer and closer to the table.

He never looked away from Angelica now, focusing only on her and ignoring everything else around him.

His world narrowed. Only her.

Aris's arm began to twitch, his shoulder twisting as his hand neared the table.

Angelica returned his stare.

Something inside Aris came to life, set aflame by the light he saw reflected in her eyes. Flashing back to their special tree and the many nights they spent together under the stars, he felt the energy ripple between them now in the plaza. He could hear nothing of the crowd roaring around him, nothing of their taunts and jeers.

All he knew was Angelica, radiant as she stood pregnant with his child. And when she nodded, his smile grew wider. In contrast to the rippling muscles in his right arm, his face smoothed out in tranquillity.

Adonis must have noticed the exchange. He howled and threw everything he had into what remained of the contest.

— ◇ —

"Stop smiling and pull yourself together!" Uri shouted.

"Don't give up!" came John's encouragement.

Holding Angelica's gaze, Aris's arm ceased shaking. He took a deep breath and pushed back against his admirable opponent.

Slowly, but in a smooth advance, Aris drove back Adonis's lead until he pushed past the vertical and kept going.

John chuckled. "Where did that come from?"

"Where else?" Uri replied, raising one eyebrow in Angelica's direction.

Aris pushed harder, gaining momentum as the back of Adonis's wrist crept closer to the tabletop.

With a final grumble, Adonis yielded, his shoulders slumping.

Unwilling to look away from Angelica, Aris didn't seem to realise he had won. His grip stayed locked on Adonis's hand.

A soft, sad smile worked its way across Angelica's face. It was her only concession to show her congratulations in front of such a large crowd.

"Aris won. Aris won!" came shouts of joy from Uri and John.

Angelica glanced away to notice Adonis trying to hide a grimace. Aris had continued to pin his arm to the table.

"Aris," she called out, but he didn't respond. She stumbled forward and yanked at his hand. "Enough, Aris. You've won. You can let go now."

Aris twitched his head as if awakening from a deep trance, and let go.

Adonis released a brittle laugh. He stretched his fingers and arm. "I told you that you were stronger than me."

Uri leaned to John and whispered, "Judas's kiss."

Both men rose to their feet. Adonis wrapped his hand around the back of Aris's neck and pulled him in to kiss him on the top of the head. "We've both won something today."

"You're wrong," Aris whispered, turning his head to Adonis's ear. "You've won nothing. I am not leaving tomorrow."

Adonis's expression morphed to one of anger.

Uri poked John's shoulder. "What's happening?"

"I'm not sure," John replied, chewing his lip. "But I think Aris is starting to fight back!"

The two combatants dropped back into their seats, their faces grim.

Zoe forced her way into Aris's lap and kissed him once on the cheek. Turning, she smiled at Adonis. "Don't worry, you can still expect the two kisses you earned."

Aris laughed. "Shouldn't the winner get more kisses?" From the corner of his view, he saw Angelica disappear amid a throng of people. He tried to lift Zoe off his lap, but she wouldn't budge. By the time he'd picked the girl up in his arms, Angelica was gone.

Zoe offered him a wicked grin. "You should pay more attention when I speak, Aris! I clearly stated what the winner gets."

61 The Fun

Aris was stopped suddenly by a guest he didn't recognise. The man had expensive boots, fashionable clothes, and a riding crop in one hand. Over the chattering of the crowd, he introduced himself as Mr. Flasi from one of the larger towns further along the coast.

"Mr. Aris, you are a strong man. Would you care to compete against my champion, Patri?" he asked, a lecherous grin on his face while he flicked his short crop out to the side.

Turning, Aris followed this visual cue to Patri, a short man with stumpy legs but a massive back, and thick bulging thighs. He was giggling like a mischievous child.

Noticing Aris sizing him up, Patri eagerly invited two friends to sit on chairs, and then he extended both arms and picked them up off the ground.

Patri cackled, showing off, but it was much to Mr. Flasi's dismay.

John hurried forward to intervene. "Aris just had a long match. He's tired."

"I will give you fifty to one in a bet, Mr. Aris," Flasi provoked.

Zoe pulled at Aris's hand, her voice trembling. "D-d-don't do it. He just wants to embarrass you. I don't like him. He's a rich man from a big village."

Aris reassured her without hesitation, before placing his hand on John's shoulder. "To earn the right to compete with me, your champion must first defeat my friend here. He's a long-time arm wrestling champion."

Patri burst out laughing when he saw John's slim build. Everyone stared at Aris in shock.

"So you are a rich man, Mr. Flasi. Are you still offering fifty to one?"

Flasi pulled out a thick stack of money with a manic grin, flashing the cash as a crowd gathered.

"No!" John whispered in Aris's ear. "He's going to break my hand, my arm… my shoulder!"

"You're flashing around two hundred American dollars," Aris said, ignoring John's concern. "That means you will have to pay me ten thousand American dollars if your man loses. Are you sure you can afford it?"

"Aris," John hissed, terrified. "You're going to humiliate me and it will cost you money. What are you doing?"

Aris squeezed his friend's shoulder. "Don't worry," he whispered to John. "I will make sure that the more Patri tries to push, the weaker his arm will become."

John's eyes grew wide. "How?"

"Hypnosis," Aris murmured.

"That won't work against this monster."

"Just trust me. Start warming up your arms."

Smirking, Flasi's pride lifted his voice above the din of the crowd. "If you think you will make us refuse the match by betting big money, you are wasting your time, Mr. American."

Angelica pushed through the crowd, slipping the ring off her finger. When she breached the front row, she stepped into the eye of the storm, holding it out. "My ring is not expensive, but it is worth at least five hundred. Will you take it as a bet against your man for one hundred or even fifty dollars, Mr. Flasi?"

Bemused, everyone watched as Manolios called out, "You've seen Patri's strength."

Aris couldn't bring himself to look at Angelica, but clearly heard her reply, "I have full confidence in Aris. If he says John will win, I believe it. If you don't, then bet against him."

Several villagers placed small bets in favour of Patri, which Aris agreed to underwrite.

Turning to Flasi, Aris said, "Before the arm wrestling begins, I would like a word with Patri to make sure he understands the rules."

Flasi waved his hand in agreement.

Aris threw an arm around Patri's shoulders, casually escorting him away from the others where they wouldn't be overheard.

Facing Patri, Aris gripped the big man by the shoulders and began to mumble. Patri nodded as Aris squeezed his arm at the shoulder joint. Patri kept nodding and smiling.

Afterward, Aris led him back to the table where John was waiting. Patri and John took their seats, facing one another as opponents.

Sweat had already soaked through John's shirt. "M-m-may the best man w-w-win," he stuttered, bracing his arm on the table in position to begin.

Patri lost no time meeting John's grasp.

Zoe bent over the table to place her hand atop the men's fists, raising her hand and dramatically shouting, "Begin!"

From the first second it felt like John's fingers would be crushed under Patri's gorilla grip. John remembered how he had faced down demons in the past year at Aris's side, and determined to put all his strength into this current fight. He looked deeply into Patri's eyes, trying to portray a confidence he didn't fully believe.

Patri made eye contact immediately but his gaze became glassy. John felt a weakening in the other man's grip.

Pushing the momentary advantage, John released an animalistic growl and pushed with all his might against the meatier muscles of his opponent.

Patri tilted his head like a confused puppy, now looking at his own arm being propelled downward against the tabletop. His focus became blurry, and despite everything muscle memory was telling him to do, he allowed John's puny arm to force his own into near immediate defeat.

John hopped out of his seat, jumping around in triumph like a prized boxer in the ring after the knockout punch.

Flasi's face grew dark and tight. "You've poisoned my man to take away his strength!" he accused.

Aris opened his mouth to refute, but Patri reached out toward two festivalgoers and, clamping them up by the backs of their shirts, he lifted one in each hand.

Flasi froze. Any defence he might have made had just been squashed.

Manolios stepped forward, levelling the man with a firm stare. "Mr. Flasi, we all witnessed it. The American won fair and square. You have to pay."

"Of course I will honour my bet," Flasi huffed. "I just don't have that kind of money with me now. I will send it in two days."

Manolios turned to his daughter. "How did you know John would win?"

"It is called faith, Father! I had full faith in Aris... something you are incapable of understanding."

Adonis swallowed painfully, his Adam's apple jerking.

Nodding for John and Uri to follow him, Aris walked away.

Angelica wanted to weep, but she was duty bound. Looping her hand around Adonis's elbow, she announced, "I am going home. The festival is over for me." With heavy steps and a heavier heart, she let her future husband escort her from the plaza.

62 The Departure

The sun had just peeked over the horizon when John and Uri stood at the front door of the rental property with their belongings, looking out over the village dyed a soft pink in dawn's light.

John shifted the bag on his shoulder, nervous to get on the road.

Uri rocked back and forth next to him. "If we don't go now, we'll miss our ride."

John twisted his head to a commotion at the end of the street.

A pair of cats tumbled out into the path.

"Just a bit longer," John sighed. "It's not like Aris not to say goodbye if he's decided to stay."

"I'm telling you, he's gone," Uri replied, slapping the doorframe. "You saw his bedroom. Nobody slept in there last night."

John curled his shoulders in tight. "Lay off. You know what he's going through."

"He's an idiot who dragged us around the world on some bullshit quest."

John shoved him back. "I've had the greatest time of my life with Aris. Before this trip, I was too scared to even voice my opinion. It's thanks to him that I'm no longer scared of everything."

Uri waved his hand around to the empty house. "That's great. So, where is this amazing mentor now? We're going to miss our ride, and I'm not walking through the woods again."

John's face sagged. "Aris didn't even want to bring us along at the beginning. We used him… remember? But because of him we both grew out of our insecurities."

"Maybe," Uri acknowledged. "I did realise I'm in love with my wife Epi."

"Maybe Aris just doesn't want to say goodbye." John twitched his head and neck, stepping over the threshold "Maybe it's best if we just go."

Uri heaved his pack over his shoulder and followed John out. They walked side by side down the street towards the meeting point.

Angelica was standing outside her own house with Despo and Granny.

"We can't thank you enough for all your hospitality," John told them in passing. "We'll never forget our time here."

Uri nodded, his foot already shifting as he prepared to continue to the plaza. "It was just like Aris said last night— you'll always be on our minds."

Angelica stepped off the porch, glancing up and down the street. "What about Aris? Has he left without even saying goodbye?"

John peeked sideways at Uri before offering her a half-hearted shrug.

Angelica moved closer, staring into John's eyes. "Are you hiding something?"

John sighed. She deserved the truth. But would it make it easier for her, or just more difficult?

Settling a heavy gaze on Angelica, he began. "Yesterday, before the festival, Aris told us he had decided to divorce his wife and stay to make a life for himself here." John saw her eyes spark like struck by a bolt of lightning. He added, "With you."

Uri grabbed John's arm to pull him away. "Come on, we're going to be late."

Angelica clutched John from the other side, preventing him from moving. "You're not leaving until you tell me everything. I thought he was going with you! Adonis said you're leaving today."

"That's just what Adonis said," John corrected. "I don't know why though."

"Enough," Uri snapped. "This isn't our place. We need to leave."

"What?" Angelica stumbled back, her mind whirling from John's confession. "Where is he now?"

John shrugged again. "He hasn't packed. His stuff is all still at the house. But we lost track of him after the arm wrestling last night."

"We really need to go," Uri repeated, raising his voice.

Granny and Despo silently exchanged glances.

"What aren't you telling me?" Angelica shook John. "There's something else, isn't there?"

Despo rushed forward, pulling her daughter off the American. "What are you doing?"

Angelica waved off her mother, turning back to John, watching him squirm.

"It's something only he can tell you," John admitted to Angelica. "It's not for me to share."

Granny stepped closer. "Are you really leaving without him? Shouldn't you wait and leave together?"

"It's more like he's leaving us," Uri argued. "He's the one who wants to stay here!"

John circled around the women, pulling Uri with him. "We have to go, or we'll miss our ride. Goodbye, ladies. We'll miss you!"

Angelica hurried after them. "Wait! Are you sure he didn't leave already?"

"Pretty sure. Like we said, all his stuff is still—"

Without waiting for John to finish, Angelica sprinted towards the plaza.

Despo tapped her fingers nervously against her thigh. "What are we going to do?"

Granny shook her head. "We've done enough damage. But whatever happens next, we must shoulder our share of the guilt."

"What are *we* going to do?" Uri mimicked, pulling John behind him to the plaza. "What were you thinking, telling all of that to Angelica? She's engaged to Adonis!"

"I didn't mean to," John said. "But someone had to. She deserved to know the truth."

———— ✦◇✦ ————

Angelica's lungs were burning and her legs cramped from the frantic run. As she reached the plaza, she saw a variety of festival visitors still milling about the open area, getting ready to depart for their home villages. One in particular stood out to her.

She headed straight for her uncle, Georgi the pedlar, who was securing the last of his goods in his van. "Have you seen Aris?" she asked, spinning him around. "Is he gone?"

Georgi blinked in surprise. "I haven't seen him. I'm just waiting for his two friends. I agreed to give them a lift to the next town."

At that, she shoved her uncle aside, darting to the next closest person. "Have you seen the tall American leave?"

Each person in turn jerked out of her grasp, shaking their heads.

She got the same answer from the next group of people she asked. She kept asking until there was no one left in the plaza to question.

In the distance, she saw Zoe playing with another girl and boy. Angelica raced to her side and questioned, "Did you see Aris. Is he gone?"

The girl's face went pale. "No, he prom—" But Zoe cut her sentence short.

"What did he promise?" Angelica completed the thought.

Zoe's head moved side to side, her lips pinched tight.

"Tell me!" Angelica shouted.

"I don't..." Zoe paused, deciding how much to share. "I don't think..." she paused again, before finishing, "I don't think he planned to leave. Or at least not yet."

Pulling at her hair, Angelica thought and thought, wondering where Aris might go if he truly hadn't stayed at the widow's rental property the night before.

Remembering the tall hill outside the village where she and Aris had shared many moonlit nights, she moved slowly at first, but then rushed past John and Uri without stopping. She ran past her own house, ignoring her mother Despo who called out to her, and sprinting up the hill until she could barely lift her legs.

Cresting the summit, Angelica collapsed at the foot of the oak tree, gasping for air. She looked all around but didn't see a single soul. The only thing remaining was the old duvet they had used as a mattress when they met under the tree.

She pushed off the ground, settling herself upon the low-hanging branch where Aris first made love to her.

"Where are you?" she whispered to the wind. "Are you all right? Please, just come back! I beg you. I will never betray your love."

The only response was the wind.

— ◆ —

BONUS!

As a special gift for you,
download your FREE copy of the novella
Assassin's Love.

Two never-fail assassins! Target and client in the same couple. The devil has drawn his double knives. There will be death! But there will also be love. Who can survive when Eros has drawn his bow and pointed his love arrows?

Claim your free copy at this website:
http://bookhip.com/GZKHQLJ

Enjoyed this novel?

Please consider placing a review!
This will help other readers find great books.

ABOUT THE AUTHOR

CHRIS NEO was born in Cyprus, migrated, and has practised in world-renowned clinics as a hypno-psychoanalyst. His experience in clinical love ailments gives him unique insight into the mysteries of the human heart, soul, and mind. Contrary to popular Freudian doctrine that most if not all psychological ailments derive from sex, his clinical conclusion is that most human psychological ailments derive from love, its lack, or its misconceptions.

A multi-talented individual, Neo has excelled in multiple industries, including tough business environments where competitors went out of business. He recently sold two of his companies and writes for pleasure, drawing inspiration from ancient storytellers like Aristotle to more current masters like Joseph Campbell, Vogler, McKena, McKee, and others.